ZANE PRESENTS

DIRTY OLD MEN

(AND OTHER STORIES)

Anthology

Dear Reader:

"Why are older men called 'dirty' simply because they still have sex drives, and are attracted to the bountiful energy, unburdened spirits, and sexual aptitudes of younger women?" That is one of the many questions that will spark conversation in this latest offering by *New York Times* Bestselling Author Omar Tyree. Tyree's thought-provoking delivery of this short story collection goes much deeper than strictly sex. He examines the psyches and motivation behind people of all "legal" ages hooking up in various types of relationships.

Internationally, there are millions of people—both men and women—who prefer to date outside of their age brackets. It is only considered an issue in America, one of the most sexually oppressed countries in the world. While older women who prefer younger men are affectionately referred to as "Bobcats" or "Cougars," older men who prefer younger women are considered "Dirty Old Men." This is a reality and Tyree has tackled the subject matter with a desire to advance the opinions and conversations about the situations presented that only a truly prolific writer could master.

I hope that you enjoy this collection of short stories. They are more than hot; they are intriguing and entertaining, but with a purpose. As always, thank you for supporting the Strebor Books imprint. From powerful memoirs like *Scared Silent: When The One You Love Becomes the One You Fear* by Mildred Muhammad and *The Day I Stopped Being Pretty* by Rodney Lofton to exciting novels like *Street Judge* by Judge Greg Mathis and *Pure Paradise* by Allison Hobbs, we strive to bring you cutting-edge, diverse, and extremely well-written books.

I am confident that you will enjoy *Dirty Old Men* by the legendary Omar Tyree. Please let me know your thoughts. You can locate me on the web at www.eroticanoir.com or www.planetzane.net.

Peace and Many Blessings,

Zane

Zane
Publisher
Strebor Books International
www.simonandschuster.com/streborbooks

ZANE PRESENTS

DIRTY OLD MEN

(AND OTHER STORIES)

Anthology

SBI

STREBOR BOOKS

NEW YORK LONDON TORONTO SYDNEY

F
Tyre

C. 1

SBI
Strebor Books
P.O. Box 6505
Largo, MD 20792
http://www.streborbooks.com

ISBN 978-1-59309-273-3
LCCN 2009933554

First Strebor Books hard cover edition October 2009

Cover design: www.mariondesigns.com
Cover photograph: © Keith Saunders/Marion Designs

10 9 8 7 6 5 4 3 2 1

Manufactured in the United States of America

For information regarding special discounts for bulk purchases,
please contact Simon & Schuster Special Sales at 1-866-506-1949
or business@simonandschuster.com

The Simon & Schuster Speakers Bureau can bring authors to your live event. For more information or to book an event, contact the Simon & Schuster Speakers Bureau at 1-866-248-3049 or visit our website at www.simonspeakers.com.

I DEDICATE THIS BOOK
*to the folks who ask for the truth
and can then take the real answers.*

ACKNOWLEDGMENTS

To be honest here, I haven't acknowledged folks in a book in lonnnnnng time. With 19 of them written and published now, it got to the point where I had basically run out of new folks to acknowledge. Then people began to take it far too personally. "You didn't give me a shoutout in your book?" So it became much less stressful for me *not* to do it at all. But if you check at the back of my first six novels alone, I must have thanked a thousand people. So it's not as if I'm not thankful for the love, help and support. I just wanted to write books without thinking about every person in the world who I forgot to give a shoutout to.

With that being said, I could create another long list of folks to thank with this one. But I won't. Due to the subjective nature of this particular book, I don't think most people would jump up and down to be included this time around anyway (smile). Talking about the fetish that older men have for young women, at my age, can be very dangerous. But if you can't talk about the truth in your art, then what good is having a voice? You think all that Viagra out there is being sold to older guys who are only thinking about their wives, who they've been married to for thirty-five years, like they suggest in those beautiful television commercials, where they dance into the bedroom? Now I dig the romantic spirit of the commercials. I really do. I just don't trust how valid they are. Do older women really want that dude up all night long, like the younger women do? Let's tell the truth here.

Anyway, I want to thank, first of all, Zane, for agreeing to publish this book of very frank short stories. The initial idea was to write real stories about men for men's magazines. But I got real tired of constantly trying to pitch to the magazine editors, especially when the first words out of most of the editors' mouths were, "We don't have much of a budget." Then you get editors who constantly want you to write "for the publicity," even though I'm a professional writer, like the people they still *pay* to write. So Zane came to the rescue. And now we can all read this thing and have something real to talk about.

I also want to thank Mary B. Morrison, Miasha, J.L. King, and J. Tremble for agreeing to read one of the stories and sliding me a book jacket review, along with Zane's. Then I'd like to thank my agent, Jacqueline Hackette, for continuing to negotiate publishing deals for me with cool, calm experience.

I want to thank the readership for continuing to buy African-American titles, even though we've honestly created an overload of similar material out there to choose from. And I'm not hating on the redundance. I'm merely telling the truth, like a pure Philadelphian. Straight up! We need some new and improved product.

Speaking of my home of Philadelphia, I'd like to thank my long-time editor, Pamela Artis-Hawkins, for continuing to work with me, and for giving me good, sound advice that I never seem to listen to (smile). Had I listened to you a long time ago on what the people want to read and simply given it to them, instead of always having a mission statement in my books, I could have made a whole lot more money. But like Popeye kicked it, "I am what I am," and that's an old school writer with a purpose for everything I put my name on. And I can go to the graveyard proud of knowing that I wrote and published exactly what I wanted. Hopefully, I won't be flat broke for it!

I wanna thank my young, Florida-based assistant, Jared Holloway, who missed having his first published story in this book by a weekend. Hell, I was already running late with this thing, dude. But when I finally kick down the door in this movie game, I got you. So hold tight.

I wanna thank the hustle and bustle of Carol Mendez, who found out how incredibly hard it is to call up the managers and staff of celebrities to try and set up meetings for business. It ain't easy, is it? But you wait until we start making these movies, how fast they'll call you back then.

On the West Coast, I wanna thank Jonathan DeVeaux, Mr. Club Owner, for all of the hospitality you've shown me over the years through your love of reading. I haven't forgotten about you. So tell your DJ to shout me out at the club, even when I'm not out there in L.A. (smile)!

Up North, I wanna thank Yvette Thompson, for always having an up-lifting conversation about the future of my success. "Omar, you're gonna do it! I know it! You're the kind of guy who won't stop until you make something happen!" I can hear your Trinidadian accent in my mind right now. And Heather Covington, too. I know you're up there in New York, marketing and promoting your tail off. Keep doing your thing!

Down South, I wanna thank Shanedria Ridley for being so real about humanity, as well as the hospitality of your father, Dr. Bilal Abdul-Alim, and his family over in Dubai. I haven't forgotten about them either. It's all coming back around. All I have to do is live to make it all happen.

Back home in Charlotte, I want to thank my right hand man, Ramon Jacobs, "The Barber," for hanging in there with me through thick and thin. We almost there, partner. And my man Big Bronze for your unrelenting talent and unbreakable spirit. My man Tehut-Nine, those film deals are coming, dude. And Kenny "The Poet" Cross in front of the camera, and Vince Paul on the Southeast casting; we're all gonna get where we want to shortly.

On the national radio scene, I'd like to thank Michael Baisden for doing it big. Thanks for shouting me out every now and then. The people always tell me, "Michael Baisden talked about you today on the radio." Thanks, dude. We're all proud of your hustle, even though I can't call you up anymore with your changing phone numbers and growing list of gate-keepers. That's how success goes, dude. I ain't mad at you. We'll get back up whenever. In the meantime, we all end up screaming like fools now, "But I know Michael *personally.* Tell him it's Omar on the line! Just tell him it's me!" Life is funny that way sometimes, dude. You gotta laugh at it and keep moving.

But you see what I mean about this acknowledgment thing? This short list can get longer and longer? And I said I wouldn't do a long one this time. But I can already hear the left-out voices now. "You didn't add a shoutout to me in your book? You didn't add so and so?"

So I'll have to end this thing right now with this; this is only a book, ya'll. My actions in real life still determine who I am and what I consider important. So even if I don't name every single person, again and again and again, if I love you, I love you, man. Period! Including my business partner, Arthur Wylie, down there in the ATL, or is it out in L.A., or is it chilling in the D.R. this week, or down in Colombia, South America, or is it over there in London, England, this time?

New business flies all around the world, dude. Let's go get it! But this ain't no business book here. This is a book to keep me in the "business of books," if you can feel me. At the end of the day, I'm still a writer, and reading adults still need strong content to read. And I'm an adult. Well, ain't I? So let's all be mature about this and read on.

This one book won't change the world. I used to actually think that way. "This book will change everything!" But for many people, it's all pure "entertainment." And the world keeps right on spinning in the same direction. So don't go jumping off the deep end of things concerning this one book, because gravity still falls to the ground, and you'll break your good leg and end up limping, all for nothing.

The bottom line is this: I'm still poised to keep making new projects happen. Plain and simple. I'm always ready to use my intellect and hustle to keep moving forward. Now watch me as it happens!

Omar Tyree / March 2009

When he was first born
he sucked on his mother's breasts for milk.

When he turned 5
he refused to even hold her hand.

At age 10
he developed his first crush on a girl.

At 15
he humped one against the wall in her father's garage.

At 20
he contracted his first STD.

At age 25
he married the one who got pregnant on him.

At 35
he became a father for the third time.

At 40
he had to beg his wife to get it at home.

At 45
he began to follow the curves of much younger women.

At 50
he opened up his bank account to pamper them.

At 55
he got divorced so he could marry one.

At 60
he discovered Viagra.

And at 65…
yup,
he's still fuckin'.

It Never Ends
by Omar Tyree

THE BARTENDER

An older man sat on a lone barstool at The Hot Spot Lounge on Eighty-Fifth Street and Cottage Grove Avenue on the south side of Chicago on a cold evening. At a quarter after six, the place wasn't that crowded. And without the competition for drinks, the man was already working on his second rum and Coke.

Up above his head at opposite ends behind the bar were two small televsion sets. On the small set to the right side of him, the ESPN network was talking NBA basketball. The sports analysts were discussing who were getting the most votes for the All-Star game that year in Las Vegas. The TV hanging from the left side paraded the latest music video from Nelly. The young St. Louis native was rapping about buying expensive, designer "grillz" of thousand-dollar jewelry across his teeth, while the hot video vixens shook what their mommas gave them across the camera screens.

The man tilted his head back, his drink in his warm palm, staring like a horny vulture, imagining how he would have swooped down and gobbled up the enticing prey more than two decades ago. He was suspended in admiration while the hypnotic video played on. And when the video finally concluded its very obvious dick tease, the old man felt as if another young piece of him had faded away.

"Shit," he mumbled to himself. Damn, he wished he could be young and single again. Next month he was turning fifty; the big five-oh. And he had been married to the same woman for twenty-seven years.

He slammed the rest of his drink to the back of his throat; the drink never tasted that good to him anyway. He only utilized liquor to take his mind off of things for a few hours.

"Hey, ah…" He didn't know the girl's name; the new bartender. But she was the finest young thing inside the lounge. And while she had her back turned to him, filling a drink at the other end of the bar in her all-black uniform, the perfect curve of her ass made him think about the worst sins in the Bible. Why, on God's green earth, were those young girls all getting those wicked tattoos etched across their lower backs? They looked like damn stroke targets. How was an old and horny man supposed to act? How could he not think about mounting and humping that young, sexy-ass broad right there in back of the bar? He could even feel his soft tweed dress pants rising and tightening up under the table while he imagined it.

I can feel that tight, young pussy right now, all wet, hot and slippery, while I nail that wrinkle-free ass like Lady and the Tramp, he mulled. It was a good thing no one could read his thoughts in the room. If he continued to stare at the girl in his obvious horniness, he was afraid that someone—or *anyone*—could read his mind. He shook his head and looked away, but not before he watched the bartender bend over and grab another bottle from under the bar.

Oh, Lawd Jesus, help me! he told himself. *I pray to God that somebody else helps me on this third drink instead of her.* But he really didn't mean it. In fact, he couldn't wait to have that young bartender in his face again with them ripe titties of hers, pushing all up against the high bar table.

Before he knew it, she was back on her hustle. That's how they were when they were young, quick and vivacious.

"You want another one?" she asked him.

She slid back into view, appearing from nowhere, as if she had a pair of roller skates on. Her eye contact was dead on and intimate. Did she want his drink order, or did she want to order his drink?

"Yeah, ah, gimme another one."

He barely looked at her when he said it. He tried to be hasty about it and mean, too, simply to get the young girl out of his face. But it didn't work. She was still standing there, all smiling and shit.

"Rum and Coke?"

Her sweet young breath even smelled like peppermint, probably from a stick of gum.

Just pour the damn drink and get out of here, he wished he had the balls to tell her. Either that or show her his balls. But that would probably get him arrested, not to mention embarrassed, in front of the talkative folks who parlayed there.

"Who's your favorite baller?" the young bartender asked him while she mixed his third drink.

Why? I don't want to talk to you, he told himself. He had no idea what he might say if he spoke to her for too long. He might ask her what time she gets off, and if she had a ride home. And he might ask her if someone was waiting at home for her arrival. But those were perverted thoughts from an old man, weren't they? Or *were* they? Hell, Denzel Washington was fifty-something, and the young broads still considered *him* sexy.

The man gazed at the bartender's face with confident boldness. He locked in on her shiny brown eyes, her arched eyebrows, baby-smooth brown skin, Colgate white teeth, curly, jet-black baby hair, and he immediately felt like grabbing his pants to stop them from bursting wide open.

"I like, ah...Tim Duncan and the San Antonio Spurs," he answered her. "That's old school balling, you know. Most of these young cats don't know how to play like that. Everything is a dunk or a three-pointer."

She smiled. "I hear that from older men all the time."

That comment threw the man for a loop.

She hears that from older men all the time, he repeated to himself.

"Well, how old are you?" he couldn't help but ask her.

"Twenty-five."

And how many older guys do you know?

He didn't ask her that one. But just when he was ready to feel comfortable in a conversation with the girl...

"Hold on, I'll be right back."

...she was off to fill another drink order at the other side of the bar, where she showed off that perfect ass and tattoo on her lower back.

Yeah, leave that damn girl alone, old man, he tried to warn himself.

But it was too late; he began to tell himself that he wasn't that old. Under the bar where he sat, he had living proof that he could still run with the younger dogs in the alley.

She ain't that damn young. And she act like she like me, he told himself. *I hear that from older men all the time*, he repeated again. *I bet she do.*

All of a sudden, he was anxious for the bartender to make her way back over to him to talk. He watched her do her magic, with her youthful energy, her rapid-fire moves, and her flexible young body.

Them damn young girls are a sin, just looking at them, he convinced himself. He began to imagine how flexible she could be, spread eagle across a nice warm hotel bed, smiling and grinning at him like an angel.

And I would be the devil, ready to burn off her pretty wings with my trident, he mused while he waited. *Aw, hell, let somebody else fill their damn drinks. You ain't the only one in here,* he found himself thinking impatiently. She was making his long, hard day at work worth the effort, without her even knowing it. Her zest and youth gave a weary old man something to come home and look forward to again.

"Hey, how you doin' tonight? You need anything?"

It was the head bartender sneaking up from his left. She was damn near as old as he was; you couldn't tell her hips from her gut, her gut from her titties, or her ass from her back. She was one big blob, reminding him of someone he knew too well back at home.

"Naw, I don't need nothing," he told her gruffly. He wasn't willing to let her destroy his fantasy. And he grew even more anxious for the newcomer to make it back over to him. It was getting late; a thicker work crowd was starting to pour in.

"Shit!" he grumbled out loud. He could already see where things were headed. The younger guys were flooding into the door, like hungry vultures. But maybe...just *maybe*...this girl didn't like younger guys that much. Maybe she liked old school men. So, he threw down his third glass of rum and Coke to get another refill from her when he saw her heading back in his direction.

She smiled and grabbed his glass.

"Be easy now," she told him. "You still have to drive home tonight, don't you?"

He grinned his ass off. "I'll be all right. I've been driving a long time, and who said I was even going home?"

She caught his drift. "Oh, now see, that's just bad."

"Bad meaning *good*, right?"

The head bartender read into his game and gave him the evil eye, but he ignored her ass and kept going.

"So ah, what team do you like?" he asked the young bartender, while she poured his fourth glass of rum and Coke.

"I like New York and Detroit. I'm an East Coast girl."

The old man broke out laughing. He told her, "Now I can see Detroit. They're playing old-school ball right now, too. But *New York*? Them boys ain't won nothing in *years*."

Nevertheless, he imagined her wearing a wet New York Knicks jersey with nothing on under it but her natural curves.

Down low, he could feel his pants growing tighter and vibrating from his stool. The young girl had him that excited. That's what they were capable of, driving an old man half crazy.

The next thing he knew—right in the middle of his scandalous fun—an unexpected friend walked up on him and dropped the bomb.

"Hey, what's going on, Harold? I figured I'd find you hanging out in here tonight. How are the wife and kids doing? Your youngest boy should be about ready for college now, right?"

Got' dammit! This motherfucking asshole! Shit! Big-mouthed motherfucker!

His boy downstairs went from strong and long to limp and wimp in a matter of seconds.

"They all right," he mumbled to his friend dejectedly. He didn't even want to look at the girl anymore. What was the point in looking at candy he couldn't have? His dreams were deferred yet again.

"So what'chu been up to, man?" his friend asked him. They were both nearing fifty.

Harold stood up. "I'll tell you when I come back. I gotta use the restroom."

"Big, stupid, big mouth," he mumbled as he moved along.

In the background, he overheard a group of younger guys who were strategically planning out their moves.

"That's the new one, ain't she? Get her over here to make a drink. Yeah, she *bad*."

Motherfucker! Harold continued to grumble as he walked.

Then he stopped and said to hell with it. He turned and faced the thirty-something guys who were quickly filling up the bar and lounge, and he gave them some worthwhile advice.

"Look here. I'm gon' tell you guys like it is. While you got them young fine girls out here running around, have fun while it lasts. And always protect yourself. But once you get my age with one woman…"

He shook his head and didn't bother to finish his sentence. Instead, he asked them, "Any one of you wanna trade places with me for a couple of weeks?"

The younger men looked around at each other and broke out laughing.

One of them replied, "Nah, that don't sound like no good trade-off to me, man."

Harold stood there and stared at them for another minute. "Well, it don't hurt to ask."

He took one last long look across the bar to the new girl, who was now smiling at another customer. She was giving her new customer the same juicy treatment, with her titties all up in his face.

Yeah, she do that to everybody, Harold told himself. And her gorgeous smile was all he needed to wake up his barrel and bullets downstairs again. So he walked into the bathroom and into a private stall, where he pulled out his proud, hard, brown Johnson, and proceeded to spray up the toilet seat and the walls, while trying unsuccessfully to hold himself steady.

"Shit!" he told himself, as he wiped down the toilet seat and the walls with a handful of toilet tissue. "At least I don't need no Viagra."

Then he laughed his ass off to stop himself from crying. A young girl could do that to an old-ass man; make him break down and cry for her sweet, young affections. And he didn't feel guilty about it either; it was only a fact of nature.

SUGAR DADDY RULES

"Clarence, I swear to God, I need a *huge* favor from you," Brenda Pittman stated with urgency. "I hate to ask you for anything like this, but if I don't pay my past due car note by Friday, they're gonna repossess my car."

She was standing outside the campus grounds of Florida A&M University in Tallahassee, decked out in ass-hugging blue jeans with a tight, titty-popping orange T-shirt. She was a fifth-year senior at age twenty-three, and the world always seemed to be falling down around her. She had called her friend Clarence there to meet her near campus that night to discuss her latest trial and tribulation.

Clarence Marbary, a divorced father of two in his late forties, listened to her with poise and understanding outside of their cars as the sun began to go down.

"Well, why don't you ask your parents for the money?" he asked her calmly, wearing his light-blue button-up, uniform shirt and dark-blue slacks.

Brenda sighed and looked increasingly frustrated. "Clarence, my parents are all tapped out. They didn't want me buying a new car in the first place. But you know how Florida is. I can't get around without a good car down here, and my old car wasn't accountable. It kept breaking down on me. It cost me more money to fix it than to drive it."

Clarence grinned. "Well, a new car is gonna cost you more to own it. Your job paying you enough to afford it?"

She frowned. "I mean, I can afford it; that's why the dealership let me have it. But I still have to pay for my apartment and school bills," she explained. "But this is my last year. I graduate in May."

Clarence looked over her apple-green RAV4 and imagined a car note in the range of three-hundred dollars.

"How much you owe?" he asked her.

She smiled. "Six hundred and fifty."

Clarence winced. "*Six-fifty?*"

"I mean, I'm trying to pay off the new bill, too, or I'll end up behind for next month," Brenda responded. "But I promise to pay you back for it in a couple of months. You know I'm not going anywhere."

Clarence looked the college undergrad over and thought about it. She looked good, smelled good, and would probably feel good and taste good, too. It was easy for him to imagine it. So he began thinking with the wrong head. But then he thought better of it.

The young woman just needs a little bit of help, he pondered. *We all need help at some point, to get ourselves established in life.*

Clarence asked her, "But happens if you fall behind again?"

"Honestly, I can't afford to. I have to stay on it," she told him.

Clarence took a deep breath and decided to do it, but for one time only.

"Okay, but look, I can't afford to do this too many times for you. I got my own kids to help raise and send to school."

She got excited. "Oh my God, thank you so much, Clarence. I didn't know who else to turn to."

Then she stepped forward and hugged him in between their cars.

Oh my goodness! Clarence told himself, taking in her fresh, intoxicating aroma, while experiencing the firmness of her curves. That got him thinking with the wrong head again. He was relieved when she quickly pulled away from him.

"Thank you, thank you, thank you!" she repeated, overjoyed. "So when can you get the money to me?"

"I'll have to write myself a check for it tomorrow. I can do it right after I get off from work, at three."

Brenda grinned. "Okay. So I can meet you tomorrow then, after four?"

When they drove off in their separate cars, all that Clarence could think about was the tremendous hug she had given him.

Damn, she felt good, he noted. He smiled all the way home imagining much more.

At the Tallahassee International Airport the next morning, Clarence overheard his coworker Maurice boasting about his latest conquest in bed to the younger guys. They were all preparing for work inside the employee break room.

"Man, I'm talking 'bout, this girl had no *idea* what I was fin' to put on her. But 'bout time she knew it, it was too damned late," he bragged. "I had her ass moaning in tongues."

The younger coworkers laughed in unison. Maurice always had some engaging story to tell. Opposite Clarence's clean-cut, no-thrills image, Maurice Benson wore plenty of old-school gold chains, new-school tattoos, and all types of attention-getting clothes, including alligator shoes, colorful Coogi sweaters, and several derby hats for afterwork hours.

"How old was she?" one of the younger workers asked.

Maurice looked the tall and slender young man over and answered, "About your age, twenty-four, twenty-five."

"Ain't you fifty-something?" one of the other young guys inquired.

Maurice stared at him. "What's that supposed to mean? You think my dick don't get hard no more?"

"I'm just saying, that's a little young for you, ain't it?"

"Not if she's legal. No woman is too young, if she's legal. That's the advantage I have as an older man now." He said, "But you younger guys got a good five to ten years before you end up arrested. So what you need to do is start dating older women and try to get some money up out of it, like a gigolo."

Clarence heard that and shook his head. In his opinion, Maurice was forever talking nonsense. The man had six children from four different women. So, how could he ever consider himself an expert on relationships? The man needed to get his delinquent house in order.

Maurice caught Clarence's twisted face of skepticism. "What, you disagree, Clarence?"

"To each his own, man." Clarence wasn't up for a philosophical discussion on dating. He simply wanted to get to work.

As the early day began with floods of passengers showing up at curbside with their luggage, a young college girl showed up, wearing a Florida State Seminoles T-shirt with a pair of stand-at-attention breasts.

Jesus Christ! Clarence thought to himself on sight.

He looked around at a few of the other men to read their responses to her. They were all stunned into submission and hesitation. But Maurice wasn't. He stepped right up and grabbed two of her three bags.

"You're heading back home from school?" he asked her. That much was obvious.

"Unfortunately," the young woman answered. She was light-brown with a face full of freckles and wild, reddish-brown hair. And all the guys wondered if her ass was as shapely as her titties. They couldn't tell through her baggy, maroon sweatpants.

Maurice listened to her and looked concerned. "Well, what's going on? You don't wanna leave?"

"No, but I *have* to," she answered. "I have to hustle up some more money to pay for next semester. But there's not that many jobs that pay enough here."

Maurice nodded in agreement. Tallahassee wasn't exactly work town USA. He asked her, "Where are you from? You got more jobs back at home?"

She nodded, while he took her photo ID to find her flight information at the computer station. "Yeah, I'm from Atlanta," she answered him. "There's a lot more jobs there, but I didn't want to stay home. You know, I wanted to get away for college."

"Yeah, you didn't want all your people in your business every day either," Maurice commented with a chuckle.

She laughed with him. "Exactly."

Once he printed her ticket and tagged the two bags, he said, "Well, let me get that last bag for you and walk you inside. I don't mind."

She looked pleasantly surprised and gave him the bag. "Oh, thank you."

"What are you studying?" he asked as he walked her inside the airport toward the security checkpoint.

As soon as Maurice left their station with the shapely college girl, the other skycaps gave themselves a knowing look.

"There goes another one," one of the younger guys assumed with a grin.

Clarence listened to them in wonder. Then he smiled and told himself, *I got one like that myself at Florida A&M,* thinking of Brenda. But then he caught himself and shook it off. *Yeah, but I can't think of her like Maurice would. That's just plain wrong.*

When Maurice rejoined them, they all wondered if he had found a way to get the girl's phone number.

"Well, what's the news?" the first young guy asked him.

Maurice chuckled. "Rule number one; you never book and tell. Always leave it up to the imagination."

That made all of the guys laugh out loud at their station. Maurice had been booking and telling forever.

At quitting time at three o'clock in the afternoon, the second shift was arriving at the airport for work, and Clarence felt guilty about his excitement. Maurice even noticed.

He read the youthful energy of his mild-mannered coworker as they walked toward the parking deck.

"What got you all skippy today? You got something tasty cooking after work?"

That assumption made Clarence feel guiltier. Was his excitement that obvious? Why was he that excited anyway? He was only giving a girl a loan.

He searched Maurice's probing, old eyes and responded, "No, why you ask me that?"

Maurice paused and started chuckling, like the sinister old man that he was. He loomed like a villain in a popular comic book series. He made Batman's Joker seem real.

"You must think I'm a damn fool, Clarence. I know when you got something going on. It bleeds out of your pores. Then you start asking me questions and shit. 'Hey, man, what do you think about this? What do you think about that?'"

Clarence objected; he didn't appreciate his insinuation. "Man, I didn't ask you *shit* out here. You making things up."

Maurice kept his cool. "Not yet. But you *want* to. I can *feel it,*" he teased.

Clarence grimaced. "Man, you can't feel a damn thing. What the hell are you talking about?"

Maurice explained, "Clarence, now you've been extra quiet all day. Then you walk out with a little bounce in your step, and get defensive with me when I ask about it." He said, "Shit, man, you're telling on your damn self. I can read you like I read these young broads out here."

Clarence frowned at his logic. "Man, get on the hell away from here. I'm not like one of these young broads. How you figure that?"

Maurice stopped and paused. "First of all, you're not normally a mean motherfucker like this unless somebody did something *wrong* to you, Clarence. And I didn't do anything wrong to you out here; I'm only asking you a few questions. So that let's me know that you got something going on that you don't wanna talk about. And it's making you happy and defensive at the same time, like a young got'damned woman would."

He said, "Now you can question me if you want to, Clarence, but I *know* what I *know*. And right now I know that you got some hot young girl on your mind," he insisted. "I can smell it all over you like a skunk."

Clarence had to watch himself. He realized the more he said, the more convinced Maurice would become in his assumptions. And the thing that made it worse was that his devious coworker was right. Clarence had been thinking about the joy and pain of Brenda's body all damn day; the joy of how good she felt when he hugged her, and the pain he felt about it being wrong.

Shit! he thought to himself. *Just leave it be, man, leave it be.*

He told Maurice, "If you say so, man," and left it at that as they reached their separate cars.

Clarence climbed into his full-sized, light-blue Oldsmobile, and Maurice climbed behind the wheel of his long, black BMW. And when they pulled out together toward the exit with Clarence out in front, he could see Maurice smiling his ass off from inside of his rearview mirror.

Clarence shook his head and ignored it.

Outside in the small parking lot of the bank, Clarence sat behind the wheel of his Oldsmobile, contemplating his emotions. It wasn't just the money he was ready to withdraw for the distressed college girl, but how he felt about giving it to her.

I didn't feel this way with her about the buddy pass flight tickets, he told himself.

But I do the buddy pass with a lot of people. This right here is something different, he reasoned. So he sat there unmoved in his car as the time inched closer to four o'clock.

"Look, either you're gonna do it or you're not," he told himself out loud. "You already told the girl that you would do it. So get on in there and take care of business."

He forced himself to climb out of his car and write a check to withdraw six hundred and fifty dollars of hard cash from his personal bank account. Then he called Brenda on her cell phone to meet up.

"Hel-low," she answered, sounding irritated.

Clarence didn't expect her sour tone, so he paused a minute. So her disturbing tone of voice created a feeling of regret and apprehension.

"Hey, it's ah, Clarence," he answered calmly.

Brenda's attitude changed instantly. "Oh, hi, Clarence. I'm sorry. I thought it was someone else calling me. But did you get the money?"

He hesitated again. *Damn. She ain't wasting no time getting to the money part, is she?*

"Yeah, I got it. Ahh…"

He continued to pause. He didn't feel as confident as he wanted to about his decision.

I got a bad taste in my mouth about this, he told himself. *Is this girl supposed to have this money or not? How well do I really even know her?*

Outside of helping Brenda with her travel back and forth to Baltimore and a few other places, Clarence hadn't hung out with her or talked much to the girl. So why in the hell was he ready to advance her a $650 loan that he felt queasy about?

"Well, let's meet up at Subway again," she suggested.

Clarence took a deep breath and nodded. "Okay." But as soon as he hung up his cell phone with her, he thought of stalling.

"Maybe I need to think more about this," he mumbled. He couldn't seem to figure out why he was so indecisive.

Six hundred dollars is a whole lot of money to loan to a relative stranger, he pondered.

But he had told her that he would do it. Nevertheless, he decided that he would meet back up with her and see how she would act when he got there. Then he would make his final decision of whether or not he would give her the money.

Well, as soon as Clarence showed up outside of the Subway shop, a little late from driving slow, he spotted Brenda in a skin-tight, lime-green T-shirt, causing her high-beam titties to shine, with a pair of black, form-fitting jeans, showing off her camel-toe high heels that elevated everything. She appeared as if she were a living statue that was ready and willing to be worshipped by mere mortals out in public. And her T-shirt nearly matched her green car, making her look coordinated in the extra glare of the sunlight.

Got' dammit! Clarence panicked, simply from looking at her. From her sight alone, he figured his decision was already made. It would take a pocket full of Krazy Glue to stop that old man from giving that young college flirt his money. He was damn near ready to hop out of his car with his money extended to her in his hand.

Jesus help me! he prayed. It seemed the young woman looked three times better than he ever remembered her from her travels through the airport.

Maybe that's because she's all out in the open now. Nobody travels all jazzed up for a airplane ride, he reasoned. *It's uncomfortable. And then they make you strip everything down for security.*

Clarence parked his Oldsmobile a few cars away from her RAV4 and climbed out before she could reach him. And when rounded off the corners of the parked cars that separated them, and walked right up to hug him again, hers curves felt even better than the first time.

"Clarence, I thank you *so much* for this," she told him. "I could just… *ahhh,*" she exhaled loudly.

Clarence had no idea how to respond. What exactly did she mean? What did she want to do? He was even tempted to ask her, but he couldn't force himself to do it.

Maurice would ask her, he thought instinctively. *But I'm not Maurice. I'm a decent and caring man.*

However, he also felt like an *aroused* man. And he could smell the aroma of Brenda's perfume again—a powdery, clean smell, as if she was giving him a clear signal that her kitten would be fresh and floral, as if flowers would float up off of the bed if he ever got a chance to fuck her.

Clarence cringed at the thought of it, believing himself to be in the wrong again.

Just give her the money and move on, he told himself. *Even if I never get it back from her, at least I can prove that I'm a decent man.*

So he dug into his pocket and gave her the bank envelope with the money in it, upside down so no one could read it. However, instead of her trusting that the money was all there and counting it later, Brenda turned the bank envelope over, took out the money, and counted every bill until it added up to six hundred and fifty dollars.

Shit! Why did she have to do that right out in the open, Clarence asked himself. She did it so quickly he didn't have time to speak up before it happened. He then looked around to see if someone else had spotted her counting it. They were out in a damn parking lot in the broad sunlight before five o'clock in Florida.

Well, maybe that was my fault. I should have gotten her to sit inside the car with me to make it a more private transaction, he mused. *Or maybe if she sat in my car, that would look a little too personal.*

Then again, he was giving the young woman more than six hundred dollars of his money. The shit *was* personal! Clarence wasn't a rich man. And he had his own children to provide assistance to, who were nearly her same age. What would his nineteen-year-old daughter think? She was in college, too, down in Tampa.

Yeah, let me get the hell out of here, he told himself. Yet, he couldn't budge from Brenda's presence. It was as if she had a Medusa spell on him that had made him immovable.

She said abruptly, "Well, I have a meeting to make tonight, so I have to go now. But call me sometimes, okay? And thanks again."

She was walking away from him with his money, and they had not even discussed the terms of her payback.

We'll get to that later, Clarence told himself. *That's why she told me to call her up.* So he was satisfied with that.

When Clarence drove off in his car, he felt good about himself. He felt that he had been a good Samaritan without any strings attached. So he smiled down the road toward home listening to his new John Legend CD.

"I'm ready to go right now / I'm ready to go right now..." he sang along with the chorus. And it was a good feeling.

But two days later, Clarence couldn't seem to get the college girl off of his mind. He was even daydreaming at work about her.

"Hey, Clarence, what are you thinking about today, man?" one of the younger skycaps asked him at the airport. "Are you trying to make some extra change today, or what?"

The old man had missed out on plenty of his usual tip money by not being aggressive enough to secure bags. On a good day, a busy skycap could make up to two hundred dollars on tips alone.

Maurice looked over and caught the conversation from the computer, while he checked in another flight.

"Mmm-hmm," he grunted with a knowing smile. *That motherfucker got that woman on his mind again. And she's messing up his money now. He better talk to me about it soon*, he determined.

On cue, Clarence eyed Maurice smiling from behind the computer station, and he could imagine what he was thinking about.

Looks like I've done it now, Clarence told himself. *I've gotten myself involved in a situation that I have to find my way back out of.*

But he still was not willing to talk to anyone about it. For what? Why incriminate himself so early in the game when he hadn't even touched the girl yet? He figured he most likely never would. But in the meantime, he was surely thinking about her, and that made it bad enough.

After work, Clarence was itching to call her.

She told me to call her up sometime, he reflected. *But maybe this is a little too early yet. It's only been two days.*

Then again, a phone call was just a phone call. Why should he feel guilty about calling a girl he loaned more than six hundred dollars to? So he went ahead and pulled the trigger on his cell phone.

"Hello," she answered more pleasantly than the last time.

"Hey, Brenda, this is Clarence. I'm calling you up to see how you been doing. You told me to call sometimes and check up on you," he told her quickly. He was still unsure about the call and was talking fast like a salesman.

Brenda responded, "Oh, hi, Clarence. Yeah, I'm good, but I'm at work right now, so I'll call you back when I get off. Okay?"

"Ahh…okay," he answered.

Just like that she was off the line with him.

Clarence shrugged and commented, "Well, she's at work. She'll call me back when she can."

By eleven o'clock that night, while he watched the latest NFL football news on ESPN, Brenda still had not called him back. He looked at his watch, and it read: 11:16 PM.

"I should have asked her what time she gets off," he commented. *But that may have sounded too pressed*, he countered. Everything was a second guess.

He finally shook it off and stated, "This is crazy. I should be able to call this damn girl whenever the hell I want. I gave her six hundred dollars."

So he dialed her cell phone number after eleven o'clock. *She's a college girl; she ain't in bed yet*, he rationalized. But there was no answer. And when her message machine came on, he hung up.

No sense in leaving her a message if she said she was gonna call me. She knows what she said she was gonna do, he told himself.

But Brenda never bothered to call him back. She didn't even call him the next day. So Clarence grew nervous about it.

Is she trying to dodge me now? he contemplated. *Nonsense! It's only been three days. It hasn't even been a week yet. What the hell is wrong with me?*

So he forced himself to leave it all be for awhile and focus on other things. He took his mind off of her, he even called up a woman he had dated on and off, who was closer to his age. He wanted to see if she would go out and grab a bite to eat with him, just for the hell of it.

"And we can take my younger kids with us?" she asked him.

Clarence had forgotten all about it. That's why he had stopped calling the woman. Everything was a package deal with her. And her kids were cumbersome.

Shit! She can never just go out on the fly? What the hell I even call her for like this? he snapped. He remembered that he was forced to plan a week in advance to go out with her. Either that or bring her younger kids along with them. But Clarence was not interested in starting the hell over with a family again; he simply had some manly needs to deal with. He wanted some pussy.

In fact, sometimes he wished that he had never gotten divorced. The dating game for an older man was not as simple as he thought it would be. Everything involved some form of sacrifice or complication. And if the woman didn't have kids to negotiate around, then she wanted to drag a good man to the altar and plan on having some. But Clarence was not fast to jump at that idea either.

So he responded, "You know what, you can ah, call me back when you feel like going out again as a regular woman and not as a momma."

"Well, I *am* a momma, Clarence. That's what it is," she refuted. "I can't make *believe*. So any man who can't understand that, well…"

Clarence didn't waste any more time with her. He said, "Okay, well… good luck with that." And when he hung up, it only pushed him closer to the college girl. He was tired of all the extra baggage of older women.

By that second week, Brenda had finally called Clarence back.

She explained, "I'm sorry I haven't called you back earlier, but I've been so busy with school and my job and everything that I ran out of time."

Clarence didn't care. He was overjoyed to hear from her again.

"Oh, believe me, I understand. That's what you're down here to do, take care of business. But I'm glad you got back to me. How is that car of yours doing?" he asked.

"As a matter of fact, somebody hit me last night while my car was parked on campus. Ain't that some shit? And my insurance deductible is five hundred dollars."

Clarence was sorry he had asked. But he damn sure wasn't bailing her out of that one. She still owed him on his first loan. And now that money seemed in jeopardy.

"Well, let me ask you a question, Brenda. Does somebody have a voodoo doll on this car of yours or what?" he joked.

That caught her off guard and made her laugh. She said, "I know, right? And just when I was starting to get back on my feet and catch up on my bills."

Clarence told her, "Well, it sounds like you're gonna have to ride around with that thing looking ugly for awhile. You can still drive it, right?"

"Yeah, I can still drive it...a little," she answered.

It sounded like a set-up. Clarence assumed that she wanted him to ask her what she meant by "a little" so that she could go into a more detailed sob story. So he began to smile at it all.

Okay, here comes the pitch, he mused. "A *little*? Well, can you still drive the thing or what?"

"Well, whoever hit me, they pushed my back bumper into the left side wheel, you know, on the driver's side. So now like, the bumper is rubbing up against my back wheel. Ain't that crazy? I can only drive like, thirty miles an hour now. And it's so embarrassing. Everybody on campus was looking at me like I was crazy. I can't keep driving around like that. I have to get this thing fixed."

Clarence shook his head with his cell phone in hand and grinned. *She's not getting me with this shit*, he convinced himself.

"Well, what it sounds like you need someone to do is to pull the bumper back away from the wheel. But you don't have to get the whole thing fixed. You're still young. This is only a starter car."

"No it's not, I *love* my car. I had a starter car two years ago," she argued. "And I'm not going back to that."

Clarence heard her out and went silent over the line. He had said all he planned to say about it. The rest was up to her.

She said, "So, I don't plan on asking you to help me out again, but I guess it'll take me a little longer to pay you back now."

Clarence figured he could kiss that money good-bye. At the rate she was going, she wouldn't see an extra six hundred dollars unless Santa Claus existed, or she lucked up and hit the damn lottery.

He asked, "Well, do you have any student loans or anything that you might be able to use?"

"Yeah, but I used all of them already. Remember, I'm in my senior year now."

Clarence remembered that she was a marketing major. "Do you have any good leads for a job, as soon as you graduate?" He was already planning to wait long-term for Brenda to turn things around for herself. It was what all college students had to do, dig themselves out of a hole. His own daughter would have to go through it in a few more years herself.

"Well, you gotta hang on in there then," he advised Brenda.

"I know, but...I wish I had some *help* sometimes, you know what I mean? But my parents can't help me at all. They're struggling right now to take care of my younger brother and sister back home. And with me being the oldest, they've gotten used to me finding a way to make things happen for myself, but I get so *tired* of this sometimes."

She was pouring the sob story on thick, and Clarence was prepared for it, as soon as she mentioned that her car had been hit.

He said, "You need some help, hunh? Well, I've already given you help." *And what have you done for me?* he asked himself. She was forcing him to think with the wrong head again.

She pleaded, "I know, but if you could like, help me out again, I swear to *God*, I will pay you *back. Honestly.*"

"I mean, you think I got like, extra money lying around like that that I can loan you for a year or two?" he questioned. *What the hell does this girl think I got going on over here?*

She said, "Clarence, you guys get tips at the airport every day. And like, in two to three days, you could get five hundred dollars easy. I *know it.* And then I would get the car fixed with my money, and by the end of the week, you could give it back to me, and then I would have to work harder, or whatever I have to do to pay you back. I mean, for real."

Clarence couldn't believe his old ears. This young college girl was really pushing him hard now. She was even counting his pocket change at the airport.

He said, "Now you really wanna get this same car fixed that bad? It seems to me that this car is gonna cause too much of a steady problem for you. You may be better off having somebody drive you to and from work every day and pay them a couple dollars each way. I mean, Tallahassee ain't but so big," he advised her.

Brenda stopped talking for awhile. She let the dead silence sink in on him. Then she said, "So you can't do that for me at all?" She remained persistent.

Clarence was even impressed with by it. She really knew how to put pressure on a man. But he also realized that he was letting her get away with it because she was young and didn't know any better. It was the spoiled and desperate recklessness of her youth talking.

So Clarence leveled with her. "You know, a young woman could really find herself in a bond with a man if you keep going like this. Because if you talk to the wrong kind of guys about helping you out with money—"

Brenda cut him off, "But that's why I'm asking *you*, because I know you wouldn't do me like that. I mean, do you know how many guys talk about helping me out. I'm not dumb; I mean, I know what they want. And I'm not going out like that, simply because I need money. But somebody has to be on your *side*. You know what I mean? I'm only asking you to be on my side and look out for me like that. I need some *help*."

Got' dammit! Clarence panicked. *What would Maurice say to this shit?* he wondered. The game had quickly climbed out of his reach. He found that he couldn't handle this young woman with his simple logic. She would eat him up alive.

He took a deep breath and thought it over. *You a damned fool, Clarence,* he told himself before he even responded to her. "I'll ah…see what I can do. But I won't make you any—"

"Thank you, thank you, *thank you*!" she exclaimed, cutting him off again. "Oh my God, I promise you will *never* regret helping me. I mean, I will make you feel so *proud* of me."

"Make me feel *proud, how*?" he asked her.

"When I become successful," she answered. "And it will be all because of your help. I mean, I can be like, your little project."

Clarence was stunned into silence. What the hell could he say to that? The girl sounded borderline *crazy*. And all he could do was smile about it. He actually liked the shit. She was a real character, and she made him feel needed. He was the only one on earth who could help her.

Clarence went back to work that next morning and found himself dodging, ducking, weaving, jumping, dipping, stretching, contorting and grabbing luggage like O.J. Simpson in an old Hertz Rental Car commercial before he went crazy for a white girl out in California.

The younger skycaps looked around at each other as if the old man had lost his damn mind.

"Hey, man, what the hell is wrong with Clarence this morning?" one of the younger guys commented to Maurice.

Maurice started giggling to himself and couldn't help it. "Don't worry about him. The boy in love and won't admit it to nobody."

"Well, you better tell his ass not to jump out in front of me again, man. And I don't give a fuck *who* he in love with. That motherfucker's fucking with my money now."

Maurice laughed it off. "Now calm down and watch your mouth out here, young'un. We got passengers to take care of."

"Yeah, and that motherfucker tryna take 'em all."

The young coworker continued pouting.

"Come on now, you know he can't take all of 'em. He's on a roll today, that's all," Maurice explained. He found it all humorous. Clarence looked as if he had drunk five cans of Red Bull on the way to work that morning. And he had a quota to make.

By quitting time, Clarence had broken his three-hundred-dollar goal. In fact, he was closer to *four* hundred. But no one was happy about it but him.

On the way back to their cars in the parking lot, Maurice made sure to have a few words with him.

"Ah, Clarence…you sure you don't have anything to talk to me about? Is your daughter doing okay with money in school? You need to bail your son out of jail or something? What's going on, man? You need me to help you out?" He was being halfway sarcastic.

Clarence looked at him and chuckled. He didn't even care anymore. He had done what he needed to do that day. And he was more than halfway there to five hundred.

So he answered, "I'm trying to make a living, man."

"Nah, you tryna do *more* than that," Maurice countered. "Last week, you was standing around daydreaming all day. Now you come back to work and turn into Superman."

"I had a good day today, that's all," Clarence explained nonchalantly.

"Yeah, I can see that. But I don't want you to hurt yourself out here on account of whatever's going on with you, man. You know what I mean? And you damn sure didn't make any of the younger guys happy about it."

Clarence frowned. "Aw, to hell with them, man. You don't see *me* complaining when *they* make a good buck or two out here."

"Yeah, but they're not out here jumping in front of us to get bags and shit either," he argued. "I mean, you looked like a gotdamned fool out here today, man. You tryna take it back to slavery days?"

"Aw, come on now," Clarence commented. "That's waaay overboard."

"Nah, man, *you* were overboard. I mean, you look like you were really Uncle Tomming it today, man. And you *know* I ain't gon' lie to ya'."

Clarence shook it off and said, "Yeah, whatever."

Maurice stopped at their cars and asked, "So you're still not gonna tell me what's going on?"

Clarence only stared at him in determined silence.

Maurice nodded. "Okay." And he walked away to climb into his car.

After only two days of gathering hungry airport tips, Clarence gave Brenda another five hundred dollars and received a kiss on the cheek with his hug. And he made certain to tell her not to count the money out in the open this time. She had to trust that it was all there, like he had to trust that she would pay it all back somehow.

She agreed and said, "Okay. Now was it as bad as you *thought* it would be?"

Clarence grinned. "Actually, it made me work a lot harder. It felt good. If I worked like that all the time, I guess I would have plenty of extra change in my pockets."

Brenda grinned and said, "You see that? I'm *good* for you. And you're good for *me*. And good *to* me."

"Yeah, *too* good," he blurted. She still was getting the better part of the deal, and he wanted her to realize that.

She told him, "So, you would rather not have me here to inspire you?"

Clarence thought about it and said, "That's a good question. But what do I inspire *you* to do?"

She looked at him and answered, "To work harder." And while her RAV4 was still being repaired at a body shop, she was driving a Chevrolet rental car.

Clarence asked, "Working harder to do what?"

"To pay you back."

He could never get much farther than that. He didn't have the balls to come right out and say it. But he wanted *more* than promises. He wanted more than money, too. What he wanted now was her companionship.

So he asked her, "Well, how 'bout you go out to dinner with me sometime? You know, whenever you're free."

He asked her the question, but he left her answer too wide open. There was no timetable on it.

"Okay," she commented with a nod. Then she ran back off to her hideaways at school and at work.

And as the days and weeks passed, Clarence found himself giving Brenda more and more of his hard-earned money only to see her long enough to give it to her. And although it was never five or six hundred dollars again, the forties, eighties, and hundreds all added up, until Clarence had run out of rope to deal with her without seeking help. So he finally broke down and sat with Maurice inside of his car after work.

"So, you finally decided to tell me now, hunh?"

Maurice couldn't stop himself from smiling and chuckling at the shit. Clarence had been a hard-headed man to his own detriment.

"Come on, man, I'm serious right now," he complained.

"Yeah, and you *should* be," Maurice told him. "So, how much money have you spent on this girl?"

Clarence added it, then he tried to subtract from the real amount. She shrugged and said, "About a thousand dollars."

Maurice stared at him and didn't budge. "Only a *thousand* dollars, Clarence? Are you sure?" He wanted Clarence to know up front that he needed to be bluntly honest with him. "Now, I can't help you if you gon' lie to me in here, Clarence. This is between me and you. And you know we've been around each other for too damn long to lie, man. Now how much you give her?"

Clarence looked away and exhaled. He grumbled, "A little over two, man."

"More than two thousand?" Maurice asked him to make sure.

Clarence got upset with him and snapped, "Yeah, man, shit."

"And you ain't touched her yet?"

Clarence answered, "I've been hugging her a lot."

Maurice stared at him like an angry demon. Clarence couldn't take the glare, so he looked away again and laughed at himself.

"You *hugged* her a lot? For two thousand *dollars*? Nigga, is you *rich* or *crazy*? You been breaking your ass out here for *hugs*?" his experienced co-worker yelled at him inside the car.

"All right, man, now look, what do I need to do now? I've already given her the money. You know that now."

Maurice began to shake his head with doom. "And that's already your problem. You gave her the money without establishing shit. So she ain't planning on giving you shit for it."

"How do you know that?" Clarence asked him.

Maurice stared at him again. "How do I know every-damn-thing else? I *know* these broads, man, if I know *nothing* else. And you got one damn rule you need to learn in this game, Clarence. Now there's a lot of damn rules to it, but this one I'ma tell ya' is the *main* one."

"And what rule is that?" Clarence asked him in haste. He realized that he had flown over to the other side of sanity by asking Maurice anything, especially concerning techniques to scores with a young woman. But that's where he was now, and there was no sense in denying that he had his nose pulled wide open.

Maurice told him, "The most important rule you need to know is this; you don't *choose* them, they choose *you*. You understand me? Now you can talk shit and proposition them all you want, but at the end of the day, if that woman don't choose to get down, then she ain't gon' *get* down. And there ain't shit you can do to change her mind. So if she don't choose you in the beginning, or when you come back to her, then you move your ass on."

"She *did* choose me. If not, then she would have gotten the money from somebody else."

Maurice started laughing again. "Clarence, understand me now...that girl did not *choose* you; *you chose her* by *going* for that dumb shit. And when you put that money in her hands, she won the game right there. And then you walked away with a damn *hug* and hard *dick*, nigga. And don't you *ever* get it confused out here.

"But the thing for honest guys like *you*, is that you scared to ask for the pussy," Maurice continued. "You feeling all guilty and shit 'cause she young. But if you ain't gon' *ask* her for the pussy, then she ain't tryna give you none. But on the *flipside*, she don't have no problem at *all* asking *you* for some money. You catch my drift? So if she can ask *you* for the money, then why can't you ask *her* for the pussy?"

Clarence didn't like his tone or his choice of words, but the facts were facts. And so far, Maurice was on point. Clarence *was* afraid to ask for what he wanted. He definitely felt guilty. And Brenda was surely not shy about asking for *she* wanted.

Maurice continued, "Look, now we too old for that innocent shit, man. These young women know what they getting into when they deal with us. And it ain't fucking walks in the park, like they might do with their college boyfriends. When they get with us, it's all about them asking, 'What am I fin' to get out of this shit?' And that's the honest damn truth, Clarence. You can't change that. And they don't give a fuck about how *nice* you are either. They know you as old as their damn daddy. So they gon' *treat* you like one unless you let them know up front that your game don't work that way. And they *do* know the difference."

He said, "So, I'm gon' give you a live sample of what I mean, when I tell you to let them choose *you*. And you don't give them *nothing* until they make that choice. So they can cry their little asses out all they want. Fuck 'em! The world ain't about charity unless you rich. And we ain't rich. So keep quiet and pay strict attention in here."

Maurice took his cell phone from his belt, dialed a number, put the phone on speaker, and set it down between them on the front seat.

"Hello?" a soft, young voice answered.

"Hey, it's Maurice. I was thinking about you coming from work. I got both my hands full with counting this tip money before I drive off, so excuse me for the speakerphone."

"Oh, okay," she uttered. "So, you made that much money today, hunh?"

"Yee-uup," he answered. "And I remembered that you needed something. But you ain't called me lately, so I figured that you must have gotten it on your own."

Clarence sat deadly silent and awaited the young woman's response.

"No, I still need it," she commented.

"Unh hunh, me too," Maurice answered with a chuckle. "So ah, we need to talk about it over at my place...or you pass?"

There was a slight pause. Then she asked him, "So...you're talking about... us having sex for it?"

"Well, you know, if you don't need it, you don't need it. But I figured I haven't seen you in awhile. You got a boyfriend now?"

"No, none of that."

"Okay, so...I thought about you, thought about what you needed, and figured I'd call you up to see how you made out with it. But you ah, call me back if you feel like it. Okay?"

She said, "Well...I mean, when you wanna see me?"

Maurice looked at Clarence inside the car and nodded to him. He answered, "I don't know. When you free again?"

"Umm...I can come see you tomorrow. But I'm busy tonight."

"Okay, well, don't have *too* much fun. You make a lonely man nervous," he suggested to her.

"Aw, naw, it's nothing like that. Me and my girlfriends are, umm, going to this comedy show, that's all."

"Well, wouldn't it be funny if you could come see me after the show. Then again, I gotta be back up before sunlight tomorrow, and comedy shows generally run late."

"Yeah, and then you won't let me stay over at your place to rest up before I go back to work."

"Aw, naw, a man gotta keep his castle sacred. But ah, so you call me up for tomorrow then, and we'll talk about that. Okay?"

"All right, then, I'll call you tomar'."

Maurice hung up and said, "You see how that works, Clarence? You see she didn't hang up the phone until she took the bait? That's how you make them *choose*. She know what she gotta do to get this money."

Clarence shook his head and said, "That sounds like prostitution to me, man. And that ain't something I wanna get involved in. I just like this girl, that's all."

"Yeah, and she likes you, too, Clarence. She likes your *money*. And she'll never like anything else."

"How can you *assume* that?" Clarence insisted.

Maurice took another deep breath and exhaled as he prepared himself to leave the car. "You're about to find out, Clarence. And if you really want that girl like you *think* you do, you would have to offer her *five* thousand dollars to fuck her now. Because she already got *two* thousand for *free*."

Clarence shook off his vile comments, while his devious coworker climbed out of his car to return to his own.

"Remember the main rule, Clarence, or get out the damn game before you end up in the poor house with a stroke and heartache from working too hard and getting kicked to the curb. HA HA HAH!" Maurice laughed like a sinister villain.

Nevertheless, his comments stuck on Clarence's mind. How could they not? He had asked him for them.

Clarence wished that he had never asked Maurice for his honest opinion. But it was too late. The man had now corrupted his mind.

"Five thousand dollars," Clarence repeated to himself at home. He continued to shake his head at the thought. *Would she actually go for something like that?*

He was itching to call her up and fiddle around to see how much truth was in it. "Nah, she would think I had lost my mind," he assumed. Maurice was right. Since Clarence had established a platonic relationship, there would be no changing of parameters.

But what if I asked once she needed something big from me again? he questioned. *I could at least try it.*

It only took another week before something *big* came up. They were nearing the Thanksgiving holiday break, with Christmas right around the corner.

"I was wondering if you believed in Santa Claus," Brenda joked with him over the line.

"Yeah, and I was wondering if you believed in having a friendly dinner."

"Sure I do," she responded.

"Well, how come we still haven't had one?"

"Because our schedules keep clashing."

"No, *your* schedule keeps clashing."

"Well, okay, I promise to go out with you as soon as I get back from the Thanksgiving break, and before Christmas."

"But you need something for when you go back to Baltimore, right?"

"Oh, definitely. It's almost shopping season. And I'll be sure to come back with at least a few pieces from D.C. that you'll love."

Clarence flipped the script on her and said, "All right, well, we can talk about that over dinner before you leave."

"I told you, *after* I get back. I got too much to do this week."

She was indeed the boss of their awkward relationship. So Clarence got bold enough to state, "I might be too busy myself to meet up with you this time. But I know I gotta eat. You gotta eat, too. So let's both eat together and talk about things."

His heart was racing while he attempted to stand tall on a new backbone.

Brenda caught on to his new game and asked him, "Are you saying you're not gonna give me anything unless I have dinner with you?"

"What's so wrong with us having dinner?" he asked civilly enough.

"Nothing is wrong with us having dinner. I don't like people giving me ultimatums and shit. And I already *told you* that I would do it once I got *back*."

Her tone was totally demeaning to a man who had helped her out with more than a couple thousand dollars, so Clarence continued to stand his ground.

"I didn't mean for you take it that way. But I guess I'll talk to you when you have time."

"I have time to talk right now," she snapped.

He said, "I meant when you're ready to pick up the money."

That made her hesitate to try and figure him out. "I mean, what do you mean, 'when I'm ready to pick up the money,' Clarence? You know I'm busy right now."

"Yeah, so when you're not busy, we can go out and talk about everything."

"Talk about everything like *what*? I mean, what are you telling me right now? Spit it out," she challenged him.

Clarence finally came out with it and said, "I'm telling you that I'm tired of you running off after I give you what you need. But you can't seem to have even an *hour* for me."

"Because I don't *have* a fucking hour," she cursed. "Every time I meet up with you, you already know that my day is already mapped out. So what are you talking about?"

It was no use. The girl was plain *stubborn*. Clarence figured he should have seen it coming a long time ago. He wasn't any closer to her than the man on the moon. And the money didn't mean a damn thing. In fact, it seemed to have made her bolder.

I don't believe how much of an idiot I've been! he told himself. *She doesn't even treat me like a friend, let alone somebody she's interested in. I'm just a walking ATM machine!*

Nevertheless, he managed to keep his poise with her. "Well, I'm here whenever you decide to see me. Okay?"

He was mimicking Maurice's tone exactly.

She snapped, "Oh, don't expect me to call you if you're gonna treat me like that. Like I told you before, I don't like when people try to lock me into shit that I already said I can't do."

"Okay, well, I'll wait for you to come around then," Clarence told her.

Finally, Brenda had run out of words to argue back and forth with him. "You know what…? Okay, whatever. I have to go."

Clarence said, "All right, I'll talk to you when you call me." And that was it.

When he hung up, he felt full of apprehension about any kind of future relationship with her. But at the same time, he felt relieved. The pressure she had exerted on him had ended. And he could breathe freely again.

Two days later, getting closer to the holiday break, Brenda called Clarence back. He immediately asked, "Are you ready to see me about everything?"

She answered, "Yeah, let's meet at our regular spot. And I need a round trip plane ticket back to BWI."

She acted as if they had never spoken about his dinner date proposal just two days ago.

"You mean over dinner, right? You told me you like Chili's. We can meet over there."

Brenda exhaled loudly over the phone and said, "*Please* don't start with that again. We're *friends*, Clarence. *Friends* don't have to go to dinner."

"And friends don't have to pay for airline tickets either."

"What? I *always* give you your money back for those tickets."

"What about for everything else I've given you money for? Is that what *'friends'* do?"

"Oh, with no *problem*. I have other friends that give me money when I need it. I mean, not as *much*, but they help me out when they can."

That was the wrong comment to make. Clarence said, "Well, you can tell them to help you out with everything else too, and until you learn to respect me more." And he hung up on her without thinking. It was a raw passion thing. She had finally taken him to that point.

Of course, she called his ass right back, only for Clarence to ignore her two return calls. But then he answered her third one.

Brenda immediately told him, "Okay, we can go to Chili's. Is that what you want? *God!*"

It was only a small victory, but a very hard-fought one.

All of that just to take this girl out to dinner once. That's absolutely crazy! Clarence thought.

But before he could comment on it, she added, "But my boyfriend will probably want to go with me."

Clarence's jaw dropped to the floor at his home. He was totally blindsided. "*Boyfriend?* Well, how come you never talked about him before?"

"I mean, what difference does it make, we're just *'friends'*?"

Clarence cursed, *This motherfucking bitch strung me along the whole got'dammed time!* He couldn't believe it. He even challenged her on it.

"You don't really have a boyfriend? Cut that out."

She had to be pulling his old-ass legs.

Then she took the atrocity further. "You wanna speak to him? Hold on."

Before Clarence could tell her no, she put a robust male voice on the line. "Hello."

Clarence didn't want to say a damn thing to him. Was Brenda fucking with him or what?

I can't believe this shit! I'ma got'damned FOOL!

Even if Brenda was joking, the joke had obviously gone too far.

MOTHERFUCKER! Clarence cursed himself. *This is what the hell I get!*

"Hello," the male voice answered again. Then he told Brenda, "There's nobody answering."

Brenda returned to the line and said, "Clarence, I know you're still there. What's wrong? I mean, you've been like a big uncle to me. So let's all go out and eat together."

Clarence calmly press the END button on his cell phone and hung up. Then he recited Maurice's number one rule: "You don't choose *them*, they choose *you*." And obviously, he had found out the hard way that he had *not* been chosen by a conniving-ass college girl.

"Fuck it," he told himself. "I guess Maurice knows what he knows... And now *I* know it."

———•———

MR. DAVID BUTLER SR.

Three eager young women walked into the downtown offices of David Butler Sr., a popular community activist who ran the Southeastern Empowerment Forum of small businesses and entrepreneurs in Birmingham, Alabama. David was a handsome power figure who could always be counted on to gather an enthusiastic crowd in the city. Recently turning forty-five, many viewed him as the next logical mayor. And although he had not yet announced his official interests in the position, everyone assumed that he would run for office in their next election. So the three excited women walked right up to his secretary at her desk inside the lobby, and inquired about summer internships for college credit in their upcoming senior year.

"We're all willing to do whatever you have available for us," the lead girl, who was the tallest, spoke up. They were all dressed professionally in women's business suits of various dark material.

The secretary was intrigued by their optimistic support. But why had they all come together?

"Well, I could see maybe one or two of you, but all *three*. What would *I* have left to do?" she joked.

The young women laughed it off.

"You'll still have your job."

"Yeah, and at least you get *paid* for it," the other two commented in unison.

The secretary countered, "Not if everyone shows up to work for *free*, I won't."

"Well, we could do a lot of things outside of the office, or after hours, while you go back home and chill more with your family or whatever," the tall leader suggested.

Everyone knew that David Butler Sr. hosted plenty of evening events. And since all three of the young women desired to be involved in event planning, they figured that mapping out functions and troubleshooting from the office of the man who may soon become the next mayor of the city was a top gig for experience.

However, his secretary frowned at their suggestion to replace her evening work. "Chill with my *family*," she repeated. "What family is that?"

"You know, your husband and kids or whatever," the second young woman responded. She was the shortest and the most striking, with sandy-brown skin and jet-black hair.

The secretary snapped, "Now wait a minute, I may be older than *you* all, but I'm not *that* old. And I haven't *found* a husband to have children *with* yet."

"Oh, my bad," the second one apologized.

Indeed, the secretary was only twenty-six herself, and she could still hold her own in the dating game.

"Well, I'll need to ask him if he has anything extra for you guys to do. Where do you go to school?" she questioned.

"Alabama State," the third one answered. She seemed to be the most reserved with the thickest body, a real meat-and-potatoes woman.

The secretary frowned again. "Oh, there. Well, I went to A&M," she bragged.

"We won't hold it against you," the tall leader joked on cue.

Her partners chuckled, but the secretary didn't seem to find her quip as humorous.

"And you want an *internship* at *my* office?" she asked sarcastically.

The three young women were stuck for a minute. How would they respond to that? The Alabama A&M rival was obviously in a decision-making position?

The second young woman finally broke the silence. "I mean, it's all in good fun. We're all black schools, and we're all trying to get ahead and do what we need to do."

"Well, you know that *David* went to A&M *too*, right," the secretary rubbed in.

"We won't hold it against *him* either, " the third woman added.

The camaraderie had been sucked out of the room. They all felt like walking back out and starting all over again.

The tall leader announced, "Well, we're not here for rivalry right now; we're here for unity."

"I bet you are," the secretary quipped back. She looked to have the last laugh. But just as their conversation seemed to have stalled, David Butler Sr. barged into the lobby while on his cell phone. Robert Clay, his childhood friend and long-time assistant, was holding the office door open for him.

"Yeah, we're on our way over there now."

The three women were all in shock and bubbled with energy.

David noticed them as he hung up his call.

"Ah, who are you?" he asked the tall leader specifically. She was in the most ready position to greet him.

She held out her hand to him like an honorable dignitary. "I'm Treena Barkley, and these are my friends, Beverly Simpson and Raquelle Freeman," she addressed.

They each smiled and shook the man's hand. He was dressed in his usual sharp suit with a stylish tie, and was groomed for perfection, with a fresh haircut, pleasant-smelling cologne, and a clean-shaven face.

"You can call me Rocki," the third young woman greeted him.

David chuckled. "Well, what can I do for you ladies?"

"We're here from Alabama State to ask for summer internships, and we're all from the Birmingham area," Treena responded.

"All *three* of you want internships?"

His secretary overheard him and grinned. It was her sentiments exactly.

"Yeah, we're The Triple Threat," Beverly stated. "We work well together."

David looked back at his assistant. "What do you think about that, Bobby?"

Robert shrugged, wearing a sharp suit and tie of his own. But he looked much older than David. "Bobby" looked more like an older mentor.

He commented, "Put 'em to work."

David then looked at his secretary. "C.J., get all their information and let's see what they can help us out with this summer."

"For real?" Treena asked him, surprised.

"That's what you want, right?"

Treena was overjoyed by the speed of his decision. "Yeah, yeah," she told him excitedly.

"Thanks!" her two girlfriends chimed in.

David nodded. "All right, so we'll see you guys later. C.J.'ll show you around the office."

And that was it. The man was out the door as if a hurricane had yanked him out.

"So...what does 'C.J.' stand for?" Beverly asked the secretary after the boss had left.

Instead of answering her, she held up her nameplate that sat on her desk. It read, "Cheryl Jackson."

"Oh, it's right there." Beverly felt stupid.

And away we go, C.J. thought to herself with a sigh. *They just made my job three times harder this summer.*

"So, you have no idea what you want them to do today?" C.J. asked David in his office, after nine o'clock the next morning.

David gave it some thought while he sat behind his large, wooden desk.

He then blew it off. "We'll think of something, it's only day one. Have them run out and buy some donuts and orange juice for the office or something."

C.J. held out her right hand and cocked her curvy hips for some money.

David smiled. "Don't I pay you enough around here already?"

"No, not hardly."

"Well, get forty dollars from Bobby to do it."

C.J. stood inside of his office with the door closed and stared at him for a moment. "Do you want me to get *everything* I need from Bobby now?" she hinted at him with a smirk.

David chuckled. "You tell me. What all can Bobby give you that you'll be satisfied with?"

C.J. stood for a few seconds and countered, "Watch yourself, Mr. Man. Or you'll get the trouble that you're asking for."

David chuckled and let the warning die down as his sexy secretary walked out of the room and immediately straightened out her walk in her business suit.

Treena, Beverly, and Rocki quieted down in the conference room when C.J. returned. She then placed forty dollars on the long, oval-shaped table. "Okay, girls, your first big assignment is to go out and get donuts and orange juice for everyone at the office."

Treena looked around at her friends, while Beverly and Rocki giggled.

"You're kidding me, right?"

"No, I am not," C.J. answered frankly.

Rocki stood up and was ready to go. "It's only our first day on the job, Treena. It'll all come."

"I hope so," Beverly added, still smiling.

C.J. had nothing more constructive to say to them. "Well, hurry up and get back with it. Maybe he wants to see how fast you can handle it."

Beverly nodded. "Good point."

Rocki added, "You see where I'm at already. I'm practically out the door. You just do what you're asked to do."

Treena retorted, "Yeah, and with no money," while she grabbed the forty dollars from the conference room table.

Rocki told her, "Well, you do the accounting, I'll do the selecting, and Beverly can do the driving."

"Why do *I* have to drive," Beverly complained as they headed out of the conference room.

C.J. shook her head. "I don't believe he's even doing this," she mumbled.

By that afternoon, David had enough free time to interview each new intern in his office about her skills.

"So, what would you say are your strengths; leadership and initiative?" he asked Treena, who he had called into his office first.

Treena thought about it and nodded. "Umm, yeah, I would say so. Yeah."

"So, what are your weaknesses; patience and high expectations?"

She began to smile and looked down bashfully. It sounded as if he had read her correctly before she even had a chance to speak. David had done deals with enough professionals to read them all quickly. It was a major part of his job skill to know who he was dealing with as quickly as possible.

"Umm ... I guess you can say that," Treena admitted.

He nodded. "So, I'll put you in charge of projects and remind you to be patient with your friends."

Next he called in Rocki to have a seat.

"So, what are your strengths and weaknesses; humor, speed, and a lack of detail and stick-to-itness?"

The question seemed loaded with the answers already.

Rocki looked at him and grimaced before she grinned.

"Well, what part of the question do you want me to answer?" she asked. "All of it."

She paused and tried to gather her thoughts. "Well, I guess I do like to lighten things up with a little bit of humor. And yeah, I just, you know, do what I'm supposed to do. But if it's something that takes a long time..."

She smiled and didn't feel the need to fill in her answer. Then she added, "Beverly is good with that part. She'll do it until it gets done."

David called Beverly in to have a seat in his office last.

"So, are you the most dedicated?" he asked her.

She looked into his eyes and felt stunned. *Dedicated to what?* she thought.

"Ahh, I guess you could say that. I don't tend to give up easy."

"Oh yeah? So how long have you been with your present boyfriend?" he asked her out of the blue.

The question threw the young and attractive college student for a loop. She suddenly felt hot and clammy, wondering if he could read her nervous body language.

She giggled. "Actually, we recently broke up, right before I left school. Honestly, I think he *planned* it that way," she added.

"Well, why would a young guy wanna do that to you? Didn't he know what he had on his hands? You would do anything for him, wouldn't you?"

With that comment, he made the young intern feel even hotter.

"He, umm...wanted other girls, I guess," she reasoned.

"Do you *guess*, or do you *know*?" David pressed her.

She paused. "Umm...I *know*."

He nodded at her. "You have to learn to be more confident. Sometimes attractiveness can mask insecurities. But you have a good heart. So learn to go with what you feel and be strong about it."

At the end of their first full day of work at his office, all three women were even more impressed with him. They sat and ate at a Burger King restaurant and discussed their separate observations of the boss.

"He is a very smart man," Rocki commented.

Treena nodded over a burger and said, "That's why we all wanted to work for him, right? So why would we expect anything less?"

All Beverly did was smile while eating fries. She didn't want to express what *she* was thinking about him. *I think we like each other*, she mused. It was as if he was using code words to let her know, ever so cleverly. But to hell if she was going to tell her girlfriends.

"So, what did he ask *you*, Bev?" Rocki asked, eating fries of her own.

"Umm, you know, about my career aspirations and stuff," Beverly lied.

"And what did you tell him?" Treena quizzed.

"I mean, I told him that we all want to learn how to plan events or whatever."

"Well, he didn't ask *me* all of that," Rocki commented. "He must like you more," she joked.

Beverly shook her head. "Here we go with that again."

Rocki argued, "But it's *true*. A lot of guys be liking your little ass."

"I'm not little, I'm just smaller than *you*," Beverly countered. "Besides, that man is married and about to run for mayor soon."

"And what is that supposed to mean, that he can't like you?" Treena questioned. "Because I can tell that something's going on with him and C.J.," she assumed.

"Oh, yeah, she's on fire for him, and be trying to play it all off. Do you see how she try not to look at him around us?" Rocki brought up. "Like, she would really do that shit if we weren't there. *Please!* It's all a damn *act*. And it's obvious that she don't want us all up in there. But I got news for her ass, this internship is a lot more important to me than her little *hurt* emotions."

Beverly only smiled again. But she didn't like the conversation about C.J. and David having feelings. Even though she assumed as much herself, if C.J. was able to bottle up the majority of his attention at the office, then where would that leave her?

"What do you think, Bev? You think C.J. got the heat for him?"

Beverly turned the question around and asked her, "Do you?"

Treena didn't hesitate. "Hell yeah!" she answered frankly.

Rocki broke up laughing and spit her soda back down her straw. She held up her right hand to high-five Treena across the table. She bragged, "I would give his ass *back* spasms in a *hot* minute."

Beverly shook her head and grinned passively. "Y'all crazy. That man is married."

"Like that ever stopped a dick from getting hard," Rocki noted.

Beverly said, "Rocki, people are eating in here."

"And they eat in the bedroom, too," she joked.

Treena laughed. "What about *you*, Bev? You didn't feel anything crazy when you were in the room alone with him? I mean, we've seen this man all up on television and in the newspapers *plenty* of times. And he looks and smells *way* better in person."

"Duuuhhh, you can't smell his ass through the TV," Rocki stated.

"Well, that's my point. Now we're all up close and personal with him. But the internship is still most important to me though," Treena established for them.

Beverly nodded in agreement. "Right." *But if he ever wanted to…*she contemplated.

When the three interns attended their first evening event, they all got a chance to meet David Butler Sr.'s wife, Krystal. She was a tall, regal woman who had put on a few more pounds than the pictures David kept of her inside of his office. Maybe he liked the curves of his younger wife and not the older one.

"Nice to meet you," she addressed them civilly. But she wasn't particularly warm to them. She more comfortable around Cheryl. In fact, she seemed to avoid her husband's secretary for the majority of the evening. That made the college students more suspicious of David's relationship with C.J.

I can imagine how she feels, Beverly told herself of his wife. She related how his wife must have felt to her own feelings of when her college boyfriend had begun to wander in other directions, and at no fault of her own.

Maybe that was the problem. David was right. She should have been more confident and straightened her boyfriend out as soon as she suspected him of cheating. But as she watched her boss work the room of Birmingham notables with his impeccable style of dress, his 100-watt smile, his fluid conversations, wit, and obvious good looks, she couldn't help but be struck by him.

"So, David, when are you gonna make the big announcement that everyone's waiting for?" a city official asked him amongst the fine suits and ties, dresses and skirts, soft music and wine, and catered finger foods, with plastic plates, cups, forks and knives that stretched from one end of the room to the other.

David realized the group of eight surrounding him would spread his answer throughout the room. "Well *if* I ever decide to make an announcement of something ah, *special*, trust me, you guys will all be the first to know." He then shared a light laugh to go down with his white wine.

Ever so often, he would look over and catch Beverly eyeing him. He made it seem as if she were his little secret inside the room. Or at least *she* felt that way.

She then took her eyes off of him for a few minutes to collect another piece of chicken, only for David to creep up beside her at the food table and slide another hint into her left ear. "Keep your eyes on the prize, young lady. You just might get it."

Beverly stood frozen at the table, wondering who may have seen him speak to her. She suddenly felt a nervous wreck, with tingles of confusion paralyzing her from the spine down. He had stopped her from moving her arm to select another piece of chicken.

He is just bad, she told herself. *I wonder how many women in this room he's been with. And his wife probably knows about most of then. But she's just in here playing wifey.*

Beverly turned just enough to her right to locate his wife, as well as C.J. and any other woman who may have been following David's moves. But everyone seemed to maintain their places, as if the man's open flirtations were all acceptable. So she began to daydream about what the boss would be like in bed.

"Hey, what's on your mind, girl? How come you're over here looking all stiff?" Rocki walked over and asked her.

Beverly shook it off. "Oh, I was just…thinking."

"About what?

Beverly grinned and fibbed, "I think that wine was a little too strong for me," to throw her friend off track.

Rocki looked her in her eyes. "Oh, well, in that case, don't talk to these men too strong in here. Because about *three* of them tried to pick me up already. And I know your little body can't defend yourself after no drinks. So I better stay right here next to you."

Beverly didn't like the sound of that. She liked her private space. "I'm not *that* buzzed. I'm not drinking anymore, that's all."

"Well, still, I need to stick by you, just in case."

"Walk with me to the bathroom then."

As they made their stroll toward the restrooms, a much younger man than the average in the room approached them. He looked no more than his late twenties, where the room average was forty-something. But the average woman in room was a decade or so younger.

"Hey, how are you guys doing? I'm Gregory Daniel."

He extended his right hand to them. He looked like a younger, taller version of the next big man in the city. And his eyes were all over Beverly.

Rocki looked him up and down and stretched her eyes wide, impressed with him. She shook his extended hand. "Well, I'm Raquelle, and this is my girl Beverly."

Beverly shook his hand and immediately caught David Butler in clear eye view from the right. He was speaking to another group of his admirers. She was paying so much attention to her cat-and-mouse game with David that she hardly listened to the younger man, who was single, flattering and closer to her age and speed.

"Oh, what was that?" she asked him absentmindedly.

Rocki told him, "Don't mind her; she's a little buzzed right now. We were headed to the bathroom to unload it."

Gregory laughed at Rocki's candidness. "Well, make sure you see me again before you leave. And take my card with you," he told them both, handing both of them his business card.

Rocki looked over his laminated card with his photo for real estate. "I'll make sure she calls you when she starts looking for a house or something." She had no confusion about who he was interested in. And it was no big deal to her. Rocki had her share of men in the room as well.

"Or before then," Gregory countered.

Beverly flipped his card over in her hands and held it out a little longer to make sure that David would see it from the distance.

Now let's see what he does about this? she pondered.

When they reached the bathroom, Rocki asked her friend, "Girl, what's wrong with you tonight? You didn't like him? He was practically *drooling* over you."

Beverly grinned and blew it off without a word. She couldn't say the young man was not attractive; he was. Her mind was simply preoccupied. "I don't really want to be in a new relationship right now. I think I need a summer break."

Rocki pushed the ladies bathroom door open. "Who was talking about a relationship? Just *date* the man and see what he's about."

Inside the bathroom, they encountered C.J., who was powdering her face in the mirror.

The secretary looked at them both and grunted, "Hey." Then she looked toward Rocki. "Who are you talking about?" She knew Raquelle was more likely to give her an honest answer. Beverly was more secretive.

Rocki grimaced. "Umm, some guy we met." She figured it was none of C.J.'s business.

David! Beverly thought of answering boldly. But she would never do that. Her private life would remain *private*. That's how she had always been, private and dedicated to her love interests.

C.J. shrugged and mumbled, "All right." She finished her powder job in the mirror, then she gathered her bag and walked out.

As soon as she was out of earshot, Rocki commented, "I wonder who she's getting all *extra* for to leave here with tonight? *Ho!*" she snapped.

Beverly grinned at the slight and thought of David Butler Sr. again. He had done a real job on her mind without even trying hard.

He's only toying with me in here, she tried to convince herself. *Nobody's getting him tonight. He's gonna go right back home with his wife. He's trying to see who's interested in him to pump up his own ego, that's all.*

Just as he kept everyone guessing about his run for election as Birmingham's mayor, David kept her—and no telling how many other women—guessing about an opportunity to sleep with him at the end of the night.

So by the time Beverly had returned to the room, she had straightened out her wandering mind. And she decided that her boss could flirt inside the room all he wanted. But there was no sense in her taking him seriously; he didn't really mean any of it.

Nevertheless, as soon she found herself separated from Rocki and Treena again, David's trusted assistant Robert Clay had caught up with her to ask how she was doing.

Beverly nodded. "I'm good."

"Are you tired yet?" He seemed straight to the point.

She grimaced. "Ahh…not really." She didn't want to sound as if she was slacking on the job, especially since they had not been asked to do much that evening. She had no time to be tired as an aspiring event coordinator. She had to expect to be up and energized at all times of the day and night. And she couldn't expect to rest or be tired until the evening was over.

Robert then handed her a room key to the Marriott as if it was a normal business card. "If you want to stay out, call him and let him know. And everyone doesn't get one of those, so put it away."

He spoke with such authority and directness that Beverly slid the room key into her small purse immediately. "Okay," she uttered.

"All right then," he mumbled to her gruffly. "Now that's yours to use or *not* to use *alone*. And you *call* him first."

Robert walked away from her as calmly as he had approached. And their fast exchange sent her mind right back into a tailspin.

Oh my God! she told herself. *He is serious!*

With all of the anxiety that she felt, she could hardly breathe.

Then Gregory Daniel popped back up.

"Hey, we meet again," he joked.

The young man had bad timing. It was the wrong night, the wrong place, and the wrong girl.

"Hey," Beverly responded. And that was it. She didn't have anything else to say to him. He was only getting in the way of her thoughts about David's invitation.

"So are you still buzzed a little bit?" Gregory asked her, smiling charmingly.

Beverly failed to even fake it. The young man was beginning to irritate her and she needed to get away from him.

"Excuse me, but I have something to do," she told him. And she then walked off toward Treena. Her tall girlfriend had been chatting up a couple dozen people and collecting business cards for herself.

"What have you been doing all night?" Beverly asked.

Treena turned and frowned at her. "Are you kidding me? What have I been *doing* all night? I've been collecting business cards and phone numbers. This is what we're here for. But what have *you* been doing?"

"Not that," Beverly leveled to her and grinned. "We have all summer to do that. I was relaxing tonight and seeing how everything works."

Treena shrugged. "Okay, suit yourself. But I'm not wasting time or opportunities relaxing. You can relax anytime. There were some major people in this room tonight. And you don't really know if they're gonna come to the next event or not."

Things were beginning to wind down at close to eleven o'clock on a Wednesday evening. The majority of the crowd had to work the next morning.

Beverly countered, "I know *somebody* will be here. The next event may have more important people than this one."

Treena paused, then nodded. "Yeah, you're right. But then I'll be right back on the grind again, collecting *more* numbers."

Beverly grinned. "Have any guys tried to get at you tonight?" She wanted to move their conversation closer to what she had been thinking about, older men who chased younger women.

Treena frowned. "Of course. That's all day, every day. But I always work my way around it. So I smile at their little comments and then ask them what kind of work they do. And by the time I get to my third question, I shift their minds back toward business."

Treena was a little *too* much business sometimes for Beverly's taste. So she asked her, "And you didn't talk to any man you may have been interested in tonight?"

Treena finally grinned. "Yeah, but I didn't let them know it."

They shared a laugh as Raquelle walked over to join them. "What are you two laughing at?"

"Life," Treena spoke up. "But it's almost time to pack it in for the night," she commented, taking a look around the emptying room.

Before she could finish her final assessment of the crowd, David popped up behind them and put his arms around them all. "Girls, it's been a good night tonight. So get back home or wherever else you have to go, and I'll see you bright and early tomorrow morning, if not sooner."

Rocki and Treena chuckled, but Beverly simply smiled. David's sly comments were tailor-made for her, and her friends had no idea what he meant by it. So as soon as he had left them, Rocki asked, "What did he mean by 'tomorrow morning, if not *sooner*'?"

Beverly shook it off to diffuse another one of Rocki's bombs. "Stop reading into everything, girl," she complained. "If you haven't noticed it yet, he likes being ambiguous. He's been doing that to people all night."

Treena caught on. "Have you been *listening* to him talk all night?"

"I've listened to him enough to *know*," Beverly countered. "He likes catching people off guard."

"Well, what he catch *you* off guard with?" Rocki asked with a smirk.

Everything! Beverly thought to herself. But she dared not to share that information with her friends. She shook it off instead and smiled.

"You really have a wild imagination, girl," she commented. "Well, let's go ahead and go."

Beverly had driven them to the downtown event that evening, and while she drove her friends back home, she contemplated if she would call David on his cell phone to find out his intentions for giving her a key to a room at the Marriott.

"Why you all quiet, Bev?" Rocki asked from the passenger seat. Treena was already knocked out in the backseat. She had practically been up for two days straight, strategizing the previous night, and had used up every bit of her energy at the event. And now that it was finally over, her body had shut down for a much needed rest.

Beverly took a breath. "I'm thinking about getting in bed and getting back up for tomorrow, that's all."

"Who you telling? I might be coming in late tomorrow myself."

"But I know who *won't* be late," Beverly teased in reference to Treena.

"Yeah, that's why she's back there sleeping now," Rocki suggested. "She's a damn workaholic and ain't even out of college yet."

Beverly dropped Rocki off at her parents' house first, then she drove Treena back home to wake her up and help her into the house. Once her driving duties were accomplished by midnight, she was free to *call* or *not to call* David Butler Sr.

"What if he's sitting right next to his wife?" she imagined to herself out loud. "That would be so embarrassing."

Then his wife would look at me the way she looks at C.J., she assumed. *But I could call him to say we all made it back home safely. His wife can't argue about that.*

She had rationalized an approach and a justification to call him. And she wanted to make the call before midnight, so she jumped on her cell phone with haste and called his emergency cell number at 11:56 p.m.

"Hey, you guys make it back home safe?" David asked her over his line. He didn't even say "hello." There was a lot of noise in the background, as if he was still out at a bar or something.

"Yeah, we all made it," she answered.

"And you're still driving?"

She paused and wondered if he could tell over the phone. "Unfortunately."

"And are you anywhere near the Marriott?"

She thought briefly. "No." She figured if he really wanted her, he would at least have to do a little work.

"Are you *planning* to be?"

"I *could*," Beverly told him. And she left it at that, prolonging their cat-and-mouse game.

"Well, what's stopping you?" he questioned. "You came this far with it. And like I tell you, you have to be confident enough to go after what you want when it's right there in front of you." He added, "You're holding the key to your own desires right now."

"Am I?"

"You answer that question for yourself and call me back with your answer. I'll be down in the lobby having a drink."

He hung up and left her to think for herself, right as she approached the exit ramp for downtown Birmingham. The Marriott was directly in view from Interstate 20 as she headed north toward home.

The hotel is right there in front of me, she told herself. *But...I mean, that's just wrong. What if it was my husband?*

That thought made her want to call him back to beef about it.

"Where is your wife? Is she there, too?" she called back and asked him immediately. She even had the gall to sound snappy.

"You know better that that. Now, are you here or are you home?"

He made the cat-and-mouse game sound finished. There was nowhere left for her to hide. Either she would accept his advances or she wouldn't.

Then she whined, "But why me?"

"I'll tell you what; I'll explain it to you when you get here. Now, let me finish up this drink."

Again, he ended the phone call. But she still wanted concrete answers from a man who seemed to be a master escape artist. He failed to give folks a straight answer to anything.

Finally, she slapped on her right-turn blinkers and headed for the ramp that was two exits past downtown.

She told herself, "You know what; he's not gonna do me like that. I need to know what he wants before this goes on for too long."

When she arrived at the Marriott and parked, less than fifteen minutes after their last phone call, she haggled over whether to use the key to enter the room on her own or meet up with him at the bar.

But if anyone else was there at the public bar with him, he may have chosen to play another game of ambiguity and have her standing there looking foolish. So she decided to call him again.

"Hello," he answered nonchalantly. Even his bland response to her call was coded. He was giving her a chance to talk without him playing his own cards at the bar.

Beverly shook her head, irritated and impressed with him at the same time. *Players are so good at this,* she analyzed. Her past college boyfriend was adept at dipping and dodging in a similar fashion.

"You want me to use the key to the room, or...meet you at the bar?"

She had already suspected his response; she only wanted to make certain.

"It's there for a reason. And I'm heading up in a minute. Then I can talk to you about everything, and explain my life to you."

She nodded. "Okay. I'll be there." And she couldn't wait to hear him out.

Beverly entered the club-level room and walked into a spacious suite with all the amenities of executive quarters. It was more than a room; it was *five* rooms, including a master bedroom, a master bath, a full office, a television and lounge area, and a guest bath. Her walk to the window revealed a beautiful skyline view of downtown.

"Damn," she expressed out loud.

David walked in while she was admiring the view.

"It ain't much to look at compared to the big cities, but she's still ours," he commented of Birmingham.

Beverly turned to face him in her plum strapless dress. "So are you gonna run for mayor? I won't tell anybody if you tell me," she promised with a grin.

David grunted and walked over to her by the window. Then he held his hands out for her to take them, which she did. "Are you gonna tell them that you were my intern?" His eyes were locked dead on hers with serious intent. His loaded sentence told her everything. She was in the real world of grown-ups now, and the stakes of rumors were far too high to chance.

She dropped her eyes. "I don't know." It was a loaded response of her own. She didn't know if she wanted to go there with him.

David kissed the back of her right hand softly with his lips. "Yes, you do. You know *exactly* what you want." He walked away from her and into the master bedroom.

Beverly stood there cold and lonely. She was cold, not from the temperature of the room, but from the lack of his soft touch. She quickly found herself desiring his warmth inside the room, no matter what the consequences would be.

She took a deep breath and thought, *What am I about to get myself into?* But it was a rhetorical question. Her decision had already been made. All David had to do now was ask her for it.

"So, you got some questions for me?" he asked her from the bedroom. He was already taking off his suit jacket, tie and shoes.

Beverly heard his question and decided to finally walk into the room behind him.

She erased all of her earlier questions, but wanted to know her worth to an older man who already had everything, and who was destined for much more.

"What do I mean to you?"

David tossed the question back in her court. "What do you want to mean?"

She shrugged. "I mean, I don't wanna be some one-night *stand*, I know that."

"Well, can you handle *more* than one night?" he questioned.

"Yeah," she answered. "Like you said, I'm *dedicated*, right? But what happens to everyone else? And your *wife*?" she quizzed.

David grunted and smiled again. "Nothing happens. Everyone plays their position, or they don't play. That's the way it is."

Beverly stood and felt cold again. His honesty had left her stranded with no coat. And she still wanted his warmth. "And what position am I?"

"You're a young rookie, an upcoming star," he spoke as if he was bragging.

The absurdity of being compared to a sports player made her grin. But she understood the comparison. She was young and brand new to his team. However, she still found herself wanting to join, like a rookie would.

"Well, are you gonna stand there trying to make up your mind…or are you planning to take off your clothes for me?"

Instead of feeling appalled by his impatient candor, Beverly felt an urge to smile. His urgency and frankness had made her feel warm again. He was finally being direct with her. And it made her feel like an insider.

She cracked, "Are you gonna take your clothes off?"

"I don't think my body is as pretty as yours."

It was a clever response on his part. So she stripped from her clothes to give him what he wanted, a close-up view of her naked body, while she aimed to feel the warmth that *she* wanted from him.

"Was that so hard to do? Look at you. You're beautiful," he expressed to her.

"And I'm *cold*."

David pulled back the overkill of quilts, sheets, and covers on the king-sized bed.

"Climb on in, and I'll be joining you in a minute," he told her.

David then took a stroll into the master bathroom to take a loud piss with the door still open.

Oh my God, it sounds like he got a big one, Beverly thought to herself, while listening to the heavy sound of his urine hitting the toilet water. She found herself in strong anticipation of his older body while she waited in bed.

When David returned to the room with condoms in hand, and stripped down to his boxers, she found that the man still had an honorable figure.

"You're not that bad yourself," she commented.

"Yeah, that's from working out and jogging. A man needs to stay in shape if he plans to run for public office. Not saying that I agree to do it yet, but you know…just in case."

He climbed into the large, quilt-soft bed with his young intern from Alabama State, and he immediately kissed her smooth shoulder, making her nipples harden.

She leaned deep into the cushioned pillows behind her and muttered, "How'd you know to kiss me there?"

David ignored her question and licked around her ripe nipples with his drink-moistened tongue.

"The same way I know how to lick you here," he answered.

Beverly then cradled his head inside her breasts, enjoying it. It felt so soft. It felt so right. It felt so gentle. And she had no doubt that he would feel warm inside of her.

"Can you put it in?" she begged him after too much foreplay.

David seemed to be blessing her entire body with soft kisses while continuously working her aroused nipples with the tips of his soft fingers. But how wet did he intend to make her before he would decide to penetrate?

"In a minute," he responded. "I like to take my time with what I do."

Beverly held her peace for another few moments of bliss before she squealed, "For how long?"

She wasn't used to the patient wait from a man. Her much younger college boyfriend would force himself inside of her in less than two minutes, and sometimes before she was even succulent. But David had her practically dripping.

"You need to learn how to make it worth it," he told her with another soft kiss on her lips. "You said you don't want a one-night stand, right?"

"No, I don't."

"Well, I don't want a quickie. But don't worry, you'll get what you need soon enough," he promised.

In the meantime, Beverly continued to massage his arms, shoulders, head, and back with her anxious hands, until David finally reached down to open a condom.

Beverly took a soothing breath and had lost all of her wrangling inhibitions. She was one hundred percent ready to submit to him now. And he entered her from on top; he was even patient with his entry, hovering around her lubricated edges with his hard-on.

She became so unnerved and desperate to feel his full thrust inside of her that she gripped him by his ass to anchor herself and push her young pelvis into his.

David then arched his back to pull his stroke away from her and avoid her clumsy rush to action.

"*Please*," she squealed. She had no idea what else to do. The man was much heavier, stronger and more experienced than she was. All she knew was that she wanted to feel him badly, all the way inside her.

David heard her trembling pleas and thought, *Oh yeah! I got her right where I need her.*

He then secured her young hips in his hands—much slimmer than his wife's or even his secretary's—and he gave her a single, strong thrust to let her feel what she could expect from him if she begged for it hard.

"Unnhh." Beverly reacted violently. She jerked back as if he had shocked her with a police stun gun.

"You don't want it like that, do you?" he asked.

Beverly was confused. She didn't want it as softly as he had started, but she surely didn't want it that hard either. Before she could respond to him, David had established his own sweet rhythm.

"I see you haven't been broken in good yet. Not like you're *about* to be. I was young and didn't know what to do myself at one time."

Beverly closed her eyes and held on tight for the ride, feeling the pain and the pleasure of his stroke. Her lack of control over the power of his thrusts forced her to trust his every move. She would trust it or fear it.

Oh my God, he's too much for me! she told herself. David was a grown-ass man, who understood exactly how to bring the heat on a woman. But Beverly was barely a woman. She had only turned legal to drink three months ago. But it was too late to turn back. She had to take it until her young body could adapt.

Fortunately, David took it easy on her and decided to work her edges. And little by little, he slid farther inside until she could take him all.

"You okay?" he asked her.

"Mmm-hmm," she hummed. She began to relax and enjoy his diligent handiwork. She even enjoyed his alcohol-laced breath as he breathed into her face. It let her know that she was really there with a man, and that she was not dreaming it.

Once Beverly began to feel comfortable, David gradually increased the pressure of his stroke.

"You still okay?" he asked her again in the middle of her pleasure.

"Yeeaahh," she squealed.

So the man began to put it on her stronger, creating a steady ruffling of the bed sheets until she reacted with whimpers of bliss to his every thrust.

"*Mmm, mmmm, mmmm, mmm….*" she moaned steadily.

David leaned into her right ear and asked, "You ever came good and strong before?"

"Unh-hunnnh," she hummed.

"I mean *strong*?" he asked her with an extra quick and deep thrust.

"*Unnhh!*" she reacted to it sharply.

"I'm ready to take you there." He shortened the intervals of his strokes.

Beverly responded immediately with the sweet noise of affirmation.

"*Ooooh, euuuw, euuw, unnnhhh…*"

"You feel it coming now?"

"*Mmm-hmmm, mmmm-hmmmmm,*" she…moaned.

The experienced man held his spot of quick, deep thrusts until she howled, trembled and clawed with the full animation of a gigantic orgasm.

"*UUNNNHHHHH….!*"

Oh yeaaahhh! David hummed to himself, smiling. *Now I got her.*

Her release was so strong and reckless that he had to secure her crawling hands with his own to stop her from scratching his back. And after the young woman had exploded into the heat, instead of relaxing to allow her to cool off, the experienced man returned the deep pressure to her wide open spot.

"You're not done yet," he told her with another deep thrust. "Mmmt-mmm," he hummed into her ear.

Beverly squeezed her eyes shut and concentrated to feel the rise of a second explosion within her body. David wasn't even there anymore. He had disappeared into nothingness. All she could feel now was her young pussy throbbing like it had never throbbed before, and opening up to a new dimension of satisfaction. She couldn't even hear herself moan anymore. She was numb with euphoria.

OH MY GODDD! WHAT IS THISSS? she asked the heavens. And the heavens answered her with a second monstrous release that was looser than the first one. At that point she was blown away physically and mentally. But the man wouldn't stop to let her recuperate. He had found her spot and continued to work it to oblivion.

"You want another one?" he asked.

She couldn't even answer him legibly. "*Euuuuuwww.*"

David went on about his business until he could feel his own climax rising. That's when his thrusts began to break from the steady rhythm he had established. His masterful stroke began to sputter like a broken-down car.

Realizing that he had likely reached the end of his road, Beverly squeezed him into her to steady his sputtering movements.

"Here it come. Here it come," he told her. "You ready? You ready?" he added in his desperate double-talk.

"Mmmm-*hmmmm*," Beverly moaned.

"*Euuuuuuw-wuu-wuuu,*" David squealed to her as he came. His hard, fully immersed dick pulsated inside of her loose pussy so vibrantly that it opened her up to an amazing *third* orgasm, causing her legs to quiver under his dead weight, like spaghetti blowing in the wind.

I don't BELIEVE THIS! she exclaimed. *Three times!*

She had not even cum *twice* in the same *night* before, let alone *three times* in the same incredible fuck. And the orgasms she did have with her college-aged boyfriend had not been *half* as strong.

Finally they relaxed, with David's full weight falling out across her body, drained, as he breathed heavily.

So what happens now? Beverly asked herself. She lay there under her boss's weight and contemplated their future together, if any. She was very doubtful of it. How could she imagine keeping such a well-respected and married older man who could fuck so well? He was bound to have many other women, including C.J. Beverly was now certain of it. However, the only certainty she expected of their own relationship was that she would be there for him whenever he wanted her to be.

Whenever he wants me, she convinced herself.

"So are you gonna run for mayor?" she asked him again, of all things.

David chuckled, with his exhausted body rumbling into hers across the bed. He gingerly released his limp, condom-covered cock from her satisfied hole and rolled over on his back beside her. Naturally, Beverly rolled to her right to face him.

"Of all the things to think about, you ask me about that. Did you hear what I told everyone else tonight?"

"I heard you put everyone on *pause*, if that's what you mean," she answered. "But you can give me a *real* answer."

"Oh, only you, hunh?"

"Yeah," she answered confidently. "I'm dedicated, remember? You don't know that yet?"

David paused and smiled. He had gotten used to the loyalty. People were volunteering their services to him left and right now, including women of all ages. And he was in a good place in his life for an ambitious man.

He finally answered, "You know…I don't know how much of my privacy I could stand to give up for that. And that's my most direct answer."

Beverly understood him now. He still wanted to eat his cake, undisturbed by the issues of morality that a run for public office would be sure to uncover. And if he actually won the office of mayor in Birmingham, which he was favored to do, his bar of perfection would rise even higher.

Nevertheless, Beverly asked, "Is that your only reason not to run? Maybe you can still have what you want on the side."

She figured if everyone else would become a risk to him, he could still count on her to be in his corner to lean on, or to lean *in*, if he wanted.

David looked down into her eyes, as she faced him with all of her sincerity, and he nodded.

"I appreciate that," he told her. "That's what I liked about you from day one. You have some people who work for you to benefit themselves, but then you have others who work to benefit the team."

"So, you have to pick the right people then," she advised him.

Then his cell phone lit up from the nightstand on the right, where he had placed it earlier. David had set the phone on mute, but the screen continued to light up whenever new calls or texts came in.

"Are you gonna get that?" Beverly asked him curiously. She was interested to see how he would treat her now that their first round of fucking had been accomplished. Would she be marched straight to the back of the bus, or would he let her sit comfortably up front as a new priority, or at least while she was still a game rookie?

David picked up his phone to read the screen and paused. Without looking at her, he said, "You can enjoy this room for the night and order breakfast in the morning, if you want, but I'll have to get up and leave in a few. Now imagine how much worse it would be if I was the mayor."

Beverly figured that making any complaint about his announcement of desertion would be in vain. She had made her bed, and she was now forced to accept the only option of sleeping in it...*alone.*

"What if I get cold again?" she cracked.

David looked down at her and chuckled a second time. The girl had a clever sense of humor. "You have the thermostat on the wall for the room temperature, plenty of covers and quilts, and plenty of pillows to block out any breeze."

"But the bed is all wet now," she whined.

David shook his head and climbed out of bed with his cell phone in hand, and he headed for the master bath. "You got enough sheets to cover it with."

Once he stepped inside the bathroom, he set his cell phone down on the marble sink, discarded his condom into the toilet, flushed it, washed himself up at the sink, and made a return phone call to his wife.

"Yeah, I'm heading back home now," he told her.

His wife paused over the line and considered his answer. What was the sense in causing a stir over the phone if he was already on his way back where she could express herself in person. "I'll see you then."

David then called his secretary, C.J., who had made several missed calls to him during the past hour. "I'm heading on in for home," he told her.

"Well, how come you didn't answer my calls?"

"I wasn't in a position to. And I didn't look at it."

She pouted, "Damn, you just...fucked up my night. I thought you said you were gonna call me."

"You know I'll make it up to you eventually. But it's another early rise and shine tomorrow, so get your rest."

"Yeah, that's easy for *you* to say. But I'm the one who's all *pent up* over here."

David was not in the place, nor did he have the time to continue a long-winded conversation with her, so he decided to cut things short.

"Get your rest, I'm gone," he told her with finality.

Beverly had not heard all of his conversations on the phone, but she already knew enough about the man to know that he would never be hers alone. There was no sense even being upset about it or having a tantrum, although she wanted to respond in some way. But small jeers of sarcasm were all that she could muster against him, knowing full well that she wanted to lie down and experience his stroke again in the very near future. She wanted to cum hard again, *three more times*, to see if it had only been a fluke, a once-in-a-lifetime occurrence. So she forced herself to relax and enjoy the spoils of the evening inside the comfortable bed. And it was big enough to roll away to one side and cover up their wet spots of passion.

By the time David had returned to the room, refreshed, and began to gather his clothes, the young college intern had accepted her fate. She would continue to ride out a relationship with him for as long as she could sanely endure it, and then she would move on.

"You all right over there?" he asked her as he redressed.

Beverly nodded and mumbled, "Yeah." She had not budged from the comfortable bed and did not intend to until morning.

"So...I'll see you back at the office then. Will you be able to get up in the morning and make it?" he teased.

She smiled. "Will you?"

"Oh yeah, business is business. The show doesn't stop for me."

"Well...it doesn't stop for me either," she boasted back.

When David left her there at the Marriott, Beverly took a deep breath, curled up with the pillows on the bed, closed her eyes, and swallowed the full reality of her decisions like a big girl.

Then she smiled in her lingering thoughts, with her eyes still closed. *So I actually fucked Mr. David Butler Sr.*, she mused. *And if he decides to run for mayor and wins, then I can say I fucked the mayor of Birmingham.*

Those were her divergent thoughts as she fell asleep that night. And if no one had ever found out or could prove that she and Mr. David Butler Sr. had engaged in a sexual relationship, then she would never tell anyone voluntarily or otherwise. Because she considered it her private business. And it would remain that way.

PRIVATE LESSSONS

Dinng-duunnng!

The apartment doorbell rang while Samuel Douglass was taking a serious dunp inside the bathroom.

"Shit. When that girl says she'll be right over, she damn sure means it," he mumbled.

Dinng-duunnng!

"Damn, the girl is impatient, too." He thought of calling her on his cell phone and telling her to wait a minute, but he didn't have his phone inside the bathroom.

If she leaves, I'll have to call her back once I get out of here, he told himself.

When he was done with his business, he sprayed the place, clicked on the bathroom fan, and shut the door. Then he gathered his cell phone to ring back his mid-afternoon visitor.

"Hello," she answered her cell phone.

"Yeah, you caught me inside the john," he told her. "Where are you now?"

She giggled, imagining the older man on the toilet. "I'm back in my car."

Samuel paused. "You leaving or you coming back?" He didn't want to seem too pressed about her visiting his new Charlotte apartment to help him unpack his things.

"Umm, I'll come back. I'll be there in a minute."

Samuel went and opened his apartment door for her before she arrived. A minute really meant a minute in her book. So he opened his front door wide and listened to her ascend the two flights of stairs before she reached him on the third.

"It's good exercise, ain't it?" he asked her, grinning. "That's how I plan to keep my legs and body young. Every little bit counts."

Candice Burton grinned with double dimples, straight white teeth, wild wavy hair, and smooth, caramel skin, wearing a peach summer dress and gold, wire-rimmed glasses. She was a bit on the healthy side body-wise, with plenty of firm handles to hold on to.

"You don't look that old," she gushed. And he didn't. Samuel had the gift of youth. Well within his fifties, the man could still pass for late thirty-something. Originally from Cincinnati, Ohio, he was a bank loan officer, who liked to dress young, with oversized blue jeans, sports jerseys and a various array of hats.

"So, how long can you help me to organize this apartment today?" he asked his young helper. He still had plenty of unpacked boxes to map out, after positioning his furniture.

Candice shrugged. "I don't have anywhere to go today. So I can stay a lot longer than yesterday."

Samuel looked her over in her nice, peach dress and commented, "And that's what you wore over here to help me in today? You don't have any regular jeans and a cheap T-shirt? You wore a dress yesterday, too."

Candice smiled and laughed it off. "Dresses are my thing," she told him. "I don't really wear too many jeans. And a summer dress is easy to wash."

Samuel nodded. "I like your attitude. I guess it is no big deal then."

He didn't know a lot about the girl yet. All he knew was that she was turning twenty-five in less than a month. She was born and raised there in Charlotte, North Carolina, and had recently graduated from Queens College with a degree in early education. Presently, she was a substitute school-teacher who had not yet applied for a full-time teaching job. She explained that she wanted to see what she was getting into before she made the leap.

Samuel had met her at a grocery store a few weeks ago, while making his transition from Ohio. Once he told her he was moving into a new apartment, and that he would love to know the hot spots around the city to eat, drink, and unwind, she kindly offered him her cell phone number and began to explain what the city of Charlotte was all about. Those conversations led to her helping him to organize his new apartment. And it was her second time over.

"So, what room do you want to start with today?" she looked around and asked him.

On the first day, they had taken care of most of the kitchen before she had to run off.

Samuel shrugged and thought about it. "What about ah, the bathrooms and the bedroom?" Then he caught himself with a hearty chuckle. "But let's do the bedroom first, because the bathroom needs a good twenty minutes to air out."

They shared a laugh as Candice agreed. "Okay, the bedroom it is." She walked into his bedroom and was ready to start.

This girl is so damn pleasant, it's unbelievable, Samuel told himself. Her good nature was also keeping his playboy instincts in check. He had had the full intention of tempting the young woman from the first moment he saw her inside the grocery store. But as he began to get to know her more, he backed down from his hunt.

"Nice bed," she told him admiringly.

"Yeah, that came right after you left yesterday."

It was a high-positioned sleigh bed of dark, pine wood.

Candice walked over and rubbed her hand over the smooth surface of the naked mattress. "You don't have any sheets or anything to put on it yet?"

"I do, but I could use some more. What would you suggest?"

"Silk or satin," she answered immediately. "I could buy some for you from the Bath & Linen store in Concord if you want. They're going out of business soon."

Samuel stopped her. "Silk or satin? Girl, what you know about slippin' and slidin' around inside the bed sheets?"

Candice grinned. "I know they feel good on your body."

That got Samuel thinking with his lady killer instincts again. *Well, maybe she ain't so innocent, just extra nice,* he mused. "Well, we'll talk about those bed sheets a little later. First I have to unpack all of these clothes."

He had left many of his boxes untouched on purpose to give them more to unpack together. And Candice didn't seem to mind. She walked over to his group of brown boxes on the floor and pulled out two arms full of colorful briefs.

"You sure have a lot of different drawers," she told him with a giggle.

Samuel laughed it off. "Yeah, I figure, why should women have all the fun with colorful panties while we wear one style of plain drawers? So I decided to mix it up a bit."

"I see," she responded to him. "So, where do you want me to put these?"

"In that top dresser drawer next to the bed."

She did as he told her and walked over to unpack the next box. By that time, the older man couldn't help himself.

"So, ah, since you know about my colorful selection of drawers now, what color of Victoria's Secrets do you like to wear?"

"All of them," Candice commented. "That's one of my favorite places to shop, actually."

Samuel looked at her intrigued. "Is that right?"

Candice chuckled and looked away. "Don't tell anybody though," she warned.

"Who would I tell?" he asked her. "And for what reason? We all have our private places to go to, right?"

Candice looked him dead in his eyes and nodded, sending a wave of shivers up his spine.

"You're right. But everyone can't understand it," she commented.

"They're not supposed to understand it. That's why it's called a *secret*."

The young woman agreed with his logic and smiled. "That's true."

Samuel smiled back. "So, what are you really telling me? You got a little freak in you that nobody understands? A lot of girls feel that way. It's only nature. But everybody wants you to cover it up all the time."

"I know, right," she agreed again. "I hate that. Where do you want me to put these?" she asked, holding up two arms full of dress pants.

"Oh, I got a bunch of hangers for those inside the closet."

Candice walked into the master bedroom closet and found a rack of hangers for his dress pants. As she hung them, she sniffed the pleasant smell of his men's cologne that lingered from a few of his slacks.

"I see you wear a lot of nice colognes," she commented after she had finished. Samuel was busy trying to decide what dressers to place most of his other things in. Brand-new furniture often created many new options.

He bragged, "Yeah, I'm pretty much a well put-together man. And with four older sisters, aunts, and nieces all around me, I figured out what women like to smell on a man."

"I'd think so," Candice teased. She was hinting ever so tactfully at flirtation.

Samuel caught on to it. It was obvious in her candid observations that she may be game to his advances. But he decided to take his time with her and keep his poise.

"What scents do you like to wear?" he asked her.

Candice shrugged. "Anything that smells good, I guess. I'm not too picky."

He looked her over again and was amused by her. Either she was too easy to read or a big tease. Nevertheless, she had him ready to speed things up to see what she was willing to accept from him.

"Sounds like you an easy girl to please."

She nodded. "Yeah, I am."

"And how well do *you* please?"

"I mean…I'm pretty much open."

Shit! Samuel thought. *Now she's making my dick hard, and we still have a lot of unpacking left to do in here. Could she be this damn obvious?*

To test out his hunch, he asked her, "You're pretty much open to what, a well-kept old man with a private young woman?"

She smiled and didn't answer him immediately. "That could be good."

"Good for who, the old man, or the young woman?" he questioned.

"Good for both."

Samuel felt like he had been sent an angel from heaven. It had never been that easy for him. Was that how the young women were in Charlotte, or did he luck up with the right one? So he became a little skeptical.

"Now how I know you're not pulling my leg in here?"

She stared at him with opened hands. "What else do you want me to do?"

Samuel was startled by her innocent forwardness. He became hesitant to speak up on his next move. But he had to. He was a playboy veteran.

"Well, unpacking boxes is one thing, but knowing how to please an experienced man is totally different."

He figured he'd try the stately approach as an obvious challenge to her.

She said, "But I can learn anything that someone is willing to teach me, right?"

"Yeah, you can. But it won't be teaching you how to unpack," he joked.

"I know that. I know what men want, even when they won't say it," she told him.

Samuel backed up on his toes. "So, what are you trying to say?" he asked.

"I said it already. All you have to do is ask. And it's either yes or no."

"So, you mean to tell me that I can ask you for whatever I want, right here, right now?"

"You're going to eventually anyway. Right?"

Samuel broke out laughing. "Shit, you a wolf in sheep's clothing."

"Sheep's clothing is easier to pull off," she teased him. "It's only one button."

"Let me see it."

Candice turned around in her peach dress and showed him the button hook at the top of the neck.

"So, if I undo this one button, the whole dress falls off?"

"Just like a bra," she told him. "All I have to do is take my arms out."

"And what about the rest of these boxes?" He was reminding her that they still had work to do.

Candice didn't budge. "I told you, I have nothing else to do today."

Well, what the hell are you waiting for then? Samuel questioned himself. Candice was a gift ready for unwrapping.

He nodded. "All right, then. I mean, it's a little unexpected but... So, you want me to undo that dress to see what I'm working with, or do *you* want to do it?"

Candice simply reached her right hand to the back of her dress and unbuttoned it. She pulled her arms out and allowed the dress to drop to the floor. Then she unclipped her yellow bra to free her twins, and pulled off her matching yellow panties to reveal her smooth, trimmed vagina.

Samuel stood there and said, "Wow. So I guess I do need some silk or satin bed sheets." He wasn't that impressed with her body. He had seen much better. But he *was* impressed in her willingness to deliver herself to him.

"Am I just gonna stand here?" she asked him.

"Well, as you can see, I don't have any sheets on the bed yet, but..." He stopped and thought about the bathroom sink. "You said you would do *anything* your man asked you to, right?" He figured he would put her to the test.

"That's what I said," she teased.

"Well, let's go inside the bathroom then."

He figured the master bathroom had aired out enough by then.

Candice walked in ahead of him, and Samuel closed the door behind them.

"Do you have any protection?" she asked.

Samuel smiled. He had unpacked his bathroom supplies, including his box of thirty-six condoms. He pulled a few out of the box in front of her.

Candice smiled. "I guess you were ready for a lot of willing visitors."

"Or, just the right *one*," he countered.

"You don't have to flatter me. I'm a big girl."

"I can see that," he told her.

"So am I gonna stand here in the bathroom and talk. Or did you bring me in here to do something?"

Samuel said, "First of all, it looks like we need to straighten out that mouth of yours. Second of all, I need you to bend over this sink, to see if you can take it."

Candice turned around and leaned over the bathroom sink without another word. She even spread her legs wide for him.

This is not fucking happening to me, Samuel told himself as he watched her. His throbbing hard-on had given him no more room to breathe inside of his drawers. So he had hurried to free his penis from his pants before it would suffocate from a lack of oxygen.

He got his pants and drawers down and slid the condom over his large erection. Then he approached his gift of a ready and willing young woman with his dick in hand, and was eager to guide himself inside of her.

He said, "You don't mind if I turn the lights off in here, do you? It's more intense in the dark."

"Do what you want to do."

Samuel chuckled and clicked off the bathroom light before he found her spot and guided himself into paradise. But once he was there, he found himself too large to slide on in.

"Oh my Lord, you're big," she told him, sounding nervous.

"Oh, don't worry about that. I know exactly what to do with a tight one."

He rubbed her nipples with the smooth tips of his fingers, and kissed up and down on her left shoulder, while he barely moved his hips to push further inside her.

He whispered into her left ear, "A woman needs to feel aroused for her natural lubrication to kick in."

Then he poked his tongue inside of her ear and shocked her.

"Unnhh," she moaned, turning away from it. It was a warm, tickling sensation that she was not at all used to.

Samuel chased her with his tongue anyway. And as he licked her more, he could feel her body become looser. That's when he began to stroke her softly from behind.

"There we go," he told her. "That's how Daddy likes it."

Feeling his big dick slide further inside of her, Candice began to move her hips back into him.

"Now you got it," he coached her. "Nice and slow."

He grabbed her wide hips for better balance before he began to pump his penis a little harder and deeper. And with every strong stroke, she moaned.

"Unhh, unhh, unhh…"

As it began to feel good to him, Samuel closed his eyes and leaned his head back in the dark. It felt like he was dreaming. But the young woman's talking interrupted him and brought him back to reality.

"Ooooh," she moaned, "you like it?"

Samuel didn't necessarily like a lot of talking when he fucked. He only talked to get her wet. But now her moaning and talking back to him was disturbing his groove.

"Mmm-hmm," he grunted back to her. "Tell me how *you* like it," he decided to add. He would much rather that *she* do the talking instead of him. He wanted to concentrate more on his stroke.

"*Ooooh*, I like it," she moaned to him. "I like it *a lot*."

"And you want me to teach you how to work it?" he asked her. What the hell? He figured he'd keep the conversation going and see how much he could slip into it.

She hummed, "*Yes-s-s-s-s*," with vibrating speech from his steady pumping.

"I'ma teach you how to suck it good, too," he told her. "You ready for that?"

"*Mmm-hmmm*," she grunted back to him.

"Tell me how you gon' suck it."

"*Goooood*," she hummed.

"And you take it all in?"

"*Mmm-hmmm*."

Samuel's imagination of her sucking him right and swallowing allowed him to reach a strong climax. He stopped talking and got a better grip on her body to push himself as deep inside of her as he could go. He wanted to feel the deepest explosion inside of her dark, warm and wet hole.

"Okay, hold still, hold still," he told her.

~~Her moving around was stopping him timing out his strong nut.~~

Samuel placed his right hand on her lower back and braced himself for it with much quicker strokes. The quicker stokes, while deep inside of her, made Candice feel something stirring within her own body.

"*Ooooh, dad-deeeee,*" she moaned.

Realizing that she was reaching her own nut, Samuel held his position and allowed her to work it all out for herself.

"Go on and cum, girl. Go on and cum."

That's when the young woman started shaking, grabbing, twisting, and howling in tongues. "*Unnhhhhnnnhhhnnn...*"

Shit, she must have never had a nut before, he pondered to himself. Then it was his turn. He choked back up on his bat, and got back to stroking her with deep, quick pumps until he could feel the pressure. And once the nut was ready to explode through his shaft, he stroked her slower and longer, pulling his dick nearly to the lips of her extra wet pussy before pushing it all the way back in. That only caused her to go crazy with a second nut.

"Unh-hunh, unh-hunh, unh-*hunnnnhhh*," she cried out again.

Samuel was pleased with his handiwork, but he still hadn't reached his own climax yet. And he had become impatient. So he pulled his penis out of her with another idea in mind, while the nerves were still jumping for completion.

"Go on and sit on the toilet," he instructed. He pulled the condom off and tossed it inside the sink. "Now suck around the head and don't go all the way down until I tell you to. Okay?"

"Okay," she agreed.

Candice held the shaft of his slippery penis and worked her lips and tongue around his massive head, like he had told her to.

"Yeah, right there," he moaned.

Before he could tell her to suck him faster and farther down, she did it on her own and shocked him.

"*Ooooh, shit!*" he responded. He then grabbed her shoulders with both hands to steady himself for a much faster than expected explosion. And *BOOM*, it hit him hard and caught him totally off guard, with warm cum spurting into her mouth. However, the suddenness of it was too strong and unexpected for Candice, so she choked on it and violently turned away. Having nowhere to turn to, Samuel quickly cupped his hands in front of his shooting stars to stop it from flying all over the bathroom.

Candice spit the semen out of her mouth and continued to choke into the bathtub to her left.

"I'm sorry," she pleaded to him. "I never did that before."

Well, you could have fooled me! Samuel thought to himself. *She may be a damn pro at it and don't even know it yet.*

"It's all right, baby girl. You did good for a first time. I have to teach you when to expect it. But you shocked me with that one, too. You worked it just right without me even telling you."

"Are you sure?" She still sounded eager to please.

"Hell yeah, I'm sure. You see how fast it came, don't you? That was less than three minutes."

Candice chuckled in the dark, as their eyes began to adjust to it.

"Okay, if you say so," she commented. "But do you have anything to drink?"

"Oh yeah, in the kitchen. I have some towels in here, too. You drink Sprite?"

She nodded. "Yeah."

"Well, I'll bring you back a can of Sprite and a glass while you freshen up."

He then grabbed a towel for her, and one to wipe up himself before he pulled his pants back up and headed to the kitchen.

"Well, ain't that just dandy," he told himself with a happy smile on the way to the kitchen. "She gave me about the best housewarming gift a guy could ask for."

He grabbed the Sprite and glass to carry back to the bedroom with him, and by the time he had made it back to Candice, she had returned to unpacking his boxes while naked.

Samuel spotted her and froze.

She looked at him and grinned. "If I help you get your apartment together like this, I won't even get my dress dirty. Then I can take a shower before I put it back on."

Samuel uttered, "Ahhh…yeah, I guess you're right." He didn't know what else to say. He thought, *That sounds great to me! And I could really get used to something like that.*

The next thing Samuel knew, Candice was willing to come over and visit him at his apartment anytime he asked her to, and whenever she wasn't busy. They would engage in consistent fucking any way he told her, and until she wore him out. Then she began the habit of taking off her clothes as soon as she walked into the door.

Samuel asked her, "You're even gonna cook for me naked?"

She grinned at him from the kitchen stove, where she planned to cook chicken tenders and fries for his Saturday afternoon of watching college football.

"Maybe that wouldn't work if some hot grease popped on me, hunh? People might ask me where I got the burn from."

Samuel advised, "Yeah, so you should at least keep your top half on. How 'bout that?"

"Anything to make you happy, baby."

"Well, what makes *you* happy?" he asked her. So far, the young woman hadn't asked him for anything, not even for him to take her out to dinner or a movie.

Candice responded, "Learning everything I need to do to please *you*."

Samuel shook his head and grinned, watching Ohio State and Notre Dame on his living room television set.

"You don't have any young girlfriends you hang out with or nothing?" he asked her curiously. She still hadn't talked enough about herself. She didn't even talk on her cell phone around him.

"Yeah, I do," she answered. "But they do their thing and I do my mine."

She walked back into the kitchen to cook, wearing another dress but with no panties or bra on. In fact, she had left her baby-blue panties and bra on the coffee table in front of him. Having her underwear sitting out in front of him like that made Samuel think more about sex than when she paraded around him butt naked.

Yeah, she's fucking up my football game now, he told himself. Suddenly, he couldn't concentrate. All he thought about was walking inside the kitchen and giving it to his young, loyal companion from the behind, while she cooked his chicken tenderloins and French fries for him.

Nah, leave it alone and finish watching your game, he insisted. *She knows what she's trying to do. She's trying to take me away from the game on purpose.*

Nevertheless, once Candice had finished preparing his football snack, and brought it over to him on a food tray, he had thought of another idea.

"You forgot the hot sauce," he told her. "And after you do that, can you do me a favor and go inside my bathroom and bring out a couple of condoms for me?"

Candice smiled and responded with a giggle, "Oh, my pleasure." She knew what was coming next. She brought three attached condoms back out to him on the living room sofa and handed them over.

"OH, HE JUST MISSED HIM!" Samuel screamed at the television. A long fly pattern was overthrown a step or two in front of a wide-open, Ohio State receiver.

"You didn't bet on the game, did you?" Candice asked him.

"No, but...I like to see the home state win, you know," he answered, chomping on his chicken tenders, smothered with ketchup and hot sauce. Then he thought of Candice standing to his right. "You ah, feel like putting one of these condoms on me? I can't do it with my hands all greasy with chicken juice, ketchup and hot sauce."

Candice laughed. "Okay. But I'll need you to lean back for me."

Samuel leaned back enough for her to undo his pants and tug them down. "You might have to lick him a little bit first to get him good and hard for you."

Candice smiled and slid to her knees to reach his penis with her soft lips.

"Ah, how 'bout putting some ice in your mouth first. That way, I'll have like, ah, hot sauce *and* cold sauce at the same time."

She laughed again. "Okay, that's different."

She walked over to the refrigerator, tossed an ice cube in her mouth from the freezer, and walked back over to please her old man on the couch.

"*Awwww, shit yeah,*" Samuel moaned. He ate, watched football, and had his dick sucked with ice-cold lips, all at the same time. What more could a fresh old man ask for? Everything seemed available with Candice.

Once he got good and hard from her cold lips, he told her, "Okay, now put one of those condoms on me and let me teach you how to ride it slow."

She complied and eased herself onto his erection, while he leaned back against the couch.

"You want me to take my dress back off?"

"Nope. And if it gets too dirty, we'll wash it right here. But I do need you to feed me that chicken and fries."

"Okay." She giggled and began to feed him the food from the tray.

"Now ease your body real slow, up and down, while you feed me."

In the meantime, Samuel continued to watch the game. Ohio State had scored its third touchdown, and was leading Notre Dame 24-6, late in the second quarter.

"Mmm-hmm, just like that," he mumbled to Candice through his food. "You need to be nice and slow, all the way up, and all the way down. And once you get the rhythm of it, you can go a little bit faster on me."

"Like this?" Candice asked him, pacing herself with discipline.

"Yeah, and don't forget to feed me," he reminded her. "Stuff some French fries in my mouth."

Candice jammed three fries into his mouth, as Samuel chomped them down and moved his hips into her slow ride.

"Mmm-hmm," he grumbled through his food. He continued to watch the game, too.

Without him asking her, Candice took one of his hands and began to suck the chicken, ketchup and hot sauce juice off of each of his fingers.

"Oooh *shit*, girl! Who taught you that?" Samuel squealed. He had no idea how good it would all feel to him.

Candice moaned, "*Mmmm*, I wanna learn it all for *you*, baby."

She nearly caused Samuel to nut prematurely again. The man prided himself on staying in control of the situation, but this young woman was making it real hard for him.

"You want another piece of chicken?" she asked.

Samuel couldn't concentrate on the food anymore. It was time for her to increase the speed of her stroke. He could feel another strong nut rising.

"Nah, just ah…go a little bit faster now."

"Like this?" she questioned, slipping up and down on his mountain-high, hard cock.

"Yeah, girl, just like that. Just like that right there," he repeated excitedly.

He watched the game with tingling nerves as halftime approached.

"Is your team still winning?"

"Yeaaahhh," he squealed, feeling his climax getting closer and closer.

By that time, Candice had figured out some things on her own. She realized how to hit her own spot while on top of him.

"Squeeze my nipples. Squeeze 'em."

Samuel reached up under her summer dress and squeezed her firm melons accordingly.

"Ooooh, yeah!" she yelled. "Ooooh, yeah!" she repeated. She romped her body around and around in circles, like a rodeo ride until she exploded.

"*Oooooooh, dad-deeee!*" she moaned. But her pleasure didn't necessarily do it for him. He needed her slower, controlled stroke again. So he grabbed her hips to guide her just right to reach his own nut.

"This is how I need you, right here," he told her.

"Okay."

They started back up again with a controlled stroke until Samuel gripped her smooth, wide hips with strong hard fingers and jerked his seed into the condom, planted nice and snug inside of her hot, wet pussy.

"*Ho-o-o-o*, you make a man's *dreams* come true!" he yelled to her as he nutted wildly.

"*Ooooh, do I?*" she asked him, moaning back.

"*Yeah*, baby girl, *yeah.*"

Her whole body grew hot, sweaty and satisfied, and so did his.

Candice then fell across his chest and chuckled, taking deep breaths. "I guess I'm gonna have to wash my dress over here after all."

Samuel chuckled. "Yeah, now you got chicken grease stains, hot sauce and ketchup fingers, sweat, cum, and fuck stains all over it. I hope it can all come off."

Candice giggled. "It'll come out. I can scrub it out."

"And if you can't, I'll take you out to buy you a new one just like it," he promised.

She shook her head. "You don't have to do that."

"Well, what if I want to? You've been good to me without asking for anything."

She leaned up and shrugged, looking him in the eyes. "That's just how I am."

Samuel shook his head. "An *angel* sent down from heaven."

"I'm not hardly an angel," Candice rebutted. "If I was, I seriously doubt I would be riding you like this. I don't think that's the work of angels," she stated sarcastically.

"And why not?"

"What do you mean, 'why not'? Angels are not sent down to earth to fuck people. In fact, I don't even think they can *use* that word."

"Well, *you* just did."

"Yeah, which proves I'm not an angel."

"Well, you still deserve to be taken out," he insisted.

"It's really not necessary," she countered. She climbed off of him nice and easy, while making sure his condom didn't spill out its semen. Then she took it off and wiped him up with a warm rag. She had made a big mess of the old man.

"Wow, I really did you slimy today," she told him, while wiping him up.

"That's all right. You see how you cleaning me up all good. I feel like I got a damn diaper on at a nursing home. *Nurrrsse!*" he teased.

She laughed. "Whatever. You're not *that* old. You don't need Viagra yet."

"Yeah, I guess not with *you* around." Then he caught himself, believing his comment may be insensitive to her. "But I mean that in a good way," he covered up.

Candice shook it off. "I don't mind. I'm glad I turn you on like that. Why would I *not* like it?"

"Well, a whole lot of women don't want to be looked at as sex objects, number one."

"Well, most people don't look at me as a sex object. Not at all."

Samuel figured she wasn't the best-looking young woman in the world, but she was at least an *eight*, and that was much better than most. So he refused to believe that no one else wanted to fuck her. She was surely attractive enough to be lusted over.

He asked her, "What are you talking about? What do you think, you're unattractive? Because you ain't hardly ugly. You're a good-looking girl."

She blushed. "Thank you. But I already know that. It's just that…I, well, when you're nice to people, sometimes they don't look at you in that way."

Samuel stared at her to imagine what she meant. "So, you mean to say that you only let your freak out with me; is that it?"

Candice shrugged, standing in the middle of his living room with a soiled summer dress and no panties or bra. "Well, would you *want* me to be like this with everyone else?"

Samuel chuckled at it. "Hell no! They can all go out and find their own angel."

"I'm not an angel," she repeated.

"Well, you're *my* angel. So I want to take you out and treat you to a nice dinner tonight, right after we finish cleaning up your dress."

She shook it off. "I have something else to do tonight."

"Well, cancel it."

"I can't. But we'll go out soon. Maybe we can take a trip up to Greensboro or something."

Samuel frowned. "I didn't move here to go to Greensboro; I live in *Charlotte* now. That's like moving to Cleveland to go to Columbus for dinner. For what?"

"Well, I've lived in Charlotte my entire life, so I'd rather hang out in other places now," Candice explained to him.

"Well, move away then," he suggested.

The young woman went silent for a spell. That's when Samuel decided that he had probably gone too hard on her.

"Or, maybe you like being around the safety of your folks," he added.

"Maybe."

After that, he got to thinking that either she was a homebody, or she didn't want to be seen out in public with him.

"You ah, not doing somebody *wrong*, are you?" he questioned.

Shit, maybe she ain't no angel, he mused. The girl obviously had some kind of secret going on. Or at least he felt that way.

"You could be a homebody," he countered, giving her another option.

Candice took the bait far too easily for comfort. "Yeah, maybe I am. I'm just a homebody. Or at least in Charlotte I am. I mean, I've seen everything there is to see here."

"Well, I haven't. I thought you were supposed to show me around this place."

"I did show you. I gave you a whole list of places to go *and* directions for how to get there," she reminded him.

Samuel could see she was prepared to dodge the real issue of being seen out with him in public. But he planned to stop his inquiry until he could catch her out and about.

"Well, let's ah, get that dress of yours cleaned up."

He finally climbed up from the sofa. And he told himself, *Something's going on here, but she's not ready to tell me yet.*

At lunch hour at the bank in downtown Charlotte, Samuel had an urge to call up his young sex pupil and ask her if she wanted to do lunch.

"By the time I get down there, I would need to rush right back to school."

"I'll come meet you at a lunch spot near campus then," he told her. "I'm not worried about how long I take off for lunch. These loan applications will still be here at my desk when I get back," he joked.

"Umm, how about dinner instead?" Candice suggested. "I mean, that would be a lot less cumbersome than trying to jam in a lunch hour."

Samuel nodded. *Okay, now we're starting to get somewhere,* he told himself. "Where would you like to go?"

"Umm, I'll decide a little later on. Okay? I have to think about it."

Samuel hung up his phone and looked forward to taking the young woman out for dinner that evening. He figured she deserved his good treatment after how well she had treated him. She had made his relocation to Charlotte smooth, inviting and down-right seductive. And he agreed to meet her at his apartment so they could travel in one car.

"Can I get some more before we leave?" Candice teased Samuel at his apartment that evening. She wore a purple blouse and skirt set, looking a hundred percent professional, like a school principal in training. But she was obviously still fresh, no matter what she wore.

Samuel laughed it off, still dressed professionally himself, in a dark sports jacket, button-up shirt with tie, and fine slacks with his shoes.

"We can have all night for that when we get back."

"But it's a work night, and I have to get up early tomorrow. In fact, we may need to take two cars anyway."

Samuel was stunned. It seemed that Candice was attempting to wiggle her way out of another date while getting sexed up before they left.

"You know, if I didn't know any better, I may start to think that you were only using me for a good sex thing." The idea sounded implausible, but it could have been karma. Samuel had been using young women to satisfy his sexual fantasies for years. And he had never been married or sired any children in four, long decades of dating.

"You don't like having sex with me?" Candice asked him innocently.

"Now, I didn't say that. I'm just saying—"

"Well, what's the problem?" she cut him off.

It was the first time he had witnessed her strong backbone, or at least while dealing with him.

"The problem is, all that we've been *doing* is fucking."

Candice stopped and started chuckling. "Oh my God, I never thought I would hear a guy say that."

"Well, I'm saying it." Samuel had had enough sex in his life to know when something smelled fishy. And for a young woman, or *any* woman to fuck him good and not even want a good dinner for it, he suspected that something peculiar was going on.

Suddenly, Candice took a deep breath and began to look saddened.

"So, you don't want to anymore?" she asked sincerely.

Shit, is this girl a closet sex fiend or what? he wondered. He could read the sadness in her eyes at even the suggestion that he would no longer want to fuck her.

"It's not that I don't want to; it's that you're making me feel kind of funny with how you've been dodging doing anything *else* with me. I mean, that's just unusual.

"I'm not an ugly guy," he continued. "So unless you're embarrassed about me being older than you, or you got some kind of a boyfriend somewhere that you're not telling me about, I don't understand why I can't take you out nowhere."

"But we *are* going out now," she reminded him.

"Yeah, after me *pushing* you for it, and only *after* you get another *fix*. And now you tell me that we need to take two cars so you can rush off afterward. Hell, I don't even know where you *live*. But you know where *I* live," he added.

The facts were all adding up, and they were convincing.

Candice looked away from him and took another breath. Then she turned and looked him in the eyes. "I'll tell you over dinner," she promised him.

Samuel nodded and agreed. "Okay."

"And we can take your car."

When they arrived at a dark Italian restaurant on the south end of Charlotte, Candice was extra quiet.

Samuel joked, "Whatever you have to tell me is not the end of the world, is it?" Her stale silence was making him nervous.

She looked up at him and grinned, while looking inside the multiple-page menu.

"I hope not."

Samuel chuckled on the outside, but on the inside he was growing increasingly suspicious. He frowned. "What exactly, ah—"

"Hey, Candice. How are you doing?" an older woman stepped up to their table to greet her. She was tall and stately. After speaking to Candice, she quickly glanced over at Samuel, with a look of investigation.

"Hi," he responded and nodded. It was obvious she wondered who he was. Samuel could read it in her quick, probing eyes.

"Hi," she greeted him back. Then she looked at Candice for an explanation.

"Samuel is a bank loan officer from Cincinnati. I'm trying to do a few things with my account," she explained.

The woman nodded back. "Oh. Well, you should bring him to church with you."

"He hasn't decided on a church yet."

The woman looked back at Samuel. "Well, he can always visit a good house of the Lord." Then she stuck her hand out. "I'm Sister Davis from the Southern Tabernacle Baptist Church, right here in Charlotte. And I guess you already know who her father is. Reverend John Burton is our pastor."

Candice stared across the table, praying that Samuel would keep his cool about it. And he did.

He nodded to Sister Davis. "Yes, of course. She told me all about him. But like she said, I haven't made up my mind on which church to join yet. I've been busy trying to figure Charlotte out first."

"Mmm-hmm, I see. Well, you couldn't find a more beautiful and willing soul than young sister Candice Burton here to talk to you about it. And you're supposed to be helping her with banking services?"

"Ahh, right now, I'm trying to pick out something on this long menu to eat," he hinted with a kind smile.

Sister Davis reacted startled. "Oh, well let me let you all get back to your menu. Don't mind me at all." She chuckled. "And Candice, I'll see you back at Sunday service."

As soon as the woman left them alone at the table, Samuel looked across at Candice and grinned.

"So that's it," he commented. "The infamous preacher's daughter."

Candice immediately shook her head in disdain. "Maybe you're right; I should leave Charlotte and start my own life somewhere else."

"Either that, or you fall into the fold and do what your father wants you to do. And I don't think that's what you want," he assumed. "So that's what you've been trying to hide out with me."

Candice sighed. She said, "My father preaches at one of the largest churches in Charlotte, and wherever I go, somebody always knows me. Then they end up telling somebody at the church. So now he's gonna want to know who's Samuel from the bank?"

"Well, you should have told me," Samuel commented. "I understand what you're going through. You're not the only pastor's daughter in the world."

"But would you have treated me the same if I had told you?"

That question made Samuel pause. He had known about nasty church women in Cincinnati, and had even slept with a few of them, but never with the preacher's daughter. And the church women he had been involved with were far too overzealous for his taste. Decisions all seemed to be a little too extreme with church women.

Noicing his longer than average pause, Candice challenged him, "You see that? How come it's taking you so long to answer?"

Samuel started laughing. It was indeed an awkward situation.

"Well—"

"See," she cut him off again. "I'm so *tired* of that. Guys either act all timid with me, like they need to marry me or something, or act all scandalous, as if I'm some wayward sex fiend, who's willing to get into trouble just to spite my father."

Samuel was speechless. He was thinking the same thing himself. Would he have been so openly sexual with her had he known she was a preacher's daughter?

He laughed out loud at the idea and couldn't concentrate on his menu.

Candice continued to shake her head, knowing that it was another mistake to allow him to know who she was, Pastor Burton's only daughter.

"I want to feel like a *normal* woman sometimes, and do what normal women do," she revealed. "That's why I was so turned on by the fact that you didn't really want ties to marriage or anything, and that you didn't go out of your way to treat me differently, because you didn't really know me. So I could, like, make my fantasies of pleasing a man come true without having to worry about all of the extra baggage of who I am or worrying about my father's influence."

Samuel nodded to her and sympathized with her dilemma. But in his mind, he still couldn't get past how openly freaky she had allowed herself to be with him. Was it overdone because she had been sexually deprived?

Her revelation seemed to change everything for him. He couldn't seem to put things back into proper perspective. Nevertheless, when they arrived back at his apartment after dinner that evening, Samuel forced himself to treat Candice no differently than he had been treating her before. So he stripped her clothes off and took her to bed.

"I'm gonna make you feel like a regular woman all right," he teased. He bent her legs all the way back, froggystyle, and commenced to tear into her pleasure spot.

"Ooooh, thank you! Thank you, Daddy! *Yes! Yessss!*" she moaned. "I want you to cum real hard. Fuck me the way you want to!"

Try as he might, the more she moaned and talked to him, the more Samuel began to think about her status as a preacher's daughter. Would he need to remain out of the public eye with her? Would her father want to meet him? Would he then ask him how old he was and why he had never been married? How old was her preacher/father? And what would her mother say?

Shit! Samuel thought to himself. The added information was clouding his mind. He began to view Candice as an innocent little church girl, wearing innocent little dresses to Sunday mass for her entire life. And there he was, pounding his big, brown dick into her innocent little pussy.

Motherfucker! he cursed himself as he pumped her, now with only one leg up. He was really confused by it all. Why should church make a difference to him? A woman was a woman. But once he began to feel the rise of another strong nut in his system, and like it, he wondered if he would be viewed as the devil's advocate, who had gotten himself deeply involved in fucking one of the Lord's dutiful little angels. Nevertheless, it felt too damned good to stop. So Samuel began to pray for his soul.

Please forgive me for my sins! he mused. Then he let out a loud, "Ooohhh God, *forgive me!*" while he came inside of her.

Candice squeezed into him and held on tightly for his overheated release of bliss. Samuel had been thinking so intently, that he had perspired more than usual, leaving his bed sheets drenched in sweat. And when they finished, Candice was usually glum.

"Why did you ask for forgiveness?" she questioned.

Samuel looked at her in bed and shook it off. "Oh, that was normal sex talk, you know."

"No, it wasn't. You're starting to feel guilty now."

He attempted to laugh. "You know, I've never been in this situation before."

"But there's a first time for everything, right?" she asked him. "I've never been in this situation before either, but I wanted to be. I mean, I've never done the things I've done with you for anyone else," she told him. "And I figured that an older man could handle it better than younger guys."

"Well, how have the younger guys handled it?" Samuel asked her curiously.

"They *couldn't* handle it," she told him. "The good ones were scared away, thinking they had to marry me, and I could tell that the bad ones wanted to sneak me a few times before they moved on. But I didn't want a bunch of one-night stands either. So I stopped dealing with all of them."

"And how many older guys have you been involved with?"

"Only you. That's why I wanted to give my all."

It sounded all so beautiful that Samuel didn't believe he deserved it.

"You mean to tell me, that everything you've been doing for me is brand new?"

"I thought you knew that already. You've been teaching me everything."

Samuel realized he had been teaching her a few things, but he figured it was only how to please *him* specifically and not how to please in general. But now everything made sense. The young woman was more open for him than he had ever imagined.

He shook his head and grinned. "Damn," he uttered. He viewed himself as a dirty old man who had been turning out a young woman more than ever now. And Candice could sense the regret in him.

She let out a sigh and asked, "Is this gonna change how you feel about me now? Because I would hate for that to happen. I feel so comfortable with you. I mean, you really take your time with me, and I feel like I could learn a lot from you."

But the more she talked and opened herself up to him, the more Samuel felt like running away from her. He didn't want all of that sentimental shit on his mind with a young woman. He wanted to date and fuck without thinking about it. But knowing who Candice really was made him second guess his relationship with her. And he would honestly rather teach a young slut to fuck than an angel. A man could rationalize turning out a slut a lot easier. But an angel?

"You still gotta get up early for school tomorrow?" he asked, changing the subject. He wanted to get rid of her so he could clear his mind without her being next to him.

"I do, but…I could stay if you really want me to. I could get up at five o'clock in the morning to go home and change then."

"So, you still live at home?" he asked her nervously. Had she been lying to her parents every time she came over his place? Hell, she was still a grown-ass woman.

"No, I have a roommate. It's my cousin, actually. And she's cool. She knows what I'm going through."

"Does she know about me?"

Candice smiled. "I mean, not about every *detail*. But she does knows."

He began to wonder if her cousin was a church freak as well, and he quickly fantasized about a holy threesome before he shook the devilish thoughts out of his mind.

You see that? This shit is driving me crazy already! he told himself.

"Well, nah, you don't have to ah, stay the night. I'm glad you finally went out with me and told me the truth, that's all."

She leaned over to face him. "Are you sure?"

"Yeah, I'm sure," he told her. "Wouldn't you want me to tell you the truth, too?"

"Yes."

"All right then."

Candice grinned and French kissed him in the mouth with a greedy tongue. But Samuel didn't feel as greedy anymore. And when his young plaything had gotten dressed and left him for home, he couldn't stop thinking about his predicament with her.

"Fuck it, just act like I don't even know," he tried to tell himself.

Unfortunately, the next few times Candice attempted to visit him at his apartment, Samuel had gotten busier with his loan applications at work. The honeymoon period at his new job had faded, and it was real work time. He even tried to explain as much to Candice.

"Look, imagine how fuller your plate will be once you start work as a full-time teacher. I need to make it through this new adjustment period, that's all."

"But why can't I come over while you work?" she pleaded.

"Because I really need to focus on finishing what I'm doing."

"So, are you saying that I would distract you?"

"Oh, *definitely*. I *know* you would," he admitted.

"And you're sure that you still want to see me?"

"Yeah, I'm sure. I don't have as much free time as I used to have."

"But if you really wanted to see me, you would *make* time. And I would stay out of your way when I'm over. I can even come later at night if you want me to."

She was trying her hardest to keep their open sessions going. But Samuel didn't feel as urgent about it any longer. He couldn't make himself feel excited anymore about seeing her. All he could think about was a church freak trying to live out her fantasies through him. His mind wasn't going for it, even though she pleased him so well.

Candice then stopped calling him altogether. When Samuel realized it had been a few weeks since he had heard from her last, and that she no longer returned his calls, he visited her father's church to see if he could bump into her again.

He listened to Reverend Burton preach the word with uneasiness, knowing full well that he had been screwing his daughter and teaching her how to swallow his seed. But Samuel was undaunted that morning. And after a few solid weeks without a word from Candice, he needed to have her back in his life. So he socialized at the church with much of the congregation, hoping to bump into her.

"Hey, Samuel, from the bank, right?" Sister Davis greeted him at the church.

"Oh yeah, Sister Davis, how are you doing?" he responded gleefully.

"Oh, I'm doing just fine. The Lord Jesus blesses me every day."

Samuel got right to the point. "Well, I haven't heard from Candice lately. Has she been doing all right? I didn't see her in here today." He had already sat through two sermons that Sunday morning.

Sister Davis looked at him cautiously. "Well, you probably won't see her back in Charlotte for awhile, except on holidays. She got a new teaching job up north. She didn't tell you?"

Samuel dodged the question. "Up *north*? In what city? New York? Philly?"

Sister Davis looked at him again, more skeptically. "Well, why don't you call and ask her? I'm sure she'll tell you all about it."

Samuel realized that his longing for Candice was maybe a little too strong. So he smiled and nodded to tone his eagerness down.

"Yeah, I'll call her and do that. Thanks."

"Well, would you like to meet her father, Reverend Burton? I can take you right on over there to meet him."

Samuel eyed the preacher a few feet away, talking to some of the other church members, and he wanted no parts of that. He backed away immediately. "Maybe next week. I got a few other stops I need to make this afternoon that I'm already late for," he lied inside the church.

"Okay, well, I'll introduce you tom him after next Sunday's service. And I'm glad you finally chose a good church now, Brother Samuel."

They both smiled at each other civilly, as Samuel nodded and backed away from her to head home.

"Now that was *crazy*," he told himself outside as he headed toward his car in the parking lot.

I gotta let the girl go, he mused. *Obviously, she's decided to move on from me.*

For weeks, Samuel wondered about Candice, hoping that she would call him back and tell him where she was and what she had been up to. Now he wished he had never told her to leave for a new city to get away from her father's reach. And he wished that he could better handle her desire to be a passionate young woman. He also wished that he had never bothered to find out who she was. He even wished that they could start their erotic teacher/student relationship all over again.

Samuel even went out and talked a new young Charlotte church girl into visiting him at his apartment. It was an attempt to play out a new fantasy. But this girl was hardly as willing or as expressive as Candice had been. Samuel tried his luck with her anyway.

"Are you confident enough in yourself to walk around without any clothes on?" he asked.

She was actually prettier and slimmer than Candice. But she was nowhere near as confident in her naked skin.

"Oh, heck no," the girl answered. "I can barely look at myself in the mirror. And I hate it when other people stare at me." Then she frowned at him and set herself on guard. "But why would you ask me something like that?"

Samuel could tell that there would be no magic with her. He forced himself to conduct his new sexual investigation anyway.

"I wanted to know if a young, church-going woman like yourself, would be as comfortable in her body as girls who may not go to church as much, that's all."

She eyed him cautiously. "Well, in *my* opinion, I think a lot of these girls out here need to feel more *shameful* about their bodies than what they do. I mean, don't *you* think? I wouldn't even *dream* about doing some of the things with my body that *they* do."

"Yeah, but come on now, every young woman wants to feel confident and naked for somebody. It's all about who you want to feel naked and confident for."

He planned to push her conscience into a corner and get the truth out of the young church girl.

"Well, I hope I can feel that way for my *husband* and *only* my husband."

"So, you're telling me you haven't had sex before. What are you, twenty-four years old right now?" he pressed her.

The young woman stopped. "Excuse me?" Then she stood up. "Oh, I think it's time for me to *go*. I don't even believe you *asked* me something like that. What is wrong with you? You think that because I agreed to come over to your place that I'm that loose, sinful and shameless. Now I may admit that I'm nobody's perfect angel, but I'm surely not bad enough for you to disrespect me like that. So I think it's time for me to make a fast exit and go."

All Samuel did was smile. "We all got here the same way, honey. Your momma laid down and spread 'em for your daddy just like you will for your man. And I'm being honest enough to say it like it is. So you can get mad at me if you want, but at least give me credit for knowing the real desires of a woman. And more than anything else, you want to feel *normal*, be a normal sex fiend, just like all the rest of us."

The young woman stood there in his living room and was speechless for a second. How could a man be so calmly outspoken about sex with a stranger? She didn't know him that well. But somehow he had cut through the bull-shit and struck a nerve. Even though she would not be immoral enough to agree with him, she at least had to admit to herself that she would remember him speaking the truth. She *did* want somebody to want her sexually. And she was too attractive not to know that men of all ages would crave her.

"Whatever," she told him meekly on her way to the front door. "I'm gonna pray for you."

"Yeah, and then you come back and get a couple of good private lessons when you calm down, okay? I'll be right here to teach you. And I promise that it'll be just between me and you."

"Yeah, when *hell* freezes over," she snapped.

"Well then, bring a heavy jacket with you, and ear muffs."

When the young woman left, Samuel sat down on his living-room couch, the same one where Candice had sucked him and fucked him, while eating chicken and French fries and watching college football. And he realized that *he* had been turned out this time.

"Imagine that," he told himself. "Now she got me fiending for the next young church girl to put her true all over me." He sighed, wishing again that he could roll back the hands of time to when he had first moved into his Charlotte apartment and invited Candice over to help him unpack...and to unwind. And after a very long period in his dating life, the teacher realized that he had become the student again.

ADDICTED TO IT

"WHOOOAAA, THIS SHIT *WORKS*! IT'S WORKING! IT'S *WORKING*! OOOHHH, YEAH!"

Marion "M.J." Jefferson was steady thrusting his sixty-three-year-old pelvis into a forty-five-year-old woman. He had taken Viagra for the first time after having problems getting his old Johnson to stay up during sex. And after recently falling limp in the middle of the act, he felt it was time to become proactive. So with a new, fully engorged dick, and a strong nut approaching, the man was in heaven, as if it was his first time fucking all over again. And when he came, boy, did he feel rejuvenated.

He gritted his teeth, frowned up his face, and hollered, "OH, *SHIT*! MOTHER-*FUCKER*!" while squeezing the woman's head like a medicine ball. It damn near felt like he was breaking something.

The woman grabbed his hands away from her scalp and bent his fingers back to stop him from crushing her brains.

"What the hell are you doing?" she cursed him.

M.J. took a couple of quick breaths to compose himself. He felt woozy.

"I was, I was..." He ran out of breath before he could finish.

The woman forced herself out from under him and pushed him aside on the bed.

"You need to get yourself some damn *oxygen*," she told him. "Maybe you just too damn *old* for this. And that Viagra's gonna help you all right; it's gon' help put you right in your damn *casket*."

M.J. had to chuckle at that one. "That ain't a bad idea. At least I can die in some pussy."

Then he looked down to make sure his condom was still on. Not that it mattered with a woman who had her tubes tied. But the nut felt so good and real, he had to make sure his Johnson was still covered.

When his partner climbed up to go to the bathroom, she stopped at the bedroom door and warned him, "Be careful what your ass hope for, you hear."

He stared at her aging body, overblown hips, sagging titties, and an ass tattooed by stretch marks. He thought, *Shit, anything is better than hoping for that.*

So while she went to wash herself up inside the bathroom, M.J. rolled over on his back and daydreamed about higher goals.

"Shit, if my dick can stay hard like this, I need to think about gettin' me some younger pussy," he commented to the ceiling.

He clicked on the color television set with the remote and changed the channel to BET for inspiration. Everyone knew the network continued to push young videos with gyrating women all over the screen. The network's most popular show, *106 & Park*, was on. A bunch of screaming teenagers watched videos while celebrity guests appeared for cheesy interviews. The show was hosted by the male-and-female team of Terrance J and Rocsi.

M.J. looked over the Latina female host from every angle and grunted, "Mmmph. Now I'd fuck her with this Viagra all night long. Rocsi, hunh? *Damn!*"

When his partner reentered the room wearing her extra-large panties and bra, he asked, "What you think about these young video girls?"

She frowned at him. "What about 'em?" She didn't understand why he was even watching them. That was like watching his three granddaughters play jump rope.

"Uhhh, nothin'," he mumbled. *She mad 'cause she never looked like them.* And he went back to watching Beyoncé's new video.

His partner looked over at the BET channel and grunted. "Lawd, don't let them damn pills get you into something you can't get out of. And if you in here huffing and puffing with me, what you expect to do with somebody else? Let alone some *young* heffa."

M.J. smiled. "Shit. Sound like you jealous. All I'm doing is looking."

"*Excuse me?* Jealous of *what?* We ain't even that serious for me to be *jealous* of somebody. Especially over *your* ass. You 'bout ten minutes from a heart attack."

M.J. got a little tired of hearing the dying jokes. "Look, now, I ain't that damn old. Besides, I got a young spirit. I feel like I'm *forty*."

His partner laughed out loud. "Are you bullshittin' me? Last week your ass was talking 'bout how you felt like your life was over. Now you dun' had some Viagra, and you all in here watching videos and talking like you Quincy Jones or somebody."

He sat up in bed excitedly. "Hey, that's a good one. Quincy Jones up in his *seventies* now, and he *still* got 'em."

"Yeah, and he 'dun had strokes, and plates in his head, and all kinds of other health problems."

"Aw, girl, now everybody got health problems. *You* got a health problem once a month until menopause. Then you'll have another damn problem," he joked.

His partner stopped and gave him an evil eye, while he laughed it up.

"Mmm-hmm, keep on laughing."

She started to put her clothes back on, but Marion wasn't finished with her yet.

"What are you doin'?"

She frowned. "I'm taking my black ass back home. I got *kids* and shit to cook for. It's almost seven o'clock."

He climbed up out of bed. "Hold on, let me see if it's still working."

"Of *course* it's still working. You think it's gon' wear off after one damn time. That shit stay in your system for *days*."

"So, why you only wanna do it *once* then? You need some women's Viagra?"

She stopped and stared at him again. "Sounds like them damn pills dun' went to your *mouth*, too."

"Aww, shit, girl, don't blame everything on them pills. I woulda wanted *seconds* without Viagra."

"Bullshit! You would'na been able to even finish the *first* time. You dun' forgot already. *I* haven't." She continued pulling her clothes on.

He cried, "So, what am I supposed to do now?"

She looked down at his still hard dick. "Well, you better do *something*. But it won't be wit' *me*. And if your ass 'bout to start hoppin' around with a bunch of women, then let me know in advance. Because I'm not trying to be a part of that nonsense."

M.J. didn't know what else to say to her. She wasn't the kind of woman to back down. And it looked as if she had already made up her mind on leaving.

Once she got dressed and headed for the door, she looked back and rubbed it in. "Well, have fun with Vaseline Shirley." Then she giggled on the way out.

"Yeah, fuck you, too," he mumbled under his breath once the front door had closed behind her. "Shit," he cursed, thinking about his dilemma. "Fuck Vaseline Shirley! I need a real woman up in this place. Who 'da hell gon' take Viagra just to jack the hell off?"

So he freshened up and got dressed to hang out in his hometown of St. Louis, looking to score twice in the same night. He drove to Petey's Bar & Grill near Interstate 70 on the north side.

"They always got a pack of hot women up in here," he noted to himself as he parked his car down the street from the bar.

He walked up to the place after eight on a weeknight, with one damn thing on his mind. More pussy. As soon as he reached the door, a group of four women walked inside in front of him.

Damn! Perfect timing! he assessed.

"Hey, girl, where you been?" another woman shouted across the room as they entered.

M.J. followed in right behind them. "Tell her you've been working out that perfect figure of yours," he cracked, jumping in their business.

The women all looked at him before any of them bothered to comment. He was a tall, ruggedly-handsome old man with plenty of thick gray hair.

He shrugged. "I'm only telling the truth."

The woman he referenced was a solid physical specimen, with a mass of curly, shoulder-length hair.

She looked back at M.J. and grinned. "Thank you."

He nodded to her. "You deserve it."

"Sounds like you got a secret admirer in here, girl?" one of her girlfriends quipped.

"Naw, this ain't no *secret*. I tells it like it is," M.J. commented.

"Yeah, that's the best way to do it, ain't it, M.J.?" one of his own friends spoke up from the bar.

"You know it. We running out of time for bullshit," M.J. shot back.

He had the women intrigued. They figured he had a lot of swagger for an old man.

"Well, where you come from, swinging like that? *Hollywood?*"one of the older women joked. She looked in her early forties, like M.J.'s sex partner, who had gone home to cook dinner for her children. But the main girl looked barely thirty. No wonder her figure was so tight.

"You don't need to be from Hollywood when you got that *juice* up in your system. And I'm *juiced* up right now," he boasted.

The ladies laughed it off.

"What juice is that, *Pimp Juice?*" one of them teased.

"Oh, now, I got more than that. I got the whole *pill.*"

The women looked around and continued laughing. They couldn't tell if the man was serious or not. But he sure had them going. He was making their night, and it was still early.

"What kind of pill are you talking about?" the main girl asked him.

With the Viagra in his system, M.J. felt as confident as ever.

"First of all, what's your name? And second …" He grabbed her left hand and flipped it over. "Are you married with kids yet?" Once he saw no wedding band on her finger, he said, "It looks like you're *not.*"

"I do have a son."

"A young heartbreaker, ain't he?" M.J. assumed.

She smiled with deep dimples. "I don't want him breaking any hearts. His *father* dun' enough of that already."

"Well, I'm sorry to hear that, ahhh…"

"Jessica," she filled in for him.

He held out his hand for a shake. "I'm Marion Jefferson, or M.J., like the famous basketball player."

"Who, Michael Jackson?" she responded hastily.

Marion paused with a gracious smile. "No, *Jordan*, the other M.J. But I guess you're right, it's a lot of us M.J.'s out here running around."

"So, what kind of pills are you talking about?" she asked him again. She seemed to be particularly interested.

"Viagra," he told her straight up.

Her girls were startled. After their embarrassed laughter, one of them stated, "Well, you ask the man a question and you get a frank answer. That's how older men are."

"That's about right," M.J. admitted. "Yup."

"Like you said, we running out of time for bullshit," his friend commented from his bar stool. He was in his late forties himself, and extra dark.

Jessica remained poised and intrigued. She smiled. "That's what's up. You're still active. I even ain't mad you."

M.J. joked, "Yeah, I feel like I'm *forty* years old again."

"Well, how old are you?" she asked him.

"Eighty-five," he teased.

One of her girls overheard him. "*Damn*! And you still walking around popping Viagra pills?"

M.J. looked at Jessica. "She didn't catch it, did she?"

"Nope, it flew right past her."

"But I still will be popping them pills if I'm alive at eighty-five. What about you, you had a kid and haven't kicked that habit yet?"

His conversation was fluid, probing, and witty. He kept Jessica smiling.

"Ahh...not quite yet, but I'm not as *regular* as I used to be."

"Shit, well, welcome to the crowd," he told her. "If I get it twice a *week* now, I'm in heaven."

Jessica grinned. "They have pills now to make you feel like that, too."

He grimaced. "Make you feel like *what*, like you having sex twice a week? They got *pills* to do that?"

It sounded incredible to him. Technology was something else.

Jessica laughed it off again with her girls. "Maybe one day. But I was talking about feeling like you're in heaven."

"Oh, here she goes with that shit," one of her girlfriends spoke up. They had all begun to give their food and drink orders from a large table awaiting nearby.

"All I need is a good woman now to keep *me* in heaven," M.J. stated.

"Well, why you taking Viagra if all you need is a '*good woman*'?" one of her girls called him out.

"I said, all I need is a good woman *now*, since I've started *taking* this here Viagra."

He had no shame to his game at all. So his friend laughed out loud at the bar.

"You tell 'em like it is, M.J."

Jessica couldn't seem to get enough of him. She stood right by him and asked, "Have you ever tried anything else?"

"What, for sex?"

She nodded, still grinning at him.

"Oh, now, you don't wanna go there with her. She'll have your ass addicted to ecstasy," another one of her girls commented.

M.J. responded, "Ain't that illegal?"

"So are weed, steroids, and underground gambling," the same woman responded.

"And *prostitution*, too," M.J. shot back.

The women laughed out loud again.

Someone said, "Well, we can see where *his* mind is tonight."

As their food and drinks began to arrive, they got comfortable in their seats at the table.

"Well, nice meeting you," Jessica told him with an extended hand of her own.

He took her hand. "So, what are these pills you're talking about?"

"Ahh...I would have to umm...contact you about that."

"Well, you need my number?"

M.J. was suddenly pressed about her. She had a great attitude and everything.

She took out her cell phone from her purse. "M.J., right? What's the number?"

"Yeah, Marion Jefferson," he told her. And he gave her his 3-1-4 cell phone number.

When Jessica joined her girls at the table, the oldest one asked her, "Now, what you plan on calling that old man about?" They all wanted to know; all five of them.

Jessica grinned. "He's just sweet. It's nothing. It's good to see an old man continue to have a sex life."

"Well, you ain't planning on calling him up about what I *think*, are you?"

her concerned older friend asked her. "Because he's still a little too *old* for that, Viagra or not. And *I* would *know*."

Jessica grinned. "I know. Don't worry about it. I'm not calling him for that." She took a sip of her drink, case closed.

Her older girlfriend gave her one final stare down anyway. She knew that Jessica liked to buck the rules and go her own way sometimes. That's why she was hanging out with them instead of women closer to her age.

"All right now," her concerned friend warned her.

Over at the bar stools, M.J.'s buddy had some questions of his own.

"Hey, man, you really took some of that Viagra?"

M.J. sat down beside him. "Yeah. I'm not walking around here with *my* dick not staying hard, Black. So, if you wanna do that, then be my guest."

Black grinned. "I have don't no problems in that department."

"Well, when you *start* to have problems, then you'll have to make your own decisions about it," M.J. advised him.

Black looked back over toward Jessica at the table, while holding his drink in hand. "Like you said, you give me a young fine one like that one, and that's all the doctor *ordered* for me."

M.J. chuckled and looked back over toward Jessica himself, longing for her.

Black asked, "You think she gon' call you?"

M.J. thought about it for a minute. In his wildest dreams, he hoped that she *would* call him But, in reality, he figured it was unlikely. So he shook it off. "For what? I basically put her on the spot right there, man. She didn't want to hurt an old man's feelings. But my sons and daughter are older than her."

With that said, he turned back to the bar and ordered his first drink.

"Now let me look around in here for somebody that I can *really* get."

M.J. didn't get lucky enough to go home with a second woman that night. But he did score a new phone number from another forty-something. Then at work the next day at the hardware store, he got an unknown call on his cell phone.

"Hmm, who's that?" he asked. He read the number on his cell phone screen inside the storage room toward the back of the store.

"Hello," he answered.

"Hey, M.J." It was the sweet, young voice of a woman.

Marion paused. "Who is this?" He had a hunch, but he didn't want to jump to any wishful conclusions.

The woman chuckled. "This is Jessica from last night. How many new women did you give out your number to in there?" she teased.

He immediately got excited. "I *knew it*." Then he had to calm himself down. He was still at work. "Now what you doin' calling *me*, and asking me about my *women*."

She laughed. "I wanted to follow up with you about our conversation last night."

M.J. spotted a coworker in the vicinity and was forced to camouflage his subject.

"About *that*?" he asked her in code, referring to sex pills.

"Yeah, you still wanna know about it?"

"Yeah, ahh, call me back after six. I'm still at work."

"You want me to meet you somewhere?"

Shit! he thought to himself. *She's putting me on the spot now.*

"What part of town you on?"

"Southside."

"Well, you can meet me at the Botanical Garden after six. I work near there, off of Forty-four. Is that all right?"

"That's perfect."

When he hung up the phone, he couldn't believe what had happened.

"Did that girl just call and ask me to meet up with her?" It felt like a dream.

"Hey, M.J.! We need you back out here on the floor. We got customers in here," the manager yelled to him through the storage door.

"All right, I'm coming," M.J. answered, strolling forward. And his smile was worth gold in there.

He pulled up in the parking lot area of the Missouri Botanical Garden after six, and Jessica had already beaten him there. She was waiting for him inside of her burgundy Ford F-150 truck.

"Shit, this girl play for *keeps*," he stated when he spotted her. "She got a damn *F-150*." She made him feel like a wimp, especially working at a hardware store. He had given up his old Dodge Ram for a Chevy a few years ago. But she had him thinking about upgrading back to a truck. She even had nice rims on it.

He pulled up in an open space beside her and rolled down his window as she rolled hers down.

"Hey, you looking good in that thing. I wouldn't have thought you had it in you," he told her. He looked up from his window; she looked down from hers.

She smiled. "You want me to follow you somewhere? I can't talk about it out here."

M.J. paused. He thought, *Shit, she must really be serious about this.*

"You don't want us to be out in the public?"

"Not if we can help it."

Damn! he thought. *She's straight up with it.* So he went for broke.

"You wanna follow me to my place?"

"Where you live?"

"Right off Page Boulevard."

She nodded and turned her engine back on. "All right. Lead the way."

Holy shit! M.J. thought. *She's following me to my house and we just met. Either this girl has a lot of trust or she's plain crazy.*

He didn't believe she would be *that* impressed with him. He was still an old-ass man. So he led her to his apartment with apprehension. He didn't need a big house anymore. After his grown kids were off and gone, he divorced his wife of twenty-six years and jumped back into the single life for the rest of his days.

Nobody's gonna tell me when I can't have no pussy. I was tired of that damn fish every year anyway, he noted.

When he pulled up into the back parking area of his low-key, third-floor apartment, atop a block of retail storefronts, he marveled again at his great stroke of luck.

"Had I known this would happen, I would have taken Viagra a lot sooner," he joked to himself as he climbed out of his car.

Jessica climbed out of her truck a few parking spaces over from his car. She walked over to join him with a large white bag over her shoulder, wearing a black skirt, a white top, and black stockings with her black heels.

She must have a can of mace or either a loaded gun in that big-ass bag of hers, he imagined. He couldn't help but to remain a little pensive and skeptical. She was making things far too easy. So there had to be a catch to it.

"So, you live in these apartments? I've passed this place before a *few* times. A couple of my girlfriends live near here," she told him.

"Yeah, a lot of people pass this place by. That's why I like it here. It's right there in front of you, but because of the storefronts on the bottom, people barely notice the apartments up on top."

He led her into a security entrance area with his key, and awaited two elevators next to the exit stairs.

She nodded. "Nice. So nobody can just walk up in here then."

"Nooo, I wouldn't live in no place like that at my age. I don't have time for the extra drama."

"That's good. Me either." Jessica grinned.

They climbed onto the elevator and reached the third floor to head toward his two-bedroom apartment. Marion grew more anxious every step of the way.

We almost at my door now, he told himself gleefully. He felt like a brand-new adult with his own personal space again. But he didn't let on how anxious he was from the outside. He remained as cool as a cucumber. He stopped at apartment 312.

"Here we go, right here."

Jessica continued to smile and waited for him to open it. Once they walked in, she took a casual walk around and nodded again.

"Nice. So, this is where you bring your women," she teased him.

Marion laughed it off. "Now, just 'cause I took some of that Viagra don't make me no gigolo. But I can't say I don't want to experiment with it." Then he smiled in her direction and added, "So, like I told you all last night, I might have to find me one good woman who can keep up with me now."

That made Jessica chuckle again. "One who can keep up with you, hunh?" she repeated.

"That's what I said."

She walked over to his kitchen table and sat down with her bag. "Okay, well, can I trust you?"

M.J. looked down into her eyes and frowned. "Trust me to do what?"

Instead of answering him, she dug into her white bag and pulled out a loaded Ziploc of separated pills in six different bottles. She set them in front of him on the kitchen table.

M.J. looked at her mini store of goods. "Shit. You weren't lying about them damn pills, were you?" He sat down at the table across from her.

She separated each bottle. "These are called Blue Dolphins. I would advise you to start off with these. They're about the most basic ecstasy pills you can get."

She placed a small blue pill into his hand to see it.

M.J. looked at the small pill in the palm of his hand. "Shit, they actually got dolphins on 'em."

She smiled at his wonder. "That's what everybody says when they see them. So, you start with one and then see if you can handle two. And always have about five to six hours to clear the effects out of your system before you go anywhere important, like work, or to a family or business event."

"Unless I plan to get my freak on there, right?" he joked.

She took the Blue Dolphin from his hand and returned it to its bottle. Then she moved on to the next pill. It was a white one with a small number "9" on it.

"This one here is called Cloud Nine. Now that one's a little stronger. It'll have you going all night and still up the next morning. But that's mainly for like, the weekend, and people who want to party all night."

"Shit," M.J. muttered. "So, that's like them Rock Star energy juices."

"Yeah, but much stronger," she warned. She continued her demonstration, moving on to the next pill.

"This one's called Business Man Trip. And it relaxes you, and makes you feel like you're enjoying a vacation."

Then she paused and looked at him. "Now, these other three, I wouldn't even sell to you. They're all hallucinogens. But while I have them out on the table, I'll tell you what they are."

M.J. sat across the table and thought, *Well, I'll be damned! She's actually a real drug dealer! And to think that she was so damn sweet.*

"Seventh Heaven, Blue Mystic, and Salvia are pills I mainly sell to white people. Blue Mystic is the safest. Seventh Heaven is a little stronger. And this Salvia stuff..." She stopped and shook her head. "I didn't even wanna sell that shit, to tell you the truth, but they kept asking me for it."

M.J. sat there blown away for a minute. "And you actually...*deal* with this stuff, like on an everyday basis?"

She shook it off. "Not *every* day, no. I mean, when I have my son with me, I don't bother with it. I have a few people who work with me. But you can't run around talking about this stuff like you talk about Viagra."

"You don't say," he quipped sarcastically. He didn't know what else to say or do. He really didn't want to get involved with sex drugs and hallucinogens.

"So, how much do you sell them for?" he figured he'd ask her, for the hell of it.

"Ten to fifteen dollars, depending on how many they want."

"And how many do they usually buy?"

"Shit, some people buy up to twenty of them at a time."

"So, you can make plenty of good money off it."

"Yeah," she admitted. "I wouldn't do it, if not. You wanna try the Blue Dolphin?" she asked. She slipped it in there as if they were talking about having a drink of coffee.

M.J. hesitated. "Ahhh...well..." He didn't want to seem like a *pussy* by backing down, but he didn't want to be a *fool* either.

"You want me to take one with you?"

M.J. looked into her face and studied her meaning.

"Now, if you take it with me..." He didn't see how he could turn that offer down.

She said, "Then I'll stay for awhile and let you fuck me."

M.J. couldn't believe his damn ears. And she was so damn *smooth* about it. So instead of responding to her, he began to chuckle.

"Shit," he let out. "Now..." He wanted to ask if he could fuck her without taking the pills, but he hesitated again. She had the old man backing up on his heels.

"I mean, I'm not gonna force you to; you're a grown man. But since you were so adamant about taking Viagra… And then you started asking me about everything else. So, I figured, you know…"

He nodded, following her logic to a tee. She was calling his bluff and basically punking him out. He was all mouth and no action.

"Well, is this how you usually, ah…"

"Hell no," she cut him off with her first frown. "I don't sleep around with these people like that. I told you, I don't get it like that anymore. But I thought that you were a nice older guy. So, you know…I thought about it and said, 'Why not?' I figured I would make your day."

Marion's Viagra-enhanced dick was already rock hard under the table. He didn't need any Blue Dolphin pill to fuck her; jut listening to her made him want to fuck.

He grinned. "Well, that's real nice of you, Jessica." He sat there and stared across the table at her. He was on cloud nine without a pill. "Are these pills addictive?"

"Is your Viagra addictive? Is good pussy? Is money addictive? You tell me," she commented with a grin. "It's all what you make of it. But I'm not addicted to anything. My *son*," she added.

She had a good point. How much control could one exert over anything? So he went ahead and challenged her.

"Well, let me see you take one of those pills," he stated.

She smiled. "You think I won't?"

"Let me see you."

Jessica opened up the bottle of Blue Dolphin pills and placed one on her tongue. Then she popped a second one and swallowed them both.

M.J. stared at her as if he were in a daze.

"But *you* just take *one* for now. That's all you'll need the first time." Then she handed him a Blue Dolphin.

M.J. looked straight ahead at her and didn't acknowledge the pill. "And you'll stay here and let me fuck you, right?"

She nodded. "Yeah. It's in my system now. So we watch TV or listen to music for a half-hour, and then it's on."

M.J. heard that and popped the pill into his mouth without looking at it. "And how long are you planning on staying?" He didn't want another woman running out on him before he was completely satisfied.

Jessica looked at her watch. "I have to be at work at eight o'clock in the morning. And I only need five hours of sleep. So you do the math."

"That's about one o'clock," he told her. "And it's seven now. That gives us less than five hours."

Jessica chuckled. "Yeah, you *are* greedy. You will need a good woman for all that. But if I had a change of clothes with me…"

M.J. smiled it off. "It's the *thought* that counts. So I'm glad you're at least *thinking* about it."

"Yeah. I like your vibe. And I know that you like *mine*," she told him.

"Damn right," he admitted. "I don't even *need* thirty minutes."

She laughed it off and put her stash of drugs back into her bag to move it from the kitchen table.

"Is that right?" she asked him. "Well, let me see what you working with. You got gray hairs down there, too?"

Suddenly, M.J. felt ashamed of his age. Why did she have to be so blunt about it? He couldn't pull his dick out on the table like that for a young woman to see it. So he reversed the challenge back to her again.

"Let me see what *you* working with. You 'da one with all the youth."

Jessica didn't mind it. She kicked off her heels under the table and stood up to take off her skirt and pantyhose. And she wore no panties. Then she started to undo her white shirt.

When she was totally naked, she sat up on his kitchen table and asked, "Now what you wanna do with me?"

First he stood up and studied her naked body. M.J. had not seen a woman's body that young and lean in person in nearly twenty years.

Got' dammit, look what the hell I've been missing all these years, he told himself. Jessica grabbed his hands and made him fondle her nipples. Then she took his index finger and made him play with her pussy.

"When it hits you, you gon' get real open," she told him. She slid her long right leg into his crotch, to rub his hardened dick with.

Why me? M.J. asked himself. *What did I do to deserve THIS?*

While he continued to fondle her breasts and toy with her pussy lips,

Jessica began to undo his light-blue work shirt, button by button. Then she slid her soft hands under his T-shirt and fondled *his* nipples.

Marion jerked in response, surprised at how good it felt. He wasn't sure if he wanted to stop her or not.

That shit makes ME feel like the damn girl! Is that how this Blue Dolphin kicks in? It's not even thirty minutes yet, he calculated.

Jessica pulled him closer to her and French-kissed him with plenty of tongue action.

Oh, shit! Imagine that on my dick, he thought. That made him throb harder and pray for freedom at the edge of the table. So he undid his belt, button and zipper to unleash his one-eyed monster.

Jessica caught him there at the edge of the table and massaged his dick, up and down and around, with her fingers.

Her soft touch felt so good to him that he backed up with slow thrusts and began to fuck her fingers.

She gon' make me cum in her damn hands! he warned himself. *How crazy would that be?* So he stopped the madness before he fucked around and wasted his first nut.

"Let me go get my protection," he told her.

Before he could move away, she gave him another forceful peck on the lips.

"I'll be waiting for you right here."

Marion damn near tripped over his undone pants as he stumbled toward his bedroom for the condoms inside of his nightstand.

"Be careful, baby," Jessica warned him with a giggle.

Shit, she ain't gon' change her mind up on me, is she? he panicked. He couldn't believe he was that close to fucking a fine woman younger than his three kids. *She's right there on my kitchen table like a damn Thanksgiving Day turkey,* he told himself.

He rushed back out with four loose condoms in his hands and dropped the extras on the floor. But Jessica stopped him from putting one on.

"Hold on, you wanna feel it hit you first," she suggested.

M.J. didn't give a damn. He still felt that she would somehow disappear like Cinderella before he got a chance to fuck her. So he was increasingly anxious about it.

"Slow down, baby, I'm not going anywhere," she promised.

"You sure?" he asked her. He sounded like a desperate beggar.

Jessica laughed at him and stood up naked from the table.

"Where's the bedroom?"

M.J. snapped to it and led her there, finally stepping out of his pants and drawers. He didn't care about the awkwardness of his age at that point. The heat was on! So he took his T-shirt off, too.

Jessica reached his bedroom and stretched out on his bed, spread eagle like an erotic freak show. M.J. stood there and watched her. He began to fondle himself, while standing at attention, seven inches long.

Holy mother of Christ! I'm going to hell now, ain't I? There's no turning back now, he told himself.

He jumped into his bed with her and got swallowed up by a seductive octopus. She was all over him. Then he felt the magic of the Blue Dolphin pill kicking in. His body felt extra clammy without the heat on. It was the intense body heat that did it. And Jessica was running her hands all through his mane of gray hair.

"You should have this all trimmed down and keep it neat and handsome. You could get a whole lot more girls that way," she advised. Even her voice turned him on now.

She began to climb down his body in bed and suck his nipples, while massaging his torso, and slipping and sliding her long, naked legs inside of his.

I'm still a MAN! Marion told himself. *I'm not a woman! But damn, her lips feel like I got TITTIES in this motherfucker!*

Then she turned him over and licked down his neck until she reached his back and kept going. Her fingers rubbed up his sides, barely touching his skin, as she tickled him into girlish submission.

Ooooooohhh, shiiiiitttt! M.J. squealed in his mind. He wouldn't *dare* allow himself to voice it. But his body told on him anyway. He shook in small convulsions as if his skin was having individual orgasms. He had turned into a hyper-sexual alien with multiple dicks and pussies on his neck, back, ribs, ass, legs…even his toes felt climactic.

"Can you feel it now, baby? The Blue Dolphin?" she whispered.

M.J. could barely speak. He was terrified of what might slip out of his mouth. His dick pressed so hard against the bed sheets that he had to reach down and adjust it before it broke in half on him. Then he felt her wet, feathery tongue inching down to the dip in his back before she licked him around his hairy ass.

WHAT THE HELL IS SHE DOING? he thought as he jerked his ass away from her. Then she clawed his body softly with the tips of her nails. He felt like the sweet devil had gotten a hold of him. But Jessica only laughed at his nervous inhibitions. She was enjoying the turnout. She already knew what the pill would do to him.

"Are you ready for me to fuck you now?"

I thought I was supposed to fuck you? he thought. But he still failed to speak. Maybe the Blue Dolphin pill had taken away his ability to communicate.

"Where are your condoms?" she asked him. She turned him over and leaned down to kiss his stomach, working her way further down and over to his hip, before she slung his dick into her mouth.

"WHHOOOO!" he jerked with it. He felt like his body was ready to fly out the window and soar with the airplanes at Lambert International Airport.

Jessica let his vibrating dick fall out of her mouth as she repeated, "Where are your condoms?"

M.J. could only point to his nightstand drawer with his left hand.

Jessica leaned over his stimulated body and reached into the drawer to pull out several condoms. She then slid one over his erection.

He could see and feel her climbing up into position. When she grabbed his seven-inch cock and balanced herself to gently ease her pussy down on top of him, M.J. shook his head as if a seizure was coming.

"You okay, baby?" She worked her body ever so slowly, while refusing to go all the way down, teasing him into insanity. "I *knew* you would love this pussy. Don't you *love it?*"

Marion nodded and reached up with both hands to anchor himself with her hips, as she bounced all the way down on his shaft.

"WHHOOOO!" he responded again, releasing his hold. Now she had him at her mercy, pumping up and down on his dick.

"This pussy is *good*, ain't it? *Ain't it? Ain't it?*" she repeated, fucking him like there was no tomorrow.

Suddenly, M.J.'s ears starting ringing, and the room seemed to spin in circles. He couldn't tell if he was at the top of the bed or at the bottom. And he could hear and feel his heart beating in slow motion.

Thoomp thoomp!..Thoomp thoomp!...Thoomp thoomp!...Thoomp thoomp!

He could barely breathe, see or hear Jessica clearly anymore. Then he panicked.

HHOOOO, SSHHIITTT! MY HEART!

"Huuhhh! Huuhhh! Huuhhh!" he panted rapidly. But the young *demon* wouldn't let him up. She kept fucking him. And fucking him. And fucking him, until his brain and body went numb.

When M.J. awoke, Jessica was flicking cold water into his face with her fingers from a filled glass. His head was propped up against two pillows on the bed.

"Oh, *shit*, thank *God!*" she said with her hands rubbing down her face in frustration. Her hair was all wrangled out now.

Marion looked up at her and asked, "What happened?"

"You passed the hell out, man," she told him. Then she laughed. "You can't take this pussy, old man."

He took a breath. "I *can* take it. I just can't take you *pounding* on me like that. Then you had me take that damn Dolphin pill. I thought I was a damn bird, flying around the room. What time is it?"

He spoke quickly now, like a man who had lost his bearings.

"Nine o'clock."

"Nine o'clock," he repeated. "Is that all?"

"Yeah, you were knocked out for like, *fifteen minutes*. But I knew you were still alive. You were breathing and your heart was still pumping. You were knocked the hell out. But your dick was still hard though," she added with a smile. "That Viagra is something else."

"So did I nut?"

She frowned. "No. How was you gon' nut? You passed the hell out."

"Well, we ain't finished yet then," he told her. "I can't be with a young broad like you and don't even cum. What you think I took Viagra for?"

Jessica laughed and rested beside him. "You're *crazy*. I thought I damn near killed you. Now you saying you still wanna fuck? What's wrong with you?"

M.J. looked over at her body. "You still naked, ain't you? Did *you* cum?"

"No."

"Well, you ain't finished yet either." And he started to play with her nipples.

"Don't start something you can't finish," she warned.

"Who said I'm not gon' finish? But I need to be on *top* this time," he suggested. "That way I can control everything. That's why I passed out. I couldn't breathe with you on me like that."

"Well, I don't weigh that much. How you figure?"

"It's not just about the *weight*. It's about the body heat and the pressure. I couldn't get enough oxygen down there like that," he explained.

Jessica didn't respond. But, as he continued to fondle her breasts, they hardened in his fingers.

"See that, you still want it," he teased.

"Yeah, I didn't get a chance to finish. And I took two of those pills to your one."

"Yeah, but you knew what you were doing with them."

"But still," she told him, "I'm still horny."

"Well, that's what I want to hear." He climbed up into the dominant position on top, and reached back over to his nightstand to pull out another condom.

"Let's finish fucking. You said it takes four to five hours to get it out of your system. Right? Well, we still got another three hours before midnight."

Jessica laughed and admired the man's mojo.

He is crazy as hell, she told herself. *But I don't know if I can do this shit with him again. He scared the hell out of me, passing out like that.*

Nevertheless, she was still in an aroused state. Both of them were. And as he continued to stroke her nipples with his masculine hands, she found herself willing to allow him to finish the job. So she reached down to stimulate the hardness of his dick with soft strokes of her fingers around his tip.

"Boy, you got a way with them hands," he told her as his penis filled up with passionate blood in a matter of seconds.

"All right, you be on top this time."

M.J. opened up his second condom, with the first discarded, and he slid it down his Johnson to get back to work. Even though he had passed out earlier, he was a lot more poised now to fuck a young, fine woman, who was less than half his age.

I'ma tear this motherfucker up now! he promised himself. *She should have packed up and quit when I passed out on her.*

He plugged his hard, vibrant dick back into her young, fresh pussy and composed himself to control his stroke.

"Now you were talking about me liking this pussy of yours before I passed out, weren't you?"

It was about the only thing he could remember, outside of the fact that she was on top.

Jessica smiled up into his face and intertwined her legs with his as he began to stroke her.

"Yeah, I said it," she told him. She reached up and ran her hands through his gray beard and woolly gray hair on his head. "I also said you should trim up your gray hair and keep it short and neat to look more handsome. Then you can get *a lot* of young pussy."

Jessica sure knew how to talk the right shit to him. M.J. had to fight himself not to nut from simply listening to her sexy-ass words. She sounded like an expert whore talking good shit to a John. Then she started squeezing her pussy muscles on him.

"Let me show you what this young pussy know how to do."

She made it so snug around his dick that M.J. found it hard to pull back from her.

Shit, she gon' make the condom slip off, he panicked. But to hell if he was gonna stop fucking her. Then she started picking at his nipples again.

"Hey, hey, don't do that," he whined like a bitch. He was tired of her making him feel like a girl. But that only made Jessica more aggressive.

She leaned up and bent her head down to suck and bite on his nipples.

"Fuck, let me just *do* what I'm doing here," he told her. She was blowing his groove by trying to turn him out again.

She smiled and slid back on the pillow like a sacrificial lamb. And her smile was still easy and incredible. Then she started to suck her own pinkie and moan.

"*Mmmmmm...*"

That damn near made Marion nut all by itself.

Shit, I'm not gon' make it! he told himself. *I'm not gon' MAKE IT!*

He wanted the fuck to last much longer, but he could already feel his nut coming from the back of his ass.

"*Ooooh, you like this pus-seee,*" Jessica moaned up to him as M.J. struggled not to come too fast. But it was no use. A strong nut was on the way.

Got' dammit, two nights in a ROW! he marveled. *But this is MUCH better than last night! This is YOUNG PUSSY!*

"*OOOOOOHHH!*" he squealed and jerked into her tight body. The force was so strong that his arm lock broke against the bed as he fell down on top of her. Jessica locked on his ass immediately like a vise grip, with her legs, her pussy muscles, her hips, her arms, and even her words locked down on his ass.

"You *love* this pussy, don't you?" she groaned into his ear. She sounded like she was angry at him, forcing M.J. to respond like a bitch again.

"*Mmmm-hmmm,*" he moaned back to her. But he needed to *breathe.* And she was sucking the air out of his old ass a *second* time.

"Wait a minute. Wait a minute."

He panted like an animal, and was attempting desperately to break away.

Realizing his distress, Jessica let him go. The man couldn't take her pressure. And he began to feel his heart beating heavy inside of his chest again.

Thoomp thoomp!...Thoomp thoomp!...

Jessica moved much faster than last time and began to fan him with the pillow to cool him down with air.

"Breathe deep! Breathe deep!" she told him.

M.J. did as she said and took long, deep breaths as his heart continued to explode with thunderous beats.

I'm not gon' make it this time! I'm not gon' make it! he told himself. He felt for sure that a heart attack was approaching. But after a few minutes of slow breathing, he realized that he was still alive. However, he *was* having chest pains. It was an omen of things to come if he kept fucking with Jessica. The woman was simply too much for him at his age, her sex drugs and everything.

"You okay?" she asked him, leaning over into his face as he rolled over on his back. She wasn't grinning either. She was seriously concerned about him.

"See, I *knew* I shouldn't have done it again," she cried. "You're just too *old* for this."

M.J. ignored what she was saying and mumbled, "Water. I need water." He could barely get the words out of his mouth to tell her.

Jessica jumped right up and went to get it for him.

When she brought a glass of cold water back to him to drink, he sat up and smiled at her.

"What's so funny?" she questioned.

He took the glass and swallowed down the cold water first. He said, "I'm all right now. We got about another hour to go."

The man refused to admit defeat. That made Jessica smile again.

She shook her head and told him, "You're crazy. How many times you gonna play with death?"

"Just one more time," he told her. "Then I'll call it a night."

"Are you serious? You *can't* be serious, right?"

"Why can't I be? I'm all right now."

Jessica continued to shake her head. She stood back up from the bed. "Let me go on and get dressed."

"See that, that's just what I mean. I need a woman who can keep up with me," he repeated from the bed.

"*No*, you need a woman who's not gonna *kill you*," she countered. "Because you can't even keep up with your*self*."

"So, what's all that talk about me trimming my hair down and going out there to get all the young pussy I can get? Ain't that what you told me?" he reminded her.

"Yeah, well, I changed my mind," she responded with a grin. "I still think that you're a nice man, and you need to be able to stay alive a little longer."

She started to walk back toward the kitchen to gather her clothes. M.J. struggled up out of bed to follow her. It was indeed a struggle too. His body felt overexerted.

"Look at you, you can barely walk now," Jessica noted, looking back at him.

"That's because I've been in bed with *you* for three hours."

"And you still want another one," she quipped. But she went and got dressed anyway.

"So, you gon' leave me now without finishing the job?"

Jessica stopped and chuckled. "Are you kidding me? Your job has been *more* than done tonight."

"Well, what about leaving me some of those pills then. What I owe you, ten dollars a pill?"

"What, for the Business Man Trips? Because that's what you *need* to do, is mellow out. Any of the other pills might kill you."

"Look, stop talking 'bout me dying so much. Okay? Now I'm still here."

"And I'm gonna make sure I *keep* you here, *too*. So we're gonna be good friends."

As she finished getting dressed at his kitchen table, Marion frowned at her. "*Friends?* Does that mean I don't get to fuck you no more with a couple of Blue Dolphins?"

Jessica cracked that easy smile of hers again. "You should be grateful I did you this time. So you can consider yourself *special*."

He smiled back at her. "Is that right?"

"Yes," she answered immediately. "Well, let me go on and go, so I can get home, take a bath, and get ready for work in the morning."

"Where do you work?"

"At Jefferson Hospital. I'm a registered nurse."

M.J. was stunned. "What? You're an R.N., and you walking 'round selling sex pills?"

She grinned. "That's why I'm qualified to deal them. I know all that they can do, *and* all of the side effects."

M.J. stated, "Well, I'll be damned! No wonder you like older men. You gotta deal with us in the hospital all the time."

"Exactly. But I thought you were one of the healthy ones from all of your Viagra talk."

M.J. boasted, "I *am* healthy."

"Just not healthy enough to deal with *me*," Jessica concluded. Then she walked toward the door. "But like I said, we can always be friends. So don't hesitate to call me."

It took Marion three days to recuperate from all the fucking he had done that week. He hadn't used all of his pelvic muscles like that in *years*! And by the weekend, he remembered to get his gray hair trimmed down nice and neatly.

"Give me one of them young man's cuts, low all around, with a nice gray goatee, Harvey," he told his long-time barber on Page Boulevard after work that Saturday evening. He had just made it into the shop before it closed.

Harvey Greenfield, a few years younger than M.J. at fifty-nine, with plenty of gray of his own, grunted, "Uh-oh. What's her name?" Then he started laughing. "That gray hair is the first thing to go when old guys like us fall in love again. Guys start dying it black and everything."

M.J. laughed with him and couldn't deny it. "She told me I would look more handsome with it trimmed down, Harvey. And you know you gotta do what a woman tell you, if that's gon' make her like you more."

"Yeah, as long as she don't start changing *everything* about you," Harvey warned. "But a good haircut and a goatee ain't bad. So, how old is she?"

M.J. grinned. "Twenty-nine."

Harvey froze. "Man, you 'bout to kill yourself. Are you *crazy*?"

"I am now," M.J. quipped with a chuckle.

"Shit, you know how many old guys kill themselves messing around with them young girls? And it may not be that same night, but the damage is accumulative."

M.J. argued, "Well, how come *Hugh Hefner* can have *three* young girlfriends and still get away with? And he's *eighty*-something."

"Hell, you know how much ass Hugh Hefner dun' had in his life? Gettin' young women is like *breathing* for him. That man just know what the hell he *doing*. But *you* ain't no damn *Hugh Hefner*. And you 'bout to *kill* yourself. You even got me afraid to cut your damn *hair* now."

At that point, a few of the other guys who were left inside the shop over-heard them and began to laugh out loud.

"Look, Harvey, go on and cut down my hair now," M.J. demanded.

Harvey stared at him for another minute before he shook his head. "Mmmt, mmmt, *mmmph*," he grunted. "You got your plot of land already picked out for your burial?"

The guys inside the shop continued to laugh hard, but M.J. only smiled. Then he joked back, "And you make sure they put it on my tombstone, 'He died in some pussy.'"

"Hey now, watch your mouth up in my shop, man. You know I don't go for that kind of language in here," Harvey told him. "Now I'll let a few small ones *slide*, but that word there is out of bounds. What if I had women and children in here?"

"But you *don't*," M.J. told him. "We all *men* up in here now. And men love *pussy*. Now go on and cut my hair down."

After getting his fresh low haircut and trimmed goatee at the barbershop, Marion Jefferson looked *damned* good! He looked like a magazine model for older men. The pharmaceutical companies could put him in a Viagra *commercial*.

Since the barbershop was only a few blocks away from his apartment building, he strolled through the St. Louis streets toward home feeling *good*. He mumbled, "I gotta do this more often, walk around and take things in."

He could even feel the cool evening breeze whipping over his head now. *I'm gon' need to wear me a hat until I can get used to this*, he told himself. He continued to stroke the smoothness of his goatee as he walked. It felt good to him.

His walk to the barbershop that evening was all a part of his change of attitude to get back in shape for fucking. He didn't look out of shape *physically*, or at least for his age, but he damn sure couldn't keep up with the circulation and respiratory he needed to stay busy in the bedroom. So he wanted to make a few changes, including more check-up trips to the doctor to make sure his heart was all right for it.

Then he decided to call Jessica back on her cell phone.

As soon as she answered the line, he told her, "You were right."

She paused. "Right about what?"

"About me getting a low haircut, and trimming up this gray goatee. I look *good* and feel even better now," he bragged.

Jessica laughed over the line. "You got it cut?"

"And I'm walking home from the barbershop now. In fact, if you don't believe me, then I can get you a second opinion right now."

He saw a group of young women with kids, having a conversation on the sidewalk in front of them. He planned to ask them.

Jessica continued to laugh. "I know you look good. That's why I told you to do it. But who you gonna ask?"

"These young mothers standing out here with their kids. They look younger than *you*."

"They probably are. But twenty-nine ain't that *young*," she noted. "Maybe a little young for *you* though."

"Not with how I feel right now. I could swing with the *rookies* tonight."

Jessica couldn't stop laughing. "I miss talking to you. You are so *crazy*."

"Crazy like an old *fox*," he bragged again. His swagger was increasing by the minute. So he asked the opinions of the young mothers out in front of him.

"Ahh, excuse me, ladies. I don't mean you no harm. I need one of you guys to tell this young woman on the phone whether I look good for an old man or not."

The young St. Louis mothers immediately looked at each other and laughed. Then they all observed him seriously.

"Yeah, I'll tell her," the boldest young mother answered. She took M.J.'s cell phone. "Yeah, he looks good. He look like he just got a haircut. And he got that smell, too, you know from the barbershop."

She listened to Jessica's response and laughed again. "Is that right?" She eyed M.J. with a grin. "Well, I'm scared'a him."

"Don't be scared of me. I'm a friendly old man," he teased her.

"Yeah, I *bet*," the bold, twenty-something mother countered with a smile. She handed his cell phone back to him. "Y'all have a good time tonight."

When M.J. got back on the line, he asked Jessica, "What you say to her?"

"I told her you think you can swing with people her age. That's why you gave her the phone, right? I'm not slow. I read people's real intentions all the time."

M.J. ignored her comments. "Well, you know I want to see you again tonight."

"I have my son with me this weekend. And you remember what I told, right?"

"What, about gettin' my haircut? I did that already," he cracked.

She chuckled. "You know what I'm talking about."

"Well, I'm gettin' myself back in shape for you right now."

Jessica laughed. "You gon' have to do a lot more than walking and getting haircuts to hang with me," she challenged.

"Well, that's what I'm gonna do then. Anything you need me to. I promise."

He made her laugh again. "Well, I'll call you back a little later. I gotta do quality time with my son right now. I answered to make sure that you were all right."

"Yeah, I'm all right," he told her. "But you call me back then."

When he hung up the phone with her, he thought about it. "Yeah, she's with her son tonight. So ain't nothing going on there," he grumbled.

Then he overheard some younger guys, standing outside of their clean and souped-up cars, talking about going to the movies.

"Yo, you see that *Notorious* movie yet? I heard it's good. I'm 'bout to go see it with my girl tonight."

"Yeah, I'll probably see it tonight. I ain't got nuttin' else to do. But why would you take your girl to that? That's where you *meet* girls at a movie like *that*. A Biggie movie'll get 'em *right*. Especially downtown when they're ready to party afterwards."

M.J. grinned, taking it all in. He hadn't been out to the movies since the past summer, with his grandchildren. They all wanted to see Will Smith flying around to save the day in *Hancock*.

Shit, maybe I need to go to the movies, he mused. "I damn sure don't wanna sit around in the house tonight," he mumbled to himself. "And I don't want no *old* pussy tonight either," he stated in reference to his older sex partner. By the time he made it back to his apartment, he decided that he *would* go to the movies.

I can go right downtown by myself, and probably head over to East St. Louis or the Riverboat tonight, he plotted.

"Then I can try out this new look and see how many phone numbers I get."

At 9:05 P.M., Marion stood in line at the multiplex movie theater downtown. He wore stylish dark-blue slacks, black shoes, a leather St. Louis Rams jacket he hadn't worn in years, and some fresh cologne patted on with his new haircut and goatee. And as soon as the line started to fill up with young folks in the teens, twenties, and thirties, three young women walked up to the stand right behind him, all wearing ass-hugging jeans

M.J. angled himself to get a look and thought, *Damn, right behind me! I don't even get a chance to concentrate out here!*

One of the girls, who were all in their twenties, gave him a quick eye to acknowledge his look, or *something*. M.J. jumped right on it.

"Hey, how you doin' tonight?"

"Oh, I'm fine," she answered civilly.

Then the other two looked at him. M.J. didn't waste any time with them either.

"So, I hear this Biggie flick is a pretty good movie. What you guys hear?" he asked them all.

They all nodded.

"I heard it was good," one of then answered. She wasn't the prettiest though. The prettiest girl had the least to say. She only stared.

"Then y'all gon' go party afterwards, right?" M.J. asked as the line moved forward.

The young women giggled like teenagers. The old man was right on point; he looked *hip*, too. And he *smelled* good.

"Yeah, probably," they admitted in unison.

M.J. chuckled. "And you guys aren't meeting anybody in here, other girl-friends, or guys or something?"

They all frowned it off. "No, it's just us," the first girl answered. But the prettiest was still the most reserved in the middle.

She's probably the one with the crazy, young boyfriend, he assumed. *It's always the pretty ones who got the biggest assholes for men.*

So he kept going after her on the sly, to find out if he was right. His swagger was that strong that night.

"You know, I don't get out to the movies much, but I know it ain't as fun watching by yourself. So if you guys would let me sit next to you, I would buy you all some popcorn or nachos just for the company."

He made it come across like a no-hands-on business deal. The young women all looked at each other and responded with receptive shrugs.

"Okay, I mean, you can sit with us," the first one responded again. She was the one who had eyed him first, and she was the second most attractive.

He thought, *I better lean more toward her if she's that open to me, in case I can't get near the finest one.*

He was mapping it all out in his wise, old head. He figured the first girl was the most confident and assertive. She seemed to be their local leader.

"All right. Good. Ladies first."

He stepped aside so they could buy their tickets in front of him.

"Thank you," the prettiest woman finally spoke up and smiled.

"Oh, no, you guys deserve it. I'm just being a gentleman," he told them. Slowly but surely, he planned to work himself into their system. Now he knew that the pretty and shy one responded to being pampered.

Yeah, this is gonna be a new ball game for me, he convinced himself. *I'm gon' keep my look right, get my wind and stamina back up, and go hard with these young ones.*

He walked into the theater with them, and they were already beginning to stand around him and chat as if he were an old friend who had known them for years.

"What was the last movie you saw?" the prettiest one asked him in the refreshment line.

Okay, she's opening up to me now, he marveled. But he kept his old man's cool and answered, "*Hancock,* with Will Smith."

"Oh, I still haven't seen that movie yet." She said it with abundant energy and a sly smile.

M.J. had to force himself to hold his sly tongue. He couldn't come off too eager with her, but he could feel her vibe already.

She's gonna let me take her out as long as she has the time, and as long as I have money in my pocket, he predicted. *And then she gon' fall right IN my pocket.*

He was already thinking about how wild she could be in bed under the influence of a Blue Dolphin pill; her *and* her lead girlfriend. They could get it both together.

Jessica is right, he told himself. *If I look right and act right, then I can catch a whole lot of these young broads. And I may not be Hugh Hefner, but I'm still alive, got' dammit! And if these young, fine motherfuckers are gonna kill me, then so be it. I'm gon' die in some pussy.*

So he dug into his pocket at the front of the refreshment line and paid for their popcorn.

THE STRIPPER CLUB BANDIT

Outside the state of Nevada—where there are hundreds of Las Vegas showgirls to entertain a voyeuristic man from sun up to sundown on the West Coast—Atlanta, Georgia, is known for its abundant list of strip clubs and adult nightlife on the East Coast. In fact, George Tatum, a shipping company worker from Decatur, couldn't seem to get enough of them; the pole climbing, sliding, spinning, bending, lap dancing, pussy popping, ass bouncing, acrobatic splits, hip twisting, pelvis pumping, and everything else. Only problem was, Georgie wanted to do more than watch. He wanted to take the strippers home with him; either that or take them to a hotel room for a more private party. But that was against most of the strip club rules, and against most of the dancers' rules, particularly with "Georgie." The man was one ugly motherfucker. And he knew it, too. So despite his constant offerings of money, the performing women were understandingly leery of him. Nevertheless, all it took was one of them to say yes to fulfill Georgie's fantasy.

"Come on, baby, I'll give you something extra. Something *way* extra," he solicited. "I know you could use the money. It's a tough economy out there."

Georgie was at it again inside Peaches & Cream, a Northwest Atlanta strip club. The place was dark and cozy, and five minutes away from Interstate 85.

Instead of responding to his desperate pleas to pay her extra for a private party away from the safe haven of business at the club, the olive-skinned stripper from Lebanon continued to ignore the wrinkle-faced man. She twisted and twirled her bare hips and ass in front of him to Ludacris' hit song, "Money Maker."

Georgie reached out from his chair, and placed his large brown hands on her smooth thighs to pull her closer to the erection that was quickly rising inside of his pants.

"No, you don't *touch me!*" the stripper turned and barked at him as if he were an unruly child.

Georgie was confused and looked up at her from his chair. "Well, you touched *me*. What's the difference?"

Her long, limber body; light-brown eyes, baby-smooth face, and thick brown hair all added to her scintillating allure. But she was all about business.

"I give you a dance, but you are *not* to touch."

Georgie sized up the foreign stripper and didn't like her attitude. No one else at the club spoke to him that contemptuously. And her hard foreign accent made it seem worse.

He snapped, "Well, go on somewhere else then. Lap dance your ass out of my face. You don't deserve my money."

The man may have been unattractive, but he still had a healthy ego. And he figured he worked too hard to be told what he could or could not do by a stripper.

The woman grabbed her bra and panties from where she had placed them on the small round table and began to redress in haste. But Georgie was already eyeing the next performer nearby, who had a much larger ass.

"This one here is more my type anyway. She got an ass I can hold onto."

The Lebanese stripper stormed off toward the dressing room without another word. And it didn't hurt Georgie's feelings at all. He still had money to spend for attention.

"Hey, baby girl, come see about me over here," he told the next woman with the large rump shaker. He took out a large wad of dollar bills and waved them in her direction.

"What, you got something you wanna give me, Daddy?" the stripper teased him. She was a satiny-smooth, dark-brown woman, in a hot-pink bra and panty set with white lace. And boy, was her ass round. It looked like two chocolate bowling balls had been pushed together.

Georgie told her, "Yeah, I need you to sit up on this brown pickle and help me count these dead presidents."

"Are they dead *Benjamins*?"

"No, but they *could* be if you treat me real nice for it."

The brown stripper smiled. "Well, what do I need to do to make that happen?" She began to work her thick brown legs inside of his at his seat, undaunted by his awful looks.

"You gotta do a little more than lap dance to get them Benjamins. But if you want 'em, you can definitely get 'em."

The stripper grinned and continued to work her rhythmic hips to the bass-thumping music, while spreading the old man's legs wider at his chair.

To his surprise, she asked him, "How many Benjamins you got on you?" She began to wiggle out of her hot-pink panties and bra like a magician performing a rope act.

Georgie raised his wrinkled brow and wondered if he had finally found a willing stripper to take him up on his fantasy.

"How many I need to make it happen?"

The huge-assed woman continued to strip, dance, and smile, while the old man's full erection began to leak with anticipation inside his pants.

"I'll let you know if you treat *me* nice," she quipped.

"Treat you nice how?"

She looked at his large wad of small bills. "How much money is that? You may want to add some *Lincolns* to it, *at least*," she added, in reference to five-dollar bills.

Georgie laughed it off. "Well, let's see how well you dance for me first."

As the next pulsating song popped on, the stripper backed up between his legs and began to bounce her naked ass up and down against his hard-on as fast as a bumblebee's wings.

"Shit, girl, you gon' make me drop the bomb up in here. Save some of that action for later on for these Benjamins."

The stripper ignored him and continued to bounce her rump shaker against his crotch. But her strong tease only made Georgie more desperate.

"What time you get off?" He could already imagine himself sticking her between her two bowling balls from behind, quick and powerfully, while she bent over the bed of a cheap hotel room. But the stripper shook her head and continued to ignore him.

"You hear me?" he pressed her.

She finally turned to face him, while still grinning. "Baby, I can't go anywhere with you. So don't worry about when I get off."

Georgie looked up at her, confused again. "Well, how you expect to get these Benjamins you want?"

"By dancing, honey."

In a knee-jerk reaction, the old man shoved his right thigh into her naked ass and snapped, "Shit, you know got' damn well you ain't gettin' no hundred dollars for no damn *lap* dancing. Where the back rooms at for privacy?"

Peaches & Cream didn't even have a back room. The strippers there made all of their money out in the open.

The woman jumped up from him, appalled. "Baby, you need to be happy I even came near your ugly ass. Have you looked in the mirror lately?"

She stepped away with her bra and panties in hand before Georgie could respond.

"Bitch," he spat toward her bare back. He still had his money in hand, so he began to look around the club for his next solicitation. Gyrating panties, bras, pussies and titties of every hue, size, and shape were all around the club. However, each man had to wait patiently for an unattended performer to move in his direction for service.

But on the other side of the club, the two strippers Georgie had already miffed, were informing the boss and his team of bouncers about the man's crassness.

"Yes, and he keeps talking about paying us outside the club. And it creeps me *out*," the Lebanese woman explained with a cringe.

Johnny, a tall, slick-haired, older white man, wearing a button-up shirt and slacks, had heard enough. He nodded his graying head and told his bouncers, "Okay, get him out of here, and tell him not to come back until he learns to abide by our rules and treat these ladies with respect."

Georgie was so focused on propositioning the next dynamite stripper for something more than lap dancing, that he never saw the two huge bouncers approaching him from his right. They were both dressed in all black and towered over six feet.

One of the bouncers kicked the right leg of Georgie's chair to get his attention through the distraction of music and exotic dancing.

"All right, let's go. You're no longer welcomed here."

Georgie grimaced and asked, "What I do?

The second bouncer, who moved to the left side of his chair to surround him, was even less cordial.

"If you don't get the fuck up right now, we're gonna carry your ass out. Now act like you wanna walk out on your own while you still have the chance."

You can't talk to your elders like that, Georgie thought to himself without voicing it. But when he viewed the bitter looks of ill intent on the faces of the two monstrous bouncers, he realized he had no choice. So he climbed to his feet to walk out on his own.

"I still don't know what I did wrong," he mumbled on his way out.

Neither bouncer responded to him. An explanation wasn't their concern.

"Well, I should *at least* get my money back if I'm not allowed to stay." Georgie pouted.

"Hey, Sherry, Johnny said to give this man his ten dollars back," the bouncer in front informed the older white woman behind the cashier's booth at the front entrance.

Sherry looked the wrinkled older man over and dug into the register to pull out a ten-dollar bill without a word.

"Thank you," Georgie told her.

Once the two bouncers made it outside with him, the lead man informed him, "Next time, you learn how to treat the women here with respect, or don't bother to come back. And we do know what you look like," he added.

Georgie joked. "All right, I've learned my lesson. Can I come back in now? I got ten dollars."

He waved the money he had gotten back from the cash register in his right hand.

"Not tonight you're not. You're lucky the man is allowing you to come back in here at all. Because I wouldn't. A bad apple is a bad apple."

Georgie said, "Yeah, well, that's why you're not the boss. And a *real* boss knows that good business is good business."

Both bouncers ignored Georgie's continuous comments and returned inside.

Georgie turned and walked toward his car, feeling incomplete and lonely.

"Shit. Maybe I should'a been easier on those girls."

He climbed into his silver Jetta in the parking lot. The man remained unmarried with one grown daughter, who lived in Macon with her relatives. Her mother had gotten pregnant after dating Georgie for two months after she had graduated from high school twenty-seven years ago. Her highly religious family didn't believe in abortion. Nor did they believe that George Tatum was a good match for their daughter. So they decided to move to Macon, raise their granddaughter on their own, and marry off their daughter for a more virtuous family, while cutting all ties to the father of her first child.

Georgie had been a bitter and untrustful man ever since. Why give your heart and soul to a woman and family who could break it so callously? So he became a scavenger of porous relationships with no ties or commitments, and found himself falling into a ridiculous fetish for strip club dancers.

With the night still young at a quarter past midnight on Thursday, Georgie drove a few miles down the road to Pony Rides, a larger, brighter and more raucous strip club. He pulled up in the massive parking lot to think it over.

"Only problem with this club is that these white girls ain't got no ass in here," he said out loud, while climbing out of his car. "Then again, they usually have a few black girls mixed in, and a few Spanish ones." *So let me go in here and see what it looks like tonight.*

At the entrance door, the cashiers and bouncers stopped him and asked him for a membership card.

"Oh, shit, I forgot about that," Georgie informed them.

The white strip clubs liked to deal more with their usual customers.

"You left it at home?" the white male cashier asked him. He looked like a tall basketball player.

Georgie hesitated. Did they have a computer list of names? He presumed that they didn't. It was a damn stripper club. So he went for broke with his hunch.

"Ah, yeah, I accidentally left it at home, man."

"Well, I gotta charge you a ten-dollar entrance fee."

Georgie shrugged. He had just gotten a ten-dollar bill back from the door at Peaches & Cream. So he dug back into his pocket and handed the cashier the bill.

There was a different style of music in the place. They were playing Britney Spears talking about being a "slave for you." There was a different type of energy and lighting in the club as well. It was much brighter with a much larger stage in the center of the room. The white-girl ratio was three to one, with nearly twenty white girls, three black, two Latinas, and two Asians.

Georgie didn't feel as comfortable in this club. The competition for the limited black women in the room was steep. All of the fantasizing white men wanted them.

"Hey ah, you wanna dance, sweetheart?" the first big-boned white girl asked him as soon as he took a seat away from the main stage. Georgie never cared to be all up in the middle of things. The chairs and tables that were placed against the walls allowed him a chance to ease out of the bright lights.

He looked over the meaty, blonde-haired, white woman in sequined gold panties and bra, and he imagined that she could break his damn leg, if she accidentally fell on him.

How the hell they let a big-ass white girl like her in here? he questioned.

"Naw, baby, let me buy a drink or something first. I just got up in here."

"Okay, I'll come back around and check on you a little later then."

"Yeah, give it some time though," he responded. Once she walked away from him, he mumbled, "A whole *lot* of time."

Then he began to survey the room to see if he could find what he liked.

Good God, look at this Asian girl! he mused excitedly. *She look as pretty as a doll baby. And she's working that little thing, too.*

He watched as a petite, Thai stripper worked her hips to perfection at the far-right end of the stage. She was much smaller than what he normally preferred, but if he got a chance to talk to her, he was willing to pay for her sexiness alone.

"I bet she get *all* the business up in here," he mumbled. The woman was that cute.

A heavyset white man at the table to his right overheard him and laughed. "You're talking about Cindy, aren't ya'?"

"Who's Cindy?"

The man pointed to their right. "The China doll up there on stage."

"You sure she's Chinese and not something else?" The Asian stripper had a strong tanned hue that hinted of a browner country.

"Well, yeah, she's probably ah, Vietnamese or something."

"Whatever the hell she is, she's *bad*," Georgie stated.

The white man laughed again. "You want me to call her over here for you when she's finished dancing?"

Georgie looked at the Asian beauty again and noticed how many eager men were tossing dead presidents in her direction on stage. He figured at least ten different customers would want her services as soon as she stepped off the stage.

"Are you sure she'll get anywhere near us back here. We might need to move the hell up to get a crack at her," he joked.

The man shook his head and grinned. "No, I know her real well. She'll come. But if she comes, she's used to being paid *well*, I'll tell you that. So if you can't afford it, then tell me now and I'll leave her alone."

The man sounded like an in-house pimp. Georgie looked him over. "How much she asking to dance?"

The man shrugged. "Fifty dollars is a good starting amount."

Georgie chuckled. "And how much do you get out of that, ten, twenty percent?"

The man looked appalled. "Excuse me?"

"You heard me, how much do *you* get out of it? You over here making the deals for her, right?"

"Nah, it's nothing like that. I know what she's used to, so I kind of look out for her."

"Yeah, that's what I mean. So what does she kick you back for looking out for her?"

The man looked embarrassed by the question. "I mean, I don't really ask her for anything like, you know, a percentage of what she makes. But if, you know, she wants to offer me something—"

Georgie cut off the man's ramblings. "So, what else does she do? I mean, I got more than fifty. But I'm not giving that up for her to dance around me in circles and shit."

The man nodded and changed his tone. "Well, what do you have in mind?"

"What can the little girl handle?" Georgie asked him.

The man began to laugh. He looked Georgie in his face for a moment of candor. "She can handle *a lot* for the right price. But how much can *you* handle?"

Okay, so he is a pimp, Georgie told himself. *I wonder if the rest of the people in here know that.* "Okay, so what exactly are we talking about—fucking?"

The white man looked around the bright room before he answered. The next hot pop song was pumping through the club speakers, Lil Wayne's *"she lick me like a lollipop"* anthem.

The man answered in lowered tones, "You don't make enough to fuck her. We're talking your whole week's salary."

Georgie felt offended. "How the hell you know what my salary is?"

Suddenly, the man stopped paying attention to him. He went back to watching Cindy entice the men from center stage.

Shit, Georgie thought. *I wonder how much he's talking. I never thought I'd end up dealing with a side-stage pimp.*

He felt the whole idea was awkward. He would rather deal strictly with the women. Otherwise, he may as well had been picking up a hooker from the street corners. But he figured the strip club dancers were sexier. And he could see exactly what he was getting before offering to pay for it.

Finally, the man leaned back in his direction calmly. "Make her a respectable offer, and I'll let you know if it's good enough."

What the hell does that mean, "a respectable offer?" Georgie pondered. *How much does he think this girl is worth?*

When Cindy made her way from the stage and into the midst of eager customers, she casually looked over in the direction of the heavy-set white man at the back. Her look was so smooth and effortless that no one suspected anything. But when the heavy white man shook his head just as casually, Georgie recognized it as an obvious sign of a no-go.

Shit! They're really working this thing, he realized.

The man then stood up to leave. "You have a good time," he commented, before he moved near another man who was eyeing the Asian beauty. Georgie watched him as he sat down and began another conversation.

So she's doing double time in here. But these motherfuckers have to know that. How could they get away with that?

Georgie imagined that someone would surely screw up sooner or later and create a leak. So he figured it must have been a fairly new game that they were playing.

And if that's the case, this opportunity may not last that long in here. She may be kicked out to find another place to scheme in, he presumed.

Time was of the essence. Georgie figured it was now or never. The Asian beauty and her smiling charm was calling out to him as he continued to watch her entertain the ready and willing customers inside the room.

Three hundred dollars. I'll start from there and see what he says, he decided. He hadn't even bothered to order a drink yet. And by the time he got up to make his move in the girl's direction, Cindy began to give a lucky man a very satisfying lap dance.

"It's all part of the business," Georgie noted to himself as he headed toward them. Before he could arrive, another white stripper stepped out in front of him and was all smiles. She was dark-haired with a much slimmer body than the first one. In fact, the young woman was so thin that Georgie could count the bones in her rib cage.

"How are you doing tonight?" she asked him. "Is there anything you need for me to help you with?"

To humor himself, Georgie smiled and asked, "Will you do anything I want?"

"Well, that all depends on what it is."

"And what if I want more than a lap dance?"

"Well, then, in that case, we have private rooms available toward the back."

His unattractiveness didn't seem to matter to the strippers in that club. So Georgie began to wonder how much they would allow a man to get away with inside the private rooms. He looked toward the black-curtain doorway on the other side of the dance stage.

But I don't want a skinny-ass white girl back there with me, he thought.

The Asian girl, Cindy, wasn't much meatier, but she was five times cuter. So he turned down the anorexic white woman and moved to next-in-line position for Cindy.

"Naw, I think I'll pass on that trip, darling."

The white stripper shrugged and moved on. "All right, suit yourself."

Feeling that he had blown his earlier chance to cut a deal for Cindy, Georgie became more assertive in positioning himself for her services. He even pulled out larger bills from his wallet to count up three hundred dollars in plain view of the white man who had propositioned him. So when the desirable Asian girl had finishing dancing for the first man, she had no discrepancies about going into a private back room with Georgie.

"I have to go back and change first," she told him in accented English.

Georgie grinned. He liked her accent as well.

"Okay, I'll be waiting right here for you."

The horde of white men, who surrounded him at front stage, viewed his hand full of large bills and realized that he wanted first bid when the girl returned. Even the side-stage pimp acknowledged him. So when Cindy returned to the main floor from the dressing rooms, wearing a tropical bra and panties set, she was all Georgie's.

"Come on," she told him, grabbing his hand and leading him toward the private rooms. Money talked loudly.

They passed through the black-curtain doorway and selected a small, open room to the right, closing a second black curtain behind them. A chair sat in the corner of the red-lighted room.

Cindy pushed Georgie into the chair and immediately climbed on top of him, placing a small white towel over his crotch.

"Yeah, I like it rough, just like that," he told her.

She smiled and worked her petite body into his massive one. Georgie grabbed her by her hips and enjoyed the ride until his crotch became too uncomfortable. He didn't have enough wiggle room in his pants for his pulsating hard-on.

"Wait a minute. Let me readjust this thing." He removed the towel to dig into his pants and tug his penis closer to center. He wanted to free it from its trapped position on the left side of his drawers. Then he got bold with the girl.

"You think you can handle one this big?" he asked, refering to his penis.

Cindy grinned and nodded. "Mmm-hmm, yeah."

"Well, let me see." Georgie placed her pussy directly on his bulge. "You sure you got something deep enough for that?"

The stripper attempted to place the white towel back between his crotch and hers. But Georgie wouldn't allow her to. He wanted to see how far he could go with things. And if he placed his dick in the perfect position, maybe she could feel how great it would be to push it all the way up inside of her. But Cindy wanted no part of that. So she squirmed to the left and right to avoid dead-on contact between her kitten and his tiger.

"No, you don't do that," she whined in her accent as she wrestled with him.

Georgie slid his large fingers inside of her panties to see if she was wet.

"No," she responded, grabbing his hand. "You can't do that."

"I'm trying to see if you're big enough. You wanna go somewhere else for this money after work?"

The stripper struggled to stand up from his lap and quickly looked up into the corner of the room. Georgie followed her eyes and spotted the tiny eye of a video camera.

"Aw, shit, they got fucking cameras in here," he blasted.

The next thing he knew, a big white bouncer pulled open the curtain on them.

"Your time's up, let's go."

"I thought these were *private* rooms," Georgie said. "Where the hell you come from? We just got in here."

Cindy didn't plan on staying around to hear his argument. The whole fiasco was embarrassing to her; she left the private room area and returned to the main stage.

The bouncer told Georgie, "We have certain rules in here that everyone has to follow to keep our club license. So if you're not gonna follow them, then we'll be forced to strip you of your membership."

I don't even have a fucking membership here! Georgie incensed to himself. He stood up with his money, still in hand, and headed to the curtain doorway. He walked back out onto the main floor, a dejected man again. And when he spotted Cindy lap dancing for the next customer, he felt even more insignificant.

"Yeah, let me get the hell out of here," he grumbled as he headed toward the exit. "Perverted motherfuckers."

Since he was not being thrown out this time, he couldn't ask for his money back. He climbed back inside his car and thought about his next destination. He remained unsatisfied with his night. In fact, after being in the private room with Cindy, he felt more anxious to take a stripper back home or to a hotel room that evening.

"Shit, I know I don't want to go down there," he contemplated out loud. "But if I really wanna take somebody's ass home tonight...then that's the place to do it."

Georgie headed on Interstate 85 for Southeast Atlanta, the opposite side of town from where he lived and liked to play.

"A bunch of got' damn *crazies* are down here," he grumbled to himself as he drove. He was referring to the multitude of drug addicts, homosexual prostitutes, muggers, car thieves, homeless derelicts, and the many other anti-social delinquents who called the Southeast Atlanta region home.

As Georgie made it to Interstate 20, and headed east toward the suburb of Decatur, he continued to mull over his plans.

Do I really wanna be down here tonight? he asked himself as he approached his exit. He traveled up the exit ramp and turned right, heading further south before supplying himself with an answer.

"Fuck it! I'm gonna go up in here, find myself a girl, see what she wants to do, and get the hell back out of here."

With his plan of execution set, Georgie pulled past the Red Light club to see how it looked from the outside first. The small, seedy club didn't have an official parking lot, just abandoned property that surrounded it, where undaunted customers parked their cars and prayed to return to them safely.

Georgie eyed the front door of the club as he drove by, spotting the usual suspects of hardcore bouncers and their convict associates posted outside. Judging from the pack of cars that were parked there that night, he suspected a pretty lively crowd inside. He found an empty parking spot and whipped his car for a U-turn to grab it. As soon as he finished parking his car and climbed out, a man approached him from the sidewalk.

"I'll make sure it stays put for you."

The man looked younger than Georgie in the face, but he was far older in the spirit. He had been beaten down by a hard life of circumstances.

Georgie passed him by. "You do that."

He quickly headed to the front door of the small club before he hesitated with his decision again.

"What's the cover tonight?" he asked the menacing bouncers at the door. He surely didn't want to be kicked out of the club by those guys. They looked like they would do much more than escort a man out.

"Twenty dollars," one of them muttered.

"*Twenty* dollars?" Georgie repeated. "You went up on the price? What, is a stripper club inflation going on down here?"

One of the bystanders chuckled. The second bouncer answered, "We got some girls down here from Virginia Beach tonight. So we got upgraded clientele."

Georgie looked and spotted a colorful tour bus that was parked in a space behind the club. "I see." And he was curious to see what "upgraded clientele" looked like.

He nodded. "All right, I'm game. Do they look good in here from Virginia?"

One of the bystanders laughed again. "Now, what do you expect them to say, 'no'? They gon' bring some ugly bitches down here from Virginia and then charge us more for 'em. Come on, man, think about it."

Georgie looked over the young, bodacious man. "Well, why are you still standing out here?"

"Man, my dick needed a *break*. I couldn't *take it*. Watch, you'll see."

Georgie thought it over, wondering if the young man was working with the club staff to entice wavering customers to spend the extra ten dollars. But it didn't make a difference to him. He had already made up his mind; he pulled out a twenty-dollar bill.

One of the bouncers patted his body up and down for weapons. The other one scanned him with a handheld metal detector. Then they waved him to enter.

"Hey, pops, have a good time in there," the young bystander commented.

As Georgie slid into the club, he overheard a second bystander joking. "That old-ass man still out here trying to get his freak on." They laughed at him, but Georgie was undaunted. A hard dick was a hard dick, no matter what age it was.

When he walked into the crowded club, T.I.'s brand-new hit song was pumping through the speakers, *"You can have whatever you l-i-i-i-ke."* And the hot Virginia Beach girls were having their way all up inside the club.

Georgie thought, *Shit, this place looks PACKED tonight!.*

He didn't remember it being as spacious inside either. But maybe the packed crowd made it appear larger. They had two L-shaped stages of busy women, and four poles, with two on each stage. That was new as well.

They must have done some remodeling in here. Georgie was impressed by their efforts. Then he studied the Virginia Beach strippers up on stage and around the club. The majority of them were yellow-skinned black women.

"I see what they're going for tonight," he mumbled. "Just push the chocolate mommas to the side, hunh?"

Georgie began a search for the darker-brown, local girls, who were sprinkled throughout the club between the invasion of redbones.

"Excuse me," an ill-tempered man stated as he pushed his way past Georgie through the crowd. The problem with the extra customers that night was that they had all run out of elbow room. Dozens of impetuous men were forced to stand up against the back walls and bulldoze their way through the dense crowd.

Georgie figured he had to make his move as fast as he could. It was all, or nothing. Once he had locked in on a chocolate dancer to his right, who searched through the crowded room unattended, he quickly made his move.

She don't look happy enough to be visiting from Virginia, he assessed of her serious grill. *She looks like somebody had trampled mud through her living room.*

He immediately approached the chocolate stripper through the crowded club.

"It's more crowded than usual in here tonight, hunh?" he commented.

She turned to face him and grumbled, "Yeah, unfortunately."

"You don't like the extra crowd? It's more money to make in here now, ain't it?"

"Not really," she uttered. "I guess it is for the *new* people. But I could have stayed the hell home tonight, for all this."

Just as she was ready to step away, Georgie asked, "Well, what do you need to make your night worthwhile?"

She looked at him again and paused. Then she shook it off and grinned. "You don't even wanna know."

"Talk to me about it. I got a few dollars."

She paused and considered it in the middle of the lively strip club. There were more than a dozen guest performers from Virginia, who were sucking up all of the attention and money.

Finally, the stripper answered, "Look, man, I'm in here trying to pay my rent for the week. That's the only reason I came tonight."

Jackpot! Georgie didn't expect to hear that much honesty from a stripper in a jampacked room. But pressure caused people to tell you the truth sometimes.

"Well, I don't know if you're gonna make that money in here tonight. But there's always money to be made outside the club."

Another patron bumped into Georgie hard on his way past. And it became the perfect prop for him to nail home his pitch to the stripper.

"You see that? It's a little too crowded in here for my usual taste, too. But I came out here tonight for companionship. But if I could have that somewhere in private…"

He stopped and allowed his words to linger on her mind. She could fill in the blanks on her own.

"What do you have in mind?"

Georgie answered immediately, "Stripping."

She looked him in the eyes. "For how much?"

"I got three bills left to spend for the night."

The chocolate stripper shook it off. "That ain't enough for me to leave, baby. I can make *eight* in here. Come at me better than that."

Georgie didn't know what to say at that point. Maybe he had played his cards too honestly. He should have haggled with her more instead of giving her a solid figure. He shrugged. "Well…every man has his breaking point. But I'll still be here for a minute, if you change your mind. What's your name anyway?"

"Sugar."

"Brown Sugar?"

She nodded and grinned. "No, just Sugar."

"I'm Georgie. And you think about that rent tonight, all right?"

She nodded. "All right."

As she faded into the crowd, Georgie gave her another look. She had incredibly long legs in her heels.

Damn! I wonder if she has deep pussy with those long legs, he mused. He started to watch her to see if she would perform any lap dances to earn her rent money, but he was quickly distracted by the stage performances of the Virginia Beach girls. Li'l Wayne's "Lollipop" song was on again.

The guys started hooting and hollering, enjoying the show while the big-money hustler types rained dollar bills onto the stage.

"Ay, you motherfuckers are gonna have to find a seat or move back to the fucking wall!" someone shouted. His forceful demand included Georgie. He was standing right in the middle of the view. Georgie began to move back toward the wall, while still eyeing the Virginia girls who were doing their thing..

"Well, at least they got the best show here tonight," Georgie mumbled and then grinned.

"I hear they gon' have different girls here once a month," someone commented.

Georgie was interested in seeing that himself. He then watched as the girls entertained only the highest bidders in the club, with the bigger bills in hand.

Yeah, these girls are getting their money's worth in here tonight, he mused. He figured there was no sense in even taking his money out. He stood to lose it all in ten minutes. So he decided to watch from the sidelines.

"You ordering anything?" a waitress dressed in all black asked him. She was somehow able to make it through all of the busy traffic in the room.

Georgie shook his head and waved her off. He didn't feel like drinking.

"It's a two-drink minimum tonight."

Georgie looked into her eyes to see if she were serious. "A two-drink minimum to stand up against the damn wall?"

"I can find you a table."

He looked around the room. "Where?" Unless she was planning on bringing out a new table from the back bar room, her offer seemed implausible.

"We have VIP seating all around the room."

"Well, I'm not VIP, and I'm not here to pay for that. Now, if I need to buy two drinks to stay in here, then at least give me a few minutes to decide on what I want. Is that all right with you?"

The waitress nodded. "I'll come back."

Georgie grumbled, "Shit, they're trying to shake you down in here, too; after I paid twenty dollars to get in, just to get bumped around and shit, and then to stand up against the damn wall. They must be *crazy*."

A younger man beside him chuckled, with a half-finished drink in his hand. He shrugged. "Hey, man, either it's worth it to you, or it's not. What's forty dollars for this kind of live entertainment?"

Georgie heard the younger man out and frowned. "Forty dollars just to watch, hunh?" It sounded like a waste of money to him.

Simultaneously, the chocolate stripper, Sugar, glanced over at him, even while she performed a lap dance.

Georgie caught her eye and told himself, *Yeah, she don't wanna be here tonight. She only wanna make enough to leave.* So he plotted on asking her again if she was ready to head out with him before the pesky waitress could return for his drink orders.

As soon as Sugar collected her dance money and moved on, Georgie made his move in her direction. She spotted him on the move toward her and slowed down to allow him to catch up. Georgie noticed and became excited again.

Yeah, she's ready! Time to go for it hard.

"Hey, ah, Sugar, you staying all night, or cutting out early?"

She searched around the room as if she had failed to hear him. "You give me four, and I'll let you meet me out back in thirty minutes."

Georgie had no time to haggle. It was her deal for a hundred dollars more. Take it, or leave it. "I'm in a silver Jetta," he told her, agreeing to her price.

She nodded and continued on her way toward the dressing rooms.

Georgie kept his cool and struggled to head back to his position on the wall. Like clockwork, as soon as he made it back to his earlier spot and began to relax for a minute, the pesky waitress headed back in his direction for the drink orders.

Okay, time to start acting, Georgie told himself.

"You make up your mind on those drinks?"

The patron beside him began to laugh.

Georgie shook his head and grimaced. He took a deep breath. "You mean to tell me you gon' harass me to order another twenty dollars' worth of drinks, with all these people you have in here tonight? I'm just one little, old man."

The waitress eyed him and was ready to answer him in the affirmative. Georgie could read it on her face, too. She was determined. Before she could answer him, he said, "You know what, I know when I'm being suckered, and there's no way in the world you got everyone in here to pay you for two drinks."

The waitress opened her mouth to argue her point, but Georgie kept on going with his argument. "So if that's how you guys wanna treat me in here tonight, after I paid my twenty dollars to stand up against the damn wall, then you can keep that money as a donation to research on cancer."

It was a perfectly dramatic scene to vacate the premises and wait out back in his car for Sugar. However, as soon as Georgie reached his car and started up his engine, he began to wonder if the stripper would actually meet him outside like she said she would.

"Well, if she don't, then...I'm on my own to decide what I want to do next." And if push came to shove, he thought of driving around downtown Atlanta to look for a hooker. But that would be his last option. He figured that strippers were much safer.

He waited a few minutes in his car at the curbside parking spot, contemplating everything. Then he drove around to the back of the club for pickup. When he arrived, the back exit door was closed and unattended.

Just give it a few minutes. But when a few minutes became a solid ten, he began to doubt the validity of the deal.

"Yeah, looks like she just pulled my damn leg," he grumbled. He didn't wanna pay an extra hundred dollars no way. "I can get a good hooker for *two* hundred."

But as soon as he decided to pull off, the back exit door opened, and Sugar walked out, wearing blue jeans and a thin, brown leather jacket, while carrying a big gold bag.

Georgie quickly pulled up beside her and swung open his passenger side door. *Shit. Now I have to hit an ATM machine to get that extra hundred dollars,* he mused.

The chocolate stripper climbed into the car.

"I'm sorry, I had to count everything up before I left."

"How much do you have to give the club?" Georgie asked.

"Forty-fuckin'-percent," she spat. "But you'll still make more here than at a lot of other clubs because their clientele is stronger."

"What, with all the drug-dealing hustlers and shit who hang out around here?"

She nodded. "Yup. And it's usually less girls in here. But, at some of the other clubs, they make your ass compete with thirty other girls to see who makes what. And in that situation, if you're not a top bitch, you might walk out with a hundred dollars after shaking your ass half the fucking night. That's why I don't feel like being up in *here* tonight. That's what they do when they invite all these new bitches to the party. But the club still makes *their* money."

Georgie smiled. "Yeah, they sure do." He had been to nearly forty different strip clubs in the Atlanta region over the past twenty years, and the only thing that stopped the owners from doing long-lasting business was greed and corruption. So many of the clubs had closed down, only for new ones to spring up.

In fact, Georgie had been propositioning strippers for a decade. But his homely looks, frugality, and sour attitude all had stopped him from being a lot more successful.

"So, where are we going?" Sugar asked.

Along Interstate 20, there were plenty of exits with cheap inns and hotel rooms, so Georgie shrugged at the question.

"Once we hit I-Twenty, we'll pick a place off the road. It don't matter to me."

"Well, let's go to the Quality Inn," she suggested. "They usually have good breakfast."

Georgie wondered, *How long did she intend to stay with me tonight? How many times has she visited the Quality Inn with a stranger?*

Sugar read his mind through the silence. "I don't do this all the time; you know, go home with someone from the club. I don't feel like being bothered with all that shit tonight. I need to pay my damn bills. You know what I mean?"

Georgie nodded. He wasn't in a position to judge. They both needed what they needed. And he needed some fantasy pussy that evening.

"Well, I do need to stop at one of these gas stations for an ATM machine to get that extra hundred for you. But ah, if I'm doin' a little extra for you, then maybe you'll be fine with doin' a little extra for me."

Sugar looked at him. "Say what you want then."

Georgie looked down between her long legs. "Now you know what I want. I want to *feel it*, every inch of them long legs of yours."

Sugar chuckled. "Well, you might want to withdraw more than a hundred dollars from that ATM machine, for all of that."

"I got a one hundred-dollar limit," he lied.

"Oh yeah, well, I got a limit, too. And you can touch it, but you can't fuck it, unless the money is right."

Georgie found himself in another quagmire. Now the price was more than four-hundred dollars to fuck—maybe five or *six* hundred.

"Can I ask you question?" he mumbled.

"What?"

"How old are you?"

She had a young woman's looks and an old woman's ways.

"I'm twenty. Why?"

Georgie looked at the chocolate-skinned stripper in his passenger seat and was shocked. "*Twenty?* Well, you ain't even legal enough to be in there."

"You ain't see me *drinking*. And us young ones get more money in the clubs."

But with her being that young, it changed everything for Georgie. There was no way in hell he was giving a twenty-year-old five hundred dollars for some pussy. He figured she was at least *twenty-five* with some responsibilities at home, like a kid or two. Age twenty was totally different, even if she *did* have a child.

"You got any kids?"

She shook her head vehemently. "No. I don't have time for kids."

"So, what you need all that money for, shopping?"

Sugar paused. "You know what, you just reminded me to stop telling people my damn age, because they always get it confused. I've been on my own ever since *sixteen*. And nobody gave me *nothing* that I didn't *work* hard for. I got *bills* like everybody else. And I don't even *do* a lot of shopping. *Grocery* shopping, maybe."

"So, you got your own place and everything?" All of a sudden, she became a lot more interesting. She was more of a case study to him now.

Sugar pointed to a twenty-four-hour gas station at the exit ramp off Interstate 20. "Don't you need to go handle that money? There's a gas station right there."

Georgie was now hesitant to get more money for her. "You know, three hundred is good enough."

"Well, let me out right here then," she told him. And she meant it. Georgie looked her into her eyes and knew it.

Shit! he cursed himself. *This night just keeps getting longer on me.*

He decided to stall. He needed time to figure out how to handle the situation. But he was leaning toward paying the girl. "You don't really want me to let you out right here."

She nodded and agreed with him. "You know what, you're right. I would want you to drive me back to the club, so I can find somebody else to finish off my night with."

"That makes it sound like you do this a lot," he commented.

"No, but if I already made that decision, then I go with it; not like some *other* people who change their damn *minds*," she hinted.

Georgie chuckled. "Well, if you remember, we started at three, and agreed on four. So that's where we need to stay. That way, neither one of us changes our minds."

"Yeah, but then you started talking about needing more than a dance."

"Yeah, if you need more than three hundred. That's a whole lot of money for a dance. And I figure what *I* want would be *easier*."

She looked at him and grimaced. "*Easier?*"

"Yeah, you can lay down and relax. You don't have to move as many muscles."

"All right. That's what I'ma do, too."

"Well, that don't mean you don't have to move *nothing*."

"Umm, are you gonna get the money or what?" she questioned.

Georgie turned inside the station and pulled up into a parking space.

"So, we agree on four hundred then," he concluded.

Sugar nodded. "Yeah. Four hundred."

Georgie walked inside, feeling defeated. He still didn't want to pay that much. "At least I'm not paying more," he mumbled at the ATM machine.

He pulled out a hundred-forty dollars in cash and separated the extra forty. *I have to pay for the damn room, too*, he pondered. *But I can do that with my card.*

They pulled into the parking lot of a Quality Inn a few miles up the road, and Georgie paid for the room before he drove the young stripper around to the back entrance. He didn't want to walk in the front with her. It would look too obvious.

They climbed out of the car and walked up to the room without much discussion. They had said everything they needed to say.

As soon as they entered the room, the stripper announced that she needed to take a quick shower.

"That sounds like a good idea," Georgie told her. "Go wash all of that club smoke off of you."

Sugar looked at him and smirked. "And what are you gonna wash off of *you*?"

"Hard work," he quipped.

"Whatever."

While the young stripper took her shower, Georgie thought again about his night. Four hundred dollars was a bit more than he wanted to spend, but at least he was getting what he wanted, another successful roll in the hay with an enticing stripper.

I should lock down one girl instead of going through all of this other shit, he contemplated. *But once you lock down a girl, the shit can become even more expensive. At least a stripper makes her own got' damn money. Maybe I should keep one of them.*

He had no idea what he wanted to do regarding women. He had been sleeping around as a scavenger for so long that he didn't know what a real relationship was like anymore. He presumed that a man paid for everything.

Sugar walked out from the bathroom wearing a white bath towel and nothing else, and Georgie's dick got hard immediately.

"So, I don't have to dance at all, right? You want me to lay down and be still?"

Georgie didn't like the sound of that, especially for four hundred dollars. "As a matter of fact, with them long legs of yours, I might want you to bend over that desk right there and put them high heels back on."

It was what he had been thinking about.

Sugar looked at the office desk to the right of the television cabinet and grinned. "You got condoms?"

Georgie pulled them out of his thick wallet. "Never leave home without 'em."

"Do you mind if I put the television on? I don't like it dead silent. It's a pet peeve of mine."

Georgie shrugged. "Turn it on then."

Sugar clicked on the color television set with the remote control and turned the channel to late-night videos. "I'm so used to music now," she told him. The new T.I. video was on.

Sugar dropped her towel and slid her heels back on, performing a few snake-like dance moves to the music.

"Mmmph," Georgie grunted, watching her. He moved to undo his pants and expose his excitement to her.

The young stripper stopped dancing and held out her right hand.

"Um, where's the money?"

Georgie dug back into his falling pants pocket and gave it to her. She counted the four-hundred dollars and slid it into her bag. Then she snake-danced back over to the desk to lean over it for him.

Georgie grinned like the devil and slid a condom over his happy erection.

I've been waiting all night for this, he told himself. He took the young stripper by her smooth brown hips and held his penis in position to enter her, while she poked her ass out for him.

"I might be a little tight, but that's a good thing, right?" she teased.

"Hell yeah, that's a good thing," Georgie told her. "Who wants to swim with a whale? A baby seal is always better."

Sugar chuckled. "Well, I'm just letting you know. So I can't do all kinds of tricks and stuff."

Georgie began to ignore her and went on about his business. They had done enough talking already. So he worked himself into a comfortable groove from behind. He could definitely feel the stripper's tightness. Her snug kitten caused him to lose his rhythm. It was feeling too good too fast. Nevertheless, he found himself struggling to keep his poise with the girl. He was all over the place with his stroke; sideways, back and forth, up and down, on his toes, and back on his heels, while smacking his hips into her ass like a wild, brown chicken.

"Shit, you ain't lying. This *is* some tight pussy, tight and *strong*," he told her. He was still fighting to control the sensations.

"I told you," she moaned over the desk.

Fuck it, I can't hold it no more! Georgie admitted. He figured he would let himself explode in less than eight minutes. So he began to push himself deeper and deeper into her tight hole until he could no longer feel the difference between his body and her body.

"Wait a minute," the younger stripper moaned, attempting to slow his urgent thrusting from behind. Georgie was pounding her tight pussy too hard. But there was no way to stop a moving train once it started chugging at full speed. He would have to crash it.

"This is gonna be a good *nut*," he stated through his hammering stroke. He was pounding her body into the desk. "I can *feel it*. I can *feel it*! *Ooohhh*," he moaned.

He hadn't even reached his climax yet. It was all from anticipation.

Sugar pleaded, "Wait, wait," while struggling to twist herself away from him. But it was no use. Georgie went into hydraulic mode and started bouncing on his toes until his thighs and ass cheeks cramped up on him.

"SHIT!" he howled through painful muscle spasms.

"It feel like it *popped*!" Sugar insisted. "Wait a minute."

"HUNH!" Georgie responded non-sensibly. He didn't care what she had to say at that point. He was ready for his rocket ship to blast off to the moon, so he could howl like a wolf.

"The condom *popped*!" Sugar let out again.

Georgie finally comprehended her plea. In the nick of time, he pulled his penis out of her, and shot fresh, hot sperm all over her back, ass, and long legs.

"AHHH, FUCK!" she yelled, feeling his seed splatter all over her. She stood up straight and cringed, running back to the bathroom.

"SHIT!" she continued to curse, locking the bathroom door behind her.

Georgie didn't know what to do. First, he backed up and fell across the bed to work the cramps out of his legs. He stretched them in every direction, trying to find the best position to relieve the pain.

"Arrgghhh!" he growled, twisting and turning on the bed.

Once he had found a safe position to relax his thighs and ass muscles, he inspected his penis and found the popped condom pushed down on his shaft with blood on it.

"Oh, *shit*," he panicked. "Was your fucking *period* on?" he asked. It didn't smell so good to him either. He failed to notice the stench while he was stroking her. But there was no answer, only shower water running from inside the bathroom.

Ignoring the pain he felt in his cramped muscles, Georgie climbed back to his feet and moved toward the bathroom, only to find that the door was locked.

"Hey, let me in there," he demanded, with urgent knocks on the door. He wanted to wash himself up as quickly as possible. *What if the girl had AIDS?*

The stripper continued to ignore him, with the shower water still running.

Georgie knocked urgently on the door again.

"Hey, I need to wash up, too, in there."

"All right, wait a fuckin' minute!" the young stripper yelled from behind the door. "I'm taking a *shower*!"

Georgie barked, "Well, I need to take a damn *shower*, too."

Sugar went back to ignoring him. His ass would just have to wait.

Realizing as much, Georgie leaned up against the wall next to the bathroom and waited there anxiously. He shook his head and grumbled, "Got' dammit. Damn, she stink." He looked over at the girl's bag and thought about taking his money back.

But I gotta wash this shit off first, he reasoned. The putrid smell seemed to get worse as he continued to stand there.

He squeezed his nose shut with his left hand and breathed out of his mouth. "I thought her ass just *took* a fucking shower," he grumbled. *How could she smell this damn bad after washing up?*

One thing was for sure, Georgie couldn't wait to get the fuck out of there. He felt embarrassed and in need of a lecture.

"This is what the hell I get," he told himself. "So take it like a man now." And he waited there to wash himself up, while still thinking about taking his money back.

But she might make a big got' damned scene while I'm in the bathroom, he imagined. *What if she even called the cops in here? And I still have to go back to work tomorrow.*

Ultimately, he decided to finish his night without any further turmoil. So he planned to wash himself up, drive the stripper back to wherever, drop her stinky ass off, and go on back to his life, with a checkup at the health clinic.

"I'm gon' leave these damn strips clubs alone for a while," he mumbled.

When Sugar finally walked out from the bathroom, with another towel around her body, she scowled at Georgie. "I told your ass to wait a minute."

Georgie didn't want to hear it. He stepped into the bathroom and closed and locked the door himself. Then he commented through the locked door, "You didn't tell me your damn *cycle* was on."

"It's not. That was just *you*, pounding me like a fucking maniac. I told you I was too tight for that."

"Yeah, whatever. It don't smell too good out there either," he told her. "What's your excuse for that? You took a shower."

Sugar heard him and thought about it. She couldn't deny the stench lingering inside the room. She shook her head and mumbled under her breath, "Fuck you, motherfucker." Then she hurried to get dressed before he could finish his shower. She planned to leave his ass there and get herself a taxi home. That's exactly what she did. She already had her money. And that ugly-ass old man didn't mean a damn thing to her.

"Fucking pervert," she yelled toward the bathroom as she walked out and slammed the door.

Georgie had counted on that. He didn't want to drive her ass anywhere anyway.

"Good riddance," he mumbled inside the shower, hearing the hotel room door slam.

Later, without returning his key to the front desk, Georgie pulled out of the hotel in his silver Jetta and spotted Sugar climbing into a yellow taxi at the front entrance.

"Yeah, at least she found her own ride back home," he told himself. "And now I gotta get a damn checkup for AIDS, or whatever else she may have."

Less than a week later, George Tatum was diagnosed with chlamydia, otherwise known as a sticky-drawers, penis drip, acquired after intimate contact with a woman's yeast infection. It was a minor sexually transmitted disease that could be cleared up after a dose of strong medication and two weeks of abstinence.

The worst part for Georgie was being asked whom he may have gotten it from.

"The wrong damn woman," he told the doctor inside private quarters. That was all he was willing to reveal.

The doctor told him, "You may want to let her know, so she can get herself checked out."

"I already *did* let her know. I told her what it smelled like in the room. That's why I knew that something was wrong before it even showed up in my system. But it takes a full two weeks for the AIDS test to come back, hunh?"

The doctor nodded. "We'll let you know when we get the results back. In the meantime, you see why it's important to know everything you can about your partner. Causal sex can be clearly dangerous, and as you've found out, condoms are not always foolproof."

"Oh, you don't have to tell *me* twice," Georgie commented. "I'm too old for this shit."

The doctor nodded. "Yes, but you still need to try and convince the woman to get checked out as well. She could do a lot more damage to her reproductive track, if her infection is not treated. So you think about that for me. Think about it for *her*. All right?"

Georgie nodded and didn't argue with the doctor. But he didn't plan on hunting Sugar back down at the strip club. If she was smart, she would get herself checked out on her own. Then again, she was still relatively young, and she had been living on her own for four years. Maybe she hadn't been taught the importance of staying in touch with a gynecologist for monthly checkups.

Georgie walked out of the doctor's private clinic and thought to himself.

What if the girl don't know what she's supposed to do? But would she listen to my ass if I tried to tell her?

"Shit," he expressed out loud as he reached his car in the parking lot. "I thought you had to be inspected to even *work* in a strip club. But I guess *not*."

He climbed into his car and wondered exactly how he would map out a conversation with the young stripper who had burned him. And hopefully, she wasn't carrying AIDS as well.

Damn, Georgie mused as he drove in silence. *This is the reason why we're forced to live right. It's crazy out here. And I've been crazy right along with it.*

—•—

JAIL BAIT

Henry Morgan headed home from another hard day's work at the *Richmond Journal* newspaper in Virginia, where he slaved as a low-level ad salesman. He was forty-seven years old, slightly overweight, balding, and separated from his estranged wife. He had two children in their mid-twenties, and three young grandchildren he barely made time to see.

Henry continued to feel self-conscious and distant after his inability to send his two kids to college upon their graduation from high school. His daughter, the oldest, found a few grants and student loans to attend Virginia State for the first few years, but she had not secured enough funds to finish a four-year education in social services. She then joined the work force as an administrative assistant in downtown Richmond before she became pregnant by her unemployed, off-and-on boyfriend of three years.

Henry's son, the youngest, had not even tried to attend college. He ended up impregnating two different girls over one long, hot and restless summer.

The family's continuation of economic shortcomings soon created a rift between Henry and his wife, with constant battles over money, until they could no longer live in the same house together.

"You need to do either one of two things," his wife told him before their split. "*One*, you need find a better *job* that pays you more for your time. Or *two*, you need to learn how to do the one you *have* better than what you've *been* doing it."

Henry chose option *three* and moved out into a studio apartment, where he was more able to focus and live in peace. Nevertheless, he thought constantly about how differently his life could have panned out, if he had found the courage to search for better employment.

But I like the newspaper business, he told himself. The newspaper industry was filled with great perks, including invitations to nearly all of Richmond's local events. He had even gotten his two-toned, Ford Expedition truck at half its value due to his relationships through the paper. And as he drove home that night behind the wheel of his vehicle in silence, he continued to weigh the pros and cons of his loyalty to the local newspaper.

Halfway home, he received a call on his cell phone. He looked down and read an unrecognizable number. He frowned and answered the call anyway. "Hello."

"Hey, it's Tasha. Where you at?"

It was the young woman he had met during a recent car show promotion. Fresh images of her black jeans and tight white T-shirt immediately popped into his mind. Boy, did he admire her hot, young body. Her figure had more dangerous curves than the cars that were at the show. So Henry began to flirt with the girl through several X-rated phone calls made over the past couple of weeks.

"I'm coming back home from work," he told her. "Where are you calling from?" It wasn't the same cell phone number he had called her on before.

"My phone needs charging, so I'm calling you from my girl's phone," she explained. "You gettin' off work at eight o'clock? I thought you work in the morning."

"I did a little overtime tonight to get a few things finished for tomorrow's paper."

"Oh, you did a little *overtime*, hunh? Are you tired then? What are you doing now?"

Henry heard a giggle in the background and didn't like it. He wanted to keep his conversation with her private.

"Ahh, like I said, I'm going home. But call me back a little later, once you've finished charging your phone."

"But I wanted to talk to you now. My charger's back at home."

Henry heard more giggles in the background. "Well, it sounds to me like you've got yourself some company," he hinted.

He hoped she would get the point; he didn't feel comfortable talking to her around other people.

"Okay, hold on," she told him. A few seconds later, she added, "Okay, we can talk privately now."

"And what do you want to talk about?" he asked her bluntly. With his thoughts on his family at the moment, he didn't feel up to having flirtatious conversations with the young woman. Or at least not that evening.

"Umm, remember all that you was telling me about, you know, eating my pussy and stuff? Umm, when you wanna do that?"

Henry was shocked by it. And it wasn't that it was a new subject for them. He had indeed bragged about what he would be willing to do as an older man that some of the younger men would balk at; her timing was just wrong. Nevertheless, she created an unexpected rise out of him.

"Ahh, you know, it doesn't really matter to me." He wasn't backing down from it, but he wasn't exactly stepping up to the plate either. It would ultimately be her decision to take things to the next level. In Henry's book, flirting and fucking were two separate things. And he had flirted with plenty of women, but he had not taken them to bed, even after the separation from his wife.

Tasha asked, "What about tonight? Can you come get me?"

Now that got Henry excited. She had him speechless for a moment.

"Tonight? Well, ahh—"

She cut him right off. "Yeah, I'm horny as hell right now. Do you smoke?"

She continued to speak to him in rapid fire. Henry struggled to keep up with it.

"Yeah, I still have the bad habit of smoking," he admitted.

"You smoke weed?"

Henry paused. *That's what it is! She's been out smoking with her friend, and now she's calling me up high and horny, and ready to do something about it.* But he didn't necessarily view that as a *bad* thing.

"I haven't done that in a while," he told her. "You know, most office jobs have urine checks from time to time."

"Oh, so that means you have to wait until the weekends to smoke." She chuckled. "So, what's up? You wanna come get me, or what?"

Henry continued to stall. Even though she had him intrigued, her sudden invitation was still too unexpected for him to grapple with at the moment.

"I mean, where you live at?"

"I told you, I live on the southwest side."

"Yeah, but you also told me you're not at home."

"I told you I don't *feel* like going home to charge my phone up, that's all. But I'm right around the corner near my girl's house."

And why would I want to drive around there? Henry questioned.

"You know I live all the way on the north side."

"*And,*" she challenged him. "Look, if you not serious, then don't talk that stuff to me no more. All right? Because I thought you were a man of your word."

Henry wanted to tell her that she had simply chosen the wrong night, but he couldn't bring himself to do it. Instead, he said, "I'm almost home right now."

"So, what does that mean? You don't wanna come get me then?"

He could not deny his hard-on. She had him going. He just didn't feel up to driving back in the opposite direction of Richmond to get her.

"Let me get home and think about it."

Tasha sucked her teeth and snapped, "All right, man," before she hung up on him.

Henry figured that was the end of it.

"Now she's mad at me," he mumbled as he continued to drive home. "So be it."

But by the time he made it in and took off his tie, sports jacket, dress slacks and leather shoes, Tasha was calling him back at nearly nine o'clock. "Did you drive back home and think about it yet?"

Henry chuckled. The girl sure was persistent.

"As a matter fact, I have."

"So...you're not coming to get me then?" she pressed him.

Can you believe this? Henry asked himself. *This girl wants me to go down on her that damn bad tonight.* "Are you that serious about that tonight?"

"If I wasn't, I wouldn't have called and asked you to get me."

Finally, Henry nodded. "You know, I'm gon' see how serious you are then. Where do you want me to meet you?"

"Umm, you can meet me on the west side of Broad Street at Popeye's. You know the one I'm talking about?"

Henry knew all of Richmond. "Yeah, I know it. But you gotta give me at least thirty minutes to get dressed and make it back down there."

"All right, thirty minutes then," she agreed.

He hung up the phone with her and shook his head. "Shit. What have I gotten myself into?" He realized this girl wouldn't take "no" for an answer. She wanted it. And she wanted it *now!*

Henry arrived at Popeye's fast-food restaurant on the west end of Broad Street, and he peeked through the glass windows, while remaining inside of his truck.

"It don't look like she even here," he grumbled. Then he looked into his rearview mirror and noticed the young woman climbing out of a dark-gray Subaru in a parking space behind him. She was wearing tight white pants and a *black* T-shirt.

Oh my God! Henry told himself as he watched her walk across the small parking lot and toward the passenger side of his truck. *I guess there's no turning back now.*

Tasha climbed into his truck and was all smiles, in short straight hair and chocolate brown skin.

"What took you so long?" she asked him. Her teeth were a perfect row of white, but her smoked-out eyes were as cloudy as a red storm.

"It took me a minute to get here, that's all." He couldn't believe an old, balding, overweight guy like himself could luck up with a fabulous young girl like Tasha. He was surprised she had even called him, after he had handed her his cell phone number at the car show. He figured she would have tossed it in the trash with her bag of cheese fries. So when she actually called him and was game to talking fresh over the phone to him, Henry fell right into the fun of talking dirty to her. But now she had climbed into his truck, for real, and she was horny.

"So, where are you taking me?" she asked him.

Henry watched the dark-gray Subaru pull out of the lot behind him. He dodged Tasha's question to ask her about it.

"That was your ah, girlfriend in that car?" He felt leery about it. He would have rather met up with her somewhere alone.

"Yeah, that's her."

"And you were out here getting high with her?"

Henry could read it in her eyes. She was all loose and giddy in the passenger seat.

"Yeah, we, ah, had a little something. And then we started talking about oral sex and shit, and how guys be wanting girls to go down on *them*, but then *they* don't be wantin' to go down on a girl. And then I started thinking about you, because you told me that, you know, you wouldn't have no problem doin' it. And you said you would like it."

Henry remembered the conversation more as him talking shit to a young, hot woman than being truthful. Nevertheless, she did have a look that made him want to back up his talk. And she was definitely acting like she wanted him to do it.

Henry placed his gears in reverse to back out of his parking spot, and he joked as he drove off. "So, you just want me for my *tongue* tonight."

Tasha laughed. "Yup, I do. But if you give me some, I'll give *you* some," she promised.

That got Henry rock hard again.

"That sounds like a deal to me," he told her.

"So, where are you taking me to do it?"

She had no shame in her forwardness, at all. But Henry remained uncertain about everything. He didn't want to take her to his studio apartment and have her see how cheaply and disorganized he lived. Nor was he willing to spend money on a hotel room.

He asked, "How badly do you want it?"

Tasha looked into his eyes and chuckled as they headed east on Broad Street toward Interstate 95.

"Let me see your hand," she told him. She reached for his right hand from the steering wheel and stretched it toward her crotch to rub her spot. She was already moist through her white pants.

"Is that serious enough for you? Or do you need me to put your hand inside my pants?"

Henry looked back into her cloudy eyes and couldn't believe it. She had him ready to wet up his own pants. But he still had no idea where to take her.

"No, I don't think you need to do that. I think you're serious enough already." He retracted his right hand to drive.

Tasha grinned in silence and looked out the passenger-side window.

Shit, if she's that ready, I could pull over somewhere nice and dark, and do it inside the truck. Fortunately, he had cleaned out the back that same week. "You mind if we climb inside the back of this truck?"

Tasha looked back into the truck to inspect its roominess.

"Oh shit, we got plenty of room back there. What's this, an Expedition?"

Henry answered proudly, "Yeah." His large truck was one of his few uplifting assets, especially after getting it washed, waxed and vacuumed.

"Well, it's wherever you wanna go then. This truck has tinted windows, right?"

"Yes, it does."

Tasha looked at him and shrugged, grinning through her high. "It's up to you."

Henry thought of the ideal place; a picnic and park area off of I-95 North. No one went there after dark. It was perfect.

When they arrived at the deserted park, Henry parked the truck, shut off the ignition, and quickly killed the lights.

Tasha took a strong look at their surroundings and joked, "I hope Sasquatch don't come out the bushes and get us out here." Then she laughed.

Henry chuckled with her, but he still felt apprehensive. However, Tasha had already undone her seat belt and climbed into the back of the truck.

"Are you coming back here with me or what?"

Henry took a final deep breath before he moved. *Well, here we go,* he told himself. He was too big to climb over the seats to reach the back like Tasha could. Henry had to step out of the truck and reenter from the back door.

"Let me put these seats down in the back to give us more room."

Tasha helped to fold down the back seats, creating plenty of room to lie down.

"God, you could put a twin-size *bed* back here." She remained silly and laughing from her high. Then she began to pull down her white pants and multi-colored panties.

Henry was still dazed by it all, even while eyeing the small bush of hair that popped into view at the unveiling of Tasha's young, wet pussy.

Am I really here doing this? he asked himself once more. He had packed a couple of condoms in his wallet from home, just in case.

By the time he confirmed that it was all real, Tasha had taken her pants, panties and shoes completely off inside the back of his truck. She spread her legs wide open for him to go to work downtown.

"You still think I'm playing?" she quizzed.

Obviously, she was *not*.

"Ahh, it doesn't look that way," Henry answered.

"All right, so let me see what it feel like."

"You mean to tell me you never felt your boyfriend's tongue inside you before?"

"I don't have one of those. I'm trying to make *you* my new boyfriend."

Henry ignored her flattery. "I meant with your *past* boyfriends."

"No, I was too busy doin' it. I wasn't thinking 'bout all that. But I would hear people talk about it and stuff. But umm, are you gonna do it or what?"

She was tired of all the talking.

Henry grinned and climbed into a kneeling position between her legs. He then placed her naked brown legs over his broad shoulders.

"Are you still high right now?" he asked.

"Hell yeah, man. It ain't gon' fade away that fast. I had just smoked some more with my girl right before you pulled up. But if you don't hurry up and lick me, you gon' blow my horny high," she added with a giggle.

Henry leaned forward into her sweetness and licked her from the bottom to the top of her wet pussy hole.

"Oh shiiittt!" she squealed, jerking forward to brace herself.

Henry grabbed her hips to steady her while licking her up and down again. Tasha tossed her head back and squeezed her eyes shut in bliss. She was trying her hardest not to act a damn fool. She had never imagined a wet tongue could feel that good. And with the increased sensations of her high, Henry's pussy licks were incredible.

Then he went ahead and stuck his whole tongue inside of her juices. Tasha felt so good that she grabbed his balding head and pushed her hips into his face to feel his tongue reach further inside of her.

"*Dam-yumm*," she moaned.

Once he got himself into a rhythm, Henry found comfort in pleasing her. It had been awhile since he could actually see, feel and hear a woman's appreciation of his sexual services. For far too many years, sex with his wife had seemed more like a chore for both of them. There hadn't been much moaning, groaning, or twisting between them. But Tasha was wide open and giving him her all. Henry didn't know a young woman could get so wet.

"*Ooooh*, eat that pussy. Eat that *pussy*," she began to wail. And eat it, Henry did, until his tongue and neck began to hurt from his position of servitude.

Soon he leaned up to stretch his neck, then he arched his back, and exercised his tongue from a muscle cramp.

"I'ma go ahead and put it in now," he told her, and began to pull down his own pants.

"Hurry up," she moaned, squirming in heat.

Henry got his pants and drawers down before he rolled a condom over his hard dick, and aimed it between her legs.

"*Oooh shit!*" Henry moaned himself. He slid right into her wetness like a kid down a swimming pool sliding board. He jackhammered that young pussy as if the cops were coming.

"Henry, you fucking me *good*. You fucking me *good!*" she told him.

"The pussy is good, too," he told her back. "It's wet. It's *real* wet," he repeated.

"I know," she bragged with a chuckle. "I'm always wet like this, when I want it."

"You gonna make me want it more now."

"*Goooood*," she squealed to him. "I *want* you to want it like this. I *want* you to want it."

Henry was pounding so urgently into her slippery pussy that he ignored the burn of his knees on the backseat carpet. His truck was literally bouncing up and down like a comedy movie.

This is the best pussy I've had in a loonnng time, he told himself while he fucked her. *It might be the best pussy I've ever had!*

He began to feel his nut approaching as he poured it on even stronger, with the windows fogging up from the heat.

"Give it to me, baby; give it to me."

"Oh, I'ma give it to you all right. I'ma give it to you, *right now!*"

They both squeezed each other hard, as sweat dripped, and clothes became mangled. They panted, nerves reaching a peak in their climactic release. It was the strongest nut that Henry could remember since he had first started having sex more than thirty years ago.

That's what fucking is supposed to feel like! he told himself. *That's how God intended it to be, I'm convinced!*

When he was done, his poor, old knees had been rubbed raw. They were burning with fresh white meat, feeling the sting of oxygen.

"Shit!" Henry whined. "Look what I did to my damn knees."

Tasha leaned up and looked at them. She chuckled. "Looks like you gon' need some Band-Aids for work tomorrow. And I know my hair is all sweated out now. Look at your windows."

They were both thrilled, observing all that their great sex had given them.

"So now I know what being ate out feels like…Thanks."

Henry only chuckled and thought, *Now I know what young, wet, pussy feels like. And it's great!* But he didn't have the gall to say it out loud.

For their third sex date, Henry finally invited the young woman over to his cleaned-up place. It wasn't much to brag about, but he figured he would explain everything to her to make it all make sense.

"So, you mean to tell me that you let your wife have the house, while you moved into this little place?"

The apartment studio looked no bigger than a college dorm room, with a private kitchen, a full-sized refrigerator, and a full bathroom added on.

Henry shrugged. "I don't need much. How much room do I need with no kids or a wife around anymore? This is the perfect size for me to concentrate."

Tasha shrugged back. "Okay, it's your life." Then she began to strip from her clothes in front of his bed. "I see I finally get to lay down in a soft bed this time, hunh?" she teased.

"Yeah, my knees can't take the burns from the truck anymore."

"Nor can my beautiful ass," she countered.

Now that they were in a normal home setting with light, a bed, and the comfort of private space, Henry was able to witness all of Tasha's fabulous young body. He felt self-conscious about his own.

"Okay, so, how does an old guy like me end up with a young, hot girl like you? That's what *I* want to know," he asked.

She hadn't asked him yet for money, time, or anything. She only wanted his sex.

"I told you already. I wanted to have my pussy licked. And a lot of other guys weren't trying to do it, or not without all kinds of other *drama* attached. And I don't feel like dealing with all that shit."

"So you decided to have an older man to do it for you?"

Henry was still trying to validate the facts.

"I mean, you was talking all that shit about it to me. So I said, 'Why not?'" She laughed. "And like I told you, I was high and horny that night."

Her logic was straightforward. He said, "But you're not high and horny tonight."

"Yeah, but now I know how good the shit feels, so I don't *need* to be high no more. But I'm still fuckin' *horny* though. And you can fuck, too," she told him. "You seem like you be really in to it, and I like that. Other guys act like they doin' you a favor, or either they only out to please themselves. So I'd rather give it to you."

Henry began to wonder how long she would deal with him before she found someone else to please her. But he figured he'd take full advantage of it, while it lasted. So he climbed into the bed and took his place between Tasha's legs again. He began to lick and suck, up and down, in and out, and around her young, wet and throbbing pussy.

I can't complain too bad about this, he convinced himself as he continued to service her. *She always smells clean, she tells it like it is, and she's constantly horny for me to eat her and fuck her.*

It was amazing what great sex with a young woman could do to an old man's passion and ego. Henry's good fortune and cheerful attitude extended to the workplace. He then found himself landing bigger advertising contracts for the newspaper. He had upgraded his existing accounts, and he was bouncing around the office now like a teenager. He felt as if he had lost *fifty* pounds and was able to float up and down the hallways.

"Hey, ah, Henry, you get back in good graces with your wife?" one of his coworkers asked him at the office. After awhile, they could all tell that something was different about him.

"Nope. And I'm no longer worried about it either." He now refused to allow himself to be punished for the decisions of his past. He had moving on to do.

After work that evening, Henry walked out to his Ford Expedition as usual, climbed in with his briefcase, started up his engine, and drove out of the newspaper parking lot toward home. He had no idea that a plainclothes detective had been waiting for him in a brown, unmarked sedan. The sedan followed his truck onto the highway and off the exit ramp toward his apartment. When the detective finally flipped on his police lights behind him and pulled him over, Henry had no idea what he had done wrong.

He looked at the flashing police lights through his rearview mirror and snapped, "What the hell?" He knew he had not been speeding.

He slowly pulled over to his right and parked on the side of the road, and waited for the officer to explain.

He watched through his side-view mirror as a no-nonsense black man in his forties, climbed out of the sedan and headed toward the driver's side door of his truck. He had a pen and pad in hand, and was dressed in a dark-blue sports jacket, brown slacks, and soft leather shoes.

Once he had reached the window, Henry asked him, "Is there a problem, officer? I don't believe I was going past the speed limit."

The officer smiled. "No, you're a model citizen, Henry. You weren't speeding at all. I wanted to stop you and ask you some questions about ah..." He looked down at his notepad and stated, "LaTasha Springfield."

As soon as Henry heard the name, his heart nearly jumped into his throat and choked him to death. What had *she* done wrong?

"Ahh...yeah," he responded slowly as his heart continued to pound. He still felt guilty about dealing with the young woman.

The detective said, "I need to ask you a few questions about her, that's all."

"Well, what did she do? If you don't mind me asking."

Has she been arrested for marijuana? Has she robbed someone? What is the problem?

The officer paused a minute to gather his words. "Henry, have you had sexual relations with ah, LaTasha?" he asked, glancing at his notepad again.

Henry's wide eyes told him everything he needed to know before he spoke a word.

SHIT! he cursed himself. *What the hell is this?*

Henry paused and asked, "Why?" He could hardly breathe when he spoke.

Has someone fucking told on me? Has my wife hired a damn spy? Or was it my damn nosy neighbors? SHIT!

All kinds of scenarios began to run through his mind.

"I need you to step out of the car and come with me," the officer told him. He was being extra civil about it.

Henry understood as much and did what the officer requested.

"Now I'm gonna have to put these handcuffs on you as a precaution. I know you're not going to try anything crazy. I know where you work and where you live."

Henry looked him in the eyes and started breathing even heavier, as if he were only two beats away from a massive heart attack.

"It's all right; I simply need to have a frank talk with you," the officer assured him. He then pulled out a pair of shiny steel handcuffs, turned Henry around to face his truck, and placed the cold, hard cuffs around his meaty wrists.

He led Henry to the passenger side of his umarked car and let him inside. He then walked around to the driver's side and climbed in himself.

Henry was still breathing hard when the officer finally introduced himself.

"Henry, my name is Detective Troy Patterson. I work with the Richmond Police Department's vice squad, its rape and child molestation divisions."

"Rape and child molestation?"

The detective looked into his panicked and confused eyes. "Did you not know that LaTasha was sixteen years old?"

"What? She told me that she was *nineteen*. You gotta believe me, man! I wouldn't have gone anywhere *near* a sixteen-year-old girl!"

He was overexcited and sweating, understandably. The girl had lied to him and had landed him in a world of trouble.

The detective nodded thoughtfully. "Well, how did you meet her?"

"I met her at a car show, and I handed her my business card with my number on it. But I thought she was of age. And I didn't even think that she would call me."

"Why not?" the detective asked him.

Henry looked at him incredulously. "Come on, man, have you seen her? I mean, why she wanna talk to *me*?"

The detective shrugged. "Why did you give her your number?"

These were obvious questions to Henry. He answered with a slight stutter, out of fear, "Because she was...she was *hot*." He felt embarrassed to even have to say it. But the detective kept his poise with him.

"When I saw your case come across my desk, I jumped right on it to make sure I got down to the bottom of this thing, and save you from a lot of unnecessary embarrassment. I understand our culture a little better than a lot of the other guys down at the station.

"Now, I understand that you may have a few things going on that you may need to keep a solid lid on. That's why I didn't come and get you from your office at the newspaper."

Henry nodded to him. "Thank you."

"But at the same time," the detective addressed him, "at no time in your conversations with this young lady, did you ask her more questions about her age, where she worked, went to school, or anything of that nature? I mean, I don't know, but that seems like a natural conversation to me. She didn't talk about anything that struck you as alarming?"

Henry shook his head. "To tell you the truth, once she told me she was *nineteen*, I really didn't focus on her age anymore. I mean, you know how some of these women get. They get *defensive* when you talk about their age too much. So I left it alone."

"Well, even at nineteen, that's still a little *young* for you, ain't it? I would hardly call that a *woman*. I have a *daughter* who's nearly that age. She's a senior in high school now."

The detective seemed to be getting more agitated.

Henry countered, "I have a daughter, *too*. But they're *all* somebody's daughter, Officer. My *wife* is somebody's daughter. *Your* wife is."

"Yeah, but our *wives* were old enough to make their own *decisions* for themselves, and they were not up against men who were more than *twice* their age."

"Officer, do you think this girl had any problems making her own decisions? She practically *begged* me to pick her up. I didn't even wanna do it."

"So, why *did* you do it then?" the detective pressed him. "And it's *detective*, not officer."

Henry looked down and shook his head, feeling ashamed. "I'm sorry, Detective," he mumbled. "But I...I was just *weak*. And I tried my *best* not to go. Lord *knows*, I did. I was making tired excuses and everything. And then I show up, and this girl is high and horny, man, and she's *telling* me this."

The detective shook his own head. He was embarrassed to even hear more more of it. "But even after all of that, you continued to see her, didn't you? And you *still* didn't ask how old she was?"

Henry could feel the judgment coming. The detective was beginning to pour the guilt on him. He whined, "Because she told me she was *nineteen*." Tears began to swell up in the man's eyes. He knew he was wrong, but it was too late to change anything.

"So, what do you want me to do now?" the detective asked him. "I have to take you down to the station and book you."

Henry's eyes grew large again. He screamed, "She *lied* to me, man, and you *know* she lied!" Fresh tears rolled out of the old man's eyes and down his plump face. He mumbled, "I thought you said you understood our culture."

He felt terrified and ashamed. What would his estranged wife and children think of him now?

"Yeah, I do understand it, Henry, but that don't make it *right*. You can't walk around giving out your phone number to young girls like this. And if I let you get away with it this time, you gon' go right back out there and do it again, ain't you?"

"No, man, *never*!" Henry stated. "I've *learned* my lesson."

The detective looked him over. "You've learned your *lesson*? Nothing has even happened to you yet. So you're gonna go out here and get on somebody else's daughter. And then you gon' make me look like a *fool*!"

Henry shook his head as tears continued to run down his tortured face.

He looked straight into the detective's stern brown eyes and decreed, "God be my *witness*, I will *never* get myself involved in anything like this again. *Never!*"

"You know they say that you should never say never," the detective commented.

"Well, I'm saying it because I *mean it*," Henry cried.

The detective nodded, thinking everything over.

"So, how long have you been involved with her?"

"Just over a month now," Henry admitted.

"And how many times have you been with her?"

Henry paused to make sure the detective was asking him what he *thought* he was asking him. He whimpered, "Do I need a lawyer before I answer something like that?"

"You can call one, after I take you down and book you at the station. Maybe your wife can call up a good trial lawyer for you."

Henry heard that and panicked all over again. He cried, "What do you want me to do?" His voice was cracking.

"I want you to tell me everything so I can help you," the detective answered. "Now if you wanna do this the *hard way*, I can go ahead and book you down at the station, and then let you call whomever you wanna call. But if you do it *my* way, I can get down to the bottom of this without the case ever making it to a courtroom."

Henry didn't believe him, but what choice did he have? He didn't want his family, friends, or coworkers to know what he had gotten himself into—especially after work had just begun to look up for him. So he had to roll the dice and pray for a lucky seven.

"I've been with her about…five or six times now," he confessed.

"Is that it?" the detective questioned. "You sure it wasn't more than that, in over a month. What if I asked *her* the same question?"

"She could lie to you again," Henry answered.

"Well, that sounds like you're in a bad situation then. Who is the jury gonna believe: an older man separated from his wife, or a sixteen-year-old girl who still lives with her mother and family?"

Henry sunk his head into his chest and cried even louder. "I'm telling you what you're asking me. I don't know what else to say. I made a stupid decision."

"So, exactly what did you talk about when she called you? Because you couldn't have asked her much about who she was or what she did for a living. You would have found out fairly easily that she was underaged."

Henry kept his head burrowed into his chest.

"I talked about a lot of things that I shouldn't have been talking about."

"Oh yeah, like what? Let me hear some of it."

Henry thought about acquiring a lawyer again, but he feared the detective threatening to book him down at the station. "We talked a lot about sex. And she wanted to…experience some things," he added after a pause.

"Is that right? And you told her you would be the one to help her experience it?"

Henry answered by nodding his head into his chest.

The detective shook his head. "Well, that's *pitiful*. How do you think *your* daughter would respond to hearing that you did something like that?"

Henry didn't want to imagine it. He figured he had suffered enough already. He had never been handcuffed inside of a police car in his life. And the only thing he knew about the station was what he had seen on television shows or in movies. He barely even read the crime section in his own newspaper.

Finally, the detective asked him, "Henry, you're not gonna skip town on me, or commit suicide, if I let you go, are you? I consider myself a pretty good judge of character."

Henry couldn't answer him right away. He had to think about it. Then he slowly shook his head. He told himself to have a little faith. He had told the detective the truth, and that's all that he had to offer.

"All right, so…I'm gonna stop by to pay a visit to LaTasha Springfield and her family, and I'm gonna hear her side of the story. And if I can straighten it all out without it making it into the courtroom, then you can come out of this thing and count your blessings."

Henry squeezed his eyes tightly again and mumbled, "Thank you!"

"Now I can't make you any promises," the detective added. "But one thing I *can* promise you is this; from here on out, any false moves on your part may *definitely* land you in prison. And that includes *speaking* to LaTasha about *any* of this or seeing her ever again. *Or* you trying to skip out of town on me. So what I would advise you to do, is avoid any further contact with her, go back to work and your regular routine, and wait for me to contact you with a follow-up."

He continued, "And you can contact a lawyer, if you want, but I wouldn't advise you to find one with a lawyer's ego. He may make the situation worse for you than what it already is. You know, sometimes these lawyers like to make themselves a big deal by getting all kinds of publicity. And I wouldn't advise you to play that game. You and I both know that what's *wrong* is *wrong*. But I *do* believe in an honest man getting a second chance to prove himself in life. So let me see what I can do for you."

Henry heard him out and nodded his heavy head into his chest once more. He mumbled, "Thank you."

The detective nodded back. "All right. Well, I'ma let you go now. But you remember everything I told you."

When Henry arrived at home to his small, studio apartment, he felt sweaty and exhausted, as if he had just jumped off of a treadmill at the gym. He fell back across his bed and didn't want to budge. The close call had taken everything out of him. And it wasn't over yet.

"I've really done it to myself now," he cried up to the ceiling. Nevertheless, he couldn't deny that Tasha's young, wet pussy had been incredible. That was the worst part of his ordeal. He had tasted the heavenly juices of youth.

"Fuck!" he enraged. As he lay in bed, he beat his balled fists at his sides. But his frustrations wouldn't change a damn thing. He was now forced to wait it out and continue to pray. He even thought of leaving town, or dying, as the detective had warned him not to do. But there were so many other places to live out there, and so many towns for him to start a new life. Or, if he was to be imprisoned because of his grave mistake, then maybe he would be better off if he killed himself before the detective and the police came back to get him.

At least then I wouldn't have to live with the shame of what I've done, he pondered. *But then...what would happen to me once I've reached the gates of heaven?*

He felt that his life was no longer in his hands. So he quietly began to weep, with tears rolling down the sides of his face and landing on his bed sheets.

If I could just have a second chance, he mused.

"Everyone deserves at least *one* second chance."

After countless minutes had turned into hours, Henry still couldn't find the energy to move. He even ignored his cell phone on the first two rings. But on the third ring, he read the number to see who was calling him.

However, the call was restricted, and he definitely wasn't up to answering any foreign phone calls that evening. *What if it is Tasha calling to get him into more trouble?* He ignored it.

But once the third call was followed by a fourth, and from a restricted number again, Henry waited for the call to end before he checked his messages.

He listened to the usual calls from coworkers, family and friends, before he reached the last two messages that were left on his cell phone that evening.

"Hey, Henry, it's Tasha. I know you probably don't want to speak to me anymore, but I wanted to tell you that it was my friend who told her mom, and then *her* mom called *my* mom. And before I could even say anything about it, my mom called the police station and made a fucking complaint. So I wanted you to know that it wasn't me. Okay?"

Henry then listened to her second message.

"*Please* don't be mad at me, man. It wasn't my *fault*. And I would never tell my business like that. I mean, I..."

Henry shook his head and erased the message without listening to the rest of it. He didn't want to hear it.

"Is this girl *crazy*? She makes it sound like this is a slap-on-the-wrist thing. But this detective is ready to lock my ass *up!*"

Furthermore, the young girl was not apologizing for lying to him about her age; she was only apologizing for being dimed out.

And if she didn't tell her business like that, then how would her girlfriend even know who the hell I was? Henry reasoned. *I knew that was a mistake the first time she called me from that girl's phone to pick her up that night.*

All her pleading phone calls only made him angrier.

"That damn girl has *no* fucking idea what she got me into!" he stood from his bed and shouted. "This ain't no got' damned *game!* This is my *life* we're talking about!"

Nevertheless, Tasha's desperate phone calls had given him new faith, so he vowed to fight the charges. He wasn't going to jail for a sixteen-year-old girl! Instead, he would force her to tell the judge and jury that she had *lied* to him. Plain and simple. And if his family, employers, and the citizens of Richmond, Virginia, would castigate him for his poor judgment, then he would up and leave the city for a new place to live.

Henry was determined to keep his same reserve at work the next morning. He performed his usual routines and was fortified in his faith that he would be proven innocent on the grounds of ignorance of her real age. But he could no longer fight the fact that he had an active sex drive. A sex drive was normal. And if he needed to finally divorce his wife and move on to a new relationship with a capable and loving woman, then so be it.

However, Henry was also prepared for any visitor from the police station to pop in on him at work. He wouldn't be blindsided by it again, and he would not break down and cry anymore. He was ready for it now. He even collected the names and phone numbers of three qualified lawyers in his wallet to call up and defend him whenever needed. But after the first day at work, no one came to get him.

In fact, no one came to get him after the second day. But that hardly meant that Henry would put his guard down. He figured he would remain prepared for whatever would happen to him.

Detective Troy Patterson had promised he would contact him again once he got down to the bottom of things, and Henry now believed him. He had no other choice. So when the detective finally caught back up with him after the third day of work, Henry was poised and ready for the verdict.

The detective pulled him over on the side of the road again, but this time he didn't bother to put handcuffs on him when they sat again inside of his unmarked car. That still didn't mean that Henry wasn't nervous though. Any man would remain nervous in *his* position. So he waited anxiously for the detective to give him the bitter or sweet news.

The detective nodded to him and remained stoic. "Well, it looks like you've dodged a bullet, Henry. But let this be a serious wake-up call for you in the future."

Henry exhaled without a word.

The detective continued, "I did some further research on the girl, talked to her mother, a few of her teachers at school, and some of her girlfriends. And at the end of the day, the girl refused to go along with pressing charges against you. Based on the facts that I've gathered on her, she wouldn't have stood up in court no way."

Henry asked him, "Did she tell you she lied to me?" That's all he wanted to know. Her initial lie to him held up his whole moral argument.

The detective took a breath. "Henry, the young woman is *full* of lies. And with all of the things she's gotten herself involved in lately, she has no *choice* but to lie."

Henry nodded and grinned, feeling vindicated.

The detective eyed him sternly. "Her lie still don't make your actions *right*, Henry. Now think about this for a second. If I would have skipped over your paperwork and passed it on to someone else, instead of taking it myself...You catch my drift?"

Henry nodded and understood him perfectly. The detective had gone out of his way to save him from a giagantic mess.

"Thanks," Henry muttered.

The detective leveled with him. He looked Henry square in his eyes and said, "Between me and you, you had some very fortunate timing, my friend. My oldest daughter had just put my wife and me in a similar situation. We found out she had been having conversations with a much older football player. She had told this man she was twenty-one. She had a fake ID and everything. So imagine how hurt and embarrassed *I was* to find this out about my own daughter, while I'm walking around investigating other cases."

Henry looked into the man's brown eyes and could now empathize with him.

The detective exhaled also. "But, no matter *what*, Henry, grown men have to stop *looking* to get involved with young women in the first place, because we all *know* that they're young. And *nineteen* is only *six* years away from *thirteen*. But you're nearly *fifty*, Henry. And *fifty* to *nineteen* is still a *blowout*."

He then pointed at Henry and warned, "So the next time this happens to you, I hope you have the reserve to walk away. Because you may not have another man on the case who can personally understand it. You hear me?"

"Yeah," Henry mumbled. How could he *not* hear the detective? He *felt* for the man. He felt for them *both*. They were both getting older while the women got younger. So the "blowouts" were more likely to happen now.

The detective repeated, "Well, I hope you do. And you can consider this your first forgiveness. But I can't promise you that you'll get another."

"I don't plan to need another one. I know exactly what I'm up against now. So you don't have to worry about me at all. And thanks again."

Henry Morgan drove away a free man that night in more ways than one. All of his recent thoughts about divorcing his wife for good and moving on to another city had stuck with him. He could easily transfer his knowledge and skills as a newspaper ad salesman to another paper in a different town. That's what the true go-getters did. They moved around for new opportunities, experiences and higher-paying jobs.

The next month, Henry found himself four hours north of Richmond in the state of Delaware, where he checked out the housing and employment opportunities. He liked everything he saw.

"Yeah, I can go for this town," he told himself cheerfully. "Everything is wide open here. *And* it's no taxes on the shopping."

He stopped to check out Christiana Mall off of Interstate 95. In the middle of his walk throughout the mall, an attractive mother and daughter walked out of a shoe store right in front of him and caught his undivided attention.

The mother looked in her early forties, with the full curves and maturity of her age. She walked like a stately woman of dignity and tact. Henry was immediately impressed with her, admiring her from behind. But then her daughter stopped and turned to their left, a few feet in front of him, causing her mother to stop along with her.

The daughter pointed with her index finger, right past Henry.

"Let's go to Macy's first," she suggested.

Henry looked the younger woman in her face and was stunned. The teenaged daughter had the dark, slanted eyes of an Egyptian, a face as smooth as an advertisement for cocoa butter lotion, titties like a double scoop of coffee ice cream, and a perfectly rounded ass in her blue jeans.

SHIT! Henry thought to himself. Just when he thought he was impressed with a woman closer to his age, her daughter made her look like an old leather bag. The mother was still attractive, but her curves were not as pronounced as her daughter's. The mother's skin was not as smooth. Her eyes were not as sharp. And her aura was no where near as explosive as her offspring's.

Well, you can't compare a mother to her daughter in most situations, Henry reasoned. There was no competition physically. An older woman was an older woman. *But it's the mentality part that really counts,* he insisted. *And these young women are dangerous and unstable.*

Nevertheless, he gave the daughter a second look as they walked by him. Before they disappeared from his sight to enter Macy's, he gave the daughter a third look. He couldn't help himself.

Jesus Christ! he exclaimed. *What in the world has happened to me?*

In his private thoughts, he had already begun to wonder what the daughter's sweet, young pussy would taste like.

SHIT! he cursed himself a second time. *I may need to see a psychiatrist now.*

Could he actually slip into being a child molester after his experience in Richmond? The idea scared him. Adults were supposed to have the conscious restraint to say no.

"I can't even look at them anymore," he mumbled to as he continued to walk through the mall. But then another young woman walked out of a store in front of him, and then the next one, until Henry was quickly forced to modify his new rule.

Well, just because you look at them, doesn't mean you have to touch them. Looking is normal, he mused. *Or maybe I can't go out to the malls anymore.*

After further thought, he came to the conclusion that he would refrain from going to places where younger women would congregate, like malls, shopping centers or movie theaters.

But that sounds ridiculous, he pondered. *I went to all of those places before. What's the difference now?*

Then he realized again that he had tasted the heavenly juices of youth, and he could not deny it. The experience of a young woman had been wrong…and also invigorating.

SHIT! Henry cursed himself a third time. *Maybe the detective was right.*

He figured he would have to fight for the rest of his days to make sure he never ended up in the situation he had escaped in Richmond. But he was *damned* if it wouldn't be hard; *real* hard!

He walked out of the mall and headed back to his car, terrified to even look at the young women who were coming and going from the parking lot.

SKIN DEEP

Jason Polk positioned his expensive Hasselblad, German camera on a tripod at the perfect height and distance from the pine-wood, canopy-style bed inside of an elegant, candlelit bedroom. The soft candlelight that surrounded the room illuminated the red satin sheets atop the king-sized bed just right.

Perfect! He double-checked the view and adjusted the lens of his camera. At twenty-eight years old, Jason was a rising star photographer with a director position at *The Higher End* magazine, a publication of wealth, splurges, expensive candy and grown people's toys, including his assigned shoot at a hideaway resort in the northern suburbs of Detroit, Michigan.

"Are you ready for me yet?" a buttery-smooth voice asked him from his right.

"Ah, yeah, let's ah, see how everything looks."

He fiddled again with his camera and tossed his long dreadlocks out of his face to see clearly.

Gabrielle Kasey, his tempting model for the shoot, walked out from the bathroom, wearing only a golden, silk nightgown, and she was ready to obey his artistic tastes and orders. She glided through the room like a sexy, young tigress and climbed onto the red satin sheets gingerly. At twenty-one, she had been modeling for less than a year, and had not yet been trained how to pose. But her willingness to experiment made her artless efforts irresistible. And her beauty…was obvious.

Jason took a calming breath and flexed his toned biceps, preparing himself for another splendid job of execution. He began to snap her pictures immediately.

"Oh my God, you're taking that? I'm not ready yet," his subject complained. "And I thought he wanted me to take it all off." She was still dressed in the silk bathrobe.

Jason ignored her complaints and continued to shoot her natural movements. He had prepared himself to preserve her every antic. In his professional opinion, everything she did by accident could become flawless.

"We're gonna shoot it all, step by step, to see what he likes the best," he advised. They were shooting storyboard scenes for a romantic getaway at the Oasis Resort Hotel for the magazine's December issue. And Gabrielle was the perfect getaway gift for any man.

She grabbed the silk robe above her cleavage with both hands and pulled it slightly open, just enough for a man to beg for more.

"I already *know* what he likes best," she purred. Then she laughed and covered herself up with folded arms.

"Beautiful!" Jason told her. He snapped it all, every impeccable frame of her girlish tease.

"I didn't even do anything yet."

Jason snapped the pictures and shook his head. *She is so damn dramatic,* he noted. *She could be an actress. She makes this shit seem easy. I love working with her!*

In her blatant inexperience, Gabrielle would effortlessly tell a story through her reactions, without photographers needing to tell her much of anything. She never hid herself from their views. She was always there, wide open for their lenses.

"Trust me, you're doing everything you need to do," he assured her. "Just keep being you."

She looked straight into his camera with piercing dark eyes and shrugged. "Okay, if you say so. And umm…let me know when you want me to take it off."

Dammit, she's sexy! Jason convinced himself. As he stared at her wild, unashamed and reckless beauty through his lens, her cinnamon-colored skin appeared as smooth as an infant's ass rubbed down with baby oil. No makeup was needed to cover up anything. In fact, makeup would only ruin her perfection. All Gabrielle needed was a dry towel to pad away her shine, a touch of gloss to accentuate her pouting lips, and a hard bristled brush to straighten out her thick mane of long, wavy hair.

Jason nodded and began to imagine the next stage of his work—the naked scenes. And Gabrielle seemed eager to shoot them.

"Okay, well, I'm ready when you are," he told her. "But take off the robe in stages. You know, one shoulder at a time; one side at a time, and give me angles while you do it, like a strip tease."

"Okay, I can do that."

Jason's blue jeans tightened at his crotch, while he took pictures of her disrobing, piece by piece, shoulder by shoulder, breast by breast, and angle by seductive angle.

Man, I would love to jump up in that bed and join her, he mused. But his professionalism demanded that he did not. She was only a subject; a model of seduction.

Arnold Whittingham Jr. pulled into the valet parking area at the front of the Oasis Resort Hotel while still chatting on his cell phone.

"Yeah, I'm having a staff meeting tonight, honey, so I don't know how late I'm gonna be. We're on deadline to finish this December issue. And I swear, this pet project magazine is wearing me out. Can't these people finish anything on their own?"

"I told you, you need to hire an editor-in-chief and give him or her the power to run it, Arnie. But *no-o-o,* you can't seem to let it go without wanting to run it yourself," his wife insisted over the line.

"All right, well, maybe I'll start looking for a good E-I-C. All right, baby? But I gotta go now. And I love you, too."

Arnold hung up his cell phone and stepped out of his black Bentley Arnage in a long, camel-colored cashmere coat with Italian leather shoes under his beige dress pants. He was a confident and wealthy man of fifty-six and was handsome with gray hair.

"You checking in, sir?" a valet attendant asked him.

Arnold shook it off. "Nah, I'm only here for a few hours. So give me a temporary ticket."

"All right, about how many hours?"

The tall, stately man looked down at his Rolex watch and shrugged. "Let's say, ah…six or seven hours. What does that make it, two or three o'clock in the morning?"

The valet added up the hours. "Yeah, that's about right."

Arnold tossed him the keys to his Bentley and headed inside the resort toward the registration desk.

"May I help you?" a young woman asked him in a uniform ensemble of navy blue, cream and orange.

"Yes, I'm Arnold Whittingham from *The Higher End* magazine. I believe we have an executive penthouse suite here where we're shooting for our December issue."

"Oh, yes, yes, it's room, ah…" She looked it up on her computer monitor. "Seventeen-oh-one," she told him.

"Thank you."

"You're quite welcome. And thank you for choosing Oasis."

He smiled and waved a friendly hand as he headed toward the elevators.

"As long as the rooms look as good as you advertise them."

"Oh, they do," she bragged with a smile.

Back up in room 1701, Jason and Gabrielle had gotten good and comfortable. The beautiful model was shamelessly butt naked and flopping all over the bed in various unrehearsed poses.

"Oh, this bed feels so *good* all *over*," she moaned as Jason continued to shoot her raw and naked energy. His jeans had now become moistened from pre-ejaculation. She was really turning him on.

"Okay, now lie flat on your stomach and turn slightly toward me."

She did as he told her with no hesitation.

"Now cover your breasts with your right arm and hand, while extending your left arm to the edge of the bed."

Gabrielle obeyed him again.

"Beautiful!"

"You are, too," she teased.

That made Jason pause. "What was that?"

The model chuckled. "I don't know what it is, but guys with dreadlocks seem sexy to me, for some reason."

Jason was so intrigued that he was tempted to stand up tall from behind his camera and question her like a detective. But he dared not to miss anything. He felt addicted to the poetry of her movements. And if he moved away from his lens, he may have missed an all-important line on her comprehension.

"How come you've never told me that before?" he asked from behind his lens.

She smiled at him like a Cheshire cat in cinnamon-brown human form. "You seemed like you were all about your work, so I didn't get a chance to."

He *was* about his work, almost to a flaw. How many other enticing models had he ignored, or put on ice, while giving his full allegiance to the eye of his lens?

"Well, don't you love modeling?"

He shot the lower end of her back and the round curve of her naked ass.

"Yeah, but not like *that*. I mean, I've only been doing this for a year now. But I didn't know you could make so much *money* doing this."

Jason snapped at her response and grimaced. "Where are you from again?"

She giggled at his assumptions. She had gotten the same bewildered response from many of the men who had met her.

"Minnesota," she answered. "I know, I know, it's Prince's state, right. And the movie *Fargo*."

"Oh," Jason mumbled. He was an original New Yorker.

No wonder she's so…aimless with her sex appeal, he thought. What else could a girl be from Minnesota? There was nothing there but a giant mall with an amusement park inside.

"Where else have you been?" he asked.

She was amazingly comfortable in the room with him, naked and all.

"I've been to Mexico, and Florida, Canada, New York, Los Angeles…" She paused to continue in her count. "Chicago…New Orleans."

"All on photo shoots?"

"Umm…no, not all the time."

She suddenly seemed a little guarded. Jason read it, but kept going with his calm interrogation.

"Did you go with your girlfriends?"

Gabrielle's thoughtful hesitation told him more than she imagined, and he caught it all on camera. A picture was worth a thousand words. How comfortable did she feel about telling him her personal business?

"Well, to tell you the truth…no," she leveled with him. "But…I mean, I don't really feel guilty about it. I wanted to travel."

Jason raised a brow and peeped at her above the lens with his naked eye for a second. "Feel guilty about what?"

She caught herself and laughed naughtily. "Umm, is this too much information?"

Jason shrugged. "What, you're already butt naked. Go ahead and lay it all out."

"Oh my God, why did you have to say that? Now you got me feeling subconscious," she complained. She even covered up her body.

"Okay, I apologize. Now turn all the way over on your back and stretch both of your arms out to the edge of the bed."

He was growing more authoritative with her by the second. The safety gloves were off now. It was time for raw expressiveness.

Gabrielle glared into the camera. "No. You come make me," she told him.

Jason froze and missed the shot. *Shit!* Then he snapped it late and missed the moment.

"Dammit! Do that again. The same way."

"Why?"

He ignored her question. "Matter of fact, turn your body to face me and spread your legs out on the pillows at the headboard. *Then* say it again."

Gabrielle continued to grin at him. "You're getting very kinky with me now, Mr. Cameraman. Would your *boss* want me posing for you like that?"

"He told you to take it all off for me, right? So what do you *think* he wanted me to shoot?"

"Something tasteful."

"Yeah, tasteful and naked. So don't be ashamed now. Let's get it all."

She sighed and swung her body clockwise, tossing her naked legs against the pillows behind her like he asked, while turning to face his camera.

"*There*, are you satisfied now?"

Jason snapped her picture on cue. "Very."

She smirked. "This is what you make all the models do for you, hunh? They all let you get your way?"

He started cheesing and couldn't help himself. *Man, she's great at this. I'm probably better off as a gay man with her,* he pondered.

"I wish. But we can start with you," he teased. He wondered how far she would allow him to go with their flirtations.

"I bet we *could*," she flirted back. "So how many pictures are we gonna take on this bed, anyway? Doesn't he want us to shoot the whole room?"

Her query was factual. The assignment was of the entire room. But Jason was having far too much fun with her on the bed.

"We're almost done," he told her.

Tap, tap, tap!

Gabrielle looked toward the room door behind him. Then she eyed Jason skeptically. "Are you expecting anyone?"

Jason shot that scene from her as well.

Tap, tap, tap, tap!

Shit! he cursed as the taps on the locked door persisted. *I thought he told me he MIGHT be stopping by,* he questioned of his boss. Hopefully, it was only room service. But no one had ordered any food. Jason walked over to the door to investigate.

Arnold Whittingham Jr. waited outside the locked door of suite 1701 and wondered why it was taking so long for anyone to answer.

Maybe I should have called first, he pondered. *What if they're in there doing something they're not supposed to be doing?*

That thought sent a wave of shock and panic rushing through the publisher's passionate body.

Shit! What the hell was I thinking, leaving the two of them alone while she does a naked shoot? he asked himself, and then he leaned in to listen through the door.

Jason Polk arrived at the doorway and looked through the peephole right as his boss leaned in to eavesdrop.

The photographer paused after he noticed Arnold's movements of snooping. He didn't want to startle his boss by catching him in the act, so he froze behind the doorway and waited for better timing.

"Who is it?" Gabrielle asked him from the bed.

Jason became confused by his dilemma. If he answered Gabrielle while he so close to the door, it would be an easy call for his boss to presume that he had likely been busted. Jason waited there in silence until Arnold had righted himself at the door.

The photographer then opened the door quickly enough to fake surprise. "Hey, so I see you did stop by."

Arnold Whittingham Jr. paused at the doorway long enough for Jason to wonder about his thoughts. But neither man wanted to play their cards too easily.

"Yeah, I figured I'd drop by for a minute, you know." Then he closed his eyes. "I'm not interrupting anything I'm not supposed to *see*, am I?"

Jason wondered, *Is it unethical for a publisher to drop by during the naked shoot of a professional model? Then again, if they are all professionals, why not?*

Jason shrugged. "Only if she doesn't feel uncomfortable about it."

He stopped and looked back at Gabrielle.

Gabrielle hesitated, overhearing their conversation. What was a naked, young woman to do? It was her *job* to pose. And the man who was paying her for it had a right to see the raw product. Or did he?

"I mean, is this like...*normal*? Or does the publisher usually wait to see the pictures *after* they're taken?" she asked.

Jason looked back at Arnold. The young model's response seemed logical. He was even impressed by her tactfulness. He didn't know she had it in her to be so wry.

Arnold popped open his eyes and said, "Well, how 'bout I sit over in a corner chair, and act as if I'm not here?"

Jason didn't like that idea at all. Not only would the publisher's presence be distracting, but he would no longer be able to enjoy the privacy of the shoot. What would happen to the open and playful candor he had established with his muse?

Fuck! Jason cursed. He could not allow himself to passively accept the invasion of his professional space, whether the publisher was paying him handsomely for the job or not. As a rising photographer in the world of images and trustful relationships, Jason had the normal ego that any young man in his position would have. So he declined his boss's idea before Gabrielle could respond.

"You know, I just don't think that, ah…that's a good idea. I mean, we still have a lot more to do here. And my shoots tend to move a lot faster with less people in the room. Especially in an intimate setting like this."

Arnold heard the word "intimate" and became immediately alarmed.

"Intimate," he repeated. "This here is a professional shoot, Jason. She knows what she needs to do. You photographers get a little too personal about this stuff sometimes. So just keep snapping her pictures, and I promise not to bother you."

You're already fucking bothering me! Jason snapped to himself. However, the publisher had strolled into the room and taken a seat in the lounge chair anyway.

As a last resort, Jason asked, "Well, how does *she* feel about it?" He made it clear through his rigid stance that he would not continue the shoot until they were all in agreement inside of the room. And if they were not, then the intruding publisher would be kindly asked to leave.

Suddenly, all eyes shifted toward the naked young model on the bed. When the publisher considered how seductively his young, handsome, and dreadlocked cameraman had convinced the young woman to pose for him, he became more adamant to hang around. The scene even turned him on. That was his intention for popping up on them in the first place, to get a rise out of it all.

Gabrielle looked into the eyes of both men separately; first the young, talented photographer she had been assigned to work with, and then into the eyes of the sly, old publisher who was paying her. And she was forced to choose her loyalty.

She quickly shrugged. "Well, I don't really mind. I mean, he's gonna see the naked pictures of me to choose from anyway. So like, what's the point in the argument? Let's just, umm, do what we need to do and get it over with."

It was a great answer for Arnold. He would now be able to watch. But for Jason, her answer amounted to torture. He could no longer speak to the young alluring model with the open rapport that they had established. He also agreed to speed up the pace of the assignment, with a drastic change in his attitude. "Okay, well, we're about done with the bed scene. So let's get a few more shots and move on."

Gabrielle looked confused. "Are you sure?"

The bed scenes hadn't seemed that complete before the boss had suddenly shown up.

Arnold caught on to his young photographer's haste.

"Hey, man, again, I'm not even here in the room with you guys. So just do everything you would normally do," he insisted.

Jason took a deep breath and ignored him. With the publisher sitting there inside the damn room, he *couldn't* act normal. He couldn't make believe that the motherfucker wasn't there. He was no damn actor!

Jason shook it off and focused to get the final shot that he wanted.

"Okay, ah…could you lift your behind up enough so I can see it behind your head."

Gabrielle laughed the same as she had before Arnold had entered the room with them. So she was obviously not disturbed by the publisher's presence.

"You mean like *this*?" She raised her ass higher than what he needed.

Jason checked his view and shook his head. "No, bring it back down three inches." He waited for her to position her beautiful ass at the right height before he stopped her. "Okay, right there."

While he snapped the desired shots of Gabrielle's seduction with his camera, he could see Arnold Whittingham Jr. smiling his ass off through his peripheral vision.

This motherfucker's getting off in here! he told himself. But hadn't he been getting off with his own fantasies before the boss had shown up? And wouldn't the enticing resort pictures lead to other men having their fantasies?

They were all in the same profession together, the profession of magazine illusions. And it was Jason's job to create the strongest images for everyone. So he calmed down and decided to ignore the distraction.

"Don't you want to, umm, get like some overhead shots closer to the bed? You know, like, some close-ups?" Gabrielle asked him.

Jason paused. Despite what it looked like at the moment, the magazine was not X-rated, and they were not shooting pornography. He had framed every one of her pictures inside the calculated angles of the room, and he had captured every detail of value that surrounded her. He shook off the idea.

"No, the close-ups wouldn't pick up any parts of the room. I mean, we *do* want to shoot your naked tease, but we don't want it to be that obvious," he explained. "These shots are all about the allure of a naked woman in an expensive hotel room."

Arnold tried to force himself not to comment, but he couldn't hold his tongue.

"Aw, come on, Jason, let the girl have a little fun. If she wants to shoot a couple of close-ups in here, then let her do it. I'm still paying for it, right?"

The photographer looked as his boss with ill intent. *Yeah, I knew this shit wasn't gonna work.*

"I thought you told me you wouldn't say anything," he cracked.

Gabrielle laughed it off to ease the tension inside the room before Arnold could respond. "You know he can't sit over there and not say anything. That's a big lie."

Jason paused and considered it.

"Okay, so...if you're not gonna allow me to do my job in here, then..."

He needed some new parameters for what the hell was going on. Was he supposed to veer off course to satisfy whatever they wanted him to shoot, instead of fulfilling his original assignment?

Arnold told him, "Nah, you're still doing your job, Jason, just loosen up a bit. Learn to have a little fun with it. You're always so serious all the time."

Gabrielle giggled. "I know he is. I was telling him that earlier. He took a whole hour to tell me to take my clothes off," she teased.

Arnold said, "A whole *hour*?"

I took less than ten minutes to get this girl's clothes off, Arnold noted to himself in silence. *Maybe Jason doesn't really like women. Maybe he wants another man in here with his clothes off,* he thought distastefully.

"I was trying to focus on my assignment," Jason alluded. "I didn't think the shoot was all about her being naked. I thought it was all about the *idea* of a romantic getaway."

"It *is* about a romantic getaway," Arnold argued, "but have some fun while you're doing it."

Jason sized up the beautiful, naked model on the red satin bed sheets and thought about what kind of fun he would *prefer* to have with her, had he allowed himself to be unprofessional.

"Well, how much fun do you want me to have with her?" he asked his boss sarcastically. "Because she surely looks like a whole lot of fun from here. But at the end of this shoot, I'm quite sure you expect me to deliver pictures that we can actually *use* in the magazine. But while you remain *here*, we seem to be getting away from that."

"Oh, no, we're gonna get all the pictures we need, Jason. She's willing to do it. So don't even worry your long hair with that," Arnold addressed him. Then he stood up from his chair abruptly. "As a matter of fact, you go ahead and take a break for a while. You seem to be a little tense. So go ahead and take a smoke or something."

Jason couldn't believe his ears. He looked over at his boss, then back to the young model on the bed, who seemed to find it all humorous. She was still fucking giggling.

Okay, what the hell is wrong with her? Is she liking this shit or what? Jason questioned. *Is she fucking him?*

All of the clues were pointing in that direction. How else could a young, naked model feel so comfortable around the boss? Jason failed to believe she could be that much of a sociable airhead. She had a method to her madness. *All* models did.

Jason said, "A smoke? I'm right in the middle of things."

"You *were* in the middle of things. But you go on and take a break now. You're still on the clock, and I *am* paying you. So don't worry about it."

Jason looked over at the naked Gabrielle again.

"You want me to wait here while you get dressed?"

She paused and was unsure how she wanted to respond.

Arnold spoke up for her. "For what? She can put the robe back on, but she still has pictures to take. I want to talk to her about how her day went so far. And by the time you loosen up and take your smoke, you guys'll both be able to jump back in to it and get everything done. Hell, I'll even leave you two back alone in here. I gotta get back home to my wife anyway," he added.

Jason gave Gabrielle one last look before he felt comfortable enough to walk out.

"You sure you okay?"

She grinned. "I can handle myself."

Then she moved to gather her robe from the floor beside the bed.

Fuck it! I could use a smoke after this shit, Jason admitted. *They must think I'm a fool in here. And if anything unethical happens to her while I'm gone, that's all on her.*

"All right. I'ma go and take me a smoke then," he told them both.

As soon as the photographer left out the door, Arnold walked over and peeped out the keyhole before he locked it.

Gabrielle eyed the sly, old publisher from the bed before she laughed at him.

"That's the same thing he did," she revealed. "Men are crazy."

"What do you mean, that's the same thing he did? He was listening for me at the door?" Arnold asked as he made his way back to the bed.

"He had to find out who it was before he opened it."

"So, he was standing behind the door before he opened it?"

She nodded, looking as beautiful and innocent as she had been when he had first met her in downtown Minneapolis. She was a waitress at a Greek restaurant while attending classes at a community college. Arnold asked her if she had ever modeled and handed her a business card for his magazine. And the rest was *their*-story. The enlivened publisher had been sneaking romps with the young and willing trinket ever since.

Arnold shook his head and unloosened his belt buckle as he approached her on the bed. "I couldn't wait to get him out of here. You look absolutely *edible* on this bed."

"I am." She then turned to face him and spread her long, cinnamon legs wide to receive whatever he planned to offer.

The handsome, old publisher climbed onto the canopy bed with her and went to work, face first, while still fully clothed. Gabrielle enjoyed his vibrant tongue inside of her and reached for the stars with her hands, while wrapping her legs around his back.

"You gon' make me mess up the sheets, Arnie. Get a towel to put under me," she begged.

He ignored her and continued to lap up her sweet juices, while tickling her shaved pussy with his thick mustache.

"I'll get a towel, all right; once I start the next course of this meal." He then pulled his dress pants and boxers down to reveal a hardened penis.

Gabrielle looked below at his hairy, brown crotch.

"I know you better get a towel for that. We'll mess the sheets *all* up."

Arnold stood up from the bed with his pants and underwear dangling around his ankles. "I'm going already," he told her. He shuffled his way to the bathroom, loving his life, and grabbed an extra thick, white towel.

Gabrielle watched his hairy ass and giggled. "Have you ever thought about shaving?"

Arnold shuffled back toward the bed with a towel and his hard-on. "For what? I'm not a damn model. I got hair on my ass for a reason. It keeps me warm at night. And ain't nobody going back there but my doctor."

"So, your doctor gives it to you up the ass?" Gabrielle teased.

Arnold stopped the joking and gave her a serious stare-down. "Hey, easy now," he warned her. "I'm not one of these boys out here chasing you around. I pay the *bills* up in this motherfucker."

Gabrielle nodded to him submissively. "Yes, you do, baby." She lifted her ass enough so he could slide the towel under her.

"Now don't you tell Jason I'm fucking you, you hear me? I don't want that boy getting too jealous. He seems pretty protective of you."

As Arnold went about his business, Gabrielle took the index finger of his right hand into her mouth and began to suck it like a pacifier.

"Mmmph, mmmph, mmmph…" she moaned.

The publisher poured it on her. And with her three-year shot of Norplant that he had paid for, he could feel her sweet, raw and dedicated pussy without having to worry about pregnancy.

God bless America, he told himself as he worked his hips into the young model's pleasure spot. *Damn, it's good to be a rich man!*

Outside the door of the hotel suite, Jason Polk had walked down the hallway and doubled back just in time to satisfy his suspicions. And he had heard enough. Once it got deadly quiet inside the room, he didn't need to be a rocket scientist to figure out what was going on in there.

He nodded to himself and mumbled, "Okay…fuck 'em both." Then he headed to the elevators to walk outside and catch a smoke.

"So the man is laying the pipe to her," he continued to mumble, while awaiting the elevator's arrival at the penthouse level. "Oh well. Somebody has to fuck her."

But they could at least do this shit somewhere else and not on my time and professional space, he reasoned. *And at least now I know this damn girl ain't innocent. None of them are innocent in this business.*

He reminded himself for the twentieth time to remain professional, and not to get too involved with any heartbreaking models that he worked with.

When Jason returned to the room, nearly an hour later, Arnold let him into the suite. He was neatly dressed as if nothing had happened.

"That was a long-ass smoke, Mr. Cameraman. I guess you had a lot on your mind out there," he noted.

Jason smiled it off. "Well, you told me to take a break, right? So that's what I did."

He was forcing himself to take the high road and remain professional.

Arnold nodded. "Well, let me go on and get out of your hair," he told his dutiful photographer. Then he looked back to Gabrielle. She was all wrapped up in her golden robe on the bed, just as she was when Jason had started the shoot that evening.

"You two have a good time and finish up what you need for the shoot in here," the boss told her. He looked back to Jason and added, "I'm sorry for disturbing you."

Jason nodded and thought, *Yeah, save it for the birds.*

When Arnold left them alone inside the room again, the flirtations between the photographer and model were no longer the same.

"So, where were we?" Gabrielle asked him. She attempted to start over where they had left off. But her energy seemed forced now, with a contrived smile. Or at least that's how Jason read it. Since her innocence had been foiled, he had no more patience with her. It was only a job now.

"All right, well, we don't have much time left before we end up in here all night. So let's just undo the robe and take a walk around the room to see what jumps out at us."

Gabrielle stared at him from the bed and hesitated as if she were awaiting a punch line. But when Jason detached his camera from the tripod to carry it around the room with him, she got the point. The man was all business now. His pleasure had been taken away.

At his private studio on the east side of Detroit, Jason developed the film from his five-hour shoot with Gabrielle in his small darkroom. He was still impressed with how photogenic she was.

"Damn, she photographs well!" he exclaimed. "And she doesn't even know what the hell she's doing yet."

He figured his boss had found himself a winner in more ways than one. Nearly every picture of her looked good. So he began to separate the shots with the best stories. And his pants began to harden during the process.

"Damn, that's never happened before," he told himself. He rubbed his hard-on along the length of his jeans. "I guess you're trying to tell me something. Are you the one?" he spoke to Gabrielle through her dozens of developed pictures.

He continued to rub his hard-on and sifted through the photos until he could no longer take it. He took a walk to his small bathroom and washed his hands in the sink, before pulling his pants and drawers down to masturbate with a glob of hand lotion.

"Are you the one to drive me crazy?" he asked himself as he worked his manhood. "But first, we gotta get rid of the boss. You'll get rid of him for me, *won't you*? You'll do that for me, *right?*" he asked while he jerked himself.

Right as he reached the point of climax, his cell phone rang.

Jason looked down at the number on the phone that was attached to his pants. He grimaced.

"What the hell do you want this fast?" he questioned, reading Arnold Whittingham Jr.'s number. "I'm still working on this shit."

He figured he'd call the publisher back as soon as he finished his business of fantasizing about Gabrielle.

"*Aaahhhhhh*, that's the way it's supposed to *feel*, right *there*," he expressed as he aimed his cum into the open toilet.

He squeezed it all out and wiped himself off before he washed and dried his hands to call back his boss. "Hey, it's Jason. I'm still working on picking them all out."

"Good, so you're there at the studio then. We're on our way over," the publisher responded to him in haste.

Jason frowned. "*Who's* on the way over?"

"Gabrielle and me. She wanted to look at the raw pictures with us."

"Hi, Jason. It was fun working with you again yesterday," Gabrielle spoke into the cell phone on speaker mode.

Jason paused and thought it over. *They're setting me the hell up with this shit*, he told himself. *Now he wants to rub the shit in my face that he's fucking his star model*. Nevertheless, he was curious to see her again. And it wasn't as if he could stop them. They were already on their way to his studio.

"Aaahh…all right, I guess I'll see you guys when you get here."

As soon as he hung up the line, he snapped, "Shit! Now how do I prepare for this."

He decided to pull out his photography albums of his favorite models who could compete with Gabrielle. He wanted to show her that she was hardly the only fine fish in the sea. By knocking her off her high horse with the boss, maybe he would have his own shot at her in a few more months.

When Arnold and Gabrielle arrived in the black Bentley, Jason invited them in with his favorite model albums strategically placed around the room, where they could easily be flipped through.

Gabrielle wore a light-brown sheepskin coat, with a fur hood and matching boots.

"Nice winter gear," Jason told her. "That reminds me of a photo shoot I took of this hot French girl up in Canada a few years ago. I think I have her album over here somewhere."

Gabrielle responded like clockwork. "Oh yeah, let me see it."

Jason walked right over and grabbed it.

Arnold frowned at the idea. "Look, we don't have time for that right now. We need to look at *her* pictures from yesterday. We're on deadline here, remember?"

"Well, maybe I can invite you back over to look at some of my other work, when you have more time," Jason offered to Gabrielle alone.

"Okay, I would like that."

Arnold gave her a look, but held his thoughts. "All right, so what did you pick out for me to look at?"

Jason gave them the temporary album of Gabrielle's photos, and he didn't say a word. Arnold and the young model sat down on the sofa to view them.

"They all look so *good*," Gabrielle gushed. "That's good *work*."

She looked up from the book at Jason and smiled.

"That's what he gets paid the big bucks to do," Arnold commented.

"Yeah, she takes great pictures, too. So I can't take the credit for all of it."

Gabrielle smiled again. "Thank you."

Before they all got too comfortable inside the room, Arnold stood back up and was suddenly ready to leave. "All right, well, we'll get back to you on it."

Gabrielle didn't seem ready to leave yet. She remained seated with her coat off.

"Let me see some of your other photo albums."

As Jason moved to gather them for her, the boss responded, "For what?

We don't have any time for that. I thought you told me you were hungry."

"I mean, I am, but…"

Arnold cut her off, "Well, you better get this meal while you can *get it*. I have other things to do today."

Jason shrugged. "I can order her something to eat. There's plenty of res-taurants that make deliveries around here."

Arnold gave Jason a look suggesting he back off. He wanted to establish that Gabrielle was his playmate. There was no more need for secrecy.

"Look, now, the pretty lady said that she would accompany me to dinner this evening. Now if you don't mind, Mr. Cameraman…"

Gabrielle got the point and stood up to leave.

"Well, yeah, I did promise him, so maybe another time. Okay, Jason?"

Jason shrugged again. "Sure."

All he had was time. And he planned to work his way into her skin, little by little, like her pictures had worked their way into his skin. The young woman was toxic, and the erotic thoughts of her would not easily go away.

However, as the days turned to weeks, and the weeks turned into months, with Jason assigned to work with Gabrielle on several new projects, he grew increasingly testy about their relationship, mainly because he still could never seem to get close enough to touch her. The shit was driving him crazy, just as he had expected it would. Her developing photo album had quickly become his new favorite, and he was growing tired of jerking off to it. He wanted the real got' damned thing!

But as he began to grow sour toward her, Gabrielle was finally forced to ask him, "Jason, why have you been so…*snappy* toward me lately? I thought that we were becoming good *friends*. What's been up with you?"

She was even dropping the heavy-handed "friend" word on him, which was the kiss of death for any eager man with a crush on a woman. But it was no use. The old, sly boss, with his magazine, money and bullying attitude, had an obvious vise-lock *grip* on the damn girl. And Jason was finally fed up enough to say something to her about it. Her relationship with "Arnie" had not ended like he had expected it to *months* ago. So he let her have it. She had asked him for it.

"I mean, how long do you expect to sleep with him? Don't you think about having someone your own age? Wake up and smell the Starbucks. He has a *wife* and *four* grown kids! And you have no *future* with that man. I'm just being *real* here!"

At first, Gabrielle seemed shocked. She was speechless. But then she smiled, and her smile turned into a chuckle. Then her chuckle turned into a full laugh inside of Jason's studio. The photographer couldn't understand it.

"What the hell is so funny about that?" he asked.

"Well, for a minute there, it almost seemed like you were *jealous*."

The idea seemed alien to her, as if she had no clue that Jason may have desired her.

He looked at her perplexed. "As a matter of fact, I *am* jealous," he admitted. "I have to look at your pictures nearly every day now. And frankly, it's killing me, especially with how you seem to act so open to me all of the time. Just act like a normal fucking *model*, if you don't like me. You don't have to bullshit me with the niceties. That's only making things *worse*. So let's just keep it professional, if you wanna keep going off and fucking that man."

Gabrielle covered her face with both hands as if she were embarrassed by his outburst.

"Oh my *God!* Jason, I had no idea. *Honestly!*"

Jason calmed down a bit. Maybe he had overreacted. However, he had been waiting a long time for something to start off between them. And it never did.

"Yeah, I just needed to get my feelings out in the open. I'm sorry for going off on you like that."

Gabrielle nodded and reached out to hold his hands. She seemed totally understanding of him now. "Well, have you ever told him?"

Jason frowned. "Of course not. Why would I tell him that? You two have had something going for a while now. I figured it would fade away after awhile. I mean, it's all based on superficiality. It's only skin deep."

Gabrielle nodded, while still holding on to his hands.

"So, you figure that what you have for him is much deeper?"

Jason paused. "What?" He wasn't able to follow her logic. Maybe she had mixed up her words.

"You feel that you have something deeper for Arnold than just the skin, I mean."

Jason asked her, "What the hell are you talking about? I don't give a fuck about Arnold like that. I'm talking about *you*. This is just a *job* for me. And by now, this magazine is holding both of us back. You should be on your way to New York now, where the *real* modeling jobs are. *Both* of us. But you're letting this man play you cheaply."

Gabrielle thought about everything and broke away for a minute. She cleared her head. "Wait a minute. So you're not gay?"

"*WHAT*? What the hell would give you that impression? I seem *gay* to you? Is that why you haven't responded to me for this long?"

"Well, Arnold told me that you were gay."

Jason couldn't believe it. "Arnold's full of *shit*! And you fucking *believed* that? Why, because I'm not strutting around like some kind of *alpha male* with my chest all out, ala King Kong? Why, because I choose to *respect* the women I *work with*? It's my *job* to do that. I *have* to be professional when I shoot. But that doesn't make me fucking *gay*. I have *respect* for my trade and *discipline* as a *man!* Something that *asshole* 'Arnie' never had.

"But he fucking told you that I was *gay*?" he repeated. "No wonder you were so confused. You don't know the difference between a straight and a gay man? Do I have any *gay* tendencies?"

"Well, he told me that *a lot* of men in the fashion industry are gay."

"And did he tell you that I broke off with my girlfriend in New York, right before I moved out here to Detroit? We were engaged to be married before I found out that she had cheated on me. So I broke the whole thing off and left. Did he tell you anything about *that?* He *knows* about it."

When Gabrielle failed to answer him, Jason shook his head at the whole fiasco. He shouted, "That MOTHERFUCKER! Fuck him! So this whole time he had you thinking that I was *gay*. That's unbelievable. But now you see exactly how *devious* that man is to get what he wants."

Gabrielle was speechless. She didn't know which way was up. She felt like running off to hide her shame.

"So, what are you gonna do now?"

"What do you *expect* me to do? I'ma tell him about himself. And fuck his magazine job, too! He can shove it up his ass, since he likes the *gay* talk. But I take that back, as being insensitive to gays. Because they don't appreciate *assholes* like him either."

Gabrielle thought about it and panicked. "Well, I don't want you to tell him that I told you that. I mean, let me figure out what to do. I can talk him into telling me the truth."

"And then what?"

"And then he'll be busted."

Jason shook it off. "Naw, that's not good enough. Something *extra* needs to happen to his ass. That man is just *foul*."

Gabrielle panicked again. Arnold Whittingham Jr. was still her meal ticket. She knew nothing about modeling in New York. She was still an amateur.

"Well, you're not gonna do anything to him, are you? I still have an event to go to with him tonight. So let me ask him about everything first. Okay? Let me handle it. *Please*," the young model begged him. She didn't know what else to do. She had to figure out how to hold things together between her photographer and her boss.

Jason calmed down again and agreed to it. He could see the dilemma Gabrielle was in. He needed more time to think about everything himself.

"All right. You go out with him again tonight, and you try and figure out why he told you that. But I *know* why he told you. He wanted to keep you away from me, and manipulate you at the same time. That's just what old men try to do to young women. They're *conniving!*"

Once Gabrielle left him alone with his thoughts at his studio, Jason figured there was no way possible for him to continue working for such an unscrupulous man.

"That's *terrible* to do that to *both* of us. I hope Gabby is smart enough to leave him alone now."

But if not, then I don't know what else to tell her, he mused. Then he heard a buzz at the studio's front door. He walked over to answer it, hoping to see that Gabrielle had returned to him, but she had not.

Jason looked through the peephole and spotted Jazmine Whitingham, Arnold's still fabulous wife of six years. She had a short, dynamic haircut that made her look all business, like the presidential class.

Uh-oh, the photographer warned himself. *Get ready for more drama.*

As soon as he opened his studio door to greet her, Jazmine demanded, "Where is he? He said he was working late to pick out photos for next month's magazine issue."

Jason smiled at the idea. He had had enough of covering for his boss. And it was the wrong damn night for it to happen.

"Ah, if you wanna believe that, I can probably tell you twenty other lies," he commented, while grinning.

Mrs. Whittingham walked in wearing a short, rabbit fur coat before the break of spring. "Well, I'm not here for any more *lies*; I'm here to find out the *truth*." She looked into his grinning face and added, "And what's so damn funny? I'd really like to know."

"I think everyone would like to know the truth from 'Arnie,' or as much as you can get from him," Jason responded.

"What is that supposed to mean?"

"It means exactly how it sounds. The man doesn't *tell you* the truth. He's been telling me about giving me a raise for *months* now."

"So where is he right now?"

Jason shrugged. "He didn't tell me."

Jazmine looked him over and considered him. She had no idea about Arnold's claim of Jason being gay. Mrs. Whittingham knew more of his *real* story. He was the consummate professional, and many of the models liked him for it.

"So, you have no idea when he'll be coming back?" she asked him.

Jason smirked. "Coming back where? He's never even *been* here today."

"So, he's out with *what's-her-name?*"

Jason paused. "Who's what's-her-name?"

Jazmine eyed him as if he should *know* better. "You know damn well who I'm talking about. *Gabrielle Kasey*," she confirmed. "I know his type. She's been all over the magazine these past several months."

So far, so good; Mrs. Whittingham was on point. Jason nodded to her.

"Have you asked him about her?"

"Of course I have. And he tells me the same damn thing: 'Don't be ridiculous, she's only a model.'"

Jason looked her over and wondered if she had ever been a model herself years ago. She was still hot as a grown and married woman. Hell, she was only thirty-three, and Arnold's *third* wife.

Rich men can buy all the finest women, he presumed.

He nodded to her and smiled again. But Jazmine considered him seriously.

"So, he's not coming back here then?" she repeated.

Jason paused, attempting to read where she was going with it.

"Ahh, you're not planning on waiting around here for him, are you? As you know already, the man likes to keep late nights."

"Good. Then maybe I should keep a late hour of my *own* for a change. What do you have to do tonight?" she asked.

Jason hesitated. He didn't have anything particular on his plate.

He shook his head. "Nothing. Tonight is one of my few rest nights."

Mrs. Whittingham began to take off her fur coat, revealing a physique that remained shapely in her off-white, cotton dress. The dress stopped at her sexy thighs.

Jason took it all in and thought, *Shit! The man's been leaving her unattended at home.* It looked as if the boss liked his cake *and* his pudding.

"So are you safe?" she asked him.

"Safe?"

"Yeah, are you clean from sexually transmitted diseases? I don't know what people have out here these days."

Jason considered it a peculiar question. Why was she asking him that?

"Yeah, I'm safe. I would be more concerned about your *husband* in that department than me."

She looked at his crotch. "Let me see it then."

"Excuse me."

"Let me see it. You said you're safe from diseases, right?"

Jason chuckled at her extreme forwardness.

"You just want me to drop my pants, like that, to prove that I'm *clean*."

"Well, if you are, then you should have no problem with it. You want me to show you *mine*?"

Jason was tempted to say yes, out of curiosity. Jazmine read his eyes, pulled her sheer stockings down with no panties, and kicked off her heels. Then she pulled up her dress to show him her goods.

Jason viewed her well-groomed pussy and tight abs and was stuck in his stance. Instead of looking away, he stared at it, dumbfounded. He eyed her private parts in amazement; he could feel himself getting excited.

"Okay, so let me see yours," she challenged him.

Jason remained stunned. Then he snapped himself out of his daze. "Oh, ah…" He didn't know what to say. It was either put up or shut up. So he pulled at his belt buckle and tugged his jeans and drawers down for his boss's wife to view his hard dick.

"Well, look who's excited," she teased and giggled. "That's a good-looking *dick*, too, without all the extra hair everywhere. I swear, I must've *choked* on a *ton* of hair from Arnold. But that looks like a *clean* suck on you. I'm really gonna enjoy this."

Jason's eyes stretched wide while he stood there in frozen apprehension.

Is she crazy or what? he asked himself. But he had not bothered to pull his pants back up.

Jazmine took a seat on his sofa and called for him.

"Don't just stand there looking stupid with a hard dick. Bring it on over here."

The photographer shuffled forward in her direction, with his pants hanging down around his ankles. He felt ridiculous.

Now this is some wild shit right here, he told himself. But he figured his boss *deserved* it. When Mrs. Whittingham secured his rock-hard dick in her right hand and kissed it with her soft lips, he had no intention of stopping whatever she planned to do with it unless it hurt him.

"Aw, yeah, this is perfect," she told him. Her soft kisses on his penis became small sucks at the head.

"Oooh," Jason squealed with his hands forward. He didn't know what to do with them. Did he push her head further down on him? Did he grab her by the back of her cranium to anchor himself? All he knew was that it felt *great*, and he wanted *more* of it.

He inched forward and elevated on his toes to feel more of her soft lips gliding up and down on his penis. But she stopped his forward lean by pushing him backward.

She looked up into his pleading eyes and smiled. "I know what you want. And you're gonna get it, too. *All* of it. Just be patient. Okay?"

Jason nodded like a child to his mother, and he couldn't wait for the boss's wife to continue sucking on his hard and throbbing dick.

Jazmine started up again slowly, and she pushed her mouth further down on him until Jason could feel an urgent volcano rising from the back of his toes.

"Mmm-hmm," she mumbled as she sucked him. She knew exactly what she was doing and how much the young man was enjoying it.

Jason began to tighten up and grow tense as he felt the mounting explosion about to release itself.

Is she gonna stop or what? he pondered, as he inched closer and closer to a climax. It felt much better than masturbation; that was for sure. He only wondered what she intended to do with his powerful skeet once it came.

Is she gonna catch it in her hands? Or is she gonna have me squirting all around the fucking room?

He figured they would make a mess of his studio. But there was no way in hell he was planning on stopping her to run to the bathroom for a towel. It was too late for that.

So he closed his eyes and allowed his cum to squirt free, without caring where it went. And to his sweet surprise, Jazmine tightened her lips around his pulsating penis and moaned, while he released himself into the security of her mouth.

"Mmmm-hmmm," she moaned as she steadied his release to her with both of her hands.

"Oooohhh," Jason cried out in jubilee. She was actually swallowing his spurting cum.

SHE'S INCREDIBLE! SHE'S INCREDIBLE! he marveled of her dick-sucking skills.

When the boss's wife finally released her mouth from his satisfied explosion, she said, "I told you I know what you want. Didn't I?"

Jason nodded and giggled like a girl. He couldn't help himself.

Jazmine stood up and spotted his refrigerator in the corner of the large room.

"You have any Coke or Pepsi in that thing?"

"Pepsi," he answered.

"Perfect. I'll get you one, too. 'Cause after you drink it, and recuperate for a minute, I want you to hit it from the back." She made it sound as if they were about to take a basic walk in the park somewhere.

Jason was still tickled by it all. He grinned. "Okay."

You're the boss, he told himself. *Or his wife,* he added. That thought made him smile even harder. And when Jazmine bent over the back of his sofa, less than thirty minutes later, he smiled the whole time, while she demanded him to fuck her harder. She was sick and tired of her old man's bullshit. And so was Jason. So her wish was his command—*gladly.*

————

HOT JAZZ, COOL JAZZ

SEAN ALSTON

You know, I usually don't go out on these double-date deals. That's not really my style. I'm more of a solo man who likes to work his own magic at his own pace with a woman. So going to The Revue in D.C.'s renovated U Street corridor with Alonzo and two new women was a little off the radar for me.

"Come on, S, it'll be fun, man. Let's do something different for a change. And I'll let *you* choose the place."

Everything "different" is fun for L, like all the different women he manages to date on any given weekend. But at least I got to choose where we went.

We arrived at The Revue a little late, after waiting for Alonzo and these two new women of his to find a parking spot. By the time they found one, it was after nine and the long line traveled down the sidewalk to the corner of Thirteenth Street.

Immediately, L began to complain about it. "Hey, S, you don't know nobody up in here, man? I thought this was your regular spot. Let them know who you are?"

Letting people *know* who you are was what Alonzo Bradshaw was known for. His marketing company, A.B.C. Promotions, made sure of it. "A.B.C. you at the show," was his tagline for everything. Although the line was definitely corny, it seemed to work, so he kept right on using it.

Anyway, I was busy trying to converse with the two young ladies he had invited out for the evening. To L's credit, both women were on point; a nine and an eight. The only reason the eight had slipped a point was because of her black-and-gold, two-piece dress, which was a little too revealing in the cleavage department. The dress also had a long split right up the middle.

That was a little too much attention for me. She looked to be broadcasting an open freeway between her legs. So I told myself that I'd let L handle her, while I dealt with her more tactful girlfriend in the peach wraparound. Their names were Catherine and Carol, respectively. And I was going for Carol.

I told L, "It's all right, man. We get to stand out here and socialize before we get inside and get drowned out by the music."

Catherine said, "Well, I need to get my drink on. And it's a little chilly out here, too. Do they at least let you go in for the bar?"

I could understand her being chilly with the shit she had chosen to wear that night. She was letting the draft come through from the top *and* from the bottom of her two-piece.

"Yeah, man, let me go talk to somebody about this," L announced as he walked to the front of the line.

We were both dressed in our usual grown-men gear, with dress slacks, fine shoes, button-up shirts, sports jackets and no ties.

"Are you chilly, too?" I asked Carol. She had these light-colored eyes that glimmered in the dark like a cat's.

She shrugged. "No, not really. I mean, I can wait. We *were* running kind of late."

Now that's my kind of woman. She was taking full responsibility for their tardiness instead of bitching about the outside chill or the wait. I even felt like placing my jacket around her shoulders to warm her up, but without L there to do the same with her friend, I didn't want to single anyone out.

The next thing we knew, Alonzo had found one of the doormen that he knew from the clubs in D.C., and he got us pulled right to the front of the line.

"Well, it's about *time*," Catherine grumbled as we headed to the front.

"Well, we've been waiting here, *too*," a blonde-haired white woman spoke up from the long line.

She had a point, but it didn't matter. The pecking order was in effect, and we were ready to walk in ahead of her, using the VIP status that L had gotten used to around the District.

"Don't worry, you'll get in soon. And get yourself a Bailey's Irish Cream when you do, to thaw out that your nose of yours," Catherine stated to rub things in.

L thought the shit was funny. Even Carol grinned at it. But I thought it was rather tasteless, like that revealing dress the woman wore.

Then we walked in and had no seats available at the bar. The place was so packed that no matter where we stood, we were in someone's way. I didn't feel comfortable about that either. I hated for people to stand around in my way at performances.

"Hey, maybe we should, ah, find one of the empty corners of the room, or stand by the walls and out of the way of the crowd until we can find a table," I suggested to our group.

Carol was already nodding in agreement with me.

But L snapped, "Man, fuck that. They can *hear* the music; they don't have to *see* the damn band. This band ain't that good no way. I could have booked them for a hundred dollars at *my* last event. What's the name of this band again?"

"The Blackfoot Jazz Quintet."

"*Blackfoot?* What's that, somebody's Indian name? They look like Black and White *Guys* to me. That'd be a better name for them."

I hated whenever Alonzo fell into his theatrics of entertainment. On a regular basis, he would make an obnoxious asshole of himself for the benefit of those around him. But in this case, only Catherine was amused by it. He hadn't even listened to the band long enough to make a qualified assessment of them. And our standing around made some of the patrons grumble from their seats around us.

"Hey, ah, you guys have a seat somewhere?" a brown-haired white American man asked from a table of four behind us. He was on a double-date of his own. But I knew where that conversation was going before L even responded to him.

"If we had a *table*, we wouldn't be *standing* here," Catherine snapped. She beat Alonzo to the punch. She was a match made in heaven for him.

"Well, why would they even let you in here, if you can't sit down and out of the way of people who are trying to see the performance?" the man questioned.

I felt the same way myself. That's why I wasn't so excited to cut the line. Real VIPs had restricted areas for their arrival, where they would have the best seats in the house. But we were not established VIPs. That's why it was best for us to arrive earlier to alleviate any hassles. But since L had bullied his way in, we were now stuck in the middle of nowhere, like an extra thumb.

"We'll be moving as soon as they find us a table," Carol responded civilly. I was growing increasingly impressed with her tact.

"And what if they *don't*?" the second white man commented from their table. "Everyone's here to see the band tonight."

"Look, man, they'll find us a damn seat, all right. So calm down," Alonzo told him. My friend had never failed at being a consummate hothead.

I began to shake my head. I was hoping our double-date wouldn't turn into one of those very long nights where everything goes dramatically wrong.

Alonzo stopped and looked me in the eyes. "I know what you're thinking, man. But we just got here. And we're gonna have a good time tonight. I *promise*."

If push came to shove, I figured I could at least reconnect with Carol on my own. She seemed like the kind of woman I could get along with.

After a few more minutes, one of the hostesses had found us a seat near the restrooms.

"Aw, I hate sitting next to the bathrooms," Carol finally complained. "They should never have the restrooms so close to your food."

I didn't think they were that close to us myself. The restrooms were around the corner from us. But I did see her point. We were seated at the last table next to the hallway that *led* to the restrooms. So I was ready to hold out for a better table for her.

"Well, you two can sit on the side away from the hallway to free your mind from it," Alonzo stated in a compromise.

I could tell that Carol still didn't like it. She paused for a minute as if to speak her mind. But then she decided to go along with the program.

"All right, well...okay."

"Girl, cut that shit out," Alonzo told her. "That bathroom ain't hurting you. We all gotta *use it*, don't we? Or you don't *take* shits?"

Catherine broke up laughing. "Oh, yes she *do*, too. Her shit stink like everybody else's. And I know it *personally*."

I couldn't believe they were even going there.

Carol shook her head and ignored them.

"Anyway...excuse me, do you have any menus?" she addressed the waitress who was working nearby us.

"Oh, sure, I'll go get them. Four?"

"Yes."

As soon as we all got comfortable at our table, L started to grip Catherine up on their side as if they had known each other for years. "I'll just order some naked spare ribs with barbecue sauce on 'em," he joked, while grabbing her around her waistline.

Catherine chuckled and didn't budge to move from him. That made me feel a little awkward. I began to wonder how long he had known her.

"Looks like they have a pretty good menu here," Carol spoke up to break our silence.

Alonzo looked at the menu on his side of the table. "Shit, look at the prices on this thing. A damn *salad* is *eleven dollars*."

"Jazz music ain't cheap, baby," Catherine teased.

"Well, we should'a gone to a damn *soul food* music spot and paid eleven dollars for the whole damn *meal*, *plus* the lemonade."

"Not on *this* corridor, you won't," I argued. "Maybe ten, fifteen years ago, when they were redeveloping. But now these places have to pay serious rent to stay over here."

"Bullshit, that's just what they tell *you* to raise the *prices*. I deal with these kind of guys every day; you just write about 'em," L countered.

"So, what are you saying, you're not gonna pay for my food?" Catherine asked him with attitude.

Alonzo looked her in the face and grinned. "Naw, I'm paying; I'm just saying what it is."

"In other words, you're just sitting over there talking shit," I commented. "We know what these prices are. We're grown-ass men. We're not in college anymore."

L looked over at me and smiled. He nodded. "All right. Order what you want, and my grown-ass friend over here is gonna pay for it." Then he laughed again.

That guy was a riot. Even Carol smiled at him.

She added, "So, I got the man with the *big* bucks then," and rubbed it in to Catherine.

"Yeah, whatever. As long as I'm not paying for my food in here."

Alonzo had the women engaged in the wrong conversation. They began to sound like food-grubbing, gold diggers. So I attempted to change the subject.

"Hey, man, this music ain't half bad. You should at least listen to the band before you judge them."

Everyone settled down at the table and paid more attention to the quintet on center stage. Then we had established a head-nodding groove that was more of my liking. I could even feel Carol's leg, tapping into mine under the table.

"All right, I could give this band two-hundred dollars," Alonzo joked.

Finally, Catherine looked at him more seriously. "You know what, you're starting to sound real *cheap* in here."

"Yeah, and cheap men keep money, too," he countered.

"And they also lose out on a lot of good women," Carol double-teamed him.

L looked over at me, but I planned to stay out of it. I shrugged and kept my mouth shut.

"Are you guys ready to order yet?" our waitress came over and asked us.

Catherine jumped right to it. "Yeah, we didn't even get a chance to order any drinks yet."

"Oh, I'm sorry. What would you like to drink?"

We all started to order our drinks, and Catherine started on the food.

"Give me the T-bone steak, well done, with a loaded potato."

The waitress looked at the rest of us to see if we all were ready to order.

Alonzo shrugged. "All right, give me the same thing. And bring out one of them eleven-dollar salads first with Italian dressing."

Carol and I weren't ready to order yet. So we just stuck with the drinks until the waitress made her way back around. And while we all waited, L began to dig into Catherine's ribs again.

"I told you I wanted these ribs barbecued, didn't I? What I order that steak for?"

Carol looked across the table with her cat eyes and seemed irritated. That made me realize that Alonzo *didn't* know them that well. But he was sure forcing the issue.

"You all right?" I asked Carol.

She turned to face me and smiled. She even patted my right thigh with her left hand under the table. "Yeah, I'm all right. And I think I'll order the chicken breast," she commented, flipping back through the menu with her free hand.

"The chicken breast, hunh?" L questioned her across the table.

"Yeah, the chicken breast," Carol repeated to him tartly. It looked as if he was working her nerves.

"I think I'll take the salmon," I spoke up to break some of the tension.

"The salmon, hunh?" L questioned again. Then he laughed. "So, we got a breast and a fish over there."

"And what are you trying to say?" Carol asked him.

"I'm not saying anything. *You* guys said it. I mean, that's what you ordered ain't it, a breast and a fish?"

"Well, there's no *fish* over here, baby," Carol huffed at him.

"But there's a couple of *breasts* over there."

"And there's a *dick* over there, in more ways than *one*," she snapped back at him.

"As long as you know it's over here," he countered.

"Hey, hey, hey, what the hell is all that?" Catherine finally asked them both.

Their back-and-forth volley had taken off so quickly that I didn't have a chance to respond to it.

"You sure have a way of words with women, my friend," I commented with sarcasm. Then I looked at Carol and asked, "You want me to change my fish to pasta?"

I was joking. She caught on to my humor and lightened up with a grin.

"I'm just saying, your guy's over there *insinuating* shit."

"Yeah, as long as you know what I got over here. And it's on *this* side of the table," he cracked.

"Wait a minute, what are you trying to say now?" I asked him.

"I already *said* what I'm trying to say. She *know* what I got over here."

He was obviously pulling out the dick-size game.

I said, "Yeah, well, like they say, the ones who talk the most feel that they *have* to. But I'm packing mine without all the extra fucking noise."

"Well, *excuuuse me*," Catherine growled. We all had a good laugh about it, but I wasn't trying to go there. Alonzo had forced my hand in the situation.

"So, what we gotta do, measure 'em out on the table?"

"Oh, shit," Catherine responded, instigating.

I couldn't believe we were even talking about that at a jazz club over dinner with two new women. But I could tell that L was loving that shit.

"Man, we're about to eat up in here," I told him.

He looked at Carol again. "Oh yeah, fish or chicken?"

Carol stopped and stared at him.

I caressed her by her arm. "He's tripping. This is why I like to go *solo*."

"Tell me about it," Carol grumbled.

I looked into her eyes. "All right, I will. Now if me and you were out together alone, I'd take you down to the waterfront, go dancing, look out at the moon, sip the finest wines, and say what was *really* on my mind."

L cut me off. "Aww, you corny-ass nigga. Listen to you."

"*Corny?*" I grilled. "Well, what the hell do you call 'A.B.C. you at the show'? Because I have to listen to *that* corny shit every other *week*."

"I call it a fucking moneymaker," he responded.

"On corny-ass events," I shot back.

"Oh, so now my events are *corny?*"

"If people respond to that corny-ass line, they *have* to be."

"Well, what about your corny-ass *columns* sometimes?"

"Look, it is what it is," I told him.

"And so is *my* shit."

"Ahh, boys, the drinks are here," Catherine told us as the waitress set down our four drinks with a grin.

Carol was all smiles as if she liked it all.

"Hey, I'm sorry about all that," I told her. L had me acting out of character.

But Carol shook it off. "No, you gotta say what you gotta say when you gotta say it."

Alonzo looked across the table and grunted, "Mmmph." Then he looked at me as if to say, *You better handle that shit, partner, before I do.*

I guess she must have turned him on with that line, because he took one sip of his drink and asked, "So, how do we all like our sex at this table, from the front or from the back? Because I hear that the back gets it in a lot deeper."

What could I do but shake my head and chuckle after he asked some shit like that?

Catherine said, "Damn, can I eat my *food* first? What's *wrong* with you?" He had even gone too far for *her* now.

"Just two drinks is all you need tonight, man, *Seriously*," I told my friend.

Alonzo ignored me and looked at Carol. "How many drinks are *you* gonna have?"

"As many as I *want*," she told him, and took a sip of hers. "I'm not driving, *Catherine* is."

Again, Alonzo looked at me and shook his head. I could read his mind. *This girl is hot, S.* And maybe she was. But you could never read all of a woman's intentions in just one night. Some women liked to test you and turn you down, once you jumped out too far in the wrong direction. So I continued to play it smart and patiently.

"I gotta go to the restroom," Catherine announced.

"Are you sure?" L asked her. He acted as if he didn't want to move to let her by.

"Yeah, I'm sure. I gotta go to the fuckin' bathroom," she snapped.

L shrugged and moved to stand up. "All right." When she walked by him, he pulled her back into him playfully. Catherine looked back at him with an evil eye.

L let her go and raised up both his palms to surrender. "My bad, I just had to test the Charmin for a minute."

He was really fucking up, man! And he wasn't even drunk yet.

Then he sat back down with Carol and me at the table.

"So, ah…y'all two like each other?" he asked us out of the blue.

Now he was putting us on the spot.

I looked at Carol. "You introduced me to a good girl. I give her two thumbs up and a high-five." I wasn't gonna wait to comment on that at all.

She smiled at me. "Thank you." Then she squeezed my arm.

Alonzo shook his head across the table again. "Man…" He started to say something and stopped. "Let me get another drink in here." He stood up from the table and walked back toward the bar area. Carol and I both watched him.

"He didn't want to order another drink from here?" she asked me.

I shrugged. "I guess not." And I guessed that Alonzo wasn't having as much fun anymore. He seemed to be more preoccupied with Carol now than with Catherine. But Carol was with me. Or *was* she?

"So, what do you, ah…think about what he asked us?" I questioned.

Carol smiled at me. "What, about us liking each other?"

"Yeah." I had already said *my* part. She was a lady worth the effort.

Carol continued to grin. "We get along."

For the life of me, I didn't quite like how that sounded. But I decided to leave it alone. I had just met the woman. What more could I expect her to say in only a few hours?

"Okay. I can take that…I guess."

I just *had* to add that last *part*, didn't I? And I knew it was a mistake as soon as I said it. It sounded unsatisfied and whiny.

Carol jumped right on it. "You *guess?*"

"Well, it just doesn't sound like, ah…too committed of an answer, that's all."

She frowned. "*Committed?* I mean, I'm just now *meeting* you. How do you expect me to commit to something already?"

I was sorry I had even asked her. L had influenced me in the wrong way. So I shook it off and grumbled, "All right."

"All right, what?" she pressed me.

"All right, I'll leave it alone," I snapped. I didn't want to talk about the shit anymore. It was the wrong line of questioning.

Catherine joined us at the table and spotted Alonzo over at the bar with a second drink in his hand. "Why is he over there? He wanted to get a closer look at the band?"

No, he just doesn't like your ass anymore, I thought of telling her. *He likes your girlfriend now. And I'm starting NOT to like her.*

As a grown man about to reach my thirties, I could sense when a woman was a hard catch and a possible tease. So once I heard her bullshit answer, I had that vibe about Carol. She wanted things on *her* terms, and I didn't like the prospect of that. She seemed spoiled by her options, like a lot of D.C./Maryland women. They made it seem like the world revolved around them instead of the sun. I didn't realize that until I started dating women from other places.

"Why are you all quiet over there?" Catherine asked me.

"Oh, I'm just listening to the music," I lied.

Carol grinned. "Whatever. He's mad now because I won't *commit* to liking him yet." She was egging me on now.

"Well, we just hanging out, kicking it," Catherine stated. "Guys get too fucking *serious* out here."

That was *it* for me. I was ready to leave those ungrateful bitches with the *check* and see how serious *they* got. Then the food arrived.

"It's about *time*," Catherine stated.

"Well, we wanted to bring it all out together," our waitress explained.

"*Why*? We didn't *order* together. They ordered *way* later than we did," Catherine reminded her.

"Um, well, you know, we figured it'd be *easier* to bring it all out on one tray."

"Yeah, and now my damn steak and potato is probably *cold*, while their shit is *hot*," Catherine continued whining.

"Ahh, no, we kept it pretty hot, actually," our waitress countered.

Alonzo popped back over to the table. "I see the food is ready? Right on time, too. I'm ready to eat a *horse* in here. But the cow'll do for now."

"As long as it ain't *fish* and *breasts*, hunh?" Catherine teased him, sparking the conversation back up again.

L shrugged. "Nah, I'd eat some fish and breasts if I *had* to. But I ordered *steak* tonight. So I'm gon' eat *that*."

I no longer had anything to say about it. As far as I was concerned, it was a wasted night with wasted money on the table. I didn't even have an appetite anymore. All I could think about was how women could get a free-ass dinner before leaving a man hanging. I could feel it before the dinner was even finished. The only thing I could do was waste *more* money trying harder to chase the bitch. So I figured that maybe I should take one for the team and let Alonzo have her back. They were both his women anyway.

"Hey, man, what you thinking about over there?" he asked me on cue.

I was considering leaving the place and calling up a few women of my own before it got too late. One bird in the hand is better than two in a bush, right?

But before I could answer, I could feel Carol staring at me. I turned to face her. "What, you wanna answer that for me?" I was in a grown man's attitudinal, survival mode. It was the same reason why Alonzo had to step away from the table for a minute. When your ego can't take the shit, you step away to recuperate.

Carol shook her head and read my emotional manhood. "Guy's egos are so damn *fragile* sometimes. I can't *stand* that. I mean, be a fucking *man* about it!"

L and I looked at each other and laughed over our food to break the tension. The woman was really challenging us like suckers. And I thought that she was the *tactful* one.

L asked me, "What the hell happened when I left?"

Carol continued to rub it in on me. "He got his little *feelings* hurt."

I shook my head and kept grinning. What else could I do? But then I got real frank on her. I said, "You know what, you're the kind of woman who *really* makes a man wanna..." And I stopped it right there.

Everyone at the table started laughing but me. I was too serious to laugh. Carol was the kind of deceiving woman who made a guy want to fuck her, while standing up against a brick wall in an alleyway somewhere. She made you want to be *violent* with her!

"Well, say what you wanna say then," she teased me.

Now I could see why Alonzo had walked away from her.

I opened my mouth and said, "You make a man really wanna fuck you *hard*." She had *asked* me for it, right?

They all broke out laughing again. Even I chuckled. But I didn't want to go there.

Carol looked at me. "You *wish*."

"You wish I'd bend your ass over *backwards*, too," I told her.

I didn't know what had gotten into me, but it was all coming out in a rush. That cat-eyed woman was like an beautiful *devil*, I *swear* to you.

L joked, "Yo, dog, slow down over there. We just met these girls."

The joke was all on me now. I was the fool who had lost his cool at the dinner table.

"She asked for me it, man. You heard her."

I was embarrassed by it, but it felt good, to be honest. You had to say what you had to say sometimes. Then I got back to eating my salmon to ease the edge I felt at the table.

"Now he's eating the fish again, hunh?" Catherine teased me.

I kept eating my food and ignored them all. And Alonzo was laughing his ass off. That was his kind of "fun"; unadulterated caveman shit. He couldn't eat his food or drink without laughing more.

"Yeah, I feel you, man," he uttered through his giggles.

"You feel him *how*?" Catherine asked him. She had long been forgotten about that evening. Not even her cleavage or freeway dress could enhance her lack of allure that night. Her girlfriend had bested her for *both* of us.

"I feel what he's taking about," L answered.

Catherine looked across the table at Carol.

Carol was still smiling, seemingly amused by it all.

All of a sudden, Catherine asked her, "Bitch, what's so damn *funny?*"

Carol paused. She seeemed surprised by her friend's outburst. Then she snapped, "Whatever the hell I *think* is funny."

"So, you were obviously out here trying to be all *cute* again," Catherine presumed.

"Oh, I don't *have* to try. I *am* cute. It's *your* bitch-ass who needs all the *attention*. Just look at how you *dress*," she countered.

At first, I thought they were engaged in rough girlfriend talk, like when black men call each other *nigga*. But once Catherine tried to reach across the table and grab Carol by her hair, that idea was off.

"Oh, shit," L responded. He grabbed Catherine back across the table. I moved my hands to protect Carol from her friend as well. But that all seemed to make Catherine more adamant to get at her.

"*Bitch*, I'm tired of your *fucking ass, showing off!*" Catherine shouted across the table.

"Well, why don't you stop *calling* me up to go out with your ass, and learn to get a *real* personality?" Carol shouted back. "Then maybe all your *niggas'll* stop trying to *get at me* so much!"

The shit was loud and embarrassing at that point. People were starting to turn away from the music and look back at our table. Then the bouncers rushed over.

"Hey, what's going on over here?" one asked.

"Oh, we got it," L told them. He stood Catherine up to pull her away.

"Get the fuck off me!" she cursed at him. "If you want that bitch, too, then go get her then!"

Alonzo let her go as she turned and looked toward the exit. At least a *third* of the people inside the jazz club were watching *us* now.

Catherine turned back and hollered, "Have a nice night, *bitch!*"

"Yeah, *fuck you, too!*" Carol screamed with her middle finger up.

L and I were both shocked by it. We looked at each other and said, "Damn," in unison.

"I guess that's your *ride*," I commented to Carol.

She frowned and shrugged it off. "I know how to catch a fucking *cab*."

"Well, you don't have to do that, if you don't want," I told her. "I can drive you back home."

"I don't think my man would like that shit. In fact, I *know* he wouldn't."

Alonzo heard that and started chuckling. I wondered if he had known the shit all along.

"Well, how come you didn't say that *earlier*?" I asked.

She grabbed her purse from the table and snapped, "I didn't *need* to. We don't know each other like that."

"Oh, but I can pay for your damn *dinner* though, right?" I snapped back at her. I didn't understand the fairness of women sometimes.

But then she pulled out two twenty-dollar bills and threw them at me.

"*Here*, motherfucker! You satisfied now? Eat your fuckin' *fish* wit' it!"

I looked over at Alonzo, standing there staring, and he started laughing his ass off as Carol headed for the door.

I shook my head. "Man...don't you *ever* ask me to go on another *blind* double-date again in your *life!*" Then I tossed a fifty-dollar bill on the table with Carol's twenties.

L took all of the money off the table and placed a hundred-dollar bill down to pay for everything.

"Look, man, what do you want me to say?" he asked me. "I didn't know they had a *feud* like that. Women are *catty*, man. And homegirl even had catty *eyes*."

I started toward the door myself. That was one of my favorite spots to relax in. But someone else in there could write a column about *me* now.

"Yeah, you didn't help matters much by getting into it with her," I reminded Alonzo. He had started it all.

As we walked back out after the commotion, Carol was already jumping into a taxi, and Catherine was nowhere to be found.

Alonzo told me, "Look, man, it's just one of them nights, S. But it's *early*, man. Let's go do something else."

I frowned at him. "Are you *bugged*, man? I'm not going out somewhere else after *this*. I need to relax with people I already *know*. And I don't even think I know *you* sometimes."

I was already walking toward my car on V Street to leave.

L screamed across the street at me. "Come on, man, stop girlin'!"

I could still hear him laughing.

I immediately jumped on my cell phone and called a woman who really knew how to *act* with a man.

"Hey, Felicia, is it too late? It's Sean."

"No, I was just about to go out," she answered.

I looked at my watch. "At *midnight*, you just going out?"

She chuckled. "Well, I didn't feel like going to sleep yet. What are *you* doing?"

"I'm coming to see you," I told her. The adrenaline of the night had me all pumped up for it.

Felicia paused. "Umm…okay. Where are you?"

"I'm down on V Street. So I could hit your place on Connecticut in like, ten minutes. *Tops*."

She laughed. "You in a hurry?"

"Nah, I'm just, ah…tired of all this extra *commotion* for one night. So don't leave yet. I'll be there."

She paused again. "Oh…okay. I'll see you when you get here then."

"Now *that's* a fucking woman," I grinned and told myself as soon as I hung up her. Felicia was originally from Memphis, Tennessee, and she was a real *dime* piece, too.

ALONZO BRADSHAW

Naw, naw, *naw*, man, that ain't even how it *went*. First of all, S called *me up* asking what I was about to get into, because he was tired of sitting around in the house with his girl, Felicia. Well, she's not really his *girl*, but he fucks with her the most. He goes over there and plays chess, board games, cards, watches movies on DVD, and all other kinds of shit before he tightens her up. But he wanted to get out and do something else that night, because the girl is *boring* as hell. I mean, she look good and all that, but she's just a damn *homebody*. So I told him I had these two girlfriends I had met a week ago, and he said, "All right, let's do it."

So I told him he could pick the place, because I knew he would bitch about where I would want to take them, like to Hooters or the ESPN Zone. And this guy chooses a damn *jazz club* on U Street. Now, I don't mind the new U Street corridor, because that shit is happening now the way Georgetown used to be. But a *jazz club* with two new women? That's the kind of place you go with a woman you've already known for a while; because it's too laid-back for new conversations, you know? It ain't like the old jazz clubs up in Harlem where couples would throw down on the dance floor and really get to know each other. These new jazz clubs remind me of fucking museums. They lack *excitement* to me.

Anyway, we show up at this place called The Revue a little late, after waiting for these girls to park their car, and there's this long-ass line going all the way to the corner. Now I promote and throw parties in D.C., and I know everybody who works them, so I'm not standing in no damn lines. But this guy actually walks to the back of the line like he's a damn nobody. And I told his ass to let them know that he's a nationally syndicated columnist for the Gannett newspapers in there, and that he could put their spot on the map all over the country with just one article.

He tells me, "Nah, man, I'm a regular customer like everybody else." That's the way Sean is; he never tries to bring attention to himself.

But as I watch the damn line at this place, I can see that it's not moving, so there's no sense in us waiting there. Either we're gonna get in or we're not. Then I spotted my man Reggie Mack inside, working with security. So I called him out to talk to me.

"Hey, what's up, man? What can you do to get me in the bar?"

Reggie Mack owed from many prior occasions, so there wasn't even an argument.

He looked back inside and said, "Let me see what I can do. How many you got?"

"Four." And that was it. I called S and the two girls to the front of the line.

Now the girl Catherine, who I knew the best, was the loud type. So she walks to the front of the line and starts running her damn mouth.

"It's about *time*. It's chilly out here."

She was wearing this damn two-piece, black-and-gold outfit, looking like she wanted to fuck anybody who asked her that night.

Then she started beefing with the white couple at the front of the line.

"You'll get in soon. And make sure you order some Bailey's Irish Cream when you do to thaw your cold-ass nose off."

I thought the shit was funny myself. But I knew that S wouldn't want to deal with her. He doesn't like shit like that, especially around white folks. He thinks black people should always be on their best behavior. So I already knew to let him have her light-eyed girlfriend named Carol. She seemed a lot more civil for him. *And* she was fine! So I figured I'd take one for the team and let him have her. She was a little *thin* for my taste anyway. She was one of them slim, *classy* bitches.

So anyway, we go inside, and of course, we didn't have anywhere to sit yet, not even at the bar, and these white folks started tripping.

"Hey, guys, you're all in our way over here."

Catherine turned around and let this motherfucker have it, *quick*.

"Well, if we had a damn *seat*, we wouldn't *be* in your way. Unless you wanna give us *your* seat."

Then her girl Carol tried the civil approach. "We'll be moving out of your way as soon as we have a table."

S was backing down and shit. He started talking about, "Let's just hang in the corners of the room, or near the back walls until they find us something."

I tell you, man, Sean is my boy and all, but that nigga need to take some *swagger* pills every once and awhile. Because I wasn't standing against no fucking wall in there.

Then the second white boy at the table came off at Carol, like he had a personal beef with her or something.

"Well, what happens if they *don't* find you a table?"

I looked over to S to see if he was gonna speak up on that shit, and he seemed embarrassed by it. So *I* said something.

"Hey, man, calm your ass down. They gon' *find* us a damn table, all right."

That white boy ain't say *shit* to me. So Carol looked over and grinned at me. And my boy S was already losing his cool points with her.

Then they found us a table near the bathroom hallway, and Carol started talking about, "Aw, this is *nasty*. I *hate* being near restaurant bathrooms."

Now, we wasn't all *that* damn close to the bathrooms. Those bathrooms were way down the hallway. Carol was just trying to get some attention because S was *boring*, like his girl, *Felicia*. He acted like he didn't know what to say to this fine-ass girl. He tried to act way too cool sometimes. So I tried to spark shit up for him.

"Aw, cut it, girl. You know we all gotta use the bathroom. Or you don't *take* shits like that?"

I mean, I was only kicking the *truth*, right? Then Catherine jumped in on it.

"Oh, she takes *shits*. I've smelled them *personally*."

Now I wasn't trying to go *that* damn far with it. That shit sounded *foul, for real*. What kind of bitch smells another bitch's shits? But I was only trying to mix things up at the table a bit. A jazz club wasn't my kind of place to take these girls to begin with.

Well, Carol didn't like that shit. So she eyed us down across the table and started asking for the menu. Since this was a damn jazz club, instead of a sports bar, everything was overpriced on there. So I let everybody know.

"Damn, eleven dollars for a *garden* salad?"

But Sean jumped on me about that. "Look, man, we grown men in here. We're not college students at Maryland anymore. And these finer restaurants have to pay the rent."

He was always talking that grown-man, price-of-living shit, as if I didn't *know*. I knew we were both turning thirty soon. I was just trying to save us both some money by putting it in these girl's heads that it wasn't a free-for-all on *us* in there. We could've ended up spending a few hundred dollars in there, *easy*, and on some girls we barely *knew*.

So I told him, "That's bullshit, man. I know what all these guys have to pay around here. And they all raise the prices, claiming that high-rent shit. But if they're not getting a good deal on the property, then they're not gonna be in business long."

I knew a lot more about stretching a dollar and doing good business deals than what Sean knew. He was just a damn *writer*. So I forgave his ignorance on the issue. But the next thing I knew, he hauled off and called my marketing slogan *corny*.

"I said, *corny*? Sean, if the shit *works*, who gives a fuck if it's corny or not? 'A.B.C. you at the show' *works*. I don't say shit about your corny-ass *columns* sometimes. But some people think the shit is *good*."

Then he started calling my events corny. So we got into the shit for a minute, talking about who made what, and who was willing and able to pay more for shit.

That's when Carol said, "So, I got the man with the *big* bucks." She was fucking with her friend Catherine across the table.

The shit didn't faze me, because I made my own money on the regular, while S had to wait for a damn *paycheck* from the newspaper. And there were several times when I had to loan his ass money in between checks. But I didn't bring *that* shit up; we were *boys*!

Catherine finally chilled us all out when we got our drinks. "Ah, guys, can I get my drink on without getting a damn headache from all this unnecessary arguing?"

I mean, imagine the *nerve* of that loud-mouth bitch saying that? But I understood it. She wanted some attention, too. So I dropped the issue with S and squeezed up on her.

"My bad, lil' momma. Let's get these orders on. And I'll take me some barbecue spare ribs over here." I was teasing her in front of the waitress, and making her feel good.

Catherine smiled and said, "I'm ready to order my food." Then her ass went right ahead and ordered *steak*. Well, I wasn't gonna let her order more than me on *my* bill, so I ordered the same steak *and* a salad.

S looked like he was still confused on his side of the table. In the meantime, Carol looked over at me as if she was jealous that I was holding her girlfriend. And Sean basically didn't know what the hell to do with her. She was too *fast* for his slow ass.

So when they finally decided on what they wanted to eat, I started teasing them both to spark shit up at the table again. I mean, my boy *needed* it, man. His conversation was bone *dry*.

"So, y'all want *fish* and chicken *breasts*, hunh?" I fucked with them.

Then Carol gave me this evil-ass eye and said, "Well, I don't have no *fish* over here, baby." She was obviously defending the scent of her pussy.

And I can't even lie, man, that shit got me going. That girl had more spunk in her than what I thought. So I kept fucking with her.

"There's a *breast* over there though."

She came right back at me. "And there's a *dick* over *there*, *too*, and in more ways than *one*."

Shit! Fuck *Catherine*! That girl *Carol* had my dick hard. She had these cat eyes that just *did* something to you when she *stared*. So I looked at S to see if he was reading the shit right. He had a damn *tigress* sitting over there next to him, and I don't think he was ready to handle her.

So I said, "Well, as long as you know I *got* one over here. And it's on *this* side of the table."

Finally, Sean woke his dead ass up. "What are you trying to say, man?"

I was just making sure he knew what *time* it was. That damn girl had the *heat* up in there! I was ready to fuck her across the table myself, skinny or not. But she wasn't *that* thin, just wasn't as thick as her girl.

I told S, "I already *said* what I'm saying." That nigga needed to *recognize* what he had over there, before I took her ass from him. And Catherine didn't really have shit to say anyway. It was all about Carol now, for *both* of us.

Sean said, "Well, I'm holding mine over here, *too*. And you know what they say, the ones who talk more feel like they *need* to. But I'm packing strong over here *without* all the extra noise."

I actually liked that damn line. So I smiled and nodded at him. Carol looked all satisfied and shit across the table herself. And Catherine finally had something to say about it.

"Well, *excuse me*, big boy," she told Sean.

He was winning some cool points back. So then I got loose with the shit. I took a sip of my drink and asked, "So, how do we all like our sex, from the front or from the back? Because I hear that from the *back* gets you in a lot *deeper*."

I was sending my messages straight to Carol to let her know that I had a *lonnnng dick* over that table. And she smiled and chuckled at the shit. But I was fucking up the chemistry with Catherine with all that.

I peeped her looking across the table at Carol with one of them "bitch, cut it out looks." But Carol ignored her ass and kept smiling.

"Shit, can I at least eat my *food* before y'all start talking all this *extra* shit?" Catherine complained. She was mad because no one was fucking with *her*.

It was too late to lie at that point. I wasn't interested in Catherine. I wanted to fuck her girl Carol something *fierce*. Then S started talking about how many drinks I had, as if I was drunk, but I wasn't. I knew *exactly* what I was doing.

I watched Carol sip her down drink across the table, and I asked her how many drinks *she* planned to have that night.

"As many as I *want*. I'm not driving, *Catherine* is." Then she licked around her straw with her pink tongue.

Got' dammit! I looked back over at S, and this slow-game nigga didn't have a *clue*! That's when Catherine shoved me and said that she had to use the bathroom.

I at least tried to give the girl a hug to let her know that she was still a good-looking woman, and sexy and all that. But she broke from my arms in a silent tantrum. So I raised up my hands in surrender and let her go to the bathroom.

When I was all alone with my man and this tigress I had tried to hook him up with, I realized that I was getting in the way. We couldn't *both* fuck her. Or *could* we?

So I asked them both, "Are you two liking each other over there yet?"

I wasn't sure if Sean even liked the girl, since he was so damn quiet. Did she scare his ass off or what?

He said, "Hey, man, she's a nice catch. I give her a two thumbs up and a high-five."

Now you talk about sounding *corny*. That's the shit that came out my boy's *mouth*. At that point, I *knew* he wasn't gonna get any pussy from *her*. His game was mad *weak*. I even started to say something about it. But I changed my damn mind. I could still at least *hope* for my nigga, you know. So I nodded to them and left the table to get another drink from the bar, and to clear my head and listen to the music for a minute. You can't have every woman. But I was hoping that my man could somehow figure out that Carol was *hot*, and take advantage of that shit.

Nevertheless, when I returned to our table when the food arrived, it seemed like S had a falling-out with the girl. He didn't even want to look at her.

Catherine was back to talking shit about how late the food was, and how come we didn't receive our steaks first after ordering before them, and a bunch of other shit that nobody wanted to hear. She was all out the loop, and Sean and Carol got busy eating their food without another word.

So I asked S, "What are you thinking about over there, man?"

He turned and asked Carol to answer my question for him, and I realized that I was right. He had fucked something up as soon as I had left him alone at the table. But the truth was, he couldn't handle the damn girl. He was not in her league.

So she shook her and said, "Guys' egos are so damn *fragile*. I can't *stand* that. I mean, be a fucking *man* about it! If a girl don't *like you*, she don't *like you*."

God damn! I thought to myself. She was a much bigger and badder tigress than I even *imagined*. I felt sorry for my boy. But what could I do but laugh it off?

"Well, what happened after I left the table?" I joked.

"He got his little *feelings* hurt," Carol answered again. She was pouring *salt* in my man's *wounds*. That gave S no choice but to go hard on the girl. And that wasn't even his style.

He told her, "You know what, you're the kind a woman who really makes a man want to fuck you *hard*. And I *mean* that."

"Don't you *wish*," she teased him.

He said, "You wish I'd bend your ass over *backwards* across this table."

I started laughing my ass off. We were *all* laughing in there.

"Yo, slow down, man. We just met these girls," I joked again.

"She asked for me it, man."

And he was *right*. She *was* asking him for it. He just didn't know how to give it to her. But *I* did. Only I was being paired up with her damn *girlfriend*.

So we all killed the noise and started eating our food. Then out of the blue, Catherine opened her dumb-ass mouth and said to S, "Damn, you're tearing up that *fish*."

I started laughing again, not because of her tease, but because I knew how Sean thought. And if I know my man, he was already thinking about getting the hell out of there, wishing he had never come. Neither one of them girls were his type.

"I feel you, man," I told him. It was an inside joke. S was ready to eat and run and make it back to Felicia. That's what he always did when things didn't go his way. That girl was like his damn security blanket.

The next thing I knew, Catherine asked me, "You feel him *how?*"

I mean, nobody had been paying any damn mind to her. She didn't have much of a personality. Even S had more of a personality than *she* did. At least he knew who he *was* and what he wanted to do. But Catherine was confused, man, and dying to be held by somebody who could understand her rude ass.

I told her, "I feel what he's talking about. He's my *boy*. I know what's on his mind right now."

Catherine looked across the table at Carol again. She had been wanting to get at her all night. It was only a matter of time. And Carol was still smiling, having a good-ass time with the shit.

Finally, Catherine snapped at her. "Bitch, what's so damn *funny?*"

"Whatever the hell I *think* is funny."

"Unh-hunh, you out here trying to be *cute* again."

"Oh, I don't have to *try* to be *cute*. I *know* what the hell *I* look like. It's *your* bitch ass who needs some *attention*. Just look how you *dress*."

I was sitting there, thinking, *Wow!* The beef was on, for real. Then Catherine tried to reach across the table and grab Carol by her fucking hair. I moved on reflex to stop her. Sean moved to stop her, too.

And that was the end of our damn night, dog. Them bitches started cussing each other out across the table and making a big-ass scene in there. And I had to admit that I was partially at fault. But what the hell could I do? Shit goes like that sometimes. I didn't know them chicks had *beef* with each other like that. S and I just wanted the same damn girl.

So after the night was ruined, S probably held true to form and called

Felicia back up for his usual as soon as he climbed in his ride, and I walked to my own car, up the street and around the corner.

I told myself, "Shit, if I ever bump back into that girl, Carol, it's *on!*" I was planning to lock that motherfucker *down!* She's *my* kind of *woman.* And I wasn't concerned about that boyfriend shit she started talking. She was only saying that for *Sean's* ass.

But I mean, it was a fun night. That's what going out is all about. Sometimes you don't *know* what the hell is gonna happen. And you're not *supposed* to. You just learn to go with the flow.

———

SEX EDUCATION

"Oh, yess! Oh, *yesss*! Come on with it! *Come on!*"

"It's coming, girl! It's *coming*! Hold on tight! *Hold on!*"

"Oh, yeah! Oh, *yeeaah...*"

Nine-year-old Marcus Gamble sat outside his father's locked bedroom door at their condo in the Skyway section of Seattle, Washington, at close to midnight, listening to his father and his female companion make nasty noises from inside.

Marcus had first noticed the noises a few months ago, when he had moved in with his father; the loud moans and squeals had unnerved him at night. He thought his father was killing someone. But once he had gotten used to the desperate cries of adult pleasure, he learned to believe that his father was giving women what they wanted. So whenever a new female companion would drop by the house past his bedtime, Marcus knew there was only a matter of time before his father would have his company moaning and groaning from inside of his locked bedroom.

The boy then became interested in comparing how loud each woman could get. He ranked the present woman a six out of ten, with a ten ranking as the loudest. And whenever the bedroom noise would settle back down after reaching a high point, Marcus would sneak back to his own bedroom and close the door, as if he hadn't heard a thing. But he had heard it all, and he had heard it clearly enough to memorize it.

Inside the master bedroom, Derrick Gamble climbed out of his extra-long, king-sized bed, and stood six feet tall and seven inches. He had a slim, wiry basketball-player frame with square shoulders.

"Girl, you really know how to work it there," he complimented his female friend. She remained stretched out and naked across his massive bed.

"You're not bad yourself."

"So, can I expect a couple of encores every now and then?"

"We'll see," she teased. "But like you said, you don't have any rings on *your* finger, and I don't have any rings on *mine*."

"I heard that," Derrick commented. "Well, any time you want me to break them walls in, let me know."

His lady friend laughed. "Ah, yeah, I'll be sure to remind my *'walls'* every now and then that you *said* that."

"Yeah, you do that," Derrick told her. He walked into the master bathroom to discard his condom in the toilet and to wash up his private parts at the sink. Then he muttered to himself casually, while taking a piss, "Man, I *love* Seattle."

A former professional basketball player for the Seattle SuperSonics before the organization moved to Oklahoma and renamed the club The Thunder, Derrick had gotten used to entertaining scores of women. However, the women he had gotten used to in Seattle were stress-free as compared to those in his home of New York or in Washington, D.C., and Atlanta—where he had played ball in college, and for the Wizards and Hawks, respectively. Derrick had an accidental son with a woman in his first professional season with the Washington Wizards. Then after he had become involved in a series of controlling, stressful relationships with women on the East Coast. Derrick settled into the Seattle area during his three-year career with the 'Sonics. He fell for the tranquil spirit of the women out west.

"They're just so *cool* about everything out here," he told anyone back east who would listen to him.

More than anything, the women out west allowed Derrick to be himself, unapologetically. And they seemed to be all inclusive; black, white, Hispanic, Asian, Canadian, and every mixture in between. So he dated them all equally, sleeping around as if it were still the free-love hippy era of the 1970s.

Derrick then invested in a coffee shop, inspired by the Magic Johnson example in Los Angeles with Starbucks. And when the SuperSonics franchise began its struggle over a new arena, ownership, fan support, and city finance disputes, Derrick felt secure enough to retire from the game and settle into the Seattle area for good. He was no more than a support player by that time anyway. He found a lot more excitement in running his popular coffee shop near downtown Seattle.

Then out of the blue, his son's mother called him from D.C. and decided that it was too much of a hassle to raise their fast-growing son on two separate coasts.

"Well, I'm not moving back to D.C. I like it out here in Seattle," Derrick argued.

"Well, look, you may have to take him out there with you for a while then, because I have some things I need to focus on. I can't do it with him stressing me about his father all the time, especially since you're not traveling with the team anymore, where he can get a chance to see you at the games like we *used* to do."

Derrick then realized that his son's mother still wanted to run the streets, while their son demanded more attention from her. So he would ask to see his father instead. And at first, Derrick balked at the idea of taking on his son long-term. But then he figured he would have more peace of mind that way, without having to argue with the woman on update phone calls. He grudgingly agreed to take his son for a year to see how he'd like it. However, Derrick refused to change his lifestyle for his son, and that included heavy dating. Besides, Marcus was a boy, so he would have to learn that his daddy liked women; and plenty of them.

So there they were, father and son, in an elaborate condo with non-stop female company from the Seattle region. And Derrick didn't apologize for any of it. Getting girls was how he lived.

The next morning at his coffee house, Derrick was at it again, flirting with one of his many female customers.

"So, how many espressos do you need to stay up at night?" he teased from the counter.

The young blonde tossed her hair out of her face and giggled. "Well, I can't really say. I guess it would all depend on my energy level that night."

"And what would raise your energy level?"

"Mmmm, who knows? Maybe a tall cup of *dark* coffee," she flirted back.

"With a little bit of cream and sugar in it?"

She grinned into Derrick's medium-brown face. "Yeah, but just with a little bit of cream and sugar, not *too* much."

"Yeah, you don't want to lose all of the strong, dark *flavor*, right?"

"Exactly," she agreed with a chuckle.

At his towering height, Derrick was hard to miss. And even though he couldn't do every woman who entered his shop for coffee, beverages and pastries, the fantasy of a six-foot-seven-inch, black man's dick, enticed many of them to continue to frequent his establishment. Derrick presumed as much and led their fantasy parade to the tune of very good business, as well as abundant pleasure after work hours.

Before he could get out another word in flirtations with his pretty customer, Derrick's cell phone went off. He looked down at the foreign number and grimaced.

Who is this? he asked himself of the number.

"Excuse me a minute," he told the blonde. "I'll be right back with you." He then stepped inside the storage room for privacy.

"Hello," he answered.

"Yes, can I speak to Mr. Derrick Gamble, please?"

The woman sounded very professional.

"This is Derrick Gamble. Who's calling?"

"This is Elizabeth Hammond, the principal at Renton Elementary School, where your son Marcus attends. And we have a very serious issue on our hands at school that I need to talk to your son about."

Derrick paused and wondered what Marcus had done.

"Well, what did he do?" he asked.

"We would much rather talk to you about it in person."

Derrick looked down at his expensive wristwatch and read that it was just after eleven o'clock.

"Okay, I can be there in a good...*twenty* minutes."

"Thank you. We'll see you then."

Derrick hung up the phone and felt apprehensive.

Was he in a fight or something? he pondered. *Couldn't she have told me that over the phone? Did he beat a kid down that bad?*

He walked back out into his coffee shop and let his staff members know he had a run to make.

"I'll be back in an hour or two." He then eyed the blonde as he headed toward the door. "We'll finish that coffee discussion the next time I see you here. Okay?"

"All right," she agreed and smiled.

When Derrick arrived at his son's school in the hills of Renton, southeast of downtown Seattle, he was still confused about what the principal wanted to discuss with him. He hoped and prayed that it wouldn't be anything too major.

He parked his white Cadillac Escalade in the visitors parking lot and walked toward the school entrance feeling nervous and anxious with every step.

When he arrived at the main office, Marcus saw his extra-tall father walk in. His eyes immediately hit the floor with shame from the chair where he sat.

Derrick looked at him and relaxed. At least his son looked normal. He wasn't battered and bruised, he hadn't been crying, and he appeared worry-free. However, he didn't want to make eye contact with his father, and that was understandable, considering the situation. His father hadn't been called to the school for a picnic.

"I'm Derrick Gamble and this is my son, Marcus," he announced to the office staff of mostly white women.

"Oh, yeah, let me get Elizabeth for you," the secretary responded. She hustled off to the back office while the rest of the staff looked up to the tall man with intrigue.

"You used to play for the SuperSonics?" the lone black woman asked.

Derrick nodded. "Yeah."

"And you own that popular coffee shop downtown now."

"It has my name on it," he stated with a grin.

"Yeah, but a lot of celebrities and athletes allow their names to be used," one of the other women spoke up, overhearing the conversation.

"Well, not this one. I even retired from basketball to help run my own place every day now," he added.

"So you retired from basketball to run a coffee shop?"

Derrick had gotten used to that question. "Basically, the 'Sonics weren't going anywhere but to a new city. We couldn't make the playoffs regularly, and we didn't have enough fire power in the West to stay in the hunt when we did. And my career had already seen its better days. So instead of riding the broken-down car until the wheels fell off in Oklahoma, I decided to jump ship and stay here to run my business."

It all made perfect sense to Derrick, and if it didn't make sense to others, then that was *their* problem. He was even looking into franchising his shop after a few more years of studying the coffee market in other areas.

"Ah, Marcus, and Mr. Gamble," the principal called from her back office.

Marcus stood to his feet and began to walk forward. Derrick followed behind him.

When they stepped inside the principal's private office, she closed the door behind them and moved to shake Derrick's hand.

"I'm sorry to disturb you in the middle of your day like this, Mr. Gamble, but we really do need to have this conversation."

She took a seat behind her desk, while Marcus and Derrick took seats in the chairs in front of her. She was a regal, hard-faced woman with graying hair, but she remained energized and youthful in spirit.

Derrick asked her, "So, what seems to be the problem?"

"Well, his fourth-grade teacher, Ms. Pavel, has been monitoring the situation for over a week now. But it seems that Marcus here has continued to use inappropriate language when addressing the girls inside of his classroom, and even *more* so while out at recess," the principal informed him.

Derrick heard that and grimaced. What exact language was she referring to?

The principal continued before he could ask her. "So I gathered a list of them here to discuss with you." She looked down at a printout of sentences and began to read them:

"'*Come here, girl, you know you want it.*' '*I got just what the doctor ordered for you.' 'Take your medicine like a big girl.' 'Hey girl, do you think you can handle this?' 'Get up in line for this, baby.' 'I'm all night long with mine.' 'Call me whenever you need me, baby.'"*

The principal stopped and looked into Derrick's face. "I mean, this is all *blatant* material. And these are just some of the more *disturbing* comments that he's used. But Marcus has constantly referred to the girls in his class-room as 'babe' or 'honey' or *'girl,'* and I mean not like a normal 'girl,' but like a guy would say to a woman in a pick-up line. You know what I mean?"

Derrick was ready to explode in laughter. He had done a great job of listening to the older white woman run off a list of familiar statements to him, and with a very studious diction at that. But he maintained his straight face instead of breaking into a smile. It was no time for smiles. His son had somehow picked up his language to women, and it was now an embarrass-ing situation for him to have to deal with.

"Now if this inappropriate behavior continues, then I'm going to have to suspend him for three days," the principal warned. "And if it continues after that, then I'll have no choice but to ask you to transfer him to another school. Now some of his comments have already begun to make it back to the girls' parents at home. But others think that it's funny, which I'm sure has caused Marcus to continue to want to do it.

"So I called you here today to allow you to take Marcus with you for the rest of the afternoon to have a real father-to-son talk with him about in-appropriate language. Then he can come back to school tomorrow and start over. But I'm really concerned about this," she concluded.

She then paused to hear any comments from Derrick. She had done all of the talking and was ready to listen to him now.

Derrick said, "So...he's excused from class for the rest of the day?"

The principal nodded. "He's been given all of his homework and his assignments for the day, and he'll be all caught up for tomorrow. Ms. Pavel has said she has no problems from him regarding his work. It's just his *mouth* that gets him into trouble. So I figured that either you take him home early to talk to him, father to son, or I'll have to suspend him right now. We simply can't have that here, and I wanted to give you a fair warning."

Derrick nodded in silence. He immediately understood that she was giving his son a break. She could have suspended Marcus on the spot. But Derrick was also concerned with how long they had allowed the language to go on before they contacted him.

"Well, if he does this again, you can contact me immediately," he offered.

"I hope he doesn't," the principal commented sternly.

Derrick could read her body language and her serious tone of voice. Marcus had already reached the end of the road without realizing it. And the next incident would get him suspended.

Shit! That's just fucked up, Derrick thought to himself. *She's only giving him this one chance. That's like a set-up.*

However, he couldn't complain about it. He knew that the white woman was judging them both now. It was a set-up for father *and* son. It was like having to stop a cigarette smoking habit, cold turkey, in one day. Nevertheless, they had no choice in the matter.

Derrick stood up tall and said, "Thank you. He'll be back tomorrow."

As Marcus followed his father out of the school and into the parking lot to his truck, he had no idea what to expect from him. Derrick hadn't said a word.

As they approached his truck, the father wondered what the principal expected from him. He surely would not whip his son, if that's what she expected. But obviously, she expected a drastic change.

Maybe he is around too many grown-ups and situations with women, Derrick mused.

Marcus had been allowed to hang out and do his homework at the coffee shop after school. But maybe having so much exposure to adults wasn't such a good idea for a young and impressionable boy. And maybe it wasn't so cool for Derrick to openly entertain so many women around him. His defiant dating practices were quickly being tossed back into his face.

As father and son drove away from the school, Derrick commented, "I'm gonna have to start taking you to an after-school program instead of the coffee shop."

Marcus didn't say a word either. He was fearful about what to expect.

"Or maybe I can get you into a YMCA sports program after school," his father added.

Marcus turned to face him and was excited by the suggestion. He had been thinking about getting into a youth basketball league since the moment he had arrived out in Seattle. Only, he was bashful about not being so great at sports. He figured his father would soon teach him how to play better.

"But first we need to deal with these *comments* you've been making at school," Derrick stated, and changed his friendly tone.

"Marcus, there's a difference between what grown-ups can do and what kids are allowed to do. You know that, right?"

Marcus eyed him and nodded. "Yes," he mumbled meekly.

"For instance; you can't drive this truck. Your feet wouldn't even touch the pedals. And you could barely see over the wheel," his father told him.

Marcus understood him with a nod. His father drove a big truck and he was a tall man.

Derrick continued, "Kids are not supposed to smoke cigarettes, drink beers, hang out in bars, go to certain movies, or certain events. And how would you feel if you had to play a game of basketball against a bunch of teenagers. Would you like that?"

Marcus thought about the speed, toughness, height, and skills of teenagers on a basketball court and shook his head. Without getting his growth spurt, he could barely see himself getting a shot off.

Derrick continued, "I know I didn't like playing against older guys when *I* was a kid. I wanted to play against kids my own age until I was strong enough to hang with teenagers. But once I was able to bang inside with the older guys, I knew that I was ready for it."

So far, Marcus felt comfortable. His father hadn't jumped on him hard yet about his language at school.

"So, you picked up some of those things from me, right?" Derrick suddenly asked his son.

He was smiling when he asked the question. Marcus didn't know what to make of it. Was his father trying to set him up before he pounced on him or what? Therefore, he remained apprehensive when he spoke.

"Yes."

Derrick continued to smile. He was amused by it. He didn't realize his son was paying that much attention.

"You've been listening to me talk to women all this time? And you've been sitting over there taking it all in, like a mini tape recorder. So now I have to watch what I say around you, because what I talk about with women is all *grown-up* stuff."

Marcus didn't deny that point. It *was* grown-up stuff that his father talked about. He didn't even know if he *liked* girls the way his father liked *women*. He found that girls seemed to respond to it all, so he used it to gather their collective attention. However, Marcus did have some questions about grown-up dating habits, conversations, and terms that confused him. He looked at his father, with his heart racing from nervousness, and he decided to ask him about it.

"Ahh…if it's grown-up stuff, then how come you call women 'baby' all the time?"

Derrick couldn't stop himself from smiling. It was his first frank talk with his son about the birds and bees. And the boy was only nine years old. Derrick couldn't remember having any conversations about sex with *his* father until after he had gotten an STD at seventeen in high school.

"'Baby' is just a figure of speech to let a woman know that she's *sweet* like a baby," Derrick explained to his son.

So far, so good. Marcus then thought about it more.

"Well, how come, umm, women say it to guys, too?"

"It doesn't have a gender to it," Derrick told him. "There are girl babies just like there are *boy* babies, right?"

Marcus nodded. "But how come I can't say it?"

The word seemed innocent enough to him. Babies were babies. So what was the big deal?

That was a more difficult question. Derrick could see where his son was confused about it. "Baby" wasn't a bad word by itself. It was all about how you *used* it.

"Well, if you say, 'Hey, that's a pretty baby,' and you're actually talking about a *real* baby, like an *infant*, then that's okay. But if you tell a girl in your class, 'Hey, baby, come here,' then that's grown-up talk that your teachers are not gonna like. Because that girl in your classroom is not actually a baby anymore, and your teachers and the girl's parents are gonna understand that you're using it in a grown-up way. And they're not gonna allow you to do that, because you're not a grown-up yet."

With that answer covered, Marcus stopped being nervous. His young mind was moving fast to comprehend it all.

"But the women at your coffee shop call me 'baby' all the time, and I'm not a real baby either," he commented.

Derrick finally stopped smiling. The contradictions were getting serious. He looked away from his son for a minute and at the steering wheel. "Yeah, I'm gonna have to get them to stop saying that to you then, if it bothers you," he mumbled.

"It doesn't bother me," Marcus told him.

Yeah, but they're still acting fucking fresh when they call you that, Derrick mused. He knew exactly which women his son was referring to, and they were all fresh-minded.

I wonder how much they really think about my son becoming a mack daddy? He had never really thought about it before. "Like father, like son" was a real issue. And Derrick remembered that he had fucked a few grown women as a teenager himself.

Shit! he blasted. It was more honesty than what he wanted to deal with at the moment. His son was still only *nine.*

"You know what, I'm gonna tell them to call you *Marcus* from now on. You're nobody's baby."

Marcus told him, "My mom calls me 'baby,' too."

Derrick eyed his son and smiled again. "Well, you *are* her baby. She can call you that for the rest of your life, whether you like it or not."

"But it doesn't bother me though," Marcus reiterated.

"Yeah, but you still can't say it to the girls in your school, because the teachers and parents will consider it *wrong. Period!* You hear me?"

His son nodded. Then he thought about his next question.

"Now what else you wanna ask me about grown-up stuff?" Derrick asked him on cue. "Because I don't want you going back to school confused about anything. Now you heard what the principal said, right? She's ready to suspend you next time. So you need to understand everything you *can* and *can't* say at school."

Marcus looked back up to his father and asked him, "Did my mom ever call *you* 'baby'?"

It was a crafty question. He wanted to know how close his parents were. So Derrick took a deep breath and told him.

"Of course she did, at one time. I mean, she won't call me that *now*, but you know…"

"You don't like each other anymore?" Marcus asked him.

Derrick had to stop and take another deep breath. "We still like each other; we just understood that we wouldn't work out as a couple, that's all."

His son nodded his head again. "You don't work out with a lot of women."

It was another blunt observation that had caught the father off guard.

Damn, this kid is mature as hell, he thought. *But how could he not think that, with all the women he's seen me around?*

"Well…I like women, son. I'm not gonna lie to you about that," Derrick admitted. "But again, I'm a *grown man*, and I can *choose* to like whatever I want. And when you get your chance to be a grown man, then you can choose whatever *you* want. But while you're still young and in school, nobody's gonna allow you to *do* that. That's just the way it is in life. You don't see *me* going to school now, do you?"

Marcus shook his head and stopped. "Umm, but some older people go to school."

"Because they *choose* to," Derrick insisted. "But young people *have* to go to school. Do you think you can live out here by yourself, and pay your own bills like other grown-ups do?"

Marcus paused and thought about it. He tried to imagine what he could do to make a living. Maybe he could sweep up restaurant floors. His father made him sweep and empty out trash baskets at the coffee shop on some days.

Derrick cut his son's thoughts short. "No, you can't, Marcus. You're *nine years old*. You can't even get an apartment yet."

Marcus smiled at the idea. His thoughts had been busted.

"Now let's deal with these other things you said at school," Derrick alluded.

"Now what do you mean when you say you gon' give a girl what she wants?"

Marcus shrugged his shoulders like the innocent kid that he was. "I'on know, like...make her feel good and stuff."

Derrick had to hold back his smile again. It was time to be a responsible father and set his son straight, even though the conversation was awkward.

"Make her feel good, how?"

"I'on know, wit'...grown-up stuff."

"*Exactly*," Derrick pounced on him. "That's why you shouldn't be *saying* it. You don't know what you're talking about. And what did the doctor order for little girls in your class?"

Marcus quickly became gun-shy again. His father was now giving him the hard reprimand that he expected.

"Nothing," he whimpered.

"You said you had what the doctor ordered, right? So what do you have?" Derrick pressed him.

"A dick," Marcus answered meekly.

Derrick wasn't expecting that. So when his son looked up to catch his eyes, they were *both* shocked by it. The father was so stunned that he had to look away.

"You don't *use* that word," he told his son sternly. But he couldn't look at him when he said it. "That's a *real* grown-up word, and you *know it*." He then looked at his son and added, "And if I ever hear you say it again..."

Derrick then paused, feeling guilty. But so what? He was a grown man who reserved the right to *be* grown.

"When you get to be of age, you're gonna find that there's a right and a wrong time to use certain words. But since you're still in *grade* school, *now* is definitely not the *time* for it. You hear me?"

Marcus nodded obediently. They were now pulling onto Interstate 405 toward downtown. Derrick was far from finished with him.

"So, what do you mean when you say you can go all night long? Did you really say that?" he asked his son.

Marcus attempted to sit there quietly again. The open and honest approach wasn't working so well for him now. But there was no way around it. His father was right on top of him inside the truck.

"Marcus, did you say that or not?" Derrick pressed him.

"I said it," he mumbled.

"And what do you *mean* by that?"

Marcus felt trapped. He knew that his honest answer would only lead to more reprimand. Nevertheless, he let it out.

"Umm...I can make her..." He paused and looked his father in the eyes before he finished. "...talk all night."

"Talk about what?"

"You know...how it feels."

"How *what* feels?"

Finally, Marcus shrugged again. "I don't know."

"*Exactly*," Derrick repeated. "You don't know what the hell you're *talking* about. And what's a 'big girl' supposed to be able to handle from *you*?"

His father was grilling his ass hard now. And it was all coming out on instinct.

Marcus sat there in the truck as stiff as a statue. He couldn't even look his father in the eyes anymore.

"Now you see why you can't talk like a grown-up in school? Because you don't know what you're *talking* about," Derrick repeated. "So you want to be a *boy*, and enjoy yourself doing sports, playing tag, marbles, and other things that little boys *do*. You hear me? You're not *ready* to be a grown-up yet."

After his rant, Derrick calmed down and allowed his son to breathe again.

"You hungry. You want something to eat?" he asked him.

Marcus nodded. "Can we go to Wendy's?"

He saw the Wendy's sign on the upcoming exit as they reached Interstate 5 for downtown.

"All right. Wendy's it is," his father agreed cheerfully.

As soon as they pulled into the parking lot to move into the drive-thru line, a big-behind woman in black jeans climbed out of her car and bent over to fix her shoe strap. She did so right beside the truck as they passed her by.

"Jesus..." Derrick stated and immediately caught himself.

Okay, now I have to watch everything I say around him, he thought.

They received their food and drove back out into the street to return to the interstate for downtown.

Marcus took one bite of his burger and said, "Daddy, what's a blow job?" as if he were asking about flavors of bubble gum.

Derrick took a sip of his large drink and chilled. Then he set it back down in his cup holder. *Now ain't this some shit,* he pondered to himself. He thought that the worst of their talk was over, but evidently it was not.

"Where'd you here that word from?" he asked his son.

"Two women were talking about it at the coffee shop."

Marcus continued to chomp down his Wendy's burger as if it was nothing.

Yeah, we're definitely gonna have to find him a new after-school hangout, Derrick convinced himself.

"First of all, don't *ever* repeat that question or use those words again. They are *very serious words,*" he emphasized.

Marcus had a look of intrigue on his face. *But what do the words mean?* he still seemed to be asking.

But that one was out of his father's range to answer.

"You don't even *think* about those words. Those word are...*off limits,*" Derrick insisted. He felt guilty and ridiculous at the same time. How utterly embarrassing were adults and the things that they chose to *say* and *do?* At the same time, he realized that the more he backed down from explaining the word, the more his son would probably think about it.

Fuck! Derrick cursed himself. *This little motherfucker gon' back school and...*

He didn't even want to think about it, but he *had* to. What if Marcus slipped up with some even *nastier* words at school?

Yeah, I gotta nip this shit in the bud, right now, Derrick told himself. His son's intrigue in grown conversation and sexuality was so important to him that he pulled over on the side of the highway and slammed the truck in park.

"Okay, son, how many other words and things do you know about that we need to talk about? Because you got me a little concerned right now. And if you go back to school and say *any* of these things, you may not be able to go *back* there, and you'll have us *both* looking crazy."

"I'm not gonna say anything," Marcus promised his father.

However, there was no way for Derrick to believe him. He wasn't sure if Marcus understood what to say and what *not* to say.

Derrick said, "Look, son, I don't know what you *know* right now. And if you don't know the difference between *grown* conversations and *kids'* conversation, then you're about to scare me to death, man. Now tell me everything."

Marcus looked at him and whined, "*Everything?*"

Derrick nodded. "Yes, *everything*. Now give me all the words that you know."

"You're not gonna be mad at me?"

"I'm gonna be mad, if you let these words slip *out*. Now I need to know what you *know* so I'm not *blindsided* by it. And then I can help you to understand what you can't *say* and *why*."

Marcus took a deep breath and muttered, "Fuckin'."

"Now you know you can't say that, right? Now what else?"

Marcus paused and added, "...Pussy."

Derrick grimaced from simply hearing the words. Each time his son let one out, he peeked at his father's face to see how he would respond to it.

"Ass."

"Keep 'em going," Derrick told him.

Marcus obliged. "Suck my dick. Eat my pussy. Oh, shit. Fuck me right. I'm cummin'. Give it to me harder..."

Finally, Derrick shook his head and covered his face in shame. "You've been listening in through my door at night, haven't you?"

Marcus looked into his father's eyes again before he answered. "Yes."

Derrick took another calming breath and continued to shake his head, not at his son, but at himself. He had been a reckless, damn *fool*!

"What the hell was *I* thinking?" he asked himself out loud. "I can't blame you for hearing this stuff, man." Then he looked his son in the eyes and said, "But you *do* know that you're not supposed to *say 'em*. Don't you? That's why you're telling me these words now. You *know* they're wong."

He son nodded. "Yes," he admitted.

"Good. And in the meantime..." Derrick stopped himself in mid-sentence. He didn't want to tell his son out in the open that he planned to stop dating so many women, just in case he would change his mind. But he did need to find a more secure way of dealing with the women that he *did* date.

"So...how do you feel about me having women over at night?" he asked his son.

Marcus shrugged. "I don't know... They just *noisy*, I guess."

Maybe I'll just tell these women to shut up, Derrick mused with a grin. But that would take away from the whole fun of love talk. *Maybe I'll fuck 'em now at their house*, he thought. He surely didn't plan to give up fucking all together. He had to figure out what to do with his midnight-roaming son.

"So, how long have you been listening in?"

"For weeks," Marcus noted.

Derrick came to the only sane conclusion. "Well, I'll tell you what, if you stay away from these words, and don't get into trouble at school, then when you're ready, I'll answer all of your questions about grown-up stuff. But right now, son, you're only nine years *old*. And you really need to leave these words *alone*. Okay?"

He looked into his son's eyes and awaited his response.

"Okay."

"Good," his father told him. He then slapped his Cadillac Escalade in drive and returned to Interstate 5 toward downtown. Derrick had no idea whether or not his son would make it through the rest of the school year without slipping up with his words again. But he was forced to have to trust him. In the meantime, he figured he had a lot of changes to make regarding his lifestyle and daily routine. He had a young and impressionable son to look out for now.

We need to check out the YMCA's after-school program as soon as possible, he told himself.

But before going to check out the Y, Derrick wanted to make sure his staff was set at the coffee shop. And as soon as he stepped foot into his shop with his son in tow, Jennifer Selig, his notoriously flirty staff manager, blurted, "Hey, baby, how was school today?"

Derrick shook his head on cue and said, "His name is *Marcus* Gamble. And he just told me that he's not a '*baby*' anymore."

Jennifer looked at them both to see if her boss was only teasing. But once she read that he was serious, she said, "Well, *excuuse me*. Hey, *Marcus*, how's it going? How was *school* today?" she asked sarcastically.

Marcus looked up at her and smiled. She was a freckle-faced redhead with an enticing body, dominated by pert titties that always seemed to climb out into his face.

"It was okay," he answered. "My dad picked me up early today."

Derrick looked around at the normal high-traffic crowd inside of his coffee shop. He wondered if he should have left his son inside the car, reading one of his books for homework.

Let me make this fast, and get him registered at the Y, he plotted. The usual atmosphere of his Seattle coffee shop was very sexy. Pretty women were everywhere, and that made more confident and assertive men show up. It was all great for business. However, the happening pick-up place that Derrick had obviously created was hardly a safe haven for a boy with great ears and a sharp memory. His father could see that more clearly now.

"Ah, Jennifer, I'm gonna be gone for a few hours, making some runs with Marcus, so hold down the fort in here for me. Okay?"

Jennifer looked at him incredulously. "Honey, you need to let your attachment to the shop go. We all understand you have other things to do. You're the *owner*, for cyring out loud. So have a little *faith* in your girl. I can do it, I really *can*."

Everything Jennifer said was flirty and sarcastic, and so were her grins, her eyes, and her curves. The fact that Derrick had been intimate with her on a few occasions didn't make matters any better for him. So he grimaced at every word of out of her mouth, knowing that his son held a deeper understanding of it all.

Derrick nodded in haste, ready to leave her as quickly as he could. "Yeah, so I'll be back then." He started to move and pushed Marcus toward the door.

"Hurry back soon, Big D," another customer teased him. "You know I come down here every day to have my *fix*," she emphasized with a devilish chuckle.

Now there's another word I gotta watch out for, Derrick assumed. *Come and get your fix, baby*, he imagined Marcus stating next at school.

All of sudden, his coffee shop seemed borderline pornographic. With all of the sexy, professional women and opportunistic men inside the room, with a giant, athletic, and sociable black man in the mix as their ringleader, Derrick fantasized that an all-out, verbal *orgy* could pop off at any minute in front of his son.

Marcus smiled at it all. He could clearly see his father's new struggle. And he really liked being around grown-up talk. But an after-school program at the Y was still a much better deal for him. Nevertheless, Marcus would miss the place.

"Come on, man, let's go," his father said, pushing him urgently toward the door.

Once Derrick got his son back out into the fresh, downtown air of Seattle, he thought, *This is crazy! I've really built a swinging place in there. But it's definitely not a place for a kid. I almost feel like a coffee-shop pimp.*

He even smiled at the idea. He liked the sexiness of his shop. He needed to separate his son from it. But then he thought about his bedroom, and the late-night visitations of horny women.

Yeah, fuck that! I'm not giving up getting pussy, Derrick persisted. *So if his little ass won't let me get mine in peace, without going back to school with the shit on his mind, then I might have to send his ass back to his mother.*

And as they walked back toward the truck, he wondered if his son had ever listened in on his *mother* fucking someone in *her* bedroom. But he became gun-shy himself about asking.

Yeah, I don't think I want to know that, he told himself with a smirk. That seemed like too much information for him. And some things were simply meant to be left alone, like grown-up talk.

———•———

A GOOD MAN

"Where are you going?" Antonio Greene asked his young wife. She was his second, at thirty-two years old, and he was fifty-four. He stood at the kitchen sink, washing off dirty dishes to place inside the dishwasher.

Suzanne Smith-Greene, his wife, pulled on her long, black overcoat at the closet and answered, "Out."

"Does '*out*' have an actual name?" her husband asked her softly.

"I'm running out with some friends, Tony. What's the problem?"

"Well, where are you headed?" All he needed was a simple answer.

Instead, Suzanne let out a long, irritated sigh. "Sometimes we make up our minds on the fly. We don't always know where we want to go. We're just out having girl talk."

"You can have '*girl talk*' over the phone."

That was the last irritable straw for Suzanne. She told him, "You know what, I'll see you when I get back. Because I can tell you're in a *funky* little mood of yours again, where you wanna ask a *million* questions, like I'm doing something *wrong*. And if you *think* that way, then why not come right out and *say it*?" she challenged him.

Tony looked away from her and couldn't bring himself to accuse her in person. But he knew that she was out there running around on him. He loved the woman's company too much to press the issue. What if, after being discovered, she decided to divorce him and leave? He would be left heartbroken and lonely again. And at his age, a piece of a beautiful woman was better than none. So he backed down from his wife's heated glare.

BLOOM!

The heavy door shut behind her as she walked into the garage and over to her black Mercedes. The garage door raised with a push of her automatic remote, and out she drove into the night for another rendezvous in Boston from her cozy home in the Brookline suburbs.

Imagine crossing the border of a million-dollar, five- and six-bedroom home community, and driving into the heart of the seedy, project apartments of Boston's infamous Roxbury, where the crime, despair, hard living and tough breaks of poverty still ran rampant?

Suzanne Smith-Greene had talked herself into doing exactly that. Her fetish with Roxbury had become her hard dose of reality, to reclaim the edge she felt she had lost in her relationship with a good man in the suburbs. She had lost her feelings of urgency there, and the vital rush of passion. There wasn't enough excitement in her college professor husband, Harvard tenure or not. The university luncheons, dinners and events that she had attended with him in her mid-twenties had become the exciting stuff of yesterday, where soft men spoke of soft issues and the cerebral world of ideas and academics. However, Suzanne still desired the active lives of real *men*, the hard hands, hard bodies, hard work, and the sweaty funk of physical exertion. She desired their brazen forwardness and lustful stares. She longed for a man's unapologetic ruggedness, and a forceful, bedroom appetite. And she had found it all in Roxbury.

As soon as she arrived at the familiar sights of Washington Street from Arbor Way, she made her usual right turn and headed farther south, passing an engaged police cruiser to her left.

WHURRPP! WHURRPP! WHURRPP!

The police cruiser's loud, short chirps warned the traffic to move out of its path, while the illuminated car accelerated up the street in the opposite direction.

"Something is *always* going on over here," Suzanne mumbled. But the commotion of the 'hood had never fazed her. In fact, she *liked* it. The everyday drama there reminded her that she was still alive and a part of a much bigger, imperfect world.

She made another right turn into the Chesterfield Homes Apartments complex and spotted a busy mother with a beautiful young daughter, walking hand-in-hand. The little girl of nine looked Suzanne right in her face from the sidewalk, with twinkling, expressive eyes. She didn't seem concerned about the poverty there in the projects at all.

"Awwww, isn't she *adorable*," Suzanne cooed from the safety of her car.

The mother noticed the stare and shook her daughter gently to stop it.

"Cut it, girl, we don't know her. She might be out here trying to kidnap you," the mother warned her daughter. "Them rich people do that to little girls, you know. They try to make you into their little dollbabies."

Suzanne noticed the heavy-set mother jerk her daughter's attention away from her car, while giving the little girl a verbal reprimand. Suzanne continued to watch them from her rearview mirror as she headed toward her destination.

She was a young, reprimanded daughter herself years ago, while growing up in the Bronx, New York, where her half-Dominican mother warned her never to trust anyone who smiled at her too hard.

"You are a very pretty girl, Suzanne. So you must watch out for people who are too nice to you. A lot of them will try to take advantage of you and think that you are weak because you're so pretty."

Suzanne believed her mother and learned to fear everyone, right up until graduation from Boston College, where she studied psychology. She then began to make her own assessments, form her own rules, and devise her own loyalties and beliefs, while going on to study law. And in the middle of finishing up her law school degree, she met Professor Antonio Greene at an intellectual property discussion at M.I.T. in Cambridge. She was smitten by his decency and his dedication to intellectual pursuits. But now that seemed *ages* ago.

I need more in my life than that academic shit now, she mused distastefully.

Although her mother had learned to love and respect her daughter's husband, after an initial leeriness over their age difference, Suzanne began to despise his impotence. He had been robbed of his ability to reproduce, and with it, he had been depleted of any swagger. Adding insult to injury, Antonio had put off any real actions toward artificial insemination to sire children. Talking about researching a sperm bank, and actually going to one, were two different things. So his young and unsatisfied wife began to stray in the inner-city terrain of Boston, finding herself a much younger man who *was* active with his words.

To take her mind off the hard realities of her past, she called to alert her destination on her cell phone.

"Hello," a gruff voice answered.

"Hey, I'm about to pull up now. Sorry I took a minute. My husband started acting up with the questions again."

"And what's up with the panties and bra? You came how I told you to come?"

She smiled. *Now that's a man!* she declared to herself. "You'll see."

"Aw'ight, well, the door'll be open for you."

And that was it. The man hung up the phone and left her to her thoughts.

Suzanne clicked off the line and couldn't wait to see him, with no panties or bra under her gray, women's business suit, just like he liked it.

She pulled into an open parking spot outside of his building and eyed the young convicts-in-training, who often congregated near the entrance of the apartments. They were all in their late teens and early twenties, wearing the national hip-hop gear of winter jackets, hats and hoodies, designer sneakers and boots, and oversized blue jeans. Knowing who she was there to see, they nodded to her respectfully and created a crease for her to walk by.

After she had entered the building, one of the young men commented on her frequent visits to the projects. "Yo, that bitch is crazy, man."

"The man just got *game* like that, player," another guy disputed with a chuckle.

"Shit, ain't that much *game* in the world. That bitch just *crazy*," the first guy insisted.

"Yeah, crazy for that *dick*," a third young man joked. They all shared a hearty laugh, fascinated that such an established, married woman would stoop so low for obvious lust.

"I mean, that's just an experiment for that ho, man. You know how it is with them educated hoes. I had a few of 'em like that myself; white ones, too," one of the oldest of the group added. "You know, they'll fuck you and give you a few dollars for a minute. Then they'll go back to their regular lives when the experiment's over."

His final assessment seemed to appease them all.

"Yup, that's how that shit is. You got it right there."

Oblivious to their conversations about her, Suzanne ascended the apartment stairs to the third floor, and every step on the hollow floors sounded amplified, like the surround sound of a state-of-the-art movie theater.

*CLIP-CLOP, CLIP-CLOP, CLIP-CLOP...*her heels sounded up the steps.

Why are these steps and floors so damn LOUD in this place? she questioned. *They need some carpeting, better wood, more insulation or something!* But it still beat taking the elevators. She didn't trust the elevators at all; the long wait, the slow mechanics, the overall safety, or the stench. So she would rather walk up.

When she arrived at the door, she took a deep breath before she grabbed the doorknob to let herself inside.

Well, here we go again, Suzanne, she told herself.

She walked into the overheated, two-bedroom apartment and double-locked the door with the latch and chain, like he had always told her to. Then she walked into a spaghetti and meatball meal inside the kitchen.

Raymond "Big Ray" Cummings sat at his small kitchen table, wearing oversized blue jeans and an ultra-clean wife beater.

"You hungry?"

He was an extra-chocolate black man with a low haircut and the body size of a hulking football player. He had played defensive line in high school, but he never applied himself enough in his classes to attend college.

Suzanne shook her head and turned down his offer of spaghetti.

"I just finished eating at home before I left out." She didn't like that *he* was still eating either. It would only slow down the process of what she was there for.

Big Ray shrugged and continued to eat his spaghetti and meatballs. He had a half roll of Italian garlic bread and a two-liter bottle of Mountain Dew, with a tall glass of ice on the table.

"So, your old man asked you where you were going again?" he asked with a smile.

Big Ray was only twenty-five years old, but he had a commanding quality about him, with the poise and authority of a man of forty.

Suzanne took off her long coat and set it across the back of one of his kitchen chairs.

"He always asks me extra questions when he gets in those funky little moods of his."

"I would *too* if my wife was running out on me to fuck somebody once a week," Ray admitted. The young and boastful man was so frank that Suzanne was no longer shocked or offended by it. His delivery was always raw. But he gave her the honesty that she wanted.

"So, did you plan to feed me earlier, or did you just decide to eat because you didn't know the exact time that I would arrive here tonight?"

"Yeah," Ray answered vaguely.

Suzanne looked confused. "Yeah, what?"

"I was hungry from waiting, so I cooked something to eat. I was about to run out somewhere, but since you said you was coming..."

"Again, I apologize. But I never really know sometimes when he's about to act up."

"What about when you go back home late? What does he ask you *then*?"

Suzanne took a breath and paused. She didn't feel like playing a game of a hundred questions with him either. She was there to be serviced sexually and that was it. But Big Ray didn't seem to be cooperating, or at least not on her urgent time schedule.

"You need me to, ah, make a run and come back when you're ready?"

Ray stopped eating his spaghetti and looked at her with a hard grill. "Everything is about *you*, hunh? You want what you want right now. Some people say the same thing about me," he told her. "My baby's momma says it."

Suzanne looked at his muscular biceps and viewed the tattoos he had of his two daughters, one on each arm. Every time she looked at them, she imagined having daughters of her own, but only under the right circumstances. And those circumstances seemed to be passing her by.

"So, you want me to go right into it and stop eating and everything, right?" he asked her.

"Well, like I said, I can go grab a drink and come back."

"And how long would that take you?" Ray continued to stuff his mouth with food while he asked her. He was nearly finished with his plate now.

"I mean, twenty, thirty minutes."

The hulking young man stood up and shook his head. He grabbed his finished plate and took it to the sink, while munching down his garlic bread.

"Naw," he told her. "I'm done." Then he walked to wash his hands at the sink.

Big Ray worked in construction now, so he was rarely without work. But he claimed to like living in Roxbury's projects for the same reason that *she* liked coming there to visit him. It felt like a real slice of life there. And after his girlfriend and baby's momma began to act a little too demanding in their new place in Hyde Park, Ray moved out and returned to Roxbury on his own.

"Nobody fucks with me like that. I give you a better life, and then you try and turn around and become the *boss* on me. Fuck that," he had explained to her. "We only got *two kids* and I'm not the fucking *third*."

After he finished washing his hands at the sink, he walked back over to the table to finish off his large glass of Mountain Dew with ice.

"You gon' get what you need," he promised.

"Are you certain your food's all digested?" she quizzed him. She wasn't so sure about sexing him so early after finishing his food.

"What you think, I'ma take a shit by accident while we fucking?"

His unabashed candor was simply humorous to her. Her husband would *never* say anything like that, even if he was thinking it. That's what made Raymond so interesting to her. He was a man of uncommon truth in a world of lies. And as a practicing lawyer, she had heard them all.

She grinned and asked, "Have you always said anything that comes to your mind?"

"That's why I keep a job," he answered. "These construction bosses know they can count on me to say what the hell I need to say to the other guys on the site, *and* to them. So I keep everybody in check. And they know that's important to get shit done. Somebody gotta do it."

He wiped a clean spot on his kitchen counter and grabbed her by her hips to sit her there.

"What are you doing?"

"I'm setting you on the counter."

"*Here?*"

"Yeah, we fucked everywhere else in here already; the bathroom, living room, bedroom, the hallway. So I came up with this idea while I was sitting here waiting for you. At first I was gon' fuck you up against the doorway as soon as you walked in."

His rawness never failed to raise her libido. Maybe it had something to do with her strong Spanish blood from the Bronx. But his barbaric mentality turned her on. It had been the same way since she had first met him down-town at the Green Room Bar, nearly a year ago.

He then attacked her right earlobe with his tongue.

Suzanne dodged it. "Sorry, but I don't want any spaghetti and Mountain Dew in my ear."

Ray leaned back to face her. "You want a dick in your ear instead? Now I'm trying to get you wet so we can do this."

"Maybe I want a dick in my mouth," she responded with a chuckle.

A bold man caused a woman to respond just as boldly.

"Oh, well, we can do that, too. I can hop right up on this table, pull my drawers down, and let you go right to work."

"Maybe later," she told him, backing down from it. "I would need a few drinks first to do that."

"You didn't need a few drinks the last time. You slobbed me up good. *Real* good."

"That's because we were already in the thick of things. I was in heat."

"You damn sure was. You gettin' me in heat right now, just thinking about that shit."

She giggled and grabbed for his crotch. "Really? Let me see it."

Big Ray was not only his namesake; it was a biological fact. The young man had a big ray of pleasure lurking between his muscular legs.

"Oh, you 'bout to see it, all right. You know how this monster sends you back home at night," he boasted. "That's why it's good you wear them busi-ness skirts over here. You don't want your husband to see that ass coming back home *bowlegged*, with your pussy hurting."

Talking shit to her like that had Suzanne wet without the need for fore-play. It was *mental* fucking that she liked. And Big Ray's mental penetration was raw and unprotected. So she pulled open his pants and freed his massive, dark dick from his money-green boxers.

"Fuck me how you want to then," she told him, stroking his shaft with her long, feathery fingers.

Big Ray got hard in a hot second and went from nearly six inches soft and squirmy to nine inches hard and thick. Her husband, Antonio, couldn't compete with that at home either. Professor Greene was only six inches and still thin on his *best* night.

"Put it where you want me to put it."

She pulled him closer and hiked up her business skirt to her stomach.

"This is where you wanted me to be, right? Well, what are you waiting for? Have your fantasy."

When she started talking dirty to him, as sexy and as professional as she was, Raymond couldn't help but feel special. So he choked up on his bat and guided himself into the lips of her lightly haired pussy without a condom. She was even on birth control now, just for him. He then gripped her ass cheeks and smooth, honey-brown thighs to anchor himself.

Suzanne slid to the edge of the counter top, so he could fit his long, thick dick all the way inside of her. She was used to his length and girth now. Then she wrapped her legs around his bare ass so he couldn't get away.

Raymond Cummings backed up his dark ass and stroked forward into the kitchen counter and a lawyer's tamed pussy.

"*Ooooh*," she moaned.

Big Ray backed up real easy and did it again.

"*Mmmmm!*"

It felt as if his dick was poking out the back of her head, it was so strong. She began to lean backward on the countertop, while raising her legs higher on his back, like a wrestler.

"Is this how you want it?"

Suzanne liked his dick size so much that her body seemed to conform to it now. So Ray began to stroke her more urgently, as her firm, suction-cup pussy increased its hold on him.

Damn, she can take it ALL now, he marveled. *I could fuck around and really get used to this.*

He began squinting his eyes blissfully as his long, powerful strokes felt better and better.

"Oh, *shit*, girl! What, you put some extra *spices* in this pussy tonight?" Raymond wanted to nut on the spot, but he held it. He wanted the fucking to last longer.

"Fuck me *good!*" Suzanne cried. "I want you to."

She was making it extra hard for him not to cum too soon. But he continued to hold on and stroke her deeply with poise.

I don't believe I got this bitch like this, he mused. *And she lets me fuck her raw dog now, and cum all up in her until her ears pop. Damn, I'm a lucky nigga!*

Suzanne thought about her experience with him as well.

Oh, my GOD, his dick is so fucking GOOD! I can feel every wall in my pussy. He's hitting them all.

As the feeling in Ray's balls began to tighten with a rising nut, he rose up on his toes and lost the steady rhythm of his stroke.

"Okay. Get *ready.*"

"*Oooh,* I'm ready, *baby.* I'm *ready.* Give it to me. *Give it to me!*" she squealed, reaching to squeeze his broad shoulders.

Then she broke into convulsions, with her legs vibrating and squeezing around him. And while she came, she made the ugliest faces of pleasure imaginable, all contorted and twisted, with teeth gritting like an extraterrestrial.

Big Ray watched her with intrigue, allowing the satisfied woman to jerk her juices out of her system. And when she relaxed, he poured on his heat again to feel his own release.

"Your husband can't do it like *this,* hunh?"

"Only *you,* Ray. Only *you,*" she groaned, squeezing his hulking arms.

Raymond had to make certain he loosened up his grip over her neck before he came. Releasing his joy with too strong of a grip around her neck may have caused him to accidentally strangle her. Nor did he want to leave fingerprints of passion around her neck. So he ran his hands *wildly* through her soft, brown hair instead.

Got' dammit, this nut gon' bust out her fucking eyeballs, he imagined as she squeezed his hot love juice into her receptive body. It felt that *strong.*

"*Oooh, yeaaahh,*" Suzanne responded to his squirting heat, filling up inside of her.

"*Dammmn, you nasty, bitch!*" Ray squealed back to her as his cum continued to squirt freely into her overheated and wiggling body.

"I like it *nasty,*" she panted.

But when Raymond had finished his phenomenal nut, he realized where they were and was hesitant to move.

"Ah...how do we get the hell out of here now? You need me to carry you to the bathroom like this?" He could imagine their combined secretions running all over the kitchen counter as soon as he pulled out of her.

"Maybe I should have gotten a towel before we started this shit," he commented.

Suzanne agreed and laughed. "Yeah, maybe you *do* need to carry me to the bathroom."

"Aw'ight, hold on tight," he told her.

She leaned up into his face and wrapped her arms and legs tightly around him. Big Ray heaved her body off of his kitchen counter and began to shuffle his feet with her toward the hallway bathroom.

They made it into the bathroom with cum dripping down their legs, before Ray could lower Suzanne into the cold, waterless bathtub.

"Shit, give me a towel," she asked immediately.

Ray smiled and moved to get her one. Suzanne moved the towel in between her legs and wiped herself up, while he wiped himself up with a second towel. He then ran hot water for a washcloth.

"This is a whole lot of cum," she complained from the bathtub, where she continued to wipe herself.

"What did you expect? With good pussy like yours, you bring a nut from my toes and fingernails."

Suzanne chuckled and asked him to wet a hot washcloth for her as well. Ray got her one and handed it to her inside the tub.

"That was real good...and *nasty*," she teased. "I had no idea it would feel that good on the kitchen counter."

"Yeah, now you know," Ray responded.

By the time they had washed up and toweled off inside the bathroom, they were both horny again.

Suzanne looked down at Big Ray's hard and throbbing dick. "Damn, that was *fast*. Did you have some kind of Viagra gel in that water?"

Raymond laughed. "Naw, he likes what he just had."

"Well, does he want some more?"

"Definitely."

Suzanne turned around to face the bathroom sink and mirror.

"You want it from the back?"

"That'll work."

With the bathtub only a few feet away from the sink, Suzanne climbed up on the tub and leaned onto the sink with her arms to give Big Ray a new angle to fuck her from.

"Oh, shit, acrobatics," he said excited. "You sure you can stay up there like that?"

She laughed. "We'll see. But remember not to ram my head through the mirror. So you may have to take it lightly and let *me* do most of the work this time."

"All right," he agreed. Then he climbed up under her legs to position himself behind her with his hard-on.

"And I want you to call me a bad girl while you fuck me," she suggested.

Ray paused. "What?" She hadn't suggested that to him before either.

She looked at him through her reflection in the mirror and repeated herself.

"I said, I want you to call me a *bad* fucking girl when you fuck me."

She said it with such violent fierceness that she sounded possessed.

"Okay, *Sasha*," he joked, alluding to the alter-ego of R&B singer Beyoncé Knowles.

Suzanne grinned into the mirror.

"Every girl has a *Sasha* in her. And I wanna let mine out *now*."

Big Ray shrugged. "Okay."

This bitch is crazy! he thought to himself as he entered her from the back. But he still planned to give her what she wanted.

As he pushed inside of her from the back, he told her, "You a bad-ass *girl*, you know that, right?"

"*Nooo*," she whined, shaking her head in the mirror and pretending. She looked like a tortured actress in a horror movie.

Raymond got in to it and barked, "Yes the fuck you are! You's a bad *bitch*!"

"I'm *not*," Suzanne squealed as he pumped her.

"What the fuck I say?" he shouted back. He looked into the mirror himself now, a dark, big-dicked assassin, killing a married lawyer from behind.

"I'm not a bad girl. I just like *dick*," she told him.

"Yeah, well, you *get* this dick, *too*. You gon' fuckin' *get it*, girl! You hear me?"

"*Yesss, yess!*"

"Shut the fuck up! You *bitch*!"

"I'm *not* a bitch," she whined.

"Yes the fuck you are! You's a *bitch*! And I'ma fuck you right!"

"Yeah, *do it*," she told him.

Caught up in the moment, Big Ray began to pound in to her with a fierceness of his own, until the bathroom sink and tub seemed ready to break apart.

Shit, this ain't fuckin' bad, he told himself. *But I hope we don't break my fucking bathroom up.*

Not only that, the steady pounding inside the bathroom was sure to alert the other tenants, who lived upstairs and downstairs.

Oooh, this shit feels GOOD! Suzanne told herself inside the mirror. *I need some of this every night!*

"*Damn*, you feel so *good*!" she expressed to him. "I can't help it. I can't *HELP IT*!" she yelped.

"I *know* you can't," Ray responded to her. "And you know why?"

"*Whyyyeee?*"

"'Cause you's a *bad fucking BITCH*!"

He then reached and palmed the back of her head with his hands, pushing his fingers through her soft brown hair. Suzanne leaned back into him, pulsating with joy.

Oh, that feels good! she repeated to herself. *This young motherfucker can FUCK!*

"*Ooooh, yess*," she moaned as she began to cum from the sink.

Ray could feel her extra looseness as he continued to stroke her.

Damn, she's LOVING this shit! he observed. *This dick is CRAZY for her!*

"You want me to nut in your mouth?" he asked her.

He began to think about other fantasies of his own.

But Suzanne shook her head. "*Nooo*," she squealed. "I don't do that."

That confused Ray for a minute.

Okay, she does suck dick in the heat of the moment, but hasn't let me cum in her mouth yet, he pondered. *But while I got her wide open like this, Im'a try this shit anyway.*

"You gon' do it *tonight,*" he told her. He waited to see how she would respond to it.

"Nooo, don't make me do that," she cried.

Oh, SHIT, it's ON! Raymond convinced himself. Just hearing her response to him, nearly made him nut already. So he prepared himself to pull out.

He teased the tip of his head around the edges of her pussy to trigger his nut, and when he felt it rising, he pulled her down from the sink and moved her over to the toilet seat.

"What are you doing?" she asked him with bulging eyes.

Raymond wasted no time. His nut was ready to shoot free with only a few licks of his head. So he pushed his ready-to-explode dick into her mouth.

"*Mmmph,*" Suzanne responded to it. She tried to turn away, but Raymond grabbed her head with both his hands and stroked his dick into her mouth until his cum shot out like a bottle of champagne on New Year's Eve.

"*Oooooh!* Swallow it! Swallow it! *Swallow it!*" he told her repeatedly.

Suzanne didn't have much of a choice. Either she would find a way to swallow his cum, or she would choke on it, because the hulking man was not allowing her to escape him. He held her head steady between his strong hands until the nut jerked all out of him. And indeed, the married lawyer forced herself to swallow down his cum.

Yeah, this bitch is the bomb! Raymond told himself. To have her swallow such a strong nut was *fabulous!*

I did it! I actually did it! Suzanne expressed of her work. It was her first time. *Now I need to get something to drink before I throw up.*

She stood up immediately and announced, "I need that Mountain Dew," while heading for the bathroom door.

"Drink it *all,*" Ray told her with a chuckle. He was so spent that he walked over and sat on the toilet seat himself to recuperate. He shook his head, grinning. "Damn!"

Suzanne hit the kitchen, grabbed the two-liter bottle of Mountain Dew from the table, and drank it without a glass.

"Mmmt, mmt, *mmph,*" she grunted to herself as she drank. Then she smiled.

She wasn't upset or embarrassed by her actions at all. She couldn't get pregnant by it. And Big Ray hadn't given her any diseases before. So she felt safe. It was safe fun. And she found that she enjoyed it.

If only Antonio could figure out how to do something like this, she pondered. *But his dick is so much smaller, and he could never bring himself to talk to me like that.*

She was in a quagmire. How long could her sexual relationship with a twenty-five-year-old construction worker—who still lived in the projects— last before it would become an embarrassment to her marriage, and the peers of her professional circles? She knew in her right mind that it was only a matter of time before she would need to break away from the insanity.

But he's so yummy, she insisted. Her fix for Big Ray had become insatiable.

When he walked out to join her from his hallway bathroom, she looked at him and grinned. "Don't get too used to that," she teased.

He chuckled. "Yeah, I *can't.* I'd fuck around and not wanna go back to work in the morning, if you keep giving me head like that."

"I didn't *give* you head. You *forced* me to do that."

"Naw, I forced *Sasha* to do it, right?"

Suzanne took another gulp of the soda and grinned. "Whatever."

After two o'clock in the morning, Suzanne Smith-Greene walked back inside of her Brookline home and was freshly loaded with rum and Coke from a quick visit to a late-night bar. There was no mistaking the distinctive aroma of rum and Coke. The strong drink would easily mask any other scents.

Once he heard the garage open and close, followed by a slam of the kitchen door, Professor Antonio Greene looked at his office clock for about the fortieth time that evening. Not able to rest his mind, while his attractive wife ran the streets, he remained up late, rereading all of the term papers and grades that he had given to his political science students.

Finally! he told himself upon his wife's return. Now he could go on to sleep. The term papers had been finished *hours* ago.

Antonio waited until his wife had made it well into the house before he began to restack the papers in alphabetical order. And before he could finish them, Suzanne walked into his open office door.

She looked down at her dutiful husband behind his office desk. "You're still up with those papers?" But at least he was dressed in his white bathrobe for bed.

He looked up at her and grinned. "I wanted to make sure that everyone gets their deserving grade, that's all."

"Awww, isn't that nice of you," she cooed. "I'm sure they'll all love you for it."

In a flash, she was out of the room and headed for bed.

Antonio finished stacking the term papers in order. He set them in their separate files for the morning, and he stood from his chair to click off the light and head for bed himself.

When he arrived in their luxurious master bedroom, Suzanne had locked the bathroom door behind her. Antonio could hear her brushing her teeth and gargling mouthwash.

"I can still smell the alcohol," he mumbled to himself. "You must've gotten *toasted*!" he decided to yell through the door. "How'd you even drive home like that?"

"What?" Suzanne hollered back out. "I'll be out in a minute, Tony. I'm trying to get myself together for bed."

Antonio nodded, pulled off his bathrobe, and climbed into bed to wait for her. While he waited, he clicked on the flat-screen television set to the sports channel. ESPN highlights and commentary lasted all night long. The latest in sports gossip concerned baseball's superstar, Alex Rodriguez, in an alleged affair with the pop icon, Madonna.

"Madonna strikes again," he joked, right as his wife walked out from the bathroom. Suzanne looked at the news and paused.

I know exactly how she feels, she pondered. *Guy Richie looks like a pussy next to A-Rod. But she married him for her sanity and family stability, until she found that shit won't hold her over forever.*

I know EXACTLY how she feels, she insisted.

Her husband broke her from her daze. "What do you think about that?"

Suzanne turned to stare at him. She even dared to tell him the truth.

Then she thought better of it. "What do *you* think?" she asked him instead.

Tony thought about it and shrugged. "I don't know. I was surprised that someone like Madonna would even marry a British guy. She seems to commit to men who are her total opposite, while having flings with guys who are more her type."

"Yeah, because her *'type'* is not *stable. She's* not stable. So it makes sense for her to crave that," Suzanne explained, sounding like the logical lawyer that she was.

Her husband nodded. "Well, that makes sense. But how long can you expect a woman like Madonna to really, you know, go for that?"

Suzanne stared at him with glassy eyes again from her late-night binge. The alcohol was all up in her system.

So, he totally doesn't get what kind of woman I am, she mused. *He doesn't see me as the Madonna or Sasha type at all. I'm just a sensible, good girl to him.*

"And how do you view *me*?" she finally asked. "What's *my* type?"

Tony considered it. "Well, celebrity women are different in that way. They expect for their guys to be as high wired as they are most of the time."

"Yeah, but you didn't answer the question. I asked you, what's *my* type?" Suzanne grilled him.

"Well, I mean, you're a professional woman. It's not all about the high-wire acts for you; it's all about the proficiency," he responded.

But I have a pussy, too! Suzanne blasted to herself. *It's not just about success and career moves all the time. It's also about loving every minute of the one you're with!*

"So, that's all I am is a careerwoman?"

"No, not hardly. You're *much* more than that, of course. But that *is* your *'type,'* since we're talking about types here."

Well, your 'type' is a boring-ass old man who can't keep up with me! she snapped to herself. She climbed into bed and remained on her left side, closer to the bathroom.

"And what is *your* type?" she couldn't help but ask.

Her husband smiled. "I guess I'm the gentle-hearted gentleman."

Suzanne thought about it with a pregnant pause. *And why did I ever think that I could be satisfied with that?* she mused. *He sounds like a pussy! And I already have one.*

So she continued to ponder her dilemma. After a few minutes, Tony clicked off the television and rolled over in his wife's direction, placing his left hand on her hip.

"Don't do that right now, I have a headache," she told him. She didn't even want to feel his touch that evening. For what? He couldn't do anything with it. Her pussy was already sore and dry from Big Ray.

Antonio nodded his head and removed his hand from his wife's hip. He mumbled, "Okay." Then he asked, "Have you taken any Tylenol yet?"

"Yeah," she lied.

Her husband exhaled softly to himself and accepted his fate.

I've lost her, he admitted. He had known that for nearly a year now. He just didn't know what to do about it.

"So, what do you think I should I do?"

Antonio had a private conversation with Professor Scarsdale at his Harvard University office, with his heavy wooden door closed behind them. Scarsdale, a Boston-raised and bred instructor of forty-nine, shook his head and chuckled at the dilemma.

"Well, that's kind of like the boat you put yourself into when you marry a younger woman. And sure, it's fun in the beginning to have a young woman, just like it is with any other new relationship. But you have no idea how she's gonna change as *she* grows older as *you* grow older. And there's no way for you to know that."

"You don't know that with any wife," Antonio countered.

"Yeah, but what you *do* know with a woman who's closer to your age is that she'll be going through a lot of the same middle-aged crises and panics that you'll be going through at the same time. So the both of you can have a little more understanding and empathy."

Antonio nodded in his chair and took the information in. Scarsdale sat on the other side of his desk in one of the three visitor chairs. His opinions on relationships and age were not new to Tony; the troubled professor only needed to be reminded of the obvious.

"But what about, you know, the sex part?" he asked his peer.

Scarsdale laughed. "The great sex part will always be a fallacy, my friend. And sure, some of these young college students would be hot in the sex department as newbies, but a lot of them don't know what they're doing yet."

Antonio heard that and smiled. His wife, Suzanne, sure knew what she was doing, whenever they were intimate, that is. However, lately, she hadn't been feeling up to it.

"My thing lately has been getting my wife to *want* to perform. She keeps running out and around the city with girlfriends and coming back home drunk and tired—so she would have me to believe."

Scarsdale raised a brow. "It's really gotten that bad? For how long?"

"For nearly a year now."

Scarsdale shook his head again. "Wow. That doesn't sound good. And again, since she's nowhere near your age, you really have no way of knowing what she's saying with that. She might be saying, in her own little way, that she wants to enjoy her youth again, while she still has it. Which, in itself, is not all a bad thing if she grows out of it. But if a young woman is too tired or adverse for intimacy *now*, then what does that say about your *future* sex life?

"And what about *you*?" he added. "Will you even be able to satisfy her in the years to come, if she gets a second wind? Those are things that older guys marrying younger women need to think more about. How do you *sustain*, over *time*, all of the intangibles of her *needs*?"

Antonio nodded in his chair again. "Those are all valid points, James. But when you first marry a person...I don't know, you figure that you'll work everything out as situations occur. I mean, despite our age difference, we're both logical people here."

"Logic has nothing to do with each person's life cycle, my friend. Either you're both in sync with where you're going in a relationship, or you're not. And you could actually agree with most of the same things of importance as far as a destination is concerned, but then disagree on *how* or *when* you wanna *get there*."

Antonio thought about his young wife's desire to have children and went silent. He hadn't exactly been forthcoming in his attempts to oblige her. He felt he was too old, too busy, and too comfortable in his lifestyle to raise children, which was a major blow to Suzanne becoming a mother.

That's a destination we definitely don't agree on, he leveled himself. So how could he blame her for going astray? It was an unfulfilled relationship for her.

So he agreed with his friend. "You're absolutely right. And if one of you doesn't have the same destination as the other, it's only a matter of time before you start going your separate ways."

Professor Scarsdale grinned. "Welcome to America and the free world, my friend. But let me ask you question, Tony. Is marriage mostly about companionship for you? Because I know that you don't have any children from either of your marriages. And if that's the case, then maybe it's better for you to have committed girlfriends, you know. That way, you don't have to go through the extra legalities and the fall-outs of divorce."

Scarsdale already presumed his friend was headed for a second divorce. Without kids and a family to hold his union together, what else was there for a young woman to hold on to?

"And you may want to start dating older women, who have less of a reason to flake out on you," he added.

Antonio looked amused. "You sound as if you believe my marriage is already over with."

James shrugged again. "Well, when the writing's on the wall…what are you gonna do about it?"

Only Professor Greene wasn't as certain that his second marriage was over with yet. He smiled and said, "Before you put the final nail in Dracula's coffin, let me at least see if we can make it back to daylight a few more times."

James grinned back at him. "Why, of course."

Back on the southwest side of Boston in Roxbury, Suzanne was butt naked with her legs bent over backward on Big Ray's bed, while he pounced into her wet, sweet spot like a jackhammer, disturbing the neighbors below him with the pulsating bed pressure against the noisy apartment floors.

"Oohh, oohh, oohh, *ooooohh…*" she moaned while he pounded into her.

Big Ray closed his eyes, feeling his fast nut mounting. Due to a new building site that was ahead of schedule, he worked a half-day and decided to call
up Suzanne to see if she wanted to sneak by for an afternoon quickie. And
the lawyer jumped at the chance, taking a long, late lunch hour after two.

"Aww, baby, here it *cuuums!*" Ray squealed as he let it all out to her.

Suzanne squirmed her body into the hot nut as it filled up her tank. Then
she pulled her legs down around him and breathed easy to relax.

"That's the best lunch hour I ever had."

Big Ray chuckled into his pillow. "Shit. Ditto for me."

Then Suzanne's cell phone went off from her purse. She moved to answer
it immediately, to see if it was the office. She grabbed her phone and read
the number.

She recognized it and paused. It was her husband. She frowned and wondered, *What is he doing calling me this time of day?* Not that Tony never called
her during her work hours, but it was usually involving something specific
when he did. She had told him a while ago that she didn't need the everyday, "Honey, how's your day going?" or "I love you" calls. She decided to
answer his mid-day call on an emergency basis.

"Okay, it's him, so I'll be off in a few minutes," she warned Raymond.

"Mmm-hmm," he mumbled. He was curious to hear her conversation
with her weak husband himself.

"Hey, Antonio. Is anything wrong?"

"No, I just had a thought. Now bear with me a minute," Antonio explained
before she could cut him off with talk about her work. It was all her regular
M.O.

"Okay, but I only have a second," she countered.

"I want us to go out for dinner tonight and have a real face-to-face talk
about where we are as a couple, be honest about what we mean to each
other, and discuss where we would both like to go."

Suzanne heard him out and considered it. *He's been talking to his friends at
Harvard about us again,* she presumed. Suzanne knew Tony's M.O. as well.
He would always seek an opinion before trying a new direction.

This could be it, she told herself. *Do I tell him the truth, that I'm ready to
move on? Or bullshit by talking about trying to work something out?*

She exhaled and responded, "Okay. Well, is the plan for right after work, or do we go home and get dressed first?"

"Let's make it right after work," he told her. "We're both professional people. So let's meet at John Cabot's Steakhouse downtown and go from there. I'll make reservations for seven."

John Cabot's was a top-of-the-line restaurant. That made Suzanne look forward to the idea. She could already taste her darkened, peppercorn steak, medium broiled. She could taste the fine, dark wine, the baked potato, and enjoy the decor of an elegant dinner at a social hub, where she would feel ten times more comfortable with Dr. Antonio Greene than she ever would with Raymond "Big Ray" Cumming. In the arena of John Cabot's Steakhouse, Big Ray was not in competition.

"All right, I'll see you then," she told her husband.

As soon as she hung up, Ray asked her, "So, you're going to a fancy dinner to talk it all out, hunh?" Antonio's voice had been loud enough to carry so Raymond could hear both sides of their conversation.

"That's what it looks like."

"Well, have fun," Raymond told her with a grin. It didn't matter to him. If he never saw the woman again in his life, she had already given him a hell of an experience with plenty of stories to tell. But he was certain that she would be back again.

Suzanne walked into John Cabot's dark, pine-wood steakhouse, right off the Boston Harbor, and gave her name. It was slightly after seven o'clock.

"Oh, yes, right this way," a male host addressed her. He led her to a table at the back of the restaurant, with a perfect view of the Boston Harbor. Professor Greene sat in the chair to the left of the table. He rose as his wife arrived with the host and pulled out her chair on the right. He'd already asked their waiter to pour her favorite red wine into her glass.

"Hey, Sweetie," he greeted her with a kiss.

Suzanne nodded to him and smiled, impressed with everything.

"Take a few minutes to look over the menu and your server will be over," the host stated.

As the host moved away, Suzanne asked her husband, "How did you manage to do this?" referring to the hard-to-get, window-view seats.

Antonio grinned. "I can still pull a few strings when I need to."

"Is that right?" She took a sip of her dark wine and continued to smile. She even liked his striking red tie that evening.

"That's a presidential red?" she stated. "A Barack Obama tie."

The thought of presidential authority turned her on. She was quickly reminded why she had married the man. Professor Greene had a little bit of style and pizzazz when he wanted to show it. And he appeared to want to that evening.

"Yeah, you didn't see me put it on this morning. You were still in bed."

She nodded and grinned. "Yeah, it's a very strong statement on you."

"So, how was your day today?" he asked her.

Suzanne shrugged. "Same as it ever was. I do my part and leave."

Antonio grimaced. "You know, you used to have a lot more passion for your work. Don't you think? That's part of what I wanted to talk to you about tonight."

He sounded like a rejuvenated man, and he was putting his agenda right out on the table for her to swallow. That was pretty direct of him.

Suzanne sat back in her chair and thought, *Shit! Who gave him his Wheaties this morning?*

Tony even ordered their steaks with swagger, forcing Suzanne to ask him, "What's gotten into you today?"

"What do you mean?"

"I mean, you really seem...on top of things today."

Antonio took a breath. "Well, I figure I have to allow us both a chance to express ourselves in this relationship, because lately, we've both been going through the motions."

Suzanne paused and remained speechless. She didn't want to tip her hand too early in the conversation.

"What do you want to talk about first?" she asked him.

She realized they had a long list of issues to address.

"Well, first of all; are you still happy?" her husband asked. He was starting the conversation with a hand grenade.

Suzanne composed herself and wondered if she should tell him the truth.

Well, since we're being up front about it, she mused. So she shook her head and answered, "I haven't been too excited about things lately. No."

Antonio kept his poise. "Well, is it the *job*, is it *me*, or is it something else you're going through right now?"

Suzanne saw a flash of Big Ray, naked in his apartment hallway, with his big, dark dick in hand. She then shook off her thoughts.

"I mean, it's a little bit of everything. I don't know. Maybe we need to go on a great vacation somewhere."

"At the end of the semester?"

"Yeah."

"To Trinidad and Tobago?" he suggested.

"Anywhere warm where I can really unwind."

Antonio nodded. "Okay. We can do that. Now what else is bothering you? Are you still thinking about raising kids?"

It was a question he *had* to ask.

Suzanne forced herself to stop and pause again before she answered. The truth was, she only thought about kids sparingly now, and mainly after eyeing someone else's kids.

"Well, I *am* getting older, Tony. But now that you ask me, I don't think enough about children for it to really be a major issue for me anymore," she admitted.

"Then again, you could be feeling bad about a number of things now because you were not able to fulfill that one goal," Tony countered. "You could be experiencing emotional diffusion."

Suzanne hadn't thought of that. She just figured she was getting her mid-life freak on. "I don't know about all of that," she told him.

Both of their steak meals arrived and halted their conversation.

"Thank you. It looks and smells fabulous," Antonio told their server.

Suzanne looked across the table and asked herself, *Who is this new man? And how long will he possess my husband?*

They tore into their meals, while watching the Boston Harbor waters beside them.

"This is a really beautiful view," Suzanne commented.

Antonio stared across the table at her longingly. He had the look in his eyes of pleasantry and pride.

"So is the view of you," he responded.

Suzanne's cold, damaged heart seemed to open up again. Or at least it tried to.

"Thank you." Nevertheless, she became a bit skeptical. "So, why all *this*, all of a sudden?" she questioned in reference to the restaurant and his zestful demeanor.

Antonio viewed it as either the beginning of a new day, or the ending of an old one. He was doing his best acting job to stay upbeat. James Scarsdale had strongly advised him to: "Who wants to stick it out with a begging and defeated man? You have to act as if you're the best thing since sliced bread to your wife. You know, flaunt who you are a little bit. I find that women, even married ones, like a man to be who he really is every once in a while. It's patriarchal liberation," he called it with a laugh.

Antonio answered, "We just needed to *do it*. Because it seems as if we're moving apart. So I wanted to stop our drift in opposing directions, and pull our boats back together to discuss what's going on."

Then he looked into her deep, dark eyes. "And I still love you, Suzanne. *Dearly*."

She looked at his neatly, low-cut head, smoothly shaved face, innocent eyes, unblemished skin, and his look of sincerity, and she melted.

Awwww, he's so adorable, she thought to herself with a smile. She even reached out and touched his face.

"I still love you, too, honey. And I'm sorry if I've been…a little *distant* lately."

She thought, *Maybe I could…I don't know, turn him into the man I need for him to be. And this is a good start.* She inspired to at least try it.

A month and a half later, after trying desperately to get her husband to be a little rougher, sexier, and uninhibited in their love life, Suzanne had gone astray in Roxbury again. Antonio just couldn't get the job done, especially since she knew where to go for a most satisfying substitute. She ended up back over at Big Ray's place.

He opened his apartment door for her with a smile. "I *knew it*. It was only a matter of time. His dick is too small now, ain't it?"

Suzanne nodded without a word. She stepped into his apartment and allowed him to close and lock the door behind her. Then she let out a long sigh. "I shouldn't be here, Ray. I've been trying my hardest not to come anymore."

Raymond laughed at her. "It don't matter how hard you try to make a *mouse* into a *man*. It ain't gon' happen. So unless you train yourself to want a *house* cat over the *big* cat, there ain't shit else you can do. Now come on in here and take them clothes off."

Suzanne shook her head and remained inside the doorway.

"Don't make me do this, Ray. I really don't want to."

Raymond read her dark, sexy eyes to see if she were role playing again. Once he noticed the same insane twinkle she had from before, he went right along with her game.

"Oh, it's too late for that shit now. You already here," he told her. And he began to undo his jeans right there inside the doorway.

Suzanne shook her head and whined, like a powerless little girl, "*Donnn't*, *Raaay*." She extended her hand to his crotch to stop him. "*Pleeease*, don't do that."

Her tease made Raymond's dick nearly jump out of his drawers and flip into her hands like an acrobat. He was hard as hell in there.

Shit, this bitch is still crazy, he thought to himself. *And I like that shit!*

"Naw, fuck that. You gon' *get it* tonight," he told her as he pulled his pants and drawers down. "Did you come with no panties and bra like I like it?"

"I don't know why, because I can't *do* that anymore, Ray. I just *can't*."

Ray went ahead and grabbed her dark-blue business skirt and pulled it up to reveal her beautiful, honey-brown ass, with no panties on to protect her from him his hard, throbbing dick.

"*Stop it*, Ray. People can hear us through the door," she told him.

So, that's where she wants it this time, he mused, *up against the doorway. That was my idea.*

He pushed her back against his locked door and lifted her into the air by her spread legs.

"*Nooo*, Ray, *don't do this*. I have a *husband*."

Ray found her sweet, wet pussy hole that he hadn't felt in a while, and rammed his raw dick up inside of her again.

"*Ooooh, Ray*," she moaned. "This is *baaaddd*."

"No it ain't," he told her with his first pump, up against the front door. "This is *good* dick. And you got some good *pussy*. And good *pussy* should never be wasted on a motherfucker who don't know what he doin' with it. Right?"

Suzanne failed to answer him as Raymond continued to pump her up against his front door.

BLOOM! BLOOM! BLOOM! BLOOM!

"Right?" he repeated to her forcefully.

"*Yesss, Raaay, yesss*," she moaned, enjoying his lost and found dick.

Big Ray continued to stroke her violently into the doorway and talk shit to her, exactly like she liked him to. She didn't care who heard them outside of his door either. That's what made it fun for her. It was raw and sexy, and the shameless passion of real life.

ARRESTED
DEVELOPMENT

Officer Jill Jacobs watched a young college student switch his way up Pennsylvania Avenue on the west side of Baltimore. She was inside her parked squad car at nearly ten o'clock at night. Everything was normal about the kid outside of his quick-footed, left-to-right walking pattern. He wore the same baggy blue jeans, designer jacket, winter boots, and carried the same style of backpack book bag that every other young guy his age carried. But his obvious walk was a dead giveaway to extracurricular activities, and a sure advertisement for homosexual come-ons.

"That's a damn shame," Officer Jacobs mumbled to herself as she continued to watch him. "Somebody needs to show that boy a better path to follow before he messes around and catches *AIDS* out here."

As the young college student continued on his way up Pennsylvania Avenue, he eventually made it out of her sight. That's when the mean streets of Baltimore stopped looking so rosy for him.

"Ay, yo, look at this faggot-ass motherfucker walking up the street switching and shit," a teen juvenile mentioned to his crew of hardcore friends. The five of them were full of bravado and swagger, while out on a street corner that intersected the main avenue. By the time Derrick Wilcox had spotted them eyeing him, he tried to change up his walk and revert back to something normal. But it was too late. The gang of troublemakers had already pointed him out.

"Aw, he scared now, yo. You see him just stop switching and shit," one of the young troublemakers noted.

Derrick thought of crossing the street instead of walking by them. But that idea seemed far too obvious. So he prepared himself to walk through them and pray that they wouldn't bother him.

"Hey, faggot ass," one of the troublemakers spat as soon as Derrick approached them on the sidewalk. So much for slipping by.

He ignored the ill-willed kid and continued walking forward.

"You heard me talking to you, motherfucker."

The unruly teenager jumped out in front of him.

Derrick attempted to walk around him to avoid further confrontation, but the boy jumped directly in front of his new path like a basketball player on defense.

"What do you want?" Derrick finally snapped at him.

"Aw, he even *sound* like a pussy. What do you *want?*" another of the five boys mocked him. They were all in the same range of Derrick's height and weight, but they were a few years younger, and definitely more rugged.

Derrick tried again in vain to walk around them; only for another one of the boys to block his path to the street.

"Where you goin', faggot? Nobody said you can leave yet."

The rugged teenager leaned back to his right as if he were ready to throw a hell of a right cross.

"I'm going back home to my dorm room," Derrick expressed and backed away from him. He knew what a hard sucker punch looked like, and he was preparing himself to dodge it.

"To do what, get fucked in the ass?" another teen to his right commented.

The troublemakers all broke into laughter as they surrounded him. Derrick then looked around to survey the street. Surely they wouldn't attack him on the sidewalk as traffic was busy with cars up and down the street. But in a flash, one of the troublemakers kicked him in the ass and knocked him forward.

When Derrick reached out to regain his balance, his hands grabbed the arm and shoulder of the boy who had leaned back to swing a punch at him. And that made the rugged teen lash out with a barrage of furious punches.

"GET THE FUCK OFF ME, FAGGOT!"

By the time Derrick realized what had hit him, he was stretched out across the pavement with kicks, punches and stomps pummeling every part of his body as they cursed at him.

"PUSSY!"

"PUNK!"

"BITCH!"

"FAGGOT!"

The beating was over with as quickly as it had started. And when the boys ran off, Derrick was left on the sidewalk, covering up his head and shoulders with his arms.

"Oh my God! Are you okay?" an older woman asked him. She had her cell phone out to call the police. "Yes, I want to report an assault on Pennsylvania Avenue... Yes, there's a young man on the ground in front on me, and he just got *jumped* by a gang of boys who ran off down the street." She listened to the operator and answered, "No, he's still on the ground bleeding right now, so you're gonna need to call an ambulance, too."

Officer Jill Jacobs received the 9-1-1 call in her vicinity and mumbled, "That's right up the street from..."

She clicked on her siren and lights and zoomed up Pennsylvania Avenue toward the scene of the crime. When she arrived in under three minutes and doubled-parked her squad car in the middle of the street, she hopped out with her gun holster open, and headed to the pavement. Then she spotted the same hot-footed college boy from ealier, sitting up against the wall of a closed storefront. His face and head were bruised and battered with fresh injuries.

"Some boys just jumped on him, and ran off," the woman who had made the call informed her.

Officer Jacobs took a breath and leaned down to inspect the young man's injuries.

"Does anything feel broken?" she asked him.

It took him a few seconds to respond. "I don't know," he finally grumbled. He seemed ticked off about it all.

The officer took in his sour mood and rose back up on the sidewalk. She stood at nearly six feet with a solid frame. Her hair was wrapped in a pony-tail under her hat.

"Okay, well, there's an ambulance on the way," she told him. The kid wasn't dying, and she blamed him for switching up the sidewalk—late night in a tough Baltimore neighborhood, anyway. She didn't have much sympathy for him.

"Did you get a good look at the guys who did this to you?" she questioned.

The young man hesitated. Then he mumbled through this busted lips, "Yeah, they were a bunch of young *thugs. Ouww*," he whined, tasting the bloody sting from his lip.

Officer Jacobs shook her head, growing noticeably irritated. Despite the young man's busted head, lip, and battered and bruised body, she didn't feel like being bothered with his attitude. It was her *job* to gather the needed information from him. He had been *assaulted* while walking through her *area* while she was on *duty*. She *had* to get his report.

"About how young were they?" she asked him.

She took out her mini notepad and pen to began taking notes.

"I don't know… Sixteen, seventeen, eighteen, *young*," he told her.

Officer Jacobs took another calming breath. "Okay, let's do it this way and start over. What's your name?"

"Derrick Wilcox."

"Where do you live?"

"On campus."

I knew it, she told herself. *He doesn't even look like he's from Baltimore. He looks like he's from a suburb in Virginia somewhere.*

She looked up from her notes and asked him, "What campus? Coppin State? Morgan? Or what?"

"No, Johns Hopkins," he answered snidely.

The officer couldn't tell if he was still sour about taking a beat down, or if he was being a plain smart ass.

Finally, she told him, "Look, I'm trying to help *you*, okay? So just answer the questions when I ask you."

The woman with the cell phone stopped, looked and gave Jill an evil eye.

"Look, you see how he's talking to me, don't you?" the officer pleaded to the woman. "He acts like it's a *crime* to do my *job. I'm* not the one who *beat him.*"

"Well, he just needs some medical attention right now, more than anything," the woman responded.

"Well, his medical attention is on the way," Officer Jacobs informed her. "In the meantime, I need to file my report to help us find the kids who *did it*. You don't want these boys to get away with it, do you?" she addressed the young college student.

Right as she asked him, two more Baltimore squad cars pulled up with an ambulance hot on their tails.

Out jumped two male officers from their squad cars; one African-American and one Latino.

"Is he all right?" one inquired.

"I'm trying to find that out now."

"Did he describe the guys who did this to him?" the other officer asked.

"I'm trying to find that out now," she repeated.

Both of the male officers looked over at her notepad and figured she had the report well underway without any further questions on *their* part. Officer Jacobs' cold-eyed glare informed them *both* that she knew how to do her *job*.

"Okay, well, you need anything else from us?"

"You can direct the traffic and get this ambulance in and out," she suggested.

The two officers looked at each other and grinned. She was what they called "a tough bitch."

"All right," they both agreed in unison.

Officer Jacobs then got back to her victim and his report. "So, what did these guys all look like—tall, dark, short, light, heavy, thin?" she ran off at him. "I want you to think about that, and I want to call you. What's your cell phone number?"

The paramedics arrived with the ambulance and pulled a gurney to the sidewalk as soon as Derrick began to give her his number.

"It's seven-oh-three..."

I knew it, Officer Jacobs told herself again as she wrote his Virginia-based number in her notebook. *Damn, I'm good!* she bragged.

Once the medics took over, Jill shrugged her shoulders and walked back to the woman to see what *she* had seen. She figured she'd catch up with the college student later.

"Ah, Ma'am, do you mind if I ask you a few questions?"

The woman immediately became hesitant. "About what? I only saw the boys run away when I saw him lying out on the pavement like that."

"Can you describe any of their coats and colors?" Officer Jacobs asked her.

"Well, you know, it's dark, and my eyes aren't that good from a distance. They never were. And I need to buy me some glasses."

Jill took a deep breath and knew that the case would be difficult. *Who would bother to talk about a basic beat down of a college boy, who may or may not be a homosexual?* Jill figured the case could also be upgraded into a *hate* crime.

"Well, can you tell me which way they ran?" she asked the woman.

"Oh, I just saw them run down the street. I didn't see which way they turned. I was too busy being concerned about *him*."

Jill looked down the block and to the corner, presuming that the boys had turned *left*. She doubted they would turn right and run across to the other side of the street. She also doubted that they would run two straight blocks.

"Thank you."

She walked over to the two male officers out in the street, who were still directing traffic for the ambulance to leave.

"Hey, I bet you if we rattle the cage around the corner, a few birds'll fly out," she suggested to her fellow officers.

"Don't we know it," one responded. They both grinned; they liked rattling cages.

"Well, as soon as we clear this all out, let's go get to it," she told them.

It didn't take long for the three officers to round up seven teenagers to scare into confessions. They were still out running the streets after ten o'clock at night. Baltimore stayed up all night that way.

"So, how many of you beat him down and stomped him? And if you don't tell, you're going to jail by yourself," Officer Jacobs threatened. She was the ringleader of the interrogation.

"Yo, I don't know what y'all talking about, man. What boy? I didn't beat up nobody," an older, rugged young man snapped. He looked out of high school and ready for the work force, the service, jail, or the graveyard. But he definitely wasn't in grade school anymore.

As the loudest protester, the guy was telling the truth. He had nothing to do with it. He was nowhere near Pennsylvania Avenue when the beat down had occurred. But *two* of the seven *were* there. They had participated in it, including the first boy who spotted Derrick and his hot-footed walk. And it was only a matter of time before something shook loose.

"Nobody bragged about beatin' down a *faggot* tonight? A *bitch*. A *girl*. A *sissy* in *pink panties*?"

Officer Jacobs was going hard on them. She understood how young men thought. She had to deal with them every day of her life, young *and* old. And she knew that the guilty would soon tell on themselves.

Sure enough, one of the boys began to smile helplessly. He was the one who had kicked Derrick Wilcox in the ass to initiate the beat down.

Jill singled him out immediately and snapped, "So, you think it's *funny*? What if you *killed* that boy tonight? *Then* what? You think *homicide* is a damn *joke*, something for you to *smile* about? Well, I hope you weren't there, because you're gonna be a part of the line-up," she informed him.

When the boy heard that, he panicked. "For what? I ain't do *nothing*," he screamed. He tried to act as hard as he could to camouflage his fear, but his heart was practically jumping out of his chest.

Jill placed her hand right on his pounding chest and said, "Uht, oh. I think we got one. So, who else was there with you? We know it was five or six of you. Or are you going down to the line-up by yourself? Let's check and see who else's heart is beating."

At that point, the first teen who spotted Derrick, and who had started the whole mess, began to panic as well. He looked straight down and refused to acknowledge his friend. He didn't want the officers to see any eye contact between them. However, the rest of the suspects didn't have a problem with looking. They all knew that they were innocent, or at *least* of *that* particular crime.

"Go on, tell us who *else* was there with you," Officer Jacobs continued to jeer the smiling boy.

"Man, I'on know what you talking 'bout." He refused to look at his friend, his partner in crime, as well. But when the other officers noticed the one kid who refused to look in his friend's direction, they connected the dots between the two.

"What's wrong with you? *Hey*, I'm talking to you," the Latino officer addressed him. In the boy's panic, he was confused with what he needed to do to act normal. And when he finally raised his head to make eye contact with the officers, it was too late.

"So, you got a problem looking at him? What does that mean? You were there, too?" the black male officer asked him.

Jill jumped on the bandwagon. "Well, you look at him right now. *Look* at him!" she shouted. When the two friends finally looked at each other, they tried their best to fake indifference.

"Do you two know each other?" Officer Jacobs asked the two line-up suspects.

Both boys were confused again. *Of course*, they knew each other. They were all hanging out together when the police rounded them up that night. But how closely did they dare to associate?

Jill stretched her hand out to feel the second boy's pounding heart, and she commented, "We got another one. That's *two* for the line-up now."

The second boy tried to shake it off by speaking calmly. "I wasn't there, man. You got the wrong guy."

"So, how come your heart is beating like that?"

"Because y'all jumped out here and started rounding people up for no reason," he explained.

"Oh, we *got* a reason. Somebody beat down a *faggot* on Pennsylvania Avenue tonight, and we're gonna find out who *did it*."

"Isn't that wrong for you to call him a 'faggot'? You supposed to say *gay*, right?" one of the other boys spoke up. That caused the guys to chuckle.

"I'm calling him what *you* call him. Did you call him *gay* when you beat him up tonight?" Officer Jacobs asked the smart-mouthed boy. "Step on up here. You're *next* in the line-up. Now we got *three* of 'em. Who's left?"

Before the smart-mouthed boy could respond to her, the first older protester responded for him.

"Yo, he wasn't out there, man. That boy just came back from the movies," he commented.

"Oh, yeah, what did you go see?" one of the male officers asked him.

"I saw that *Underworld* movie, *The Rise of the Lycans*. You know, the one with the werewolves against the um, vampires."

"Okay, so you probably won't be picked out of the line-up then," Officer Jacobs told him.

The boy grimaced and looked confused. "Yo, you already know I wasn't there, man. I mean, you gon' grab me up just because I said you shouldn't call him a faggot? I don't have no problem with them people, man."

"*Them people*, hunh?" the Latino officer repeated.

The boy looked at him. "Yeah, man, they do what they do. That's *their* thing. To each his own. As long as they don't bother *me*."

That made a few of the other boys laugh again.

"Or *what*?" the officer challenged him. "You'll whip his *gay* ass?"

The first protester spoke up again. "Yo, man, he wasn't there." He was adamant on protecting the boy.

"What, is he your little brother or cousin?" the black male officer asked.

Officer Jacobs assessed it all. She asked the oldest protester, "Were *you* there? You step up then." She read his dominant body language and knew that he could help her get to the bottom of things.

"So, will he pick *you* out of the line-up?" she asked him.

"I'm not going to no damn line-up," he answered defiantly.

She read his body language again. He had a real chip on his shoulder for a reason.

He most likely wasn't there, and he probably has a solid alibi, she told herself. *But he can still help me to get the answers that I need.* "So, if you weren't there, then what did you hear about it? Somebody come back home bragging?"

"I didn't hear *nothing* about it. I was standing out here talking about movies."

"Well, what about *you*? What did *you* hear about it?" she asked the second line-up suspect again. She had gotten away from him for a minute.

He shook his head. "Nothin'," he said weakly.

"Well, we'll see what he says at the line-up. Now we got four down and two to go. So, who else was there? Is anyone missing?" she asked the first boy who had been caught smiling.

Finally, the oldest protester had had enough. He looked at the first two partners in crime and said, "Yo, if y'all *know* something, y'all better let it be *known*, 'cause if *I* go downtown for some shit that *I* didn't do… And I *know* that *shorty* wasn't there either. And y'all *know* that shit. So, if *y'all* ma-fuckers out here *fakin'*…"

"Watch your mouth," Officer Jacobs warned him. He was getting a little too full of himself.

"I'm just saying, man," he told her. "They *know* who they are. And I'm not going downtown for no faggot shit. Excuse my French," he apologized.

"That's not a French word," the Latino officer told him.

Once the dominant and older young man let it be known that he wasn't taking the rap on something he didn't do, the first two culprits began to cower. That's when Jill read their wilting reactions, and she knew she had picked the right two boys to work on.

"Okay, so...*you two* are *definitely* going down for a line-up. You can either tell us who else was in on it, or you can pay the price for it yourselves."

They definitely were not planning to point any fingers out there. All that was left was silence, confusion, and fear.

The second teen, who had pointed Derrick out earlier, and who had started the commotion, took a deep breath. He realized that a line-up would be his downfall, so he began to think about who else could go down with him.

Officer Jill Jacobs read the dilemma on the young man's face before he spoke a word. She knew it would only be a matter of time before he agreed to give up his friends. She stared him down with poise and patience, and she repeated to herself, *Damn, I'm good!*

After all of her excellent police work in rounding up the five boys involved in assaulting Derrick Wilcox, when Officer Jill Jacobs got in touch with the college student to perform a line-up selection of the culprits, he became non-committal.

"You know, I just don't...wanna get involved with that," he told her over his cell phone.

"What? What do you mean?" she asked.

"I mean, I don't wanna *see* those guys again."

"You don't *have* to see them. You pick them out from behind a shielded glass. You've seen cop movies before, haven't you?"

"Yeah, but I don't... I mean..."

Jill snapped, "Look, cut it out. Now I know you may be a little afraid, but you're totally safe. I can pick you up from the dorm rooms at Johns Hopkins myself, and make sure no one bothers you. Now you can't let these kids get away with this. This case can be considered as a *hate crime*, and it will protect other people against similar attacks in the future."

Derrick stuttered. "But that...that's, that's what I mean. I...I don't want all of that attention. I just want to live my life."

Again, Jill started to feel a certain bias against his sexual orientation. *If he were a straight kid who got jumped, there wouldn't be a problem. But since this kid is gay...*

She asked, "Well, what were you doing out there in the first place?"

Derrick hesitated a second time. "Ah, minding my own *business*," he quipped. "And are you trying to um, *insinuate* something?"

You know what, this boy needs a real... Officer Jacobs stopped and shook her head against the phone. She figured it was all a waste of time.

"So, that's it? After all my work of rounding these kids up, you're just gonna let them get away with it?"

"Well, they know that they've been caught, right?"

"Look, that doesn't mean *anything*, if you don't force them to *pay* for it. They'll just look at this as a dodged bullet, and they'll go right back out there and assault somebody else."

"Oh, it sounds like you have a lot of *faith* in humanity, officer. I wonder where you learned *that* from."

Jill had to stop and pull the phone away from her ear to look at it. Was that kid serious or what?

Amazing! she told herself. *The people you meet out here as a police officer.*

Finally, she told him, "Okay. Good-bye."

Before she could hang up on him, he muttered, "Thank you," and continued to be a smart-ass.

Jill hung up the phone and shook her head again. "I'll just let my superiors handle this boy," she grumbled to herself. She planned to pass his case on and go on about her life as a Baltimore City Police officer.

More than a month later, Officer Jill Jacobs spotted Derrick Wilcox walking out of the Baltimore Public Library downtown with books in hand.

"Well, looka' here," she told herself from behind the wheel of her squad car. She happened to be heading north from the precinct downtown.

She stood idle for a minute at the street corner and watched the college student as he headed back in the direction of Johns Hopkins University. But his walk wasn't as pronounced as the first night she had seen him. And it wasn't as late at night.

"I guess he's learned his damn lesson," she presumed. Then she became curious. She wondered if he still had a sour-ass attitude. Was it because he was embarrassed at being beaten for his sexual orientation that evening on Pennsylvania Avenue, or did he have personality issues?

She sped up the street in his direction to catch up to him, and alerted his attention with her siren.

WHUURRPP! WHUURRPP!

Derrick turned to his left and spotted the Baltimore police cruiser pulling up beside him in the street. He frowned at it and wondered what he had done.

"I know she's not stopping for *me*," he told himself.

Inside the squad car, Officer Jacobs rolled down her passenger-side window.

"Derrick Wilcox," she called to him, remembering his full name.

Derrick stopped and eyed the officer in confusion. Once he realized who she was, he mumbled, "Oh my God, it's *her* again. Yes?" he spoke to her, still with obvious resentment.

Jill read his face and attitude. "You know what, what is *wrong* with you? I've only tried to help you out, and all you give me is constant *beef*. Now do you have a particular problem with me or what?"

"I mean, what is it that you *want* from me?" he asked her snidely. "That incident is like, so *over* with."

Oh, he is such a fucking BITCH! Jill incensed. *Just drive the hell away from him, RIGHT NOW!* she tried to tell herself. But the young man was so irritating that she felt like slapping him around, for the hell of it.

She grumbled, "You know what? Fuck it!"

She climbed out of her squad car to get up close and personal with the boy to figure out what his problem was.

Derrick backed up as soon as she approached him on the sidewalk, as if the officer was ready to give him another beat down.

"All right, now what is your problem?" she asked him. She was right up in his face on the sidewalk.

"I don't *have* a problem."

"Yes, you *do*. And you *act* like you got a damn *period*." As she studied his face up close without the fresh bruises this time, she couldn't help but notice how pretty he was. The young man had girlish features without alterations—naturally sharp eyebrows, long and curled eyelashes, long sideburns, baby hairs; soft, pouted lips, and smooth, hairless skin.

Shit, he actually looks like a damn girl, she told herself. He made *her* feel like a man, especially while she was still in uniform. *He makes me want to pull this fucking shirt up*, she snapped.

"Why can't you speak to me with any *respect?*" she asked him. "Everything that comes out of your mouth is smart-aleck."

"That's just *your* perception."

The young man happened to smell good, too, with a mix of sweet cologne, cocoa butter lotion, and fruit-flavored ChapStick.

"Are you walking back to campus?" she asked him out of the blue. She figured maybe she could soften him up with a ride back to school.

But Derrick frowned at the question. "Heck no," he answered. "I'm catching the bus up the street."

"No you're not," she told him. "You're going with me."

She would simply drive his ass back to campus, whether he liked it or not.

"Am I under arrest?"

The thought seemed interesting. Maybe he *did* need to be under arrest to correct his foul attitude. "I can *put* you under arrest, if that's where you wanna *be*. Now walk on over there and get inside the car before I *do* arrest you," she ordered.

He studied her serious demeanor. "Well, do I even have a *choice?*"

"Yes, you have a choice. You either climb into the car *without* handcuffs, or be *pushed* into the car *with* handcuffs."

Understandably, Derrick didn't like the sound of either one of his options.

"And what's option number *three?* You leave me alone, and let me go back home to mind my own business?"

"You *wish*," she told him. "Now get inside the squad car before I have to arrest you."

Derrick hesitated again. *Is she for real?* he asked himself. But when the officer moved to grab him, he quickly picked up his feet and scampered toward the squad car before she could reach him to do it herself.

"You want me in the back?" he asked timidly.

His complete recessiveness and stance led Jill to think a few inappropriate ideas about him. She even acknowledged the ill intent of her thoughts to herself.

Yeah, he's the kind of person who just makes you want to do foul things to him. I can't even lie, she admitted.

Derrick climbed inside the back of her squad car, looking like an edible gazelle who had just been trapped by a lioness.

Oh, my God, he looks like such a little pussy back there, the officer thought. The college student was giving her a lot of crazy-ass thoughts. As soon as she popped the car in drive, she asked him a personal question.

"Have you ever been with a woman before?"

Derrick looked totally floored. "Excuse me."

"You heard me right. Have you ever been with a *woman?*"

The college student hesitated and stuttered, "What, what does that have to do with you driving me back to campus?"

"I'm just trying to figure out who you are, because you always seem to have a sour disposition with me. Do you have a thing against *cops* or is it against *women?*"

"No, I *don't* have a thing againt *women*. And my mother and I get along quite *fine*. Thank *you*."

"What about with every other woman?"

"I have girlfriends."

"Girls who are *friends*, or girl*friends?* Because there *is* a difference."

"I know that."

"So, which one is it?"

"And why does this *matter?*"

Jill stared at him through her rearview mirror. She thought, *Okay, he just needs to get FUCKED good! That's all there is to it. I wish I could take him down to the jailhouse for ONE night.*

"Okay," she finally responded. "So, you want me to do this the hard way."

"What?"

"You didn't tell your mother you got jumped down here in Baltimore, did you?"

"Why?"

"Because she would have told your behind to pack up your bags and get back down to Virginia as fast as a heartbeat, that's why. So I *know* you didn't tell her. Otherwise, we would have heard about it down at the station, I'm sure."

You damn momma's boy! she snapped to herself. Now she understood him much better, and she planned to use that knowledge against him...like a cop *would*.

Before Derrick could respond to her, she added, "She probably didn't even want you going to *school* in Baltimore. What do you have, a scholarship to Johns Hopkins, and you're studying in the medical field?"

She imagined that he was smart enough to have been awarded an academic scholarship. He came off like a spoiled, little whiz kid who still needed adult guidance.

"Well, Johns Hopkins *is* one of the premier medical schools in the country," he bragged. "*And* I get to do an internship at their prestigious hospital."

And what are you studying to be, an OB-GYN, so you can live the rest of your life with pussy envy until you can afford a sex change? She amused herself with a chuckle.

She realized that the young man could likely talk about academics all night, but not about sex—he hadn't had any.

"So, what were you doing down on Pennsylvania Avenue that night; trying to find someone to turn you out? What were you, in *heat*?" she asked brashly.

"*What*? I don't like your line of *questioning*, Officer..." He stopped and looked into the mirror to read her badge backward. "...*Jacobs*."

"But it's the truth, isn't it? You're still a *virgin*. That's why you were out there switching so hard, to get some attention. But you ended up attracting the wrong *kind* of attention, didn't you?" She was pouring a psychological profile on him to break him down.

"Whatever," he responded weakly.

"So, you can't find anyone you like on campus? Or you don't want them talking about you, especially since you like *boys*?"

Derrick began to get all flustered in the back of her squad car.

"Look, does this have *anything* to do with *anything*?"

Jill was finally at peace with the boy as she continued to drive.

His smart-ass mouth is all about getting attention, too, she pondered. *This poor boy needs a kinky friend to help turn his hot-ass out. He's flaming so hard he doesn't know what to do with himself.*

"Well, I don't want you catching *AIDS* out here just because you want a little *friend* to play with, Derrick. It's very dangerous to start sleeping around with men you don't know like that."

"What? I wasn't *trying* to. I was just *walking* back to the *bus stop*," he huffed at her, irritated by her hard truths.

"Yeah, on Pennsylvania *Avenue* of all places, near ten o'clock at night. And why, because you thought you'd run into some *action* out there? And you just talked yourself into doing it?"

She was really socking it to him now! Derrick had no defense for it.

He breathed heavily in the back of her squad car. "Whatever."

She then received a police call on her radio.

"Yeah, don't you have to get back to *work*, *harassing* people or something? I guess I *do* have a thing against *cops*," he stated.

Jill ignored him and answered her radio call.

"On a quick run, give me fifteen to thirty."

"All right. I'll call Darryl on it," the dispatcher told her.

"Good, I'll back him up in a minute."

Just like that, she was off the radio and back to Derrick.

"What if somebody gets *shot* while you're still in here *harassing me*?"

Officer Jacobs shook her head and grinned. She was approaching the campus.

"We know which calls are urgent and which ones are routine," she responded to him. "Otherwise, we'd have a bunch of officers flying around the streets of Baltimore all day long. And that would be unsafe for traffic."

"Whatever," the young man mumbled again.

Jill looked back at him through her rearview mirror and smiled. *I think I'm gonna make his day*, she told herself. *He just needs a private friend. But I can't ask him about it. I have to tell his smart-aleck ass.*

"Well, it looks like this is the end of the road for you," she announced.

"Finally."

She ignored that as well. "You have early classes tomorrow?" she asked.

"*Why?* You wanna take me *hostage* in your police car again in the *morning?*"

Jill continued to smile at him. She was no longer bothered by his attention-getting antics.

"No, I needed to see how late you could stay out tonight. I need you to meet me right back here on campus at eleven."

Derrick frowned. "For what?"

"Because you need some damn *lessons* in *etiquette*. So think of it as a private outreach program."

The young man paused and considered it. "Which entails *what?*"

"Which entails you doing what the hell I *tell you* to do," she snapped. "Now, do you have an early class tomorrow or *not?*"

"No, but that doesn't mean that I'm gonna meet up later with *you*."

Officer Jacobs paused and pulled over her squad car to face him.

"Why, because I'm a *woman* instead of a *man?*"

Derrick was speechless. Before he could gather and respond, Jill told him, "You meet me here at eleven o'clock. And if I don't see your ass out here *waiting* when I come, then I'm coming to *look* for you. Do you understand me, Derrick?"

"Well, I have *homework* to do," he protested. "This *is* a university, you know."

"So you bring your books with you then. At eleven o'clock. Now get your ass out of my car and go."

The young man didn't speak another word, in case the hard-nosed officer would decide to keep him hostage longer in her squad car. But as soon as he had climbed out and her police cruiser sped off behind him, he mumbled,

"Whatever. I don't know who she thinks *she is*." And he began to walk back toward his dorm room.

Officer Jacobs smiled to herself, while she watched him in the mirror, and sped toward her destination for backup in northwest Baltimore.

"Yeah, he'll show up," she told herself. "And I'll make sure to bring a couple of *girl* toys for him."

Right on time, Derrick Wilcox waited nervously near the edge of Johns Hopkins' campus grounds in the same spot where Officer Jacobs had dropped him off earlier.

"She's just *fucking* with me, I *know it*," he grumbled to himself as he paced. The police officer had screwed up his entire evening. The poor young man couldn't concentrate on his studies without watching the clock every fifteen minutes, and contemplating whether or not he would show up that night to meet her.

But when he thought about an insane, woman police officer, stalking around campus grounds looking for him, he figured it was best to find out what she wanted instead of trying to dodge her.

I know she could find out where my dorm room is. She's a cop! he reasoned. He felt there was no way around her. He even brought his books like she had instructed.

"I know she's just trying to *scare me*," he continued to mumble. "This is *stupid*. I should go on home."

Nevertheless, he was terrified to leave. What if she actually meant what she had said to him. She could make his campus life a living *hell*. He would start looking for her everywhere. And every Baltimore police cruiser would then send his heart racing. He was forced to face up to her.

Officer Jill Jacobs pulled up to the university in plain clothes, driving a blue and tan, special edition Ford Explorer from Eddie Bauer. She spotted Derrick waiting for her at the same location.

"Like clockwork," she told herself with a grin. "And he won't tell anybody either."

She pulled up to the sidewalk, where Derrick paced back and forth, and rolled down her passenger-side window.

"Hey you, get in."

Derrick looked at the SUV and cautiously walked over to it.

"I thought you were coming in your squad car again."

She was wearing a blue jean set with pants and a jacket, and her long ponytail was out. She didn't look half bad as a regular citizen.

"The police force is my *job*, but it's not my *life*. Now get in," she repeated.

The college boy climbed into her vehicle on the passenger side and fastened his seat belt.

"I see you brought your homework," she commented.

"I *needed* to. I'm not finished *studying*. But where are you taking me to, and how long are you gonna have me out?" he asked.

Jill smiled and took off driving. *You're gonna lose your virginity tonight*, she told herself. But she didn't plan on telling him that until she got him where they were going.

"*Hel-lo.* I asked you a *question.*"

"You'll see when we get there."

Jill headed north and pulled into a hotel parking lot off the Interstate 695 beltway.

Derrick looked around at their surroundings, confused.

"Umm, what are we doing here?"

"We're going inside this hotel," she told him frankly.

The college boy shook his head and responded, "Umm, no we're *not.*"

Jill sighed deeply. "Yes, we *are*," she told him. "Now get your ass in there before I have to pull my gun out."

Derrick's eyes grew wide as he stared at her. But he refused to move. Jill then reached for her purse before he got the message and jumped out of the vehicle in a hurry.

"I'm not out here to play with you," she told him outside of her truck. She handed him a key to room 611. "I'll be up in a minute. So go ahead and get your homework out."

Derrick eyed her a second before he began to walk toward the hotel entrance. *What is she up to?* he asked himself. *Private outreach, hunh? We'll see.*

He entered the bare essentials hotel room on the sixth floor and stood. There was no way in the world he could focus there to study anything. He still wondered what the police officer's purpose was in bringing him there.

"So, what do I do now? This is *stupid*," he repeated to himself.

Before he could settle into the room and think things out, Officer Jacobs walked in and startled him.

Derrick jumped back and whined, "Oh my *God*, you *scared* me."

"Why? I told you I'd be up."

"Yeah, but I was expecting you to *knock* first, or...*I don't know*."

"Not when I have my own *key*," she answered, showing it to him.

"So, you checked into this place before you came to get me?"

Jill pulled a brown rubber dick out of her large tote bag and casually tossed it onto the bed as if it were a sandwich.

Derrick looked at it with wide eyes again. "What the hell is *that*?"

At a glance, the big brown, rubber dick looked nine inches long and three inches thick. It was gigantic! Then she pulled out a smaller one, six inches long and two inches thick.

"Umm, can I ask you what those are *for*?" the apprehensive college student commented.

"That's what you were looking for out on Pennsylvania Avenue, right, some dick? So I brought a couple for you. Or do you want some real *pussy*?" she questioned him.

The college student was stunned by it. He didn't know what to say. But the rubber dicks were turning him on. The officer then pushed him face-down on the bed and climbed on his back with her full body mass to hold him down.

"This is what you *want*, right, to be tied down, face first, and fucked up the *ass*?" She grabbed the large, brown dildo with her right hand and began to work it in between his ass cheeks for effect.

"Stop it," he told her.

"Are you *sure*?"

Jill began to poke the dildo back and forth into the back of his jeans.

"Unnnhh," Derrick moaned, seeming to like it.

"Are you getting *hard* from this?" the officer asked. She reached around to the front of his jeans and grabbed at his crotch to feel his hard-on with her left hand. "That's what I *thought*," she responded. The college boy was excited with a stiff one.

Jill began to rub his real dick through his jeans in the front, while she worked the rubber dildo into his ass from the back.

"Now you want these pants down or *what*?" she asked him.

Derrick had closed his eyes and opened his mouth into the pillow, feeling stimulated. Seeing his mouth open wide, Jill grabbed the smaller dildo with her left hand and brought it up to the boy's mouth.

"Suck on it," she told him. "Go on. It's a brown *Popsicle*."

Derrick stuck out his tongue and began to suck on the smaller dick, while Jill worked it in and out of his mouth. And her position of dominant power was turning *her* on. So she began to grind into the young man's thigh with her *own* crotch.

Oooh, this is kinky, the officer thought.

After a few minutes of working their combined senses into a frenzy with clothes on, Jill abruptly stood up from the bed.

"Get up," she told him. Derrick looked up in her direction from the bed and noticed the plain-clothes officer beginning to take her clothes off.

"Hunh?" he whimpered, not moving.

"Get the hell *up*, I told you," she snapped. She even kicked the damn bed with her right foot.

Derrick jumped up out of the bed, and his pants were noticeably poked out from his hard-on. Jill immediately grabbed his hard dick with her right hand and started to rub it again, while stepping out of her jeans. She then squeezed his mouth with her left hand and kissed him on it.

"Do you want a *girl* or a *boy*?" she asked while she kissed him. "*Pussy* or *dick*?" Derrick didn't know how to respond. He had never been that close to sex before, from a boy or a girl. He didn't even know how to *kiss*. But he was damn sure excited to *try it*.

Jill took her bra off and forced him to fondle her naked titties.

"Go on, play with them. They won't hurt you. They're soft."

Derrick rubbed the officer's titties with both hands. While he did that, the officer worked her panties down and began to undo his pants, all the while kissing him on the lips.

"Don't," Derrick told her, slightly pulling away.

That only irritated the officer. She was tired of his whining. So she snapped, "Shut the fuck up, *bitch*! You know you want this shit."

She yanked his pants down forcibly. Then she grabbed his wet drawers and yanked those down. The boy was so excited that he was dripping all over like a leaky faucet, but he was still hesitant to go all the way.

Jill told him, "You're gonna get *fucked* tonight. You're not going back to your *dorm room* without it. Everybody has a first time. Now take the rest of your clothes off."

She backed up from him in her full nakedness and waited. But Derrick only stared at her in fear. He didn't know how to respond. It was all too confusing and sudden for him.

"Motherfucker, do you want me to get my *gun out*?" the naked officer threatened him.

"*No-o-o*," Derrick whined, shaking his head and cowering.

"Well, then *take* your fucking *clothes* off. Or do you want *me* to do it?"

The young college boy cringed instead of taking off his clothes. That only forced Jill to grab him and strip him down for herself.

"You know what, you getting on my *fucking nerves*," she yelled, yanking the rest of his clothes off.

"Unnhh," Derrick whimpered, naked. He looked terrified, but his dick was still hard.

He has no idea what he wants, Jill told herself. "You know what, you gon' get *both* tonight; dick *and* pussy. Now get in that fucking bed and pull the covers back."

Derrick finally did as instructed without her having to force him. The officer then walked over to her bag of sex items and pulled out a pack of ribbed condoms and a tube of K-Y jelly. She then grabbed the smaller dildo as she climbed into bed with the boy.

"Shit, you in here dripping all over," she stated about all of his pre-ejaculation. "You sure you didn't *cum* yet? *Damn*!"

She grabbed his stiff dick and prepared to slide a condom on him.

"What are you gonna *dooo*?" he cried.

"I'm gonna *fuck you*," she told him frankly again. "Now you do *exactly* what the hell I *tell you* to do. Do you *hear me*?"

"Yesss," the boy answered.

"Good."

When the officer finished rolling her condom over his hard-on, she took the K-Y jelly and rubbed it around the tip and shaft of the smaller dildo. She figured the larger one would be far too much for his first time.

That shit would break his little ass open, she thought. She then moved into the center of the bed and turned on her back.

"Get on top," she told him.

The college kid moved on top of her as the officer spread her muscular legs around his tender, young body. She grabbed his dick into position between her legs with her left hand, while holding the dildo away from the sheets with her right.

When the officer looked up into Derrick's face, the young man still looked confused. *This poor boy has no idea what's about to happen to him. But I'm ready to give him the fuck of his life,* she told herself. *Better me than some whore out in the streets.*

So she quickly poked his condom-covered dick into her adult-sized pussy, and she closed her legs between his to make it tight. Then she spread his legs wide with her knees, and reached down to his butt cheeks with her left hand, inserting the lubricated dildo into his ass with her right.

"*Unnnnhhhh,*" the boy moaned, responding to it, squeezing his ass cheeks shut.

Jill fought to keep the dildo in position.

"Let it go *in,*" she told him. "You *want it,* right?"

"It *hurrrts,*" he whined.

"Because it's your first fucking *time,*" she snapped. "Now let it go in. I'll do it softer," she promised.

Derrick loosened up his ass cheeks, while Jill began to softly push the tip of the rubber dick into the boy's anus.

"*Oooohh,*" he began to moan and move with it.

Once he was able to relax, Jill started to stroke her body in unison with the dildo. When the dildo went in, she pushed her body into Derrick's dick, creating a rhythm.

She told him, "I'm jealous of you, boy. You gettin' dick *and* pussy. It feel *good?*"

"Yeaaahhh," he responded, shivering.

Once their rhythm was established, Jill began to stroke the boy harder, while pushing the dildo further into his ass. And when Derrick jerked forward from the pain, he pushed his dick deeper into her pussy. That made her jam him in the ass harder with the dildo, so she could feel his violent reactions up in the front in her pussy.

"*Oooohh, shit*, this is *GOOD!*" the officer moaned.

"*Unnhh, unnhh, unnhh,*" Derrick groaned, reacting to the feelings in his ass, as well as his dick. He was getting the best of both worlds. The police officer was loving it as well.

"Fuck me *good*, baby. Fuck me *good!*" she told him.

Derrick still had no idea what he was doing. He was mainly reacting. But then he began to feel something rising in his dick. There was a *surge* building up inside of him.

"Heeyyy...hey, *wait*," he begged. He felt as if something was wrong with him.

"What?" Jill asked him. She continued to stroke her body in unison with the dildo. She was starting to feel her *own* orgasm approaching.

"*Oooohh*, it feel, it feel...*oooohhh*, it feel *funneee*," the boy squealed.

Realizing that he was ready to cum for his first time in some pussy, Jill spread her legs wide and wrapped them around his lower back for better leverage. And Derrick began to pump his dick into her on his own, like a hot rabbit.

"*Oooooh, shit, boooy,*" the officer moaned. "That's how you *work it*! Work that *pussy*, baby!"

All Derrick knew was that something *strange* was happening with his dick. Then he lost control of himself when it finally hit him. A strong stream of pleasure squeezed itself out of his tiny dick hole and into the condom that penetrated the police officer's pussy.

"*Oooh, oooh, oooohhh,*" he moaned, shook, and panted. Jill gripped him by his ass with both hands and released her *own* juices. She made sure to keep the dildo secured in his anus with the edges of her fingers, so that the college virgin could feel it *all*. And he damn sure did, too! He was in a triple bliss; his first nut, his first dick, and a woman's orgasm all in one.

When it was over for both of them, the young college student was all out of breath and amazed.

"Well, *congratulations*," the police officer cheered. "You finally got what you *needed*. Now you can stop acting like a *bitch* all the time and get your attitude right."

Derrick giggled at it, feeling all loose and giddy. "I'm not that bad," he told her.

"What? Yes, you *are* that bad," she argued. "But once I got to know more about you, I knew just what your ass *needed*."

Derrick giggled again.

Jill told him, "Now give me a kiss."

The boy leaned over and awkwardly kissed her on the lips.

The officer shook her head at his terrible attempt. She mumbled, "Yeah, I'm gonna have to teach you all *kinds* of shit; how to kiss, how to suck these titties, eat pussy, work your hips right…"

"Is that all a part of your 'Private Outreach Program?'" Derrick asked her sarcastically.

Officer Jacobs chuckled at the idea. Then she warned him, "As long as it remains *private*. You hear me?"

"I know," he told her. "Everyone knows that police officers can't be going around fucking college students."

Jill nodded to him. "Good. Because I don't wanna have to come find your ass for the wrong *reason*. And if I come looking for you, then you want me to come looking to *fuck you*, not to fuck you *up*." She looked into his love-struck eyes and repeated, "You hear me?"

"Yes, I hear, you. And I wouldn't *tell* anybody," the college boy responded.

"Motherfucker, you better *not*," the hardened officer warned him again. "Because if I have to go to *jail* for your ass…"

"I *won't*," he promised her. "Did I tell on those guys who beat me up? I'm not like that."

"So, you're just a sweet little momma's boy, hunh?" Jill teased him.

"Whatever," Derrick hummed with a grin. His attitude had taken a one-hundred-eighty-degree turn for the better.

"Hmmph," Jill grunted, squeezing him as he lay beside her. "I'm gonna tell you something about *me* then. Okay? And you don't tell anybody about *this* either."

"Okay," Derrick agreed. He felt *great* that she even trusted in him.

"Well…when I was first trying to become a police officer, a lieutenant on the force…he thought I wasn't *rugged* enough. He thought I was too much of a *girl* for the job. So, he umm…took liberties with me."

Derrick listened. "You mean he *fucked* you?" He was straight to the point.

"In all *kinds* of ways," Jill admitted. "He taught me how to ride him, how to suck dick, how to take it in the ass. But he knew that umm…I *liked* it. And I told myself that I could *take it*. And that helped me to become one of the best police officers, knowing that I could take whatever people had to dish out to me, you know."

"So, now you're gonna teach *me* to take it, right?" Derrick asked her with a sadistic smile.

"Yeah, but *AIDS* is *serious* out there, boy," Jill warned him.

"You think I don't know that? Like you said, I *am* in the medical field," he countered.

"Well, you won't mind then, if I kick your *ass*, if I ever see you hanging out in the *streets* again."

"I'm *not*. I already *learned* my lesson about that. But I wasn't gonna go *home* with anybody. I just wanted to *meet* someone."

"Well, now you *have*," she told him. "And I'm a lot *safer* than the drug-infested *riff-raff* you gon' run into out in the *streets*. You hear me? So don't make me have to *shoot* your ass if I *catch you*."

"You *told* me that already."

"I'm just trying to make sure you *hear me*."

Derrick stared at her and didn't answer.

Officer Jill Jacobs added, "Especially if you're fucking with *me* now."

"All right already. I *get* it."

She then looked into Derrick's girlish face and leaned over to kiss his lips again.

"You're such a pretty little *bitch*; you *know* that, right?"

"Whatever."

Jill grinned and asked, "You want some more?"

Derrick smiled bashfully. "Yesss."

"Well, turn your little ass back over then."

The college boy did as she told him without a fuss. Jill then kissed and licked his tender back.

Derrick arched his back, feeling wonderful. "*Unnnhh*," he moaned.

Officer Jacobs stopped and grunted, "Mmmt, mmmt, *mmmph*." She stared down at the boy's smooth ass, before she softly bit him.

"Ouch!" he whined and jerked his ass away. "That *hurt*."

Jill rose back up to his ear and told him, "Bitch, that's what I'm gonna *do* if you *fuck* with me. I'm gonna *hurt* you. You're *my* bitch now, you hear me? And I'm a *jealous* motherfucker, *too*. Now you let me catch your pretty ass back out there doing something I don't want you to do. And I'll arrest *your ass* and anybody I catch you out there fucking with. Now you *try me*."

"How many times are you gonna tell me that?" Derrick asked her. He had heard her warnings enough. And after all that, she softly bit his earlobe while grinding his bare ass.

"I want you to be my pretty *bitch*," the officer confessed to him.

"I *am* already," Derrick confessed back. "So you don't have to tell me that."

"Good! And you better *know it*, motherfucker. I am *not* playing with you." Then she kissed him softly on his neck, and went on to have her way with the boy for the rest of their first night. And she no longer had to worry about his sour attitude.

———•———

CONFLICTIONS

Melanie Morgan had the most perfect black body you could ever imagine. But where she was attempting to find work in Hollywood, California, her body was simply too much. The camera was used to straight-up, straight-down girls with curves that barely registered. Or maybe a little extra bump up front in the titty department wouldn't hurt...for a *white* girl. But poor Melanie had the full Venus shape, with ass, hips *and* titties, which doomed her to countless come-on lines and intimate propositions from the men she hoped to find work with in the movie industry. Even a few freaky women had approached her. But none of them had given her any work.

Born and raised in Oakland, Melanie's black, satin skin and big, expressive eyes, only added to her allure, compounding her issues with professional flirtations. In fact, all of the extra attention she seemed to draw was what made her decide to try her luck in the movie business to begin with. People would constantly stare at her. So she figured, why not be *paid* for it? But since she was a practicing Christian from a strict household, she was not willing to accept any roles that included nakedness or acts of lewdness. Her loving family in Oakland would have been *mortified*. And what kind of message would that have been sending to her two younger sisters?

"But this is all *make-believe*. You *do* know that, right?" the acting instructors, film directors, and producers all informed her. "You're not really doing it, you're *acting* it out. You're in *character*."

Nevertheless, Melanie remained apprehensive, especially once she had made it close enough to the real movers and shakers of Hollywood to experience the delusional power they held over aspiring actresses. She saw, firsthand, competing women who were willing to do just about *anything* to be cast for even a small role as an *extra*.

"If you really want it, you gotta go *get it*, girl," the bolder actresses advised her. "They can't cast you if nobody *sees* you."

They explained to the innocent Oakland girl that Hollywood was not a child's game. Hollywood was the playground for grown-ups, and they all played there for *keeps*.

So Melanie continued to think about how she would negotiate her morals to accept the conditions of a film role in television, video, or *anything* where she could be seen and called on for something *bigger*.

I might have to be…a little bit wild for a minute, she told herself. She moisturized her body with lotion and got dressed for another audition up in Beverly Hills.

"Hey, are you ready today, Melanie?" her talent agency assistant called to check up on her. Melanie was on her way out the door and was eager.

"As ready as I always am."

"Well, get up there and have a *blast*. And good *luck*."

Melanie climbed into her small car on a foggy Los Angeles morning, slightly after eight. She then drove into the crowded morning traffic headed north toward Beverly Hills on Interstate 405. She took a breath to compose herself.

"Whatever happens happens," she stated. She was finally ready to loosen up and see where it took her.

When she arrived at the Bel Air studio near UCLA's campus before nine, she parked her car in the crowded lot and joined the long line of aspiring actors, who waited outside the entrance door and down into the parking lot.

Mannn, I hate these early-morning auditions. They always start off so crowded.

Usually, the all-day auditions were less crowded during the late-morning and late-afternoon hours. Many aspiring actors were anxious to be seen early, or had to work later on in the day. Melanie was there early because of her work schedule as well. She was due to check in for work at West Coast Video at one o'clock that afternoon. She had no choice but to crash the audition's long, early line with the rest of the anxious crowd.

The audition was for a pilot television show, ironically called, *New Generations*. It was based on a futuristic and multicultural high school setting, and the casting line represented as much. Aspiring actors and actresses of every nationality stood in line, from Hawaiian to Native American, Italian, Irish,

Mexican, African, Jamaican, Australian, French Canadian, Korean, Japanese and every mixture.

Nevertheless, Melanie's body continued to stand out, even in her normal clothes. She wore beige slacks and a simple baby-blue tennis shirt in an attempt to tone herself down, but it didn't work. Her dark skin, round ass, pert breasts and sexy stance compelled a production assistant to immediately notice her in the line.

"Are you here for the Annika role?" He was a blonde-haired college student. Most of the people in the line were young. And at twenty-three, Melanie considered herself one of the oldest. But she could pass for sixteen.

She looked at him and nodded. "Ahh, yeah, I guess so." He made it sound as if everyone knew their roles already. So he gave her the script for the African character.

I wonder if he asked me that because I'm the darkest girl in line, Melanie imagined. She read the one-page script and saw that they wanted "Annika" to speak about her African background.

Okay, do they want me to do an accent, she pondered. But she thought against it. All Africans didn't speak with accents. She decided to read it straight.

As the line moved rapidly forward, the show's director stepped out the door to take a look. He was a slim and balding, older white man. He noticed Melanie, too.

"Wow. Annika," he called her.

"If that's who you want me to be?" Melanie responded and smiled.

The director was actually calling her out in the character's name. She had *never* been *that* close to a role before.

"Can you *act*?" he asked her.

"I guess we're about to find out."

The director stared at her. "*No*, we will *not* find out. You must say, 'Yes, I can act.' Because if *you* don't know, then *none* of us knows."

He seemed to be speaking with enthusiasm to the entire line when he addressed her. "The answer, *yes*, is the key to all progress. *Yes* is what we're all here for. '*Yes*, I want the role. *Yes*, I can play the part. *Yes*, I can make it to my rehearsals on time.' And '*Yes*, I want to be the *next* big television *star* and an American *icon*."

Melanie was a little startled by the man.

Okay, we have another one of those types, she noted. She had been around a few other high-octane directors on some of her previous casting calls. She couldn't imagine herself having to deal with one on a daily basis. The high-strung type made her nervous.

The director looked back into her eyes. "So, you think about that confidence the next time someone asks you if you can play a role. *Any* role. Otherwise, you'll drown before you even dive into the water."

Then he stopped and smiled. "Not that you won't drown *anyway*, but... at least you can start *off* with some confidence. You know what I mean?"

All Melanie thought to do was nod. But before the director left her, he asked her more questions. "How old are you? Have you had any acting lessons?"

Melanie paused to decide which rapid-fire question to answer first.

"I'm twenty-three. And *yes*, I have had acting classes."

"And you still don't know if you're any *good* yet, at *twenty-three*?"

He made it sound as if she was already over the hill and wasting her time. *Okay, now what do I do?* He had her speechless.

"Well, I guess we *will* see," he commented. "We'll see about *all* of you. Who in this line has the chops to create what we need?"

Then he walked back inside so Melanie could exhale. But then she could no longer concentrate on the script. She continued to think about how much pressure the director had put on her now to perform.

Darn it! This is all I needed to throw me off!

Before she knew it, she was inside the studio building and at the front of the line, where she watched a final actress in front of her perform a heck of a job.

Wow! That was pretty good, she thought. The girl didn't make things any easier for her, that was for sure. Melanie felt like five thousand people were watching.

"Number sixty-seven. Melanie Morgan, reading for Annika," the casting director called out as Melanie walked into the center of the room. They had two cameras in the room, with one angled from the left and another angled from the right. A production panel sat at a long white table in between them, including the casting director, the show director, several producers, and several production assistants.

Melanie took a breath and thought, *Okay, here goes everything.*

She stepped into the hot spot to perform and cleared her throat.

"Quiet on the set!" the high-wired director yelled. He waited a few seconds more for Melanie to prepare herself with the script before he called out, "*Action!*"

Melanie began to read her script with full animation. "Oh, let me tell you, that's *nothing* from where I come from. In *my* country in *Nigeria*, it's, it's hotter than, than hot. I mean, a hundred and...*ten* degrees is normal... temperature there," she stated. After a relatively good start, she began to stutter and pause to read instead of memorizing the lines. And the nervousness of the pressure began to get to her.

"I remember a time when...it was, it was so *hot* that...the goats were, were fighting for the shade...beside the houses."

She read from the script so badly that it broke her concentration. She then looked up to view the responses from the director and his staff. Once she noticed him shaking his head in disappointment, she couldn't wait to finish her awful, cold read and high-tail-it out of there. She was *beyond* embarrassment.

What's wrong with me? I can read much better than this! she told herself.

"Next!" she heard the director shout when it was over.

Melanie handed her one-page script to the production assistant and mumbled, "I'm sorry," before she walked out the exit.

"Darn it!" she snapped to herself out in the parking lot. *I screwed that up bad!*

She drove back toward Interstate 405 for Inglewood, and stopped at a Starbucks coffee shop to buy a morning pastry and a bottle of orange juice.

"Hey, aren't you Melanie Morgan?" someone asked her from behind.

While headed out the door, Melanie turned to face a curly-headed, white man. She nodded to him and confirmed who she was. "Yes, I'm Melanie."

"Yeah, I saw you at the *Fireside* auditions in Burbank a few months ago."

"And you still remember me from that?"

"Oh, yeah," he answered strongly. "You did a really good read there. I felt you should have been chosen for *something*. I don't know why they passed you over."

She shrugged it off and held her thoughts to herself. "Well, you know, that's the Hollywood game. You win some, you lose some."

And I seem to lose them all, she mused.

She walked out to return home to Inglewood to get ready for work, only for the man to follow her out of the coffee shop.

"Hey, Melanie, my name is Brian Belgium." He extended his hand to her.

Melanie shifted her pastry bag and drink into her left hand to shake Brian's hand with her right.

"Nice to meet you." However, she was ready to head on her way. Her bad read at the audition that morning had made her more hasty than normal. Had she performed a good read, she may have felt comfortable enough to stick around and eat at the Starbucks location. But Brian wasn't ready to let her slip away so easily.

"You know, we have a set party tonight over in Santa Monica. And I'd love to invite you and a friend over as my guests. There's gonna be a lot of great film people there tonight, who, you know, you might be able to net-work with. I mean, I was really impressed with your work," he told her.

Yeah, I've heard that line before, she pondered. She nodded to him anyway.

"Well, you know, I work tonight until nine, so I have to see how I feel once I get off."

He nodded back to her. "Well, you do that. And if you decide to show up tonight, just ask for Brian Belgium."

He said it as if his name meant something. That made her stop and recon-sider. She figured she had to refrain from turning everything down and learn to go with the flow. She could at least investigate how the network parties panned out in Hollywood.

That's what I'm here to do, right? she convinced herself. *So, why not?*

"Well, where is this party?"

"So, how'd it go at the audition today?" Her talent agency assistant had called Melanie back to ask her.

Melanie had redressed in her West Coast Video uniform, and she was ready to head off for work at the store in nearby Culver City. She let out a deep sigh and answered the question honestly. "Terrible. I really could have done a much better read this morning. But at least I got invited out to a Hollywood network party in Santa Monica tonight," she added to cheer herself up.

"Oh, yeah? So they invited you back out? Well, *that* can be good thing. Who exactly invited you?"

"Well, it wasn't from the *New Generations* set, actually. I stopped by a Starbucks on the way back, and some guy named Brian Belgium invited me out. He said he remembered me from the *Fireside* auditions in Burbank a few months ago. He remembered my full name and everything."

The agency assistant repeated, "*Bri-an Bel-gium?*" in four clear syllables.

"Yeah, some curly-headed guy in his mid-thirties, I guess," Melanie commented.

"Oh my *God!*" the assistant responded excitedly. "Do you know who he *is?* Brian Belgium is like, one of the *hottest* young film producers on the market right now. He does a lot of work in action comedies."

Melanie had no idea who he was. The guy came off like an average, California hippie. "So, you're saying that I should pretty much go then?"

"Oh, you *better*. Are you kidding me? I would *kill* to go there."

"Well, he told me that I could bring a *friend*."

"And you're inviting *me?*" The assistant sounded surprised.

Melanie laughed it off. "Well, you know who the guy *is*. So, sure. Why not?"

"Okay, what time do you want me to meet you?"

When Melanie hung up the phone, she walked out of her apartment to head out for work, and she received another call on her cell phone. She read the number and didn't recognize it. But it was an Oakland area code. So she answered the call, expecting a family member with a new number.

"Yeah, is this Melanie Morgan?" a male voice asked her.

She frowned and answered, "Yes. Who is this?"

"This is Vincent Washington from the *New Generations* auditions this morning. I was one of the cameramen on the left, and the only black guy," he answered, then chuckled.

"Oh," Melanie responded upbeat. "So, they're calling me *back*?" she presumed. She couldn't believe it. "I was *miserable* this morning. I think that was one of the *worst* auditions yet."

She was jumping far ahead of him in her conclusion. The cameraman had to calm her down.

"Well, not exactly. I mean, you *did* do bad this morning," he admitted with another laugh. "But they liked your *look*. You just have to do better on your *reading*. So I got a chance to look up your file and saw that you were from Oakland."

"Oh, yeah," she told him. "You're from Oakland, too? I see you have the five-one-oh area code on your phone."

"Yeah, I'm from the Bay. Alameda. So I wanted to get back in touch with you to invite you out to some auditions for a few videos I'm shooting out here."

"Oh, yeah?"

Here we go with the video groupie thing again, she told herself. She had been through it all before, where the directors, producers, cameramen and musicians all wanted to flirt and fuck, instead of pay anyone.

"Yeah, and I can also talk to the producers at *New Generations* to see if I can get you a second audition. But you have to be *ready* this time," he warned her.

Melanie paused and shook her head against the phone. She didn't want to tell him that it was all bullshit, but she was *thinking* it. They all ran the bait-and-switch technique out in Hollywood, where they hang one goal over a girl's head while shopping another.

"Well, I'm not really into the whole *video* thing, but I *would* like to have a second chance for this television show."

Vincent paused to negotiate it, just as she had expected him to do.

"Well, I can do that, but there's no telling if they'll allow it or not. But if I could get you in front of the camera and show them more footage of you from like, a video montage..."

Melanie tuned him out immediately. It was the same old racket.

He probably won't even ask those people about me at the show, she predicted. *He's just trying to get me for these videos, and probably try to get some, or pass me on to someone else to work his own deals. I swear, this place is really disgusting to me sometimes!* she concluded.

She cut him off and said, "Well, I'll save your number and think about it. In the meantime, make sure those guys at *New Generations* don't forget about me."

"Oh, I won't. But *please* call me back. You might be the girl that everyone is looking for. Can you *dance?*"

On that note, she laughed out loud.

"Umm, I have to get to work now, Vincent. But I'll call you," she lied.

At nine-thirty that evening, Melanie was still wrangling over what to wear to the set party in Santa Monica when the talent agency assistant, Deborah Gilford, showed up and buzzed her at her apartment. She was early and eager.

"Girl, I'm still in here trying to figure out what to wear," she told Deborah at the door. "You wanna help me? I just made it back home."

Due to her history of enticing men, she didn't want to look too sexy, but she didn't want to look *boring* either. Deborah, on the other hand, looked as racy as she wanted to be in a hot-pink skirt and blouse set, with triangular cut-outs at the stomach and lower back. Even the skirt had triangular cuts.

Melanie looked her over and joked, "You look like *The Flintstones*. But it's cute, I like it." However, Deborah didn't have *half* the curves that Melanie had to deal with.

"*The Flintstones?* Are these cuts really *that bad?* I just wanted to look *different.*" She stood tall in black heels, with light-brown hair, and was pretty and slim.

"Well, you sure *will*," Melanie admitted with a chuckle. "I like it though. *I* just can't wear anything like that. I don't want Mr. *Belgium* coming on to me," she joked.

Deborah grinned. "Are you *sure?* Brian's definitely a *hottie.*"

"Yeah, maybe for *you*. But I'm thinking about *business* here."

Deborah walked through her apartment and stood there silently. She had something to say, but she was hesitant. Then she forced herself to air it out.

She grabbed her aspiring actress by both hands. "Melanie, *please* don't tell anyone that I said this to you. Okay? But this whole *disciplined*, don't-touch-me-I'm-a-professional-*actress* act, is mostly just *that*, an *act* for the media. Because if the guys are really turned off by that, a lot of times they're not gonna hire you, especially if you're a new face.

"So usually, unless they hire you the first time around, like, you're just *the one*, it's gonna take you a few parties like this one to loosen up for them to really feel comfortable enough to hire you," she commented. "And you didn't hear me *say that*, but that's the *truth*."

Melanie paused and took a calming breath. "So, by '*loosen up*,' you mean to go along with the whole casual *sex* game?"

Deborah, at twenty-seven, had been around the block a few times, where Melanie had not. She grimaced. "You don't necessarily go *along* with it, but you definitely don't act *appalled* by it either. You kind of take it as a part of life. I mean, it's just guys and girls, you know what I mean? So, you kind of act like it's high school and college all over again. But *this time* you have real *jobs* at stake."

That analogy became another issue for Melanie. She'd had only one boyfriend in high school, who tried discourteously to sex her up, and he had *failed*. She had guarded her sexuality closely ever since. And there she was, years later, still trying to figure out how to maintain her dream of becoming a professional actress, while continuing her chastity.

"Oh, okay," she muttered. Maybe the actress game was not her cup of tea.

Maybe I need to grow up and stop being so afraid of it, she pondered. *But that doesn't mean I'm gonna screw somebody just to be in a movie or on a television show.*

"Anyway, help me to pick out something to wear," she stated. They had a Hollywood party to attend.

When the two young women showed up at the densely populated set party after ten o'clock at the Subiak Club in Santa Monica, the bi-level club was in full swing, with pretty-faced girls and guys everywhere.

"Wow, this is *nice*," Melanie stated after checking in at the guest list table. Deborah advised her to wear basic blue jeans with a bright T-shirt and a sporty jacket.

"If you don't want to look too sexy, then look hip and spunky in jeans," she advised. "Make it look like you're going to a cool concert with a group of your girls, and don't think twice about it."

So that's what she did; she dressed spunky and casual. And her body *still* stood out, but in a hip way instead of enticing.

When they walked throughout the party, Deborah expressed in a hushed tone, "Oh my *God*, you've hit the *jackpot* in here! It's *loaded* with who's *who*. I can't even *begin* to tell you."

She didn't need to. Melanie also had noticed a horde of film, television, commercial, comedy and athletic stars inside the room: tennis star Serena Williams, comedian/actor brothers Joe and Guy Torre, basketball stars Paul Pierce and Derek Fisher, along with actress Meagan Goode, director F. Gary Gray, Dogg Pound rapper Kurupt, singer/actor Tyrese Gibson, and the list went on. She didn't recognize most of the white American stars in the room, but she did notice Jennifer Love Hewitt and a few of the cast members from the HBO hit *Entourage*.

"Okay, so…what part of the room do you want to work first?" Deborah asked her. "And we haven't even *looked* upstairs yet."

Melanie stood there flabbergasted. She was so happy she had accepted Brian Belgium's invitation that she didn't know what to do with herself.

"So are you feeling it yet?" Deborah asked her before she could get out a word.

"Yup," Melanie answered, cheesing. She was short with her response to remind herself to keep her cool composure.

Just keep your head screwed on straight in here, and you'll be all right, she warned herself. *And you let them do all of the talking.*

The silent act was how she allowed the playboy types to tell on themselves. The more a man said without her response, the more his contradictions became apparent. Then she would carefully pick him apart. So, for twenty-three years, Melanie had remained proudly untouched.

"You know what, let's go upstairs first to see who's up there before we make up our minds," Deborah suggested.

Melanie shrugged, as the guys began to notice her.

"Good *God*, who's *that*?" someone yelled out as she followed Deborah up the stairs. "Hey, come back here!"

Deborah looked back at Melanie and grinned.

"It sounds like someone's already *loaded* in here."

When they arrived on the second level of the spacious and dazzling night-club, Brian Belgium was right there in the thick of the crowd, taking pictures with the other popular Hollywood players.

Deborah continued to grin. "There's your guy."

Brian was taking pictures with Martin Lawrence and Ashton Kutcher. And as soon they stepped into view, Brian spotted them.

"Heyyy, Melanie Morgan. Come on over here. Let me introduce you to a few people."

He made her feel like a star attraction immediately. Everyone turned in her direction to look, including a few icy-cold, white girls and a couple of cute brownies.

Oh my God, why did he do that? Melanie questioned. He was putting a gigantic target on her for everyone else to aim it.

So, that's his game, she told herself. *He's trying to overwhelm me.* But she continued to keep her cool in unwarranted attention.

Deborah, on the other hand, was ready to lose it. She gripped Melanie by the arm and squeezed her like a fresh orange for breakfast.

"Deborah, my *arm*. You're *hurting* me."

"Oh, my bad," she responded and let her go.

"Everyone, this is Melanie Morgan from ahh…" Brian snapped his fingers toward her to fill in the missing information.

"Oakland," she answered.

"Yeah, Oakland, California," he repeated.

"And this is my rep assistant, Deborah Gilford, from Talent International."

"Yeah, T.I.A., I *know* those guys," Brian commented. Everything he said was extra loud for everyone to hear him.

Deborah looked as nervous as ever, especially when people began to take in her outfit. She didn't expect to get that much attention. She had worn the outfit to *draw* attention. But, to be right in the middle of things, made her feel overdone.

Brian then began to tell the crown and camera guys that Melanie was the next big star. "You mark my words. Black skin is gonna be back in, like the *seventies*."

Martin Lawrence and Ashton Kutcher both laughed at it.

Martin said, "Watch yourself now, B. I know you may *think* you're black, but you might get yourself into trouble making comments like that. So, you let *me* say it first. The black *joke* police won't come after *me* for it." he stated.

Then he gave Melanie a glassy-eyed look of his own.

"And I *do* declare that Melanie is one of the finest African-American princesses I've ever seen in my *life*. And I've seen a *few* back home in the Maryland and D.C. area. But you from Oakland, hunh?"

His look went right through her well-prepared clothes.

Oh my God, this is too much! she panicked. *MARTIN LAWRENCE is right here in front of me. And he's talking to ME!*

"Yeah, Oakland," she answered calmly and smiled.

"You ever think of modeling? How tall are you?" Ashton Kutcher asked her next. He stood out in the height department. He was over six feet.

Deborah looked up at him and was ready to hyperventilate. She couldn't believe Melanie was getting that much attention from Hollywood *superstars*.

"I'm only five-five without the heels. So, I've always thought that I was too short to model."

Ashton nodded. "Yeah, they can be pretty *anal* about the height thing. But your complexion is really beautiful," he told her.

"Thank you."

Then the cameramen started taking pictures of her.

Brian told her, "Suck it all up and get used to it, sister. This is how the big stars get roles. So make sure you learn how to *smile* good."

By the time Melanie had taken a few pictures, Brian's celebrity crew had moved on to the next conversation. "Heyyy, *Conrad! Over here!*"

And like that, the two girls fell from the head of the class to the back of the bus again. Nevertheless, the high of the moment was enough to keep them floating on helium for the rest of the party.

"So, what have you done so far?" another white man asked.

Melanie looked at the older man and felt embarrassed by her impending answer. Deborah jumped in to answer the question for her. It was time to get back to the business of pitching her client in the room.

"Oh, well, she's been getting auditions for a lot of great new roles all over," she gushed. "And you know how it works; she's gonna be the new face of everything in a few years. Look how fast it happened for KeKe Palmer."

The man nodded and pulled out a business card from his black leather wallet.

"Give us a call and send over her resume and head shots."

Deborah took his card. "Will do."

"How old are you?" the older man asked Melanie next.

Deborah jumped on that question as well.

"She's sixteen to twenty-five, or whatever age you *need* her to be," she quipped.

The man looked irritated and frowned for a minute. He wanted Melanie to speak up for herself. "What if I need her to be *thirty*?"

Deborah got stuck on that question. "Are you serious?"

Melanie read him more clearly. Her representation was getting in the way of him flirting with her. She could see it in his roaming eyes. His eyes were all up and down her body.

"We'll call you," Melanie promised him and moved on.

They stopped a minute and stood around the edges of the room. Every few minutes or so, Brian would play a game of peek-a-boo to spot where they were.

Okay, he's watching me now, but I'm not interested, Melanie told herself. All of the Hollywood hype and roaming eyes had not scored her a job yet.

"Let's go back downstairs now," she suggested to Deborah.

"Yeah, it's kind of died down up here," Deborah admitted.

They began to head back toward the stairs, only to be stopped again by a younger black man. He was not much older than them, dressed in a classy black sport jacket with a white, button-up shirt and blue jeans.

"So, you're the next up-and-coming girl," he commented with a drink in hand. "And you're from *Oakland*. I just helped turn a girl from the Bay area into a star a few years ago."

The young man was boastful with a sly delivery that fit his outfit.

I know his type, too, Melanie read quickly. *He expects a girl to jump because of who he is, or what he's done. So let me at least flatter him.*

"Oh yeah, who?" she asked excitedly.

"You ever heard of a singer named Keyshia Cole?"

Deborah butted right in. "Oh, yeah, everyone knows Keyshia Cole's story."

"Well, I helped to make her story happen. I introduced her camp to a few people when they were first looking for a record deal. I'm Winston Allen," he finally introduced himself.

"Oh, yeah, the song writer and music producer," Deborah stated. "You just started a relationship with BET with new television productions, right?"

He nodded and smiled, happy that Deborah had done her homework.

"Yeah, that's me."

Melanie had never heard of the guy.

"You're not from Oakland, are you?" she asked to make sure.

"Naw, I'm from out here in L.A. I just traveled a lot."

"Can you get me on BET?" Melanie challenged him. Since Winston was so full of himself, she was curious to see how much juice he was able to muster with his productions.

"You want an audition?"

Before Deborah could answer for her again, Melanie responded boldly. "I want a *role* on a show." She figured she would match his swagger with some gusto of her own.

Deborah looked back at him to read his response.

"Give me a contact for you, and let's see what we can do."

"Give me *your* contact and we'll send you whatever you need from our offices. I work for Talent International, and we represent her," Deborah responded. She even stuck her hand out for a handshake.

Winston shook her hand hesitantly. "Okay," he grumbled, pulling his business card to hand to her. Deborah was right there on top of him to stop his other intentions.

Melanie smiled and thought, *She's blocking everyone. I may have to take her around with me a little more.*

When they finally headed back toward the stairs, Brian Belgium called out to her again. "Hey, Melanie, you're not leaving already, are ya'?"

"No, we're just going back downstairs."

"Well, make sure you see me before you leave, all right?"

Melanie looked at Deborah before she answered. But the agency assistant had no response. She was in over her head with Brian. So, the client was forced to answer him on her own.

"Okay."

As soon as they reached the bottom of the staircase, Melanie asked her, "So, what was that all about? You won't help me against *him*, hunh?"

Deborah shrugged. "Well, I *am* only an *assistant*. And I would *hate* to try and mess things up with a guy of his *caliber*. So yeah, we really need to ask *Howard* how to deal with him back at the office."

Howard Stevens was the Talent International Agency CEO.

Melanie nodded and agreed with her. "Okay."

When they arrived back downstairs, the club area on the first level was five times more lively. The music was louder and everything. They were blasting Rihanna's "Umbrella," featuring Jay-Z.

"Wow, this is where the real *party* is," Melanie spoke up over the music. "Upstairs is just the celebrity meet-and-greet section."

"Yeah," Deborah agreed. The downstairs area was more aggressive, too.

"Hey, I was waiting for you to come back down," a guy grabbed Melanie's hand and commented.

She pulled away from him and cracked, "That's nice."

"It'd be even nicer if you danced with me."

"Sorry, but I'm not here to dance." Only a few people were dancing anyway.

Deborah then spotted some female friends of hers, standing near the bar area.

"Heyyy, there's my girls," she shouted, pulling Melanie along in their direction. "Come on, let me introduce you to them."

They all got to talking and drinking in the club before Melanie found herself getting woozy. She had rarely drunk at events.

Wow, I think I had a little too much, she told herself. Deborah seemed to be taking *her* drinks just *fine*.

"You need another one," a young white guy stepped up and asked her. He was a blond in his late twenties with a sharp, icicle haircut, standing four inches high on top.

Melanie looked and noticed him. "Heyyy, aren't you from that rock band, Iron Nails?"

"Yeah, you know my *music*?" he asked her, smiling.

"Not really, but I recognize your face from the posters," she leveled with him. "You guys had a concert recently on Sunset Boulevard, right?"

"Yeah, a few weeks ago."

Then Deborah and her girls noticed him.

"Michael *Dekker*!" one of them shouted at him, obviously inebriated.

"Hey," he answered. He raised his drink in hand in friendship.

"When's the next album coming out?"

Michael moved closer to Melanie while he spoke about it.

"Well, we're kinda working on some ideas right now, but we don't have like, a solid date or anything yet. We're like, still enjoying our *last* album."

He added, "We're working on some new soundtrack stuff for Brian right now."

"Brian is really big right now?" one of the girls commented.

Michael nodded, still standing close to Melanie. And she was too buzzed to move away from him.

"Yeah, he's the man right now. It's just his *time*."

When the rock star found another moment to speak to her in private, he told Melanie, "You know he's gonna have an after-party up at his house tonight in the 'Valley.' Are you gonna hang out?"

Melanie looked at him and frowned. "*Who's* house?"

"*Brian's*," he told her, as if she should have known already.

"Well, I have to go to work tomorrow," she blurted out. She wasn't *that* buzzed. A late, Hollywood house party was out of the question.

The rock star shook his head. "If you get a chance to be in the in-crowd with Brian Belgium right now, you *take it*. I mean, you're in the right place if you really wanna make it out in Hollywood. Brian has the golden touch right now. He even gave me a cameo in his next film."

So what? Melanie found herself blasting in jealousy. Michael Dekker was obviously *friends* with Brian, so he *would* benefit from their relationship. But *she*, on the other hand, could not be so certain of future opportunities with him.

"How do you even know he's gonna invite me to his house?" she quizzed.

"Oh, he'll invite you over. I just know."

Right on cue, Brian descended the stairs with a real-life entourage surrounding him. He looked around the bottom level of the club to spot everyone he wanted to see before he left, including Melanie. And instead of inviting Melanie by herself, he invited everyone in her area near the bar.

"You guys all going with us?" he asked the entire group.

"Hell, yeaaahh!" one of Deborah's girlfriends shouted.

Deborah made eye contact with Melanie and was not against the invitation. She shrugged and said, "All right."

But when they all started for the door, Melanie got close enough to Deborah to ask her, "Don't you have to be back at the office in the morning?"

She didn't like the vibe she felt to travel in a big group like that. She didn't have enough control over it.

But Deborah blew her concerns off. "We'll make it." And they exited the club toward three awaiting stretch limos outside. "Remember to go with the flow, like in high school, but that doesn't mean you have to *do* anything," Deborah reminded in a whisper.

But Melanie had never gone with the flow in high school. So she was a nervous wreck, while trying to figure out how to back out of it.

To make matters worse, Brian grabbed her hand and pulled her into the first limo with his personal crew, while Deborah and her friends were pushed toward the last limo.

"Ahh, I really need to stay with my *rep*," Melanie complained. However, the group of insiders were already pushing her toward the limo door to climb in. Her hesitation was only getting in everyone's way.

"It's all right. We're all going to the same place," Brian assured her with a grin.

She felt like she was in over her head now. The group acceptance was a hindrance to her individual decisions. But before she could count to three, she was there inside of a deep-seated, stretch limo with a bunch of wild, freaky strangers. She didn't even recognize any of them. They were all part of Brian Belgium's inner circle.

"So, are you guys ready to party all night?" someone asked them all. It must have been nearly twenty people all crammed inside the first car, with the other two just as crowded. Then they began to pop champagne and pass around glasses to pour it in.

Oh, no, I've already had my drink limit for the night, Melanie warned herself, shaking her head. So when the champagne bottles and glasses reached around to her, she passed them on. Then she noticed a few of the people sniffing lines of white cocaine into their noses.

Oh my God, they're doing it right out in front of me! she panicked as the limo drove toward Interstate 405. *What if we get pulled over by the cops or something?*

She couldn't believe her eyes and senses. She was in the belly of the Hollywood *beast*. People then started to kiss and make out, as if preparing for a moving orgy.

Melanie dug for her cell phone in her bag. *This is crazy!* She wanted to text Deborah immediately and let her know what was going on in there. But before she could begin her text message, a stern stare from one of Brian's crew members stopped her cold. He read the panic in the girl's face, as he remained sober in the crowd.

He then looked right at her cell phone. "You all right?" He didn't look the type of man to ask her *twice* either. He was an *enforcer* type, who didn't need to repeat himself. So she had to get what he meant *the* first time. And she *did*. The man was Brian's *protector*, and Melanie was the only newcomer who looked suspicious. She was also one of the few *black* faces inside the limo.

She eyed the stern-faced man and backed down from her phone text message with a slow nod. She understood exactly what he was there for.

Oh my GOD, I can't even call her now! she realized. She was tempted to do it anyway, but then she remembered Deborah's last words to her: *Remember to go with the flow like in high school, but that doesn't mean you have to do anything.*

So Melanie forced herself to remain calm. *I don't have to do anything I don't want to. And I shouldn't have drunk anything either*, she chastised herself.

Brian appeared through the chaos, crawling over the limo floor, and placed a soft hand on her leg. "Are you all right in here?" He looked glassy-eyed and wild himself. More than *half* the folks inside the limo were loud, animated, horny, and insane. They had all lost their common sense in there.

Melanie looked over at Brian's sober enforcer before she responded to him. His enforcer continued to eye her carefully.

"Umm..." She failed to gather her words. She felt as if she was finally starring in a movie, a movie role that she was grossly unprepared to play.

"What don't kill you will only make you stronger. All right, babe?" Brian advised her through the insanity. Or maybe it was all normal for him. He seemed to be at peace with it all.

Yeah, he's crazy, too, she concluded, looking into his eyes. *They're all crazy-behind white people in here. And a few crazy blacks, too.*

Brian read the disdain in her eyes. He said, "The inner circle is always sacred. You hear me? And you only get a few chances to be invited in. So when the opportunity presents itself to ya', you ask yourself if you're ready to take it. And if you're not, then what the hell are you even doing here?"

He seemed to be validating his point to everyone who listened.

He said, "There's plenty of other things that you can do in life. But how crazy is making believe that you're playing someone *else's* life? You know what I mean? And you make a good *living* from it. How crazy is *that*?"

He sounded like a fictional character. But within the insanity of the limo, he made perfect sense. You either act crazy with everyone else, or you get the hell out of there. Only, Melanie had no way out at the moment. They were entering the interstate.

Brian pulled a girl toward him and kissed her hard on the lips.

"Who's ready to venture to the other side of the world?" he asked them all.

"WE ALL ARE!" someone yelled from the back.

"YEAH!" the euphoric girls hollered all around them.

Out of the blue, Melanie began to smile at it. There was no sense in getting all riled up about something she could do nothing about. She would have to wait until they arrived at their destination to regain her individual sanity. In the meantime, she took in the wildness of the circle with a chuckle. Then someone passed her a glass of champagne.

"Go ahead, it'll help you to relax," a blonde-haired woman advised her.

Her lack of a smile seemed to sooth Melanie. The woman seemed rational, as if it made sense to drink in their company.

So Melanie took the glass of champagne and swallowed it down in one big gulp before she would have second thoughts about it.

"Wow," the woman responded to her. "Take your time, girlfriend." But it was too late. She had drunk it all up already. And she had no idea what it was. Then she began to feel warm inside.

"You okay?" the blonde-haired woman asked her.

Melanie looked confused and was lightheaded for a moment, as if she were floating on air inside the limo. The glass of champagne had jumped straight into her system.

"You're very beautiful," the woman began to tell her. She even stroked Melanie's hair. And it felt *good* to her.

"Your skin is like, *Godly*," the white woman flattered her.

Melanie began to bubble up at it with a chuckle. What kind of word was *Godly* for skin? Did God even *have* skin?

As Melanie looked the attractive white woman in her face closely, she could see the flakes of her makeup drying out her clogged pores. The woman looked to be in her early thirties, and she was still considered a hottie, despite her dried-out skin.

They may all like her in here, but my skin is way smoother than that, Melanie bragged to herself in her inebriation. She was so close to the white woman's face that it felt as if the woman had kissed her.

"You're beautiful," the woman continued to express. She had her hand on Melanie's smooth face now. And *that* felt good, *too*. Then everything sounded quiet and serene for a minute, until the blonde-haired woman leaned over and kissed her on her lips.

Did she just kiss me? Melanie asked herself. Before she could answer the question, the enchanted woman kissed her lips again. Then she began to rub Melanie's breast with her hands.

Whooaaaa, she moaned in her thoughts. *This is craaazy!* But she couldn't seem to *move* to *stop* the woman. It felt too *good* to stop her.

The next thing Melanie knew, the white woman had climbed into her lap and spread Melanie's legs to get closer to her. And as she continued to stroke Melanie's hair, kiss her lips, and titillate her breasts, ever so softly, she continued to call her, "Beautiful."

Oh my God! What is she doing to me? Melanie rambled in her thoughts. But she was powerless to stop it. Her head leaned back against the window, and her eyes met with the neon lights that changed colors on the outlined sunroof.

Ooooh, this feels so good, Melanie told herself limply. She licked her moist lips as the blonde-haired woman continued to kiss and seduce her inside the limo in front of everyone. Melanie's natural defense had suddenly flown south for the winter, leaving her unprotected for an erotic ambush. And the limo ride to Brian's hillside home, overlooking the San Fernando Valley, seemed to take them forever.

"Remember, Melanie, the inner circle is *sacred*," she could hear him repeating to her. "And nothing you do with us will ever *leave* this place. So welcome home."

Less than thirty minutes later, Deborah Gilford was all in Melanie's face at Brian's elaborate, hillside home.

"Are you okay?" she asked her for the third time. They were standing outside on the back deck, under the full moon, in a Californian nighttime breeze. And Melanie looked unstable.

"Yeah, girl, I'm good. It's just the drinks," she answered.

"You drank something more inside the limo?" Deborah asked her with concern.

Melanie shook it off. "It was just *one* drink."

"Yeah, but one more drink is all it takes sometimes," the agency assistant barked.

Melanie didn't feel like hearing it. Deborah was blowing her mood. She had been cock-blocking everyone except for Brian Belgium all night. And Melanie now thought of returning to the great feelings that the blonde-haired white woman had given her earlier.

"Are you *sure* you're okay?" Deborah asked a *fourth* time.

Melanie finally brushed her aside to walk back inside the house.

"I have to go to the restroom."

Deborah followed her back inside before she stopped with her girls.

"Is she all right?" they asked her themselves.

Deborah shook it off. "She doesn't *seem* like it. But she's always in control, so I guess she'll be all right once, you know, she gets the drinks out of her system."

"Well, isn't this house *great*?" one of her girls whispered. "I wonder what rooms he'll allow us all to peek into."

As Deborah and her girls chatted to themselves in their small group on the outside deck, Melanie made it to the hallway bathroom and caught the eye of her blonde-haired friend from the limo ride.

"I'll catch her on her way back out," the woman told people standing next to her. "Isn't she just like, *beautiful* though. I'm like, *sooo* attracted to her."

"Yeah, we *saw* that," a younger woman responded with a chuckle.

"Yeah, what was in that *drink* you gave her?" one of the guys asked.

Brian Belgium walked up before the blonde could answer.

"So, where's Melanie?"

She pointed to the bathroom. "She's inside."

Brian looked toward the bathroom and had a thought.

"You ah, wanna use a room with her?"

The pretty blonde smiled at him. "Sure."

"Can I watch?" he asked.

"If you want. I mean, it's only your house."

"And what if she lets me in on it?" he quizzed.

The blonde-haired woman shrugged. "Well…"

"All right, I'll show you to it," he plotted.

As soon as Melanie walked out of the bathroom, her blonde friend grabbed her by the hand and led her forward.

"Come here, I wanna show you something."

Melanie followed her without refusal and arrived at a secluded bedroom. And as soon as they walked inside, the woman closed the door back and attacked Melanie's beautiful black body with everything she had; lips, hands, fingers, hips, knees, shoulders, toes, ankles. She was feeling up every inch of her.

"I want to do everything to you, sweetheart, if you let me."

Melanie didn't refuse her. She was still lightheaded from the drink. She wanted to feel the woman's soft touch again. So she allowed her free roam over her body.

Oh my God! This is so crazy! What am I doing in here? Melanie pondered.

The blonde woman began to strip from her clothes and move Melanie toward the bed.

"Can I see how beautiful you are?" she asked, taking off Melanie's jacket.

She caressed her breasts and made them aroused again. Then she began to kiss her nipples through her T-shirt and bra.

"I really want you," the woman expressed to her lustfully.

With less room there to move, Melanie fell back across the bed, where the woman attacked her flat stomach and her bare belly button with her probing tongue. Then she spread Melanie's legs against the edge of the bed.

Oh my goodness. This woman is freaky, Melanie told herself. She felt the lustful woman going after the button on her jeans.

No, no, nooo, Melanie finally protested. She stopped the woman with her hands. But that only made the blonde lick each of her fingers ravenously.

God, what is she DOING to me?

Before Melanie could fight her off again, her button was popped open and her zipper pulled down.

"Wait, wait. What are you doing?" she spoke up.

"I wanna taste you, sweetheart, just a little bit."

Taste me? Melanie repeated. *With her tongue?*

She was still trying to figure what the white woman's intentions were. Now she knew.

Yeah, she IS freaky. But I can't let her do that, she told herself. Nevertheless, she found herself struggling to hold up her pink panties, while the woman's greedy tongue inched closer and closer toward the succulent lips between her legs. Then she poked a finger inside of her.

"*Oooh*," Melanie moaned, pulling back. But when she pulled away, she gave the woman more room to pull down her panties and jeans from the edge of the bed.

"Let me get you nice and wet," the horny blonde begged her. She was pulling Melanie's pink panties away from her crotch now. Before she allowed the beautiful black girl to respond to her, the white woman dipped her tongue below the panty line and licked the outer lips of Melanie's virgin pussy.

"*Ooooh*," Melanie moaned, feeling it. The woman's tongue felt like a wet feather, tickling up her clitoris. But Melanie remained against it. So she reached down with both hands to push the woman away.

The blonde gripped her by both hips and placed her chin inside of her panties, securing her head in between Melanie's legs, where she could go to work on her without obstruction. Realizing the woman's secured position,

Melanie rose up in a panic on the bed, attempting to squeeze her legs shut. But it was too late. The blonde's greedy tongue poked inside of her tight, dark sugar walls.

"*Ooooob,*" Melanie moaned again. Her body began to throb and heat up, uncontrollably, while the white woman did her business between her legs. Then she reached up under her shirt and bra and fingered Melanie's hardened titties with the soft tips of her fingers.

Oh my God! I'm HOT!

No longer able to fight it, Melanie began to run her restless hands through the woman's long, blonde hair.

"*Mmmm, yeaah,*" the woman moaned back to her. "Just relax, sweetheart."

She pulled Melanie's panties and jeans down even farther.

"Just lie back, and let me do it all."

Melanie didn't know what "*all*" meant, but she was no longer able to fight the feeling. So she fell back across the bed, while the woman pulled her jeans and panties off completely, and planted herself back in between her legs. Melanie's smooth black skin contrasted the woman's pale, white shoulders.

When her bottoms were completely discarded, the white woman's tongue action was able to work Melanie's sweet, dark pussy deeper.

"*Ooooooh*" she moaned, squirming over the bed.

The woman began to work her tongue like a miniature dick, in and out of the wet walls. Melanie balled up the bed sheets in her fists, while she squeezed her eyes shut toward the ceiling.

Ooooh, she feels so good! she admitted to herself. The horny white woman was servicing her well.

"You like it?" she asked from down below.

Melanie looked down into her eyes and mumbled, "*Mmm-hmmm.*"

The woman climbed up to her chest and pushed her T-shirt and bra up to lick and suck her titties now, while placing her knee into Melanie's wet crotch.

"Take this off. I wanna see your beautiful body," she stated, referring to Melanie's bra and T-shirt. Before she knew it, the woman had Melanie naked and squirming in ecstasy inside of a foreign bedroom.

Brian Belgium soon peeked through the door and loved what he saw. It was like an erotic, black-and-white Benneton ad. Their contrasting white and black skin became hypnotizing, as Brian continued to watch them from the cracked doorway.

Wow! I wish I had a camera to record this, he mused with a smile. *I've never fuckin' seen a body so perfect. I have to fuck her myself!* he thought of Melanie. *It'll be like, going back to Mother Africa.*

So he quietly slipped into the room and closed the door behind him. But that immediately sent Melanie into a panic when she saw him standing there.

"Oh my *God!*" she snapped, covering herself up on the bed. She was embarrassed as well as fearful. What did he have planned for her in there?

"Hey, hey, it's just me," Brian told her with his palms raised in surrender. "Remember, this is all our inner circle. It's all right."

Inner circle or not, his presence in the room had startled her. She had forgotten that there were other people in the house. But when Brian barged into the room like that, *uninvited*, Melanie remembered that there were *tons* of people at his house with them.

I gotta get dressed! she panicked. *Oh my God! Deborah's still here! What if she's looking for me?*

Her concerns all rushed out at once, as swiftly as she moved to grab her things.

Shit! Brian responded. *Look what I've done now. She's all fuckin' paranoid!*
"Hey, calm down and relax," he told her. "I'm leaving."

Melanie ignored him and continued to collect her things to get dressed in a hurry, while her new friend attempted to calm her nerves as well.

"It's okay, sweetheart, he was just being a *guy*. Brian is totally *harmless*. He's a real *doll*," she explained.

Brian quickly backed out of the room like he said he would, but it was too late. All that Melanie could think about was what *Deborah* would think of her.

What did she put in that drink? she finally asked herself of the woman. Her body remained hot and disoriented as she redressed.

Once she was dressed and ready, she ignored the woman's final pleas and walked back to the closed door, pausing there behind it.

"No one even *cares* what we do in here, sweetheart," the blonde-haired woman pleaded. "It's all the inner *circle*."

Melanie ignored her again. She thought, *Now how do I get out of here without people seeing? And how was I so stupid!* she blasted herself.

Behind her in the room, her horny friend was getting dressed herself.

"Are you gonna call me, Melanie?"

Melanie couldn't even concentrate on her. It was all an aberration, as far as *she* was concerned. She was hoping never to see the woman again.

Then she made her move and strutted out the room, looking carefully for Deborah. When she failed to spot her before reaching the hallway bathroom, she felt good about it. Then she found that the bathroom door was locked when she tried to get in.

Darn it! But at least I made it out of there, she told herself. So she stood by the bathroom and waited, while thinking up lies for where she had been. She didn't even know how long they had been inside the room.

While she was waiting there, she spotted a few of Deborah's friends down the hallway from her. They saw her and stretched their eyes wide in panic. Melanie noticed it and wondered what it was all about.

Did they see me walk out of the room? she panicked again.

She looked back to see if her blonde *stalker* was there. But she wasn't.

Okay, at least she didn't follow behind me. But why are they looking at me like that? she continued to ponder of Deborah's girls. From the looks of their stares, she could tell that something was amiss. Or maybe she was still feeling the effects from the crazy drinks she'd had.

But after awhile, she had been standing next to the bathroom for five minutes. That's when one of Deborah's girls began to head in her direction.

"I think someone's in there," she stated.

Right as she said it, Deborah Gilford barged out of the bathroom. With Melanie standing there waiting to get in, they surprised each other.

"Oh, Melanie," Deborah responded nervously. "Where were *you*?"

However, Melanie was too close to the bathroom for Deborah to get away with her secret mission. And when she spotted the rock star, Michael Dekker, inside the bathroom, she immediately understood why Deborah's friends had been staring at her with concern. Their girl had been *busted*.

Okay, now I don't have to worry about what I did, Melanie told herself. She almost felt like smiling. But she held it in.

"Umm, I didn't see anything," she lied. "It's all in the inner circle in here."

Deborah looked at her and then toward her friends before she nervously laughed it off. "Ahh, yeah, right, the inner circle."

Michael walked out of the bathroom with a smirk, and the temperature inside of the bathroom told their story.

"Well, I'll be out in a minute," Melanie announced as she walked inside and locked the door back behind her. Then she took a deep breath and stared at herself inside the sweaty mirror. She felt dirty and couldn't take a shower yet.

"What was I *thinking*?" she stressed to herself.

I've been very bad tonight, she mused. *It must have been something else in that drink that made me all loose like that!*

Nevertheless, she felt that no one had to know what had happened to her. She would keep it all to herself.

At nearly three o'clock in the morning, Deborah drove Melanie back home to Inglewood in dead silence. They were both worn out from the evening, with another work day ahead of them in six hours. And they were both embarrassed by their actions.

When they approached Melanie's apartment complex, Deborah finally said, "Well, I guess you *know* where I was over at Brian's. But where were *you*?"

She had been waiting to ask that question all night, especially since she had been caught in the act. She wanted them both to go down in infamy together. But Melanie refused to play the game with her.

"I was just watching movie footage in one of the rooms. They had a big flat-screen TV in there, and I was still a little woozy from the drink, so I didn't want to be around a lot of people like that," she fibbed.

Deborah heard her out and nodded. "Yeah, I understand." Then she perked, "Oh well, at least I scored VIP tickets to the next Iron Nails concert."

She attempted to laugh it off.

Melanie understood her embarrassment. "Don't be so hard on yourself, Deborah. It's just Hollywood. Anything can happen here, right?"

"Yeah, you can say *that* again." She searched Melanie's eyes for more information. "But where did you get that 'inner circle' line from?"

"Are you kidding me? They were using that line all night. I guess that's what they say to get people to go along with them. So they kept repeating it until it was in my head like a played-out song," she stated. Then she laughed at it.

Deborah chuckled at it herself as they pulled up to Melanie's apartment building.

"Okay, well...what happened tonight *is* in the inner *circle*, right?"

She wanted Melanie's confirmation that she would remain silent about it. She had a reputation to protect to keep her job at the agency.

Melanie squeezed her hand for sincerity. She said, "Of course. I said it earlier and I *meant* it."

Deborah exhaled and smiled weakly. "Thank you."

When Melanie climbed out of the car to end her very long night, she told herself, *I can't even begin to judge anyone now. Hollywood got the best of both of us tonight.* And she couldn't wait to give herself a long, hot shower in her bathtub...even though it would never wash away the sexual reality of her evening.

I guess Hollywood is not all make-believe after all. And now I know.

PARADISE

Brian Culpepper stood in front of the judge inside the New York County divorce courtroom and managed to keep his composure. He had lost possession of his five-bedroom home in Harlem, his dark-blue Denali SUV, his condominium in the Hamptons, and custody of his son and daughter. He had been ordered to pay $20,000 a month in alimony and child support to his wife for the next fifteen years, and until his six-year-old daughter had turned twenty-one to set up scholarship trust funds to mature when they turned eighteen. The total package of the divorce was estimated at nearly six million dollars.

Jesus Christ! his lawyer thought to himself as he stood there beside him. *He's getting hit with everything.*

Brian barely cared anymore. He was ready to wipe his hands clean from all of it. A lucrative and generous stock investor at a young age, the fast life had gotten the best of those around him; his wife, his family, his friends, *and* his business associates. And when the man had finally found an oasis to get away from it all, into the awaiting bed of a woman who he thought had loved him, he found that she was just as deceitful as everyone else around him.

Brokenhearted by her betrayal, Brian refused to agree to the woman's dollar amount in her attempt to blackmail him. That's when she followed through on her threat to confess their affair to his wife. And she told her *everything*. Not only that, but she supplied addresses, dates, pictures, receipts, gifts and stacks of telephone records. With a wife who had been less than warm, overly skeptical, and calculating to begin with, Brian never had a chance. So he bent over inside the courtroom and took his fucking like a bitch at a breeding kennel.

"Do you have anything you want to say?" his lawyer asked him hesitantly.

He had no idea what was on Brian's mind at the moment. He only hoped and prayed the man wasn't thinking about killing himself.

But Brian shrugged in his impeccable dark-blue suit and bold, colorful tie. He forced himself to appear as if he were a perfect picture of poise over adversity. So he shook his head and answered firmly, "No."

His ex-wife attempted to read his eyes from her side of the courtroom to gauge how he was taking the final verdict, but he never even looked in her direction. He didn't want to give his ex-wife the satisfaction of his emotions.

"Let's settle everything up inside the car," he told his lawyer as he turned to walk out of the courtroom.

Seeing that the man was impenetrable, his mother-in-law commented loudly from the countroom's benches, where she sat with her grandchildren, "Well, you can at *least* acknowledge your *kids!*"

Her outburst got to him. Brian wanted to acknowledge his son and daughter, and hug them and kiss them inside of the courtroom like any other father would. Yet he understood that it was all another form of their many exploits. Why would they even bring the kids to such a hostile, adult environment? So he fought his urge to give in to the shameful manipulation.

He's turning into a bitter and hard man, his lawyer assessed of him as he followed his client out of the courtroom.

As they walked toward the awaiting limousine outside of the courthouse, Brian told his attorney, "I want you to set up a power of attorney for the Culpepper trusts and accounts, where I don't have to be involved with any of it."

The attorney nodded. "No problem. I can prepare the paperwork immediately."

Brian nodded to him. "Good. And I want you to call up her attorneys and let them know that we'll deposit the full six million dollars within two years time, and be done with the whole thing."

The attorney looked at him and was startled. "Ahhh, Brian, you might not want to *do that*, even if you had all of the money *tomorrow*. I mean, that's only gonna make them skeptical of how much you really have."

Brian looked back and said, "The judge just gave us the settlement terms, right? So take it right back to the judge and tell him your client does not trust the level of stress that a prolonged settlement would endure, and that he would rather be a normal father to his kids without any bickering over money. And I'm sure that the judge would understand that and order her lawyers to accept our terms without attempting to question where the money's coming from. And you just tell them that I'd rather go *broke* paying them off, and have to start my company all over again, than to be forced to have to deal with that woman for the next fifteen years of my life. Because I'm not doing it."

Brian sounded so clear and precise that his attorney had no more room to argue.

"O-kay," he agreed to it.

Before they reached the black limousine at the sidewalk, Brian's ex-wife ran out of the building with their two children holding her hands. And she began to yell down the cement steps toward him.

"BRYY-AN! BRYY-AN! THESE ARE YOUR *KIDS!*" she yelled at him.

Brian shook his head and never looked back. He asked his lawyer, "You see what I mean? They shouldn't have even *been* here today. Even her *lawyers* know that. But she used her mother to bring them." Then he climbed into the limo without another word.

As they headed back toward his Manhattan apartment inside the car, his lawyer shook his head and commented, "Wow! If she's *that* bad, then how do you ever get a chance to see your kids in peace?"

Brian paused with his answer. "Well…the reality is…they become casualties of the divorce."

His attorney looked into his stern and meaningful brown face inside the car and thought, *Shit! He just called his kids CASUALTIES!*

He figured his client could have used a more humane word. But when they reached Brian's sky-rise apartment building in busy Manhattan, he stated, "You know…you try to give a woman, your friends, and your family members as much as they need to be happy, and then you find out that it's a never-ending cycle. Then you try to do something satisfying for yourself, and all hell breaks loose."

"So, what do you do now?" he questioned. "Do you start the cycle all over again, with a new wife, new friends, and new family members? Or do you try to fix a broken record with Scotch tape?"

Then he laughed, while his attorney sat there dumbfounded.

"Put the paperwork together for me, Wade. And I'll sign it once it's ready," Brian told him on his way out.

Wade placed his hand on Brain's arm before he could leave.

"Are you okay? You sure you wanna be left alone right now? You don't want to come up to talk, or go down to your offices?"

He was still concerned about his client's mental state.

Brian shook it off. "Nah, not today. I'll go back in the offices tomorrow. And I'm tired of talking *or* listening right now. Didn't we both hear enough today? So I need to relax a minute."

Wade, a young and sharp lawyer on his way up, had been around suicidal bosses before. And the bleak outlook that Brian discussed with him was surely a need for alarm.

Those may be the last words he ever says to me, Wade panicked. *Maybe that's why he's trying to take care of his family like, RIGHT NOW!*

"Are you sure? You don't wanna do lunch or anything?"

Finally Brian frowned at him, reading his attorney's obvious paranoia. "Wade, I'm not gonna do anything to hurt myself, okay? Now I'll talk to you later."

He climbed out of the limousine and headed into his building for the twenty-first floor.

"Hey, Mr. Culpepper? How's your day been today?" the bellman asked him.

Brian forced a smile. "I can't complain about too much. I can still afford to live in this building, right?"

The bellman chuckled at it. "Yeah, I guess you're right about that," he commented. The apartment tower was not at all a cheap residence.

But when Brian arrived in his breathtaking apartment, with the New York city skyline in view from his living room, his smiling and joking was over. He walked over to his mahogany bookshelf and grabbed the first pictures he could find of his son and daughter, and he sat down on his dark leather sofa to stare at them. Then he slowly began to weep, with his right hand rubbing the tears away from both eyes.

He broke down and mumbled, "I love you guys. I love you *so much*."

But...I can't stop from living my life, he thought to himself. *There's too much living left to do.*

He stood up with the picture of his kids and walked over to his living-room window to look out again at one of the most fabulous skylines in the world; Manhattan, New York.

"I'm gonna miss this city," he stated. His plans to move far away had already been made. Brian wasn't just moving to another city, or to another American state. He had decided to leave the country completely. He had been doing good business with well-respected men internationally, and he had traveled to countries around the world. And sometimes he envied what he saw, a world of so many different opportunities...for *everything*. All he had left to do was to break free from the shackles that held him hostage in America.

So he took another look at his kids in their smiling picture, as he took a deep breath and exhaled. Then he muttered to himself, "...I'm gonna *pray* for you guys."

Nine months later in the city of Mumbai, India, Brian Culpepper had officially changed his religion to Islam, and his given name to Khalif Raj Muhammad. From his comfortable mansion off the coast of the Arabian Sea, he paced back and forth with his cell phone to his ear in front of a scenic, second-story living room that overlooked the beautiful blue waters that were less than a mile west of his villa. He was dressed in a golden silk sari, with a white-and-gold headdress, and no socks or shoes in the comfort of his home, while engaged in a long-distance conversation with his older brother, Jacob, in Long Island, New York.

"I mean, what are you planning to do, Brian? You're never gonna come home again to help raise your kids?" his brother argued.

"With all due respect, my name is Khalif Raj Muhammad now. And I'm hoping, with your good blessings, that you'll be able to step in and help raise your niece and nephew for me in the spirit of Allah."

Khalif spoke with calm and poise, and he was free of the constant stress, the despair, the betrayal and the anguish that he had felt over the past four years in America. And he was ready to fulfill a very important meeting that afternoon. So he was anxious to finish his brother's burdening phone call.

Jacob responded tartly. "Look, man, don't talk to me with that brainwashing

Muslim shit. You could have done that in *America* if that's what you really wanted to *do*. Because my niece and nephew are not *my* responsibility."

Khalif responded to him calmly. "Nor have you been *my* responsibility as my older brother. But *En sh' Allah* (God willing), I was always able and willing to help *you* in your personal struggles."

Khalif had helped not only his older brother in *his* personal and family issues, but he had helped plenty of their family members as well; with hundreds of thousands of dollars in cash, and countless hours of sound business advice, only for them all to fail at lifting even a *pinkie* to help him in *his* times of need. In fact, it was his older brother, Jacob, who had introduced him to his eventually spiteful mistress, who had led to Brian's final unraveling in America. So Khalif began to smile to himself and enjoy how much better his life would be abroad.

Feeling guilty about their past, Jacob countered, "Oh, so you still gon' hold *that* over my head? Look, man, we all make mistakes in life. You made mistakes, *too*. Don't try to act like you all *perfect* just 'cause you helped me out a few jams. But *I* didn't just jump up and try to fly away from *my* problems. I stood here like a man and *faced* them."

"But what *if* you were able to leave America?" Khalif asked his brother civilly. "And what if you had found a better way to live with people who really *appreciate* you? Would you have given yourself a chance to make a change for a better life?"

Jacob paused before he answered. He had always realized that his younger brother had been the most driven, rational and supportive of all of their family members. So he became more *careful* with his choice of words.

"Man, when you go to another country, it's *always* gon' feel like that, Brian. You an *American*. But the grass ain't always greener. And sometimes you gotta learn to refertilize your own lawn and get the weeds out, that's all."

Khalif smiled again, impressed with his brother's analogy. Then he countered it. "And sometimes we have to be intelligent enough to know when to walk away for much better *acreage*. That's business one-oh-one, Jacob," he told his brother matter-of-factly.

"Yeah, but your *family* ain't a *business*, man. We talking about your *blood* here."

Khalif told him, "The message of Islam teaches us that our *families* are the most important business of our *lives*. So why would I *not* treat my family like a business? That was my biggest downfall in America. But now I am no longer blinded by the separation between church and state. And my business, my family and my *religion* should all work as *one*."

"Aw, Brian, Christianity teaches you the same damn thing, man," Jacob argued. "That separation between church and state shit is only for the government. But you can do what you want to in your own *house*."

Khalif responded, "Exactly. And we did. We did everything that was *wrong*. And I no longer want to live that way."

"All right, fine, you live however you wanna live. But don't cut your *kids* off, man. What did *they* do?"

Jacob had a good point. The children were innocent. But as long as they were connected to his ex-wife, and to the old weeds of the damaged lawn, Khalif felt vulnerable to touch them. So he had already convinced himself for the better, to take a tough-love approach with his American children to insulate himself against his past weaknesses.

"*En sh' Allah*, when they are old enough to make their own decisions, then we'll see if they would like to join me."

"Aw, man, what kind of cop-out shit is that? You know damn well your kids don't have a choice in something like that," Jacob snapped.

Khalif said, "And when they *do*, I will explain to them their *mother's* way and *my* way. And then they'll have their *own* choice to come and go as they *please*, as long as they respect the Prophet *Muhammad's* way and his journey to *Allah*, whenever they are with *me*."

He then looked at his eighteen-karat gold watch, and he realized that he had said enough. He would need to be leaving for his important meeting soon.

"Look, man, you can't tell your kids what to do like that, once they're already *grown*," Jacob advised him.

"Jacob, we'll need to finish this conversation at another time. I have a very important meeting to make in the next hour that I need to prepare for," Khalif informed his older brother.

"Yeah, whatever, man. It's in the middle of the damn night over here anyway. I need to get some sleep. I just wanted to make sure I caught you with the time difference. And we're *not* done talking about this *either*. So you call me *back*. Your children *need you*, man. So you think about that for a minute."

When Khalif hung up the phone with his brother, he was forced to take another deep breath to compose himself. The mental and spiritual welfare of his children was still an obvious weakness for him, as it *should* be. Nevertheless, he would not stray from his chosen path.

"I'll just have to convince my brother to help raise them to keep them close to me," he expressed. Then he gathered himself to leave.

"Nasid," he called to his housekeeper and driver as he headed down his staircase.

Nasid, a dutiful Indian man dressed in all white, popped into view from the entrance foyer of the house.

"You ready to go?" he asked in choppy English.

"Yes," Khalif answered.

"Good. I go get the car."

Khalif slid on his soft, brown leather shoes and walked outside of his earth-tone home on a pleasant and sunny day of eighty-eight degrees. As he awaited his driver to pull the car out in front of him, he stared up at the blue sky of scattered white clouds and was at peace with himself.

This is what it means to have paradise, he contemplated. *I should have done this a lonnng time ago. But it's better late than never.*

Nasid pulled up in a white Rolls-Royce Phantom with shiny, silver-and-gold rims. He hopped out of the car and walked around it briskly to open the back passenger door. And while he served his American immigrant boss, Nasid's smile was as bright as the afternoon sun. He loved every *second* of his job. It beat working in the heat of the daily, poverty-stricken markets inside the center city of Mumbai.

"The car is ready, Mr. Muhammad."

Khalif chuckled as he climbed in. "Yes, I can see that."

Nasid closed the door behind him and hustled back around to the driver's seat.

"It's a beautiful day today," Khalif commented. They drove north toward their destination.

"Yes, yes, very beautiful," Nasid agreed. He took a peek into the rearview mirror to see how Khalif was holding up his composure on such a big day.

"Are you nervous?" he asked him. "I've heard Vinod's *three* daughters are very *beautiful*, and so are his *six nieces*."

Khalif smiled and chuckled again. He *was* nervous. He said, "More than anything, I'm nervous about choosing the wrong *one*. I would much rather be asked to choose *three* instead," he joked.

Nasid broke into laughter. "Yes, that would settle *everything*. You could choose one daughter from *each* family."

Not only did Vinod Siyamesh, a long-time business associate and international investor, offer *his* three daughters to the talented, American businessman in marriage, but his two brothers, Kumar and Shyam, agreed to offer *their* daughters in marriage as well. With Vinod as the second oldest brother, he was asked to allow for a democratic process so that all *three* brothers could offer their daughters equally.

Nevertheless, Khalif assumed Vinod's two brothers were only positioning themselves and their families for good favor from him in the future. But surely, Khalif would marry one of Vinod's three daughters *first*. Then again, he worried what would happen if one of his six *nieces* was prettier, and with more talent to offer him as a wife.

"If they're so pretty, I'm amazed that none of them are even married yet," he commented to his driver with a grin.

Nasid responded quickly, "Two of his oldest daughters *are* married. But few men can *afford* any of them. And the young men who *can* are more interested in being *playboys*. So they want to get married much *later* now." He said, "But for *you*, a *rich* American man, living in *India*, and who is ready to marry an Indian *woman*, they will all worship your *feet*."

Khalif didn't know how he felt about that.

"And how does that make *you* feel?" he asked his Indian driver.

Nasid nodded, making eye contact with him through the rearview mirror. "I hope to have same one day when *I* can afford it."

Khalif responded to him with a grin. But the prospect of virtually *buying* a wife in India was much different than the dating games that were played in America. However, for the wealthy, the tables of ready-and-willing wives could turn in a man's favor in a very similar fashion. Wealthy men had far more opportunities. Yet, the *loyalty* and *service* part of a marriage to an American woman, could hardly be counted upon through income alone.

When they arrived at the off-shore estate of Vinod Siyamesh, less than an hour north of Mumbai, and near the city of Thane, Khalif became even more nervous. He had been to Vinod's large mansion to discuss business several times before, but never to select one of the man's daughters as his wife. That changed everything. So he began to breathe deeply, similar to an American teenager on prom night.

This is definitely nerve-wrecking, he admitted to himself. He had only seen *glimpses* of Vinod's daughters before, and they were always covered in colorful headdresses and garb.

Vinod and his two brothers met Khalif outside of his home, where Nasid pulled up beside the other exotic luxury cars that were parked inside of the circular driveway.

"Welcome back home, my brother," Vinod addressed him. He and his brothers were all clean-shaven Indian Muslims, with skin nearly as brown as Khalif's. And they all wore white and gold for the occasion.

The men all hugged and kissed both cheeks in their greetings.

"You Americans sure know how to pick out a car," Vinod's older brother, Kumar, commented of the white Rolls-Royce. He was also the tallest brother at nearly even height with Khalif.

"Your brother picked out this car," Khalif informed him.

"Only because I knew you would *like it,*" Vinod explained. "But it's only a small token of respect for how much investment money you have helped us to make over the past seven years, my friend."

Vinod was the middle brother in size as well, where Shyam was the shortest.

Vinod slapped a friendly arm around Khalif's shoulder and bragged, "You have made me *millions* of U.S. dollars so far, my brother. And we all plan to make *millions* more."

"Well, now he will be your *son-in-law,* if he decides to marry one of your daughters," Kumar added. "Or maybe, *my* son-in-law."

Shyam did not add to their discussion concerning the marriage. He only smiled as they made their way toward the house. And when they entered, they all left their shoes inside of the foyer.

"Come, come, we will eat lunch first," Vinod expressed, leading them into a separate dining room.

When Khalif heard the laughter of women in the dining room beside them, he became nervous again.

Man, I just want to get this over with, he told himself. It wasn't that he was not excited about choosing his first Indian wife, he did not want to prolong the issue. Indian culture had a way of prolonging everything. Even a simple lunch could become a five-course meal.

"So, Khalif, what do you think about Tata's acquisition of Jaguar from the American *Ford* company?" Shyam finally asked him over the table.

Khalif swallowed down his first bite of food with Indian pita bread. "It depends on what they do with it. Americans can be very unforgiving about too many changes in their cars. So when Cadillac got away from the big, fancy cars that they were *known* for, only the Escalade was able to recover lost ground. And the OnStar system did okay. But Cadillac still lost much ground to Lincoln, with the Town Car and the Navigator."

"So, who will Jaguar lose to as a mid-level luxury car?" Vinod questioned.

"Well, *Mercedes* continues to be strong," Khalif answered. "And Maserati is making its *own* comeback in America, like Jaguar did when Ford took over. But really, there's no particular mid-level luxury car that stands out right. People are buying a little bit of everything."

"So, what do you say, not to invest in Tata?" Kumar asked him more pointedly.

Khalif shook his head. "Not yet. Let's see where Ratan wants to go with it first. But if *I* were a part of management, I'd shop it around the world first before I start making too many changes with it. And I think most Americans will take the same wait-and-see approach."

Shyam shook his head. "That's a strong enough of a reason not to invest for *me*. A wait-and-see approach means a very long return, if *anything*."

Khalif took another bite of his meal and commented, "The best companies to invest in in America are the major sports franchises; baseball, basketball and American football. Because if Americans support nothing else, they support their *sports* teams."

Vinod agreed with him. "Yeah, yeah, you're *right*. Even when sports teams *lose*, or they move to a new city, the price of the franchises continue to increase every year."

"And so do the television contracts," Khalif added.

They went back and forth over the hot and cold investment prospects, while eating their lunch meals, until Vinod finally put an end to it all.

"Okay, enough talk about investing for now. Let's have you meet our daughters," he addressed to Khalif and his brothers.

That quickly raised Khalif's heart rate again.

Okay, here we go, he prepared himself.

First they all took turns washing and drying their hands inside the bathroom. Then they walked into the elaborate sitting room of fine furniture, artwork, and Indian rugs. Vinod left them momentarily to allow the women of the house to know that they were ready.

"Okay, you will meet *my* three daughters first," Vinod announced upon his return to the sitting room. "And remember to please ask them any questions you would like."

He sat on the sofa beside Khalif and called for the oldest of the three daughters to enter the room. She entered quietly from the right of the hallway. She wore bright red and carefully undid her headdress to reveal her long, dark hair and smooth, tan skin. She was tall and beautiful.

She bowed and greeted, "*Asalamalakim* (Peace be on to you). My name is Rani, and I am the *third* oldest daughter of Vinod Siyamesh."

Suddenly the nervousness subsided. It was time for all seriousness.

Khalif greeted the daughter back and asked her, "How old are you?"

"I am twenty-three."

"And you went to school in London for two years?" He had heard Vinod speak of his daughter's studies abroad on several occasions.

"Yes. I took international studies there."

In the past, Khalif would have *valued* her education, but presently, he didn't trust a woman with too much ambition in a marriage. And he could not believe that a traveling, educated woman would enjoy an arranged engagement.

"How long do you plan to stay in India?" he asked her. It struck Rani as a peculiar question. Did he want her to leave or to stay?

She grimaced and answered, "India is my *home*, but I can travel wherever I *need*."

"And where would you want to travel?"

For that question, she smiled and answered, "I would love to travel all over the world, where I may use my education."

"And what about going back to London?"

She grimaced again. "If I have *business* in London, or if my husband would like to go there, then I will return."

"So, you have made no *friends* in London?"

"Oh, of course," she answered. "But I have made friends from *everywhere*; the United States, Canada, Australia, the Middle East, Japan, Spain…"

Khalif nodded as he listened to her. Rani would prove to be a great asset to her father in business, but Khalif still did not trust to select her as a wife. She was Vinod's oldest, unmarried daughter now, and if she were a man, she would easily be in line to take over his estate. So Khalif kept that in mind.

"No more questions," he told her with a smile. "And thank you."

Rani smiled back to him and bowed again to Khalif, her father, and to her two uncles.

Vinod nodded to his oldest daughter and was pleased with her answers. "Good. Send in your sister, Saleema."

"Yes," she responded. She smiled and nodded to Khalif again as she left the room.

Saleema Siyamesh walked in dressed in yellow. She took off her headdress to reveal her thick, dark-brown hair and smooth, tan skin; she was even more beautiful than her older sister. She was slightly shorter than Rani, with a rounder face, and a pair of auburn eyes that glowed with illumination inside the room. And when she looked directly at Khalif with her eyes, they nearly melted his heart.

Merciful Allah! he told himself. But he had to curb his excitement. Saleema was only the second of nine daughters that he was there to choose from.

"How old are you?" he asked her.

"Twenty."

Her eyes did not budge from him, nor did she waiver in her solid stance.

"And how long do you plan to stay in India?"

She smiled. "I *love* India. India is my *home*. But I will go wherever my life takes me."

Her uncles chuckled at the passion of her answer.

Khalif commented, "But you have not gone away to school."

She shook her head and answered, "No," with no further explanation.

Khalif was forced to ask her, "Why not?"

She paused and continued to stare at him. "I did not feel a reason to. There are good universities here in India."

"And what are you studying?" he asked her.

"Biology. I want to study how to grow and select better foods."

"Better *foods*?" Khalif repeated.

She nodded and answered, "Yes, I like to *cook*."

Again, her uncles and father responded with chuckles. Saleema had an abundance of presence about her.

"But you are only twenty years old. Are you even ready for marriage?"

"I am a *good* twenty. I am *very* mature for my age."

Khalif heard her out and nodded with a grin. "But are you ready for marriage to an *American*?"

With the directness of his question, Saleema finally looked down and away from him. Then she returned her glare to his eyes. "Yes," she answered. "I am."

Khalif nodded and was unsure of Saleema as well. The prospect of an arranged marriage definitely seemed *forced*. How could he really know if Vinod's, or his brother's, daughters were really ready to *be* married? Were they even allowed to deny their father's wishes?

"No further questions. That is all," Khalif told her.

Saleema seemed to study him a bit longer with her stare before she acknowledged the completion of his questions.

"Okay," she finally answered. Then she bowed to them.

"Send in your sister, Ieesh," her father addressed her.

Saleema nodded. "Yes." As she left the room, she cut a final eye to Khalif.

He caught it and smiled at her, causing her to hesitate for a second.

She's really checking me out, he told himself. *The first daughter didn't do that. Saleema*, he repeated to remind himself of her name.

The third and youngest sister walked in, wearing lime green. She undid her headdress to reveal her silky, long hair, with lighter skin than both of her older sisters. Her face was also more acute, like a European's. But Khalif knew immediately that he would not choose her. She was the baby of the family, and she deserved to *remain* that way. Nor did she seem as stable in her stance.

"How old are you?"

"I am nineteen."

"And are you ready to be married to an American man?"

Instead of looking down like Saleema had done, Ieesh cut an eye to her father. Then she looked back to Khalif and nodded. "Yes."

"Are you *sure*?"

Her uncles began to chuckle at her instability.

She smiled, nervously. "Yes, yes," she repeated quickly.

Khalif told himself, *There's no way in the world she's ready for marriage.*

After meeting all three of Vinod's daughters, his brother Shyam asked Khalif, "How come you did not ask Rani if *she* was ready to be married?"

Khalif smiled. "Because she's the oldest. I was more interested in what her plans were for her future."

"But her *future* should be with *you*, right?" the oldest brother Kumar hinted. "Unless, of course, you find one of *my* four daughters to be more appealing."

Vinod chuckled at the obvious brother's rivalry. "We will see," he commented. "By the way, Saleema turns twenty-one, and Ieesh turns twenty later on this year," he informed Khalif.

Khalif responded with a nod and a grin. "Okay."

He thought, *This is something else. I could never imagine doing something like this in America.*

When Kumar's oldest daughter entered the room, she was dressed in much more elaborate garb. She undid her multi-colored headdress and introduced herself.

"My name is Sunita, the oldest daughter of Kumar Siyamesh. And I am very pleased to meet you, Mr. Muhammad."

She was very formal, and beautiful as well. But her regal tone sounded a little *too* formal. And her tactfulness made her seem stuffy.

"Do you dream about picking your own husband one day?" Khalif asked her.

Sunita's eyes cut to her father. "I, ah...what do you *mean*?"

Kumar frowned at Khalif himself. An arranged marriage was honorable.

"I mean, do you have someone of your own that you are interested in?"

Sunita shook her head and answered, "No. Not without my father's blessing."

Her three younger sisters seemed just as stuffy. And even though they had all worn tasteful and stylish saris and headdresses for the occasion, none of them really stood out past the oldest. They all lacked personality.

Maybe that's their way of accepting an arranged marriage. Or either their father told them to be too *respectful,* Khalif mused to himself. Either way, none of Kumar's daughters had swayed his mind past Saleema or Rani.

When the youngest brother, Shyam's, oldest daughter walked in, Khalif was rather worn out from it all. He had seen seven young Indian women, with two left to go, but he had already narrowed down his most logical choice.

Unless one of Shyam's daughter is fabulous, I've pretty much already made up my mind, he pondered.

When Shyam's oldest daughter, Priya, walked in to greet him, wearing beautiful purple, Khalif was stunned by it. However, her *height* was so much shorter than his, that she immediately seemed like a little *girl* to him.

Instead of asking her how tall she was, like he wanted to, Khalif asked her his uniform questions. "How old are you?"

"I am twenty-one."

"And are you ready to marry an American man for the rest of your life?"

She paused, smiled, and giggled. Then she answered, "I guess I am."

Khalif felt that was cute, in an Indian Barbie doll kind of way, but definitely not as a first wife.

Her younger sister, Safika, introduced herself last, standing taller, thicker, and seemingly more stable than her older kin.

"How long do you plan to remain in India?"

"Until my husband asks me to leave with him," she answered. But the sincerity of her answer seemed empty. It seemed as if she were reading from a script.

Khalif nodded at the end of the introductions and said, "Thank you. I have no more questions."

As soon as Shyam's daughter walked out of the room, Vinod asked his young American friend, "So, what do you think? What daughter do you choose?"

They all stared at him, ready for his answer. Khalif forced himself to pause. The open selection of a wife was still a foreign concept to him, and one that he needed to have patience with.

"Ah, *En sh' Allah*, if you all don't mind, could we all have dinner with your daughters without their headdresses, so that I may be around them longer to make my final decision."

The Indian brothers all searched each other for their combined agreement. They then began to nod to his request.

"Sure, sure, we can all have dinner together like a family," Vinod stated. "In fact, we'll all sit outside with our wives and daughters and have tea, while the dinner is being prepared."

That idea sounded even better. Khalif happily agreed to it.

"Merciful Allah," he cheered. "That sounds *great*."

Vinod then called to his housekeepers in their native tongue and told them all to set up the tables and chairs outside in the yard for tea.

"You drive a hard bargain, my friend," Kumar commented.

Khalif laughed it off. He said, "It's just a little hard to choose a wife after just an introduction and a few questions answered, you know."

"Oh, I understand," the Indian man responded. "It's a lot different from the many years you spend with a woman in America, right?"

"Yeah, *if* they even *get* married in America nowadays," Khalif quipped. "Shacking up *without marriage* is the new thing to do over there now."

"Yes, my friend, shacking up is the new thing *everywhere*. But for old-fashioned businessmen like us, and followers of Islam, a man's family still represents the stability of his fortune and his moral interests."

"All praise be to Allah," Khalif agreed with a nod.

When they all gathered outside on the soft, green grass of Vinod's villa estate, Khalif was allowed to meet their Indian daughters again with their mothers, and even meet a few of their brothers who were present. It was closer to the family gatherings that he was used to in America, but without the bickering. And as the daughters hovered around him amongst the comfort of their family, while making their individual personalities felt, Khalif made certain to view Vinod's daughters, Saleema and Rani, specifically.

Rani was the more busy of the two, socializing with her various family members, while Saleema spent more of her time standing still and watching. Nevertheless, her glowing, auburn eyes seemed to cut back to Khalif whenever he moved. She also made certain to give him unobstructed views of her, while never turning her back to him to whisper like her cousins did. When he met Saleema's attractive mother, Ramshicka, he noticed the second daughter had been the only one to inherit her mother's auburn eyes.

"You're Saleema's mother?" he noted.

"Yes," she told him and squeezed his arm. "She has a very strong personality."

"And Rani?" he asked.

Ramshicka smiled. "She is now the oldest unmarried."

Khalif analyzed their mother's words quickly. Just because Rani was the oldest sister now, didn't necessarily make her the most loyal to a marriage. She could likely be more loyal to her father and her Indian family, which she was already hinting at through her activities out in the yard. She barely even looked at Khalif, while her cousins gave themselves every opportunity to engage him.

Well, that makes sense, Khalif reasoned. *Their cousins understand that I still have stronger ties to Vinod than I do with their fathers. So they would need to work harder to win my favor.*

However, in contemplation of Saleema's strong personality, she could also become more of a defiant wife to her husband, much like an American woman. So although Khalif felt the strongest affinity toward Vinod's middle daughter, she posed a blessing and a curse dilemma for him.

The last thing in the world I need is another unruly woman. But I'm very attracted to her strength, he admitted.

Al-Alim, the All-Knowing Allah, please give me a sign between the two daughters, he prayed.

"Would you like some more tea, Khalif?" Kumar's oldest daughter, Sunita, asked him kindly.

Indeed, the oldest daughter will be the more dutiful, Khalif assumed.

He answered, "I thank you for your offer, but I think I should get my own tea while I'm still choosing a new wife." Then he smiled at her.

He did not want to offend her father, Kumar, or lead Sunita on by having her treat him too kindly. He knew that she was not on his short list for a wife.

Sunita responded to him with a hum, "Nooo, you must understand, that whether you choose *me* or not, any daughter you choose here today, and you will become part of the *family*. So it is not just about your *choice*, but it is about showing *kindness* to *family*."

That made Khalif even more confused. At age twenty-five, Sunita was the *oldest* of all of the unmarried daughters who were there.

She simply speaks from diplomatic authority, he reasoned. *But is that my sign? And am I choosing between the wrong daughters?*

When Sunita smiled and left him, Khalif met again with the strong-eyed glare of Saleema.

Well, why doesn't she say anything? he asked himself of her frequent stares. *I wonder if it's a shy sister thing. But if I make a move toward her first, then that would tell them all that I had chosen her, or at least that I am leaning in her direction.*

So he continued to be confused. And the prolonged process of marriage was becoming more cumbersome.

Until finally, Saleema broke away from her cousins and began to head in his direction, only for her father to beat her there to Khalif.

"I understand how hard this must be for you, my brother. But you don't necessarily have to make a choice today," Vinod advised him.

Khalif eyed him, while watching his second daughter, Saleema, who was now in their vicinity. And he spoke to her Indian father frankly.

"Let me ask you a cultural question here," he suggested in private tones.

Vinod nodded and grumbled, "Sure, sure."

Khalif asked him, "If I am not to choose an oldest daughter for my first wife, then how would the oldest then take it?"

Vinod chuckled. "The oldest daughters are sometimes the most *logical* choice, but they can also be the *hardest* choice." He said, "Ramshicka is the *third* daughter of my respected father-in-law, Prakash Adoni. And I chose her as my *second* wife because she was already used to being a younger sister. However, I also thought she was the most *beautiful* as well. So it all worked out well for me," he added with a hearty laugh.

He said, "But I did not want to choose an oldest daughter to be my *second* wife. I assumed that that would cause many problems in my household. So, if you are indeed ready to choose a *second* daughter as your *first* wife, then let that be the only daughter you choose from that family, unless the next daughter is considerably younger than her."

Khalif understood Vinod's logic exactly. There was a cultural pecking order that he needed to understand and realize before he made his decision. And it all made sense. An oldest daughter is used to being *first* in line, in *every* culture.

Then Vinod shared with him in lowered tones, "But in *this* case, the second daughter would be a good *choice* for you. Sometimes the most loyal woman is the one who stays at home."

He then looked Khalif in his New York eyes and added, "Although American men may admire the adventurous, traveling woman, it is the woman who understands how to solidify her own *home*, who often helps a man to establish the confidence and peace of mind that he needs to become more successful in his *business*, and in his *life*."

With that said, Khalif thought about his ex-wife in America, who was a first-born daughter herself, and who had been spoiled rotten through a most destructive relationship with her mother. Khalif also thought of Ramshicka's statement concerning *her* two daughters. And he felt he understood her comments better now. Where *Rani*, the older daughter, could very easily go astray on her own world missions, it was *Saleema* who was deemed as the stronger *home builder*. And her eyes were unwavering in what she wanted. *India* was her home and family. *Life* was whatever her family chose to do. And *Muhammad* would become her new family name.

Thank you, Merciful Allah, Khalif prayed. *Saleema is who I prayed to marry. And I will treat her well.*

So when he turned to find Vinod's second daughter, Saleema, who stood close by him, but not close enough to touch, he moved in her direction and took her hand in his with confidence.

Saleema looked into his handsome brown face with those glowing eyes of hers, and she searched his heart, finding that it was pure. He had chosen her over all others.

He asked her kindly and respectfully, "Do you wish for it to be, for my first Mrs. Muhammad?"

Saleema smiled calmly and melted his heart again. "Yes, I do wish it." She had a natural sense of romance and coyness about her that he recognized now. She had devised a way to create the necessary emotions of universal love, even inside the courtship of an arranged marriage. And love her, he would do.

Khalif felt giddy and hot as he held onto her hand. And he was certain that Saleema felt the positive energy through his palm. He was a satisfied man with a thoughtful and emotional choice.

Merciful Allah! This is a grand occasion, and a new beginning of my blessed life! he proclaimed.

Before he knew it, the Siyamesh family began to clap and gather around them in a circle in the yard. Saleema then became bashful and pulled her hand away from him to cover up her tremendous smile.

"Congratulations!" they all stated.

"Salee-ma! Salee-ma!" her cousins began to yell.

"Welcome to the family, my brother," the youngest brother Shyam stated. "Or should I begin to call you *nephew* now?"

Khalif immediately looked toward Vinod's older daughter, Rani, to see how she would take it. She caught his eye and nodded to him with a smile. Kumar's daughter, Sunita, nodded to him as well. And Shyam's oldest daughter, Priya, was too busy being excited for Saleema to even care.

Vinod took Khalif by the shoulders and told him, "Good choice," with a wink of his right eye. Then he led him away from the excited women to discuss it more in private.

"Saleema is so young for a first wife that you would have to wait nearly four years to marry again without causing too many problems in your household. So she is very happy now to have her own so young."

"What about her feelings toward being married so young?" Khalif questioned. He still wondered about that.

Vinod reminded him, "This is not America, my friend. In *India*, we are not afraid of being married young. A young married couple is a *focused* couple. Then they go into the world and find their way."

Kumar caught up with them in the yard and stated, "You've done it. You have restarted the rivalry of cousins. They have always thought that Saleema would be asked to be married *first*. However, she never seemed as interested in marriage as the rest of them. It must be her romance for an American," he joked.

He was a big brother indeed, forever putting his own spin on things.

Vinod responded, "Don't worry, Kumar, your daughters will get over it. And maybe Khalif will choose to marry one of the younger ones next time."

Khalif chuckled at it himself. But he didn't plan on marrying too many more of their daughters. If anything, he felt it would be more progressive to link himself to a new Muslim family somewhere else, maybe in the Middle East, or in Africa. But at the present, he was too happy with the prospect of his Indian bride-to-be for his mind to stray too far into the future. And as they were separated from each other in the yard of the estate, they continued to cut looks at each other through the joyful crowd.

Khalif had not felt that much family love since his younger years of boyhood, and before he knew that family members could have so many ulterior motives.

Yes indeed! he told himself with swagger. *Saleema has plenty of passion in her heart. And she genuinely likes the idea of being involved with me.*

He could read the passion burning through her eyes across the yard, and he couldn't wait to feel every part of her for the rest of his life. He could already imagine her stating, "I *love* Khalif Raj Muhammad. I love my *family*. And I love my *life!*" And *mean* every *word* of it.

And whether it's because I'm rich, or an American, or handsome, or whatever. I don't really care anymore, Khalif told himself as the family continued to celebrate around him. *This it what it means to have paradise. And I deserve to have it!*

———•———

ABOUT THE AUTHOR

Omar Tyree is a *New York Times* best-selling author, an NAACP Image Award recipient, and a Phillis Wheatley Literary Award winner who has been cited by the City Council of Philadelphia for his work in urban literacy. He has published nineteen books with two million copies sold worldwide. With a degree in print journalism, Tyree has been recognized as one of the most renowned contemporary writers in America. Now entering the world of feature films, Tyree is a tireless creator and visionary of few limitations. For more information on his work and titles, please view his web site @ www.OmarTyree.com.

CHAPTER 10
Narcissism

TO LUCINA'S SURPRISE, two of her girls who were familiar with the Filipino and Mexican crowd of the southeast agreed to work with Ivan. And once Audrey and Christina had settled into the San Diego area as roommates, they were in on the deal as well. A thousand dollars a month to host wealthy, bodacious men during *Monday Night Football* once a week was an easy decision for all of them. Their rents would all be paid with just sixteen hours of work.

Ivan even had the girls do photo shoots wearing the featured teams' opposing jerseys for the flyer, with Pittsburgh and Dallas as their first game. He then had Eddie K. work a deal to feature a sporting goods store on the sports spotlight page of the website, with a promise from the store's manager to advertise their next sales specials on the site.

Ivan then solidified commitments from some of the Chargers he had met at the birthday party, as well as Emilio Alvarez and a few of his friends from the Padres, to attend his "*Monday Night Football* Bash at Raymond's Hot Spot Lounge."

Ivan even invited Julio out, while his neighbor promised to spread the word to more of his Mexican friends.

Thomas Jones called him from the Urban League offices after he had heard the ads on the radio.

"So, I see you worked out another deal with Raymond," he commented.

Ivan told him, "Hey, man, I had to learn to get back up and ride that horse. It's too much money to be made over there to leave it alone, you know."

Thomas said, "Brother, you ain't said nothing but a word. Get back over there and make it happen."

ON THE NIGHT of the first big event, Ivan left work at the accounting offices early to make sure the large projection television was set up right and con-

---

nected to the stereo speaker system at the lounge. Before the game started, some of the crowd began to show up after work to catch the *ESPN Countdown* show.

"Make sure we block off that left corner area as a restricted section for the Chargers and Padres," Ivan told Christina and Audrey. He wanted them both to work the VIP section, while the two other girls worked the general floor, closer to the Filipinos and Mexicans he hoped would show up to join the crowd. And each of the four girls would spend time at the door passing out I.D. Promotions flyers.

By game time, Ivan had his wish. Emilio Alvarez showed up with Butch Clayborne, Big Deke Walker, and two other Padres players. Perry Browning, Zee-Dog, and three other Chargers showed up, including Herman "The Big Bad Hitta" Seaford. They all took chairs on the left side of the room, with a few girls and other guys who accompanied them. The Filipino locals, Mexican locals, and local blacks showed up with their money, jewelry, and girls to claim their areas of the room to watch the game. And before the Pittsburgh Steelers had even kicked the ball off, premium bottles of expensive liquor were already being ordered and popped from the tables.

The lounge was filled to capacity by the end of the first quarter, with a line still waiting out front. A hired cameraman took shots of it all for the website, while Jeff and Paul had other work to do.

"What do we do when we run out of room?" Ida pulled Ivan aside to ask him near the door. She was pleased with the turnout, but also worried about the overflow.

Ivan shrugged and said, "They're just too late. There's no more room in here."

He wore a gold knit tennis shirt under a dark gray sports jacket to keep his professional look, even among the jersey-wearing sports crowd.

Ida told him, "Well, you need to go out there and tell them something. It's a whole lot of people still waiting to get in."

"About how many?" Ivan asked her.

"I can't count them. They're all over the sidewalk."

Ivan walked out to view the crowd for himself. Sure enough, there were plenty of latecomers outside, admiring the luxury and sports cars of the athletes and other high rollers who had arrived early enough to park and make it in. They were also pleased by the girls who walked out to pass them flyers.

"Hey, Ivan, what's going on, man? Am I still good?"

It was Julio and three of his friends, including his little brother, all standing out in the crowd, late. Julio was wearing Dallas Cowboys gear, all pumped and ready to watch the game.

Shit! Ivan cursed himself. *How am I gonna work this line out?*

Everyone outside wanted to get in, but the place was fast running out of room. *And what if a few of the Padres or Chargers come late?* Ivan worried.

He thought fast and told Julio, "One minute, man." Then he grabbed the first security guard he could reach to walk inside with him.

Once they were inside the door, Ivan told him, "Hey, man, do me a favor and grab the guy with the Cowboys jersey and his friends in here. And if any other professional athletes walk up, you let them in as our special guests. But we need to tell everyone else to come earlier next week and enjoy the game somewhere else, because we're filled to capacity already."

Ivan didn't want to max the place out to elbow-room. That would only make it more ripe for a disaster.

The security guard smiled and said, "I got you, man," and walked back out to do his job.

Ida overheard him and smiled herself. She said, "You sure got your wish tonight, hunh? So I guess we can close the cash box now."

Ivan chuckled and said, "I guess so." He went back to working the crowd on his own that night. Lucina wanted no part of it. She didn't even bother to witness her partner's smashing triple. The only thing that stopped it from being a home-run hit was the small capacity of the lounge.

"Hey, what up, man? I'm Ivan David," he introduced himself to the crowd, shaking hands. He wanted to make sure they all remained sociable.

"Yeah, we know who you are," some of the crowd responded to him. "From IDPromotions.com, right?"

"Yeah," Ivan answered, grinning. "Y'all need any more bottles of that good stuff ?"

"Is the next bottle free?" someone joked loudly.

Ivan answered, "Naw, this ain't the place for that, nephew. This is high rollers only in here. So put your money where your mouth is, and we'll send one of the pretty girls over to collect it."

They laughed out loud over the football announcers on TV. And they respected Ivan as the chief of the party.

Perry Browning yelled out from the players' section on the left, "Hey, Ivan, how come you didn't bring ten of Lucina's girls? I don't see enough of 'em in here to go around for me."

Ivan hollered back to him. "Oh, that'll happen for you next week. We wanted to see what we were working with first." Then Ivan addressed the crowd. "But now we know. So make sure y'all show up bright and early again next week. The only reservations we're taking up in here is cash money."

"I heard that!" Herman the Big Bad Hitta yelled out.

"THERE GO THE BUS! THERE GO THE BUS!" Perry yelled toward the screen in reference to the Pittsburgh Steelers' massive running back Jerome

Bettis. Bettis rumbled over several Dallas defenders in the secondary for a touchdown, to give the Steelers a 16–3 lead in the second quarter.

As the crowd responded to the replays on the large screen, Perry boasted, "You wait till we play his ass in week twelve! I'm gon' knock his damn wheels off!"

The Big Bad Hitta hollered right behind him, "THE SHOCKW-A-A-A-AVE!" and high-fived his teammates.

OUTSIDE AT THE INTERSECTION OF THE STREET, Lucina pulled up in her black E-Class Mercedes and eyed the dense crowd of sports fans and exotic cars that surrounded Raymond's Hot Spot Lounge in the parking lot, as well as on both sides of the street.

"Oh shit, it looks like they did it tonight," her passenger commented. It was her girl Maya, the dark-haired Colombian.

Lucina remained speechless at the wheel. She pulled up to double park outside the lounge entrance, next to a dark blue Bentley. She pressed her hazard lights on.

"I'll be right back out," she told her girl.

"You're going in to see Ivan?" Maya asked her.

"Of course," Lucina answered snidely. *Why else would I go in?*

Maya didn't think anything of it. "Tell him I said hi."

Lucina closed the car door behind her without responding.

Out in front of the lounge, the security guards were still trying to clear the disgruntled crowd.

"Look, you all just need to clear away from here. There's no more room to stand inside."

"Man, you don't own this sidewalk," someone jabbed from the crowd.

Lucina walked right past them all.

"Hey, Lucina Gallo," one of the security guards noted.

A dark brown baller, draped with jewelry around his neck, in both ears, and across his front teeth, turned to recognize the Brazilian beauty for himself. He had only seen the much-talked-about San Diego woman before from a distance. *Twice.*

He responded, "Oh, shit, she's up in the flesh out here."

Lucina wore another expensive, eye-popping dress, with heels to match. As she walked by, she ignored the men out front as if they were all shadows in the dark.

"Is Ivan still inside?" she asked the security. She wanted them all to know who she was there for. It was more marketing for the future.

"Oh, yeah, he's still in there," the security told her.

"Take me inside to see him," she ordered.

The security guards didn't say another word. One turned to lead her inside.

One of the other ballers said, "Yo, I thought you said it wasn't no more room in there," to the remaining guards.

"There's always room for her," one of the guards deadpanned.

A few of the crowd started to chuckle. Someone said, "Well, goddamn, I wish I was Ivan."

INSIDE THE LOUNGE, Lucina strolled into the middle of the room and immediately called the attention of her four girls. All eyes were on her, just as she liked it, especially since the game had reached halftime. Her four pretty workers scrambled in her direction from their separate sides of the room, all wearing curve-hugging jerseys and heels with tight blue jeans. Then the whispers started:

"Hey, that's Lucina."

"You know who that is, don't you?"

"That's Lucina Gallo right there."

"Is that Lucina?"

"Yo, she da *baddest* bitch."

"That girl looks skinny to me."

"That's a nice-ass dress she's wearing."

"Who the fuck is she?"

"Damn, my dick is hard just looking at her, homes."

"Yeah, she's *very* pretty."

"I guess she's the boss bitch, hunh?"

"Why is everybody staring at her?"

There were nearly three hundred opinions of her inside the room.

Perry Browning hollered out above the crowd, "LU-CI-NAAA! You bring six more girls with you? I told Ivan he went cheap on us in here tonight!"

Lucina only smiled in the football player's direction. She had little tolerance for him that night.

She asked her girls in their huddled circle, "Is everything okay?"

"Yeah, we're good," they all answered.

"And are they treating you right in here?"

"Yeah, they're treating us good."

Lucina nodded to them. By that time Ivan had spotted her. She made eye contact with him and proceeded to send her girls away. "Okay, everyone go to their own homes tonight. Now let me talk to Ivan," she told them.

As soon as they all left her, Lucina stared at Ivan through the crowd and gave him a come-here finger motion.

Ivan saw it from across the room and froze.

God knows, I wanna fuck the hell out of that girl, he mused of Lucina's sexy grandstanding. *I thought she said she wasn't coming tonight. Let me go over here and see what she wants.*

When Ivan reached her in the middle of the room, Lucina turned to walk toward the exit, expecting him to follow her. And as soon as he followed her as she expected him to, he met eyes with Ida and felt a lightning bolt of guilt and shame strike his heart.

Shit! he cursed himself in a panic. *I wonder what Ida's thinking right now. I look like a fucking dog following his master out of the rain.*

To make it all seem harmless, Ivan pointed to Ida and stated, "I'll be right back in. All right?"

Ida made him feel better by nodding to him. "Yeah, okay," she told him. *Whatever,* she thought. *I know you like that damn girl. Cut your hair down for that bitch and everything. Didn't even ask me about it. But that's okay. You won't be fucking with me tonight. So you best hope she wants to give you some of that South American pussy, because you won't be touching me. Ever again!*

And as Ivan walked out of the lounge behind his seductive partner, the whispers started up in the room again:

"What the hell was that about?"

"You think he's fucking her?"

"So they're supposed to be just partners, hunh? Yeah, right."

"Man, she looked like she was mad as hell at him."

"I thought he was with the light-skinned sister."

"That's a lucky motherfucker right there, homes. Let me tell you."

Ivan walked outside of the lounge behind Lucina and was disturbed by her. She'd made him look weak in front of Ida at his own event. Then she had the audacity to walk away from him as he continued to follow her like a sidekick.

When she finally stopped and turned to face him a little ways up the street, Ivan asked her in irritation, "What's going on?" She was acting as if they were a couple who had had a fight.

She stared at him and said, "I just came to check up on you."

Ivan stared back at her. He frowned and asked her, "And that's how you do it? You looked like you were having a tantrum in there. What I do to you?" he asked her. "You wanted me to fail? I thought we're supposed to make money together."

Lucina continued to stare at him without words.

Finally, she told him, "I don't want you to fail, Ivan. I'm just concerned about my girls tonight."

"Bullshit, man. You're actually jealous that I pulled this shit off without you."

"That's not true."

"Yes, it is," he argued. "You were mad when your girls even agreed to do it with me. What do you think, you're Mommie Dearest and they gotta listen to everything you say? They're trying to get money, have a good time, and live out here, Lucina. That's all."

He calmed himself down, realizing he had said enough. He wasn't even sure if Lucina could take that from him. Was she ready to move on and mark him off as another lost business partner?

She nodded to him and said, "Okay. You did a good job. Just make sure they all get home safe tonight."

She started walking back toward her Mercedes parked in the street.

Ivan said, "You're not staying? You can make sure they get home for yourself if you stay."

Lucina looked back at Ivan from the street and shook her head. "Maya and I are expected at another event tonight."

Ivan was ready to ask her more about it, but what difference did it make? She had promised to attend someone else's event on a night when he had set up a party for them to make easy money. He thought about that and was irritated again. It seemed disrespectful to him. She knew he had planned the "*Monday Night Football* Bash." She could have at least supported him on the first one.

Nevertheless, he nodded and blew it off. "All right, then. Y'all have a good time tonight."

"Thank you," she told him.

Ivan headed back inside the lounge without another word. The third quarter would be starting after halftime.

Lucina watched her determined partner walk away and felt betrayed by her pettiness. She wanted to hurt him just to see if he would bleed. She wanted to know if he still had a heart outside of business. And if he bled, then it proved that he cared. But was it fair for her to test him in that way just to satisfy her own insecurities about their partnership?

When she climbed back into her black Mercedes she felt guilty about it. She sat there in silence for a minute behind the wheel.

"Of course, he wanted us to stay," she commented to Maya.

Maya read Lucina's volatile emotions and already knew.

She likes him, she thought with a silent nod. *So she's going through a power struggle with him now.* But there was no sense in her speaking up about it. Maya knew that Lucina liked to keep her intimate emotions to herself until she expressed them on her own. Even when they were obvious.

Finally, Lucina took a deep breath and said, "Let's go," before she restarted the car to drive off.

IVAN WALKED BACK inside the lounge and made his way over to Ida to calm the rough waters he could sense between them. Ida had already begun to complain about Lucina's blatant disrespect of her. She also hinted that Ivan gave the woman far too much leeway in their partnership. But the power-play antic Lucina had just pulled inside the lounge may have been the straw to break the camel's back.

"What did I miss?" Ivan asked Ida in reference to the football game. The game had moved into the third quarter now.

Ida shook off his question. She answered, "I wasn't really watching it." She said, "But since you have everyone in here now, I'm getting ready to go. I have some other things I have to prepare for." She handed him the cash box and the money bag.

Ivan didn't like how that looked or felt. He asked her, "What's wrong?" as if he didn't know.

Ida refused to talk about it. "Nothing's wrong, I just have some other things to do tonight."

Ivan stared at her. "Are you sure?"

He was itching to get told off, but instead of taking the bait, Ida took a breath to compose herself. She wanted to remain civil.

She nodded and said, "Yeah, I'm sure. Let me just go ahead and go now."

Ivan took a deep breath and looked away in frustration for a second and caught Christina eying them from across the room.

He turned back to Ida and nodded. "All right. I'll call you when I get in tonight."

When Ida left the lounge, no more than five minutes after Lucina had left him, Ivan felt alone in the crowd, and with a load of money in his hands.

Fuck it, let me go count up this loot, he told himself, moving toward Raymond at the bar.

As he made it through the crowd, he watched all of the girls to see how they were making out. They all looked to be enjoying themselves and working the crowd effectively. He could also see that Audrey was continuing to work her charm on Emilio. She made sure she passed him with every move she made inside the players' VIP area. Then he watched Christina to see what she was up to. As he studied her from a distance, he noticed that she seemed distracted.

She knows I'm watching her, he told himself. *And she knows that Ida is pissed at me. She's smart like that.*

"Hey, Raymond, can I use your back office for a minute?" he asked behind the bar area.

Raymond was working his ass off behind the bar, with boxes, bottles, and glasses everywhere. But he was pleased as hell to be doing so.

He looked up at Ivan while filling another drink order and noticed the metal cash box and money bag in his hands.

"Oh, sure, Ivan, one minute," he said, finishing up the drink. He grinned and led Ivan back to his office. "You really did it tonight, man. I mean, really. This is gonna be a great deal for us."

His wife was hard at work, filling drink orders with two other bartenders. Three waitresses and Lucina's girls all worked the floor.

Ivan smiled at Raymond and said, "I'm just glad you decided to do it."

"Oh, me, too, man. Me, too."

Ivan closed and locked the door behind him before spreading the money out across the floor. He sat in Raymond's office chair, leaned over, and separated the hundreds, fifties, twenties, tens, fives, and ones as usual. But this time he did it by himself. And when he did his recount, the take from the door came to exactly $5,238.

Ivan grinned and mumbled, "Either Ida let somebody in for eighteen dollars, or she took or lost two singles out of the cash box."

He wasn't going to make a big deal over that. But Ida had left without even being paid that night.

"Yeah, I know something's up with her now," he assumed.

He set the metal cash box and the money bag in a corner of the room and returned to the bar to have Raymond lock the office back up until they were ready to close for the night.

"What are you guys looking like tonight?" he asked Raymond in reference to their take at the bar.

Raymond looked at him and said, "So far, thirteen thousand."

Ivan smiled, feeling like a contestant on the game show *The Price Is Right*. His estimates were right on target. It felt like he was taking candy from a baby.

He nodded and said, "Okay." *Another G for me*, he thought. *But just imagine if I owned the lounge.*

He stepped away from Raymond and pulled Christina from her VIP duties to speak to her in private for a minute.

"Are you all right over there? You doing okay?"

She looked at him with all of her girlish innocence. "Yeah, I'm okay. Why do you ask me that?"

Ivan felt her steadiness all over him. That was what he was used to from her. But he couldn't see it from her when he was staring at her.

He said, "Maybe it's just me, but you seemed to be...*distracted* tonight."

She shook it off again. "No, I'm good. But how are you doing? Is everything all right with you?"

Ivan looked into her small dark eyes, surrounded by her beautiful brown skin and dark wavy hair, and he began to think with the wrong head. He felt like reaching out and pulling her sexy frame into him and telling her the blunt truth at that moment.

After making this easy money in here tonight, I feel like I deserve some good pussy. Seriously!

Since Ida and Lucina had left him there alone, Ivan had no other bumpers to keep him away from a payout from Chris. So instead of him playing it all business, like his normal MO, Ivan changed up his script.

He told Christina, "Don't leave here tonight before I talk to you."

She paused and then nodded to him. He was in authority.

She said, "Okay." And that was it.

When she walked away to return to the VIP area with the ball players, Ivan told himself, *Yeah, she knows what time it is. And I'm not playing Mr. Nice Guy tonight to let her off the hook, either.*

THE PITTSBURGH STEELERS held on to win the game 37–31, after a furious late comeback by the Dallas Cowboys. When the game was over, the customers continued to party, drinking and talking shit. But there were no fights, no escalating arguments, and no embarrassing incidents.

So Ivan thanked everyone for coming out, reminded them to show up early for the game next week, and made a gang of new friends. Then he went through the final bar numbers with Raymond.

The bar total came to more than fifteen thousand dollars, increasing Ivan's take to close to seven thousand. After subtracting his expenses, he and Lucina would net close to four grand to split.

At ten o'clock at night, Ivan stood out on the sidewalk with Audrey and Christina. He had already paid them all, and Lucina's other two girls had left a few minutes earlier.

"So, you're driving, Audrey?" Ivan questioned. He had to set up his getaway plans for Chris.

"Yeah, I got a little Pontiac convertible," she responded with a chuckle. "What are you driving, Ivan?" she asked him.

Audrey had watched Emilio pull off in a red Maserati with plenty of fanfare. The Latino crowd had been excited to see him there and to take pictures with him. Audrey couldn't wait to catch back up to him. She had his personal numbers now.

Ivan smiled at her and answered, "I just drove my company-man car, a black Nissan Altima. All that other stuff can wait."

Audrey heard him out and agreed. "I know that's right."

Ivan then looked at Chris. She was doing her normal silent-smile thing.

He said, "So, we're all grown people out here, right?"

He waited for them both to respond.

"Yeah."

"And grown people's business is grown people's business?"

Audrey and Chris looked at each other, wondering where Ivan was going with it all.

"I mean, what are you trying to say, Ivan?" Audrey asked him. She had a feeling of where he was going. She also had a response to it if he went there.

I hope he's not thinking what I think he's thinking with us, she thought.

Christina had a feeling as well. But she waited hers out to see what Ivan had to say first.

Ivan said, "Well, if it's all right with Chris, I'll take her home."

Both girls froze and looked at each other. Ivan didn't have to do that out in the open. He could have pulled Chris off to the side and let her tell Audrey something on her own. Even Chris was shocked by it.

Why did he make it so obvious? she asked herself. At the same time, it turned her on a little. He was getting rather bold. And he was making it known that he wanted her.

On Ivan's side of the coin, he also wanted to test Lucina's rules.

We'll see if she doesn't ask them now, he told himself. *But if I'm gonna be around all these girls all the time, they're not all gonna tell me no.*

Audrey opened her mouth and said, "Well—"

"Let me talk to him," Christina commented, cutting her off.

Audrey looked at her and said, "Okay." She figured Chris would handle it on her own. Ivan was off base.

Chris walked forward with Ivan for their privacy.

She asked him immediately, "Why did you do that?" He had put her smack inside of a dilemma. What would Audrey think? Lucina had told them all to make sure they returned to their own homes that night. She didn't say that for no reason. But there was Ivan, deliberately complicating things for all of them.

Ivan said, "If you don't wanna go, you don't wanna go. Just tell me you don't like me that way."

He doubted she would tell him that. He already knew she liked him. And he was not letting her off the hook.

Christina told him, "It's not that, it's just...I mean, we're all in business together, Ivan."

Isn't that why Ida walked out on you earlier? she assumed. *Mixing business with pleasure is just bad. It doesn't work.*

Yet she was highly attracted to Ivan's individual hustle.

He asked her, "You think my business is gonna stop because I take you home tonight?"

She knew better than that. "No, of course not."

"Are you gonna stop doing business with *me*?"

Chris had to stop and think about that one. What if she started to hate his guts for some reason? Or what if Lucina began to dislike her? She could tell that Lucina had an attraction to Ivan as well. Maybe she had even ruined his relationship with Ida on purpose.

Christina had read the whole thing. Now Ivan was attempting to take his emotions out on her. She expected that as well, just not as boldly.

She shook her head and told him, "I just don't want to be in the middle of anything."

"And how is that gonna happen?" he asked her.

Somebody would have to tell. Who would it be? Audrey?

Christina said, "I have to respect everybody in this, Ivan. I just can't up and do that."

"Up and do what?" He wanted her to spell it out to him. He said, "If you don't like me like that, then it's not an issue, right?"

She told him, "But you know I like you. I told you that already."

He said, "You told me you liked me in business. But my life is more than just business."

"I know that."

"So why would you let me go home alone tonight if you like me?"

He was killing her. But she already knew that Ivan had it in him. He knew how to press people's buttons to get them to move. She had watched him in action all night. Now he was turning his focus in her direction.

She read the situation and said, "I just don't want to be anybody's substitute, that's all."

He smiled and said, "Oh, so now you're not good enough? What, I'ma put you back on the bench after the game? You can't handle being a starter?"

Chris smiled back, knowing that he was wrong. Now he was attacking her ego.

He said, "Shit, if I got my chance to start after watching from the sidelines, I'd take that chance and go to the championship with it. But maybe that's just me."

Chris was still standing there in silence on the sidewalk. Either she wanted him or she didn't. But Ivan was going to make her choose *right now. Impulsively.*

He said, "But if you don't want me like that, then go on back home with Audrey. She's still here."

It was a big risk to go that hard on the girl. Nevertheless, Ivan was training himself. Business was a hard man's sport. There was little room for softness. Softness either lost the business or ended up on the liabilities column instead of the assets. And Ivan was only thinking about making money now, the assets.

On Christina's side, she couldn't take the rejection from him. What if he meant it? And what if she never got another chance to get that close to him? She was certain that he was on his way up. There was no question about it. So she would hate herself for turning her only opportunity down. But it still felt wrong.

She squirmed and said, "Ivan, I really do like you, but—"

Ivan cut her off with a raised hand and said, "Let me let you go, then."

Christina stopped and stared at him. "What does that mean?"

Her heart was pounding in her chest. *Did I fuck it up? I just don't...feel sure about it yet,* she told herself. *I mean, I want to, but...*

Ivan told her, "Go on back to Audrey. I'm done."

His rejection was even stronger now. She could hardly breathe.

She pleaded, "Don't be that way with me, Ivan. I'm not like that. If I say I'm down with you, I'm down with you to the end."

Ivan remained as stony as a downtown building with her.

"Well, show me, then."

The clock stopped ticking. It was all on Christina. She sized up her chances and gave in.

She took a deep breath and said, "I'll go tell her I'm going with you."

AUDREY WAITED down the street for what seemed like forever. When Christina finally returned to her, she asked her, "So, what did you say?" She assumed that she had turned Ivan down.

Chris took another breath and answered, "I'll just, um...see you later on or whatever. Okay?"

Audrey looked at her, confused. She said, "What, you're *going* with him? You know Lucina told us—"

"I know what Lucina said," Chris argued.

Audrey whispered, "And you're gonna fuck with her partner in business anyway? I mean, how is that smart?"

"Are you gonna tell her that, Audrey?" Chris asked her.

Audrey frowned and said, "Hell, no. But what if she calls tonight and asks to speak to you?"

"You just tell her to call me on my cell phone."

"And what are you gonna say when she calls?"

"You let me deal with that. It's not your concern."

Audrey backed off and said, "Okay." *I just thought you were smarter than that*, she thought. *But that's a dumb decision. You could have any of those guys in there before Ivan. Ivan is, like, off limits.*

Even Audrey could tell that Lucina liked her partner in more ways than just business. Lucina was very protective of Ivan's image. But like Christina had told her, it was not her concern.

IVAN TOOK CHRISTINA HOME with him to solidify his confidence in everything. He wanted to feel like he deserved it. And he wanted to teach everyone around him to give in, starting with the black and Japanese beauty.

But there were no more dreams about Lucina while he did her. Ivan had his full focus on the beautiful mind, body, and soul of Christina, who accepted his passionate weight.

"You like me for real, hunh?" he asked her with a strong thrust of his naked pelvis into hers. They were dead center in Ivan's king-sized bed.

Christina winced, whimpered, and moaned, *"Mmm-hmm."*

"Can I have this whenever I want?" he asked as he continued to push.

She took it and whined with her eyes closed, "If you want to."

"But do you *want me* to *want it?*"

"Oooh," she moaned, feeling it.

"Hunh?" Ivan asked her, pouring on his weight. *"Do you?"*

"Yesss," she hissed back to him, *"I want you to want me."*

Ivan was not interested in making their romp into a talkathon. Business was about action. The talk was over. So he pounded into her body without pause. And he planned to continue having things his way.